AND BABY MAKES THREE

"Is it stupid of me to say that ever since we got pregnant, I've been realizing how superficial my job can be?"

"It's not stupid, Blaine. It's sweet, actually. I'm discovering that the whole world is pretty damn superficial when you get pregnant." Gretchen lay back on her sofa, and I sat down on the floor next to her, not caring about my tuxedo. She caught me staring at her and said, "You want to touch my belly, don't you?"

"I know it's silly, but—"

"It's not. But for someone with body issues, the idea of everyone wanting to touch your stomach . . ." She shuddered and cringed, wrinkling her face like a child who was just offered Brussels sprouts. "However, I guess I have to get used to the idea. Go ahead."

She stared at the ceiling, which I took as my cue to put my hand on her stomach. Inside, my emotions were milling around and colliding like bumper cars. I looked up at Gretchen and found her staring at me with an expectant gaze.

"This is incredible," I said. "I feel so excited. Not to mention scared, thrilled, proud, and kind of nauseated."

"You should feel it from this side," Gretchen said. She put her hand over mine and added, "But it's going to be good. I know this isn't the way either of us planned on becoming a parent."

"We've been over this," I said.

"I know," she said. "But . . ."

"It's going to be good," I echoed, with an inward sigh of contentment when I realized that I meant it.

Books by Timothy James Beck

IT HAD TO BE YOU

HE'S THE ONE

I'M YOUR MAN

Published by Kensington Publishing Corporation

I'm Your Man

Timothy James Beck

KENSINGTON BOOKS
http://www.kensingtonbooks.com

KENSINGTON BOOKS are published by

Kensington Publishing Corp.
850 Third Avenue
New York, NY 10022

All Kensington titles, imprints and distributed lines are available at special quantity discounts for bulk purchases for sales promotion, premiums, fund-raising, educational or institutional use.

Special book excerpts or customized printings can also be created to fit specific needs. For details, write or phone the office of the Kensington Special Sales Manager: Kensington Publishing Corp., 850 Third Avenue, New York, NY 10022, Attn. Special Sales Department. Phone: 1-800-221-2647.

ISBN 0-7582-0787-5

First Kensington Trade Paperback Printing: December 2004
10 9 8 7 6 5 4 3 2 1

Printed in the United States of America

For Tom Wocken,
who makes the Jewel Box and Doll House
home for us all.

ACKNOWLEDGMENTS

Continuing gratitude for their help and guidance to Alison Picard, John Scognamiglio, and Michael Vicencia.

Thank you to Steve Code and James McCain Jr., who get their own line for going above and beyond.

Special thanks to Dorothy Cochrane, Caroline De La Rosa, Paul Enea, Erin Swan, and Bill Thomas. Additional recognition for support, encouragement, interest or inspiration to Noel Alumit, Dave Benbow, Shanon Best, Christine Bradley, Tim Brookover, Rob Byrnes, Jason Cabot and Jeff Heilers, the Carter family, Colin Chase, Jean-Marc Chazy, Darryl Coble, the Cochrane family, Andre Coffa, Leonard Cohen for the title, Darren Connell, Jason Crawford, Jennifer Damiano, Carlton Davis and Veronique Gambier, Jonathan De Michael, Lynne Demarest, Jone Devlin, Kim Duva, Ghalib El-Khalidi, Jeffrey Fischer, the Forry family, the Garber family, Amy and Richard Ghiselin, Lowry Greeley, Terri Griffin, Jennifer Hackett, Will Hatheway, Larry Henderson, Dennis Hensley, Lisa Hicks, Gregory Hinton, Wendy Howell, Anthony Johnson, Judge Joe B., Christine and John Kovach, the Lambert family, Marla McDaniel, Robin McElfresh, Christian McLaughlin, George Michael for the title and a great ass, the Miller family, Debbie Milton, Helen C. Morris, Riley Morris, Steve Nordwick, David Outlaw and Michael Ryan, Steven Parkhurst, Felice Picano, Ron Pratt, the Rambo family, Lori Redfearn and Bob Corrigan, Christopher Rice, the Rose family, Carmela Roth, Rhonda Rubin, Trish Rumble, Mary Russo, Terry and Allen Shull, Laurie and Marty Smith, Clifton Snider, Marc Stauffer, Denece Thibodeaux, Dana Thomas, Ben Tyler, Steve Vargas, Jeffrey Wallen, Ellen Ward and Pat Crosby, Don Whittaker, Jessica Wicks, Carissa Williams, Sarena Williams, Tracy Wilson, the Wocken family, Casper

Yaqoub, Yojo, AOL friends, especially Lora, Patti, and Michelle, A Different Light, Lobo Bookshop, and timothyjamesbeck.com.

In loving memory of Louise Wocken and Pete Martinez.

For enduring and unquestioning love, thanks to Arthur, Brandi, Guinness, Hailey, Lazlo, Margot, and Merc. Especially for Striker, who taught us how to live and who will be missed always.

We will never break the chain: Jim Carter, Becky Cochrane, Timothy Forry, and Timothy J. Lambert.

CHAPTER 1

I'd never been the kind of man who'd break a date, even one that was made over a month earlier in the previous millennium, before my life changed in ways I could never have predicted. But I wasn't thrilled about leaving my warm, dry Hell's Kitchen apartment to go forty rain-sodden blocks on a Saturday in January Y2K to a Woody Allen film festival in SoHo.

Still, a promise was a promise, and I waited as long as I could outside Film Forum for my friend Gretchen to show up before I finally bought my ticket. Feeling damp and a little surly, I made my way into the small art house to find Gretchen already there, sitting in her favorite place, just to the left of center, about midway between the screen and the door. My bad mood evaporated instantly. I should have known that Gretchen was even less likely to break a date than I was, and she gave me a bright smile when I slid into the seat next to her.

If I had to sum up Gretchen's appeal, I'd give it a yin-yang quality. She had a brisk, no-nonsense male energy, but eyes that communicated feminine compassion and intuition. She was solidly built, but moved with a woman's fluidity and grace. She was a woman's woman; it was a mystery why she spent so much time at the movies with me. She claimed to be unlucky in love. I suspected she always chose the wrong woman because she really loved nothing more than her work and her friends. Often she combined the two, to the satisfaction of anyone who wanted to be financially stable.

I'd been told that when she was in her early thirties, Gretchen was stocky because she tended to grab fast food on the run between end-

2 Timothy James Beck

less meetings, spending the rest of her time at her desk eating take-out while she helped build financial empires for her clients. She'd also endured a series of unhappy love affairs, consoling herself with her favorite vanilla bean ice cream.

By the time I met her, she'd invested in Happy Hollow, her retreat/resort in upstate New York, where she spent a lot of time outdoors renovating the property's old hotel. She'd also cut back her workload and dedicated her energy to a healthier lifestyle. She'd remade herself into a svelte, stylish businesswoman, with tousled chestnut hair cut short and streaked with blond highlights.

"Hi, Blaine! I wasn't sure you'd make it," she said, affectionately patting my knee as a welcome. "Is it still raining?"

"Yes," I said. "What's gay about Woody Allen?"

The question wasn't as strange as it sounded. For a couple of years, Gretchen had arranged dates for us that were meant to improve my cultural awareness as a gay man. Although many of these involved parties celebrating the Oscars, Pride Week, and Halloween, they often centered around movies I hadn't seen. I'd never heard that Woody Allen was a gay icon, however, so I wasn't sure how today's event fit into the gaying of Blaine Dunhill.

After thinking it over, Gretchen finally said, "Woody's synonymous with Manhattan, and Manhattan . . ." She trailed off and laughed when she saw my dubious expression. "Okay, I confess. I like *Hannah and Her Sisters* because it's quirky and sweet, but hardly anyone I know watches Woody Allen. Especially after the scandal sheets got finished with him."

"I never pay attention to that crap. If you like the movie, that's good enough for me," I said, meaning it. In the three years that I'd known Gretchen Schmidt, she'd never steered me wrong, either in her role as my financial advisor or as my friend. I'd been asking myself a lot of questions about the changing nature of my friendships. It was comforting to feel that this one was intact in spite of what it was originally based on: our mutual connection to my ex-boyfriend, Daniel Stephenson.

When the lights went down and the movie began, I became absorbed in the intertwined love stories. I refused to think about Daniel, even when Woody's character reminded us that love was "really unpredictable." Nor did I shift in my seat over uncomfortable reminders of love affairs in crisis. I knew I'd think about it later, when sleep eluded all my best efforts. But for a few hours, I could be happy to see a movie with a friend and go out afterward for good food and conversation.

After the movie, we walked down slushy sidewalks to Herban Kitchen, one of Gretchen's favorite restaurants. Though Gretchen was a vegetarian, she never inflicted her dietary beliefs on others. Herban Kitchen offered meat, poultry, and fish on their menu, all of which were organically raised. I could rest assured that my steak had lived a better life than I ever would.

After Gretchen decided on something called the Harvest Plate and relinquished her menu to the waiter, she turned to me and asked, "What did you think of the movie?"

"Carrie Fisher sang. What's not to love?"

"Wow. You almost sounded gay that time," she teased. "But you're right. I've had a crush on her for years. Women have that Princess Leia fantasy, too, you know."

"It was nice to see Barbara Hershey stay alive," I said. "After watching *Beaches* so many times, I assumed she died in all of her movies."

"No. You're thinking of Mary Louise Parker."

"Oh. She was in *Fried Green Tomatoes,* right? Or was that Maria Conchita Alonso?"

Gretchen laughed, then said, "You were right the first time. With Mary Stuart Masterson."

"How do you keep all those three-named women straight?"

"I know my girls," Gretchen said with a salacious grin. She suddenly switched gears, leaned forward, and said, "Was it awful of me to take you to a movie about love?"

"Oh, please," I groaned. "Don't pussyfoot around me. I'm a big boy. I'm fine."

"What, no rending of garments? You break up with the love of your life, and you're fine? Come on, Blaine," Gretchen urged, "this is me you're talking to. It's okay. Fess up."

"I think the worst thing about breaking up with someone is how everyone who knows you asks, 'What happened?' Then you end up repeating a condensed version of the story ten to twenty times. It's like issuing a press statement to your friends and colleagues," I complained.

"That's not the worst part of breaking up, and you know it."

She was right. There was no worst part. The arguing, going to bed together angry, the silent dinners, the final fight, the loneliness the morning after; it was all pretty awful. I felt my eyes start to well up with tears and said, "Maybe I'm not ready to talk about it."

"I'm sorry. I shouldn't have brought it up. It's just that I'm concerned," Gretchen said, reaching across the table to place her hand over mine. "I want to make sure you're okay. The circles under your eyes are darker than Sarah Jessica Parker's roots."

"Or do you mean Sarah Michelle Gellar? Seriously, I was happy that you kept our date tonight," I confessed. "When I was waiting outside the theater, before I found out you were already inside, I thought you ditched me out of loyalty to Daniel."

"That's absurd," Gretchen admonished and lightly slapped my hand.

"You were his friend first," I reminded her, "before he and I ever got together. He's known you for a thousand years. I've only known you—"

"Long enough for me to know that I like you and value your friendship," Gretchen interjected. "I know what it's like to have well-meaning friends get in the middle of your relationships. Or breakups. If you want to talk about how you're feeling, that's fine. What you say to me stays between us. The same goes for anything Daniel and I talk about."

"Have you talked to him?" I asked.

"Until tonight, this is the first time I've seen either of you since we were together at Happy Hollow for Thanksgiving," she said. "After that, you went to Europe on business. By the time you got back, I was in Barbados."

"That's right. Your trip. Did you have a good time?"

"Terrific," she said. "First chance I've had to relax in years. I spent most of my time alone. It helped me make some major decisions about my life."

"Such as?"

"We aren't talking about me. We're talking about you," she said. "When I got back, Daniel had gone to spend Christmas with his family, and you were in Colorado, undoing all my gay lessons with your straight friend. How was your ski trip?"

"Being with Jake was exactly what I needed," I said. Jake Meyers had been my best friend since we were kids growing up in Eau Claire, Wisconsin. It had been a relief to spend time with someone who didn't know Daniel except through me and didn't ask any questions about the breakup, letting me decide how much I wanted to say. However, I understood that Gretchen wasn't merely being curious. She genuinely cared about Daniel and me, and I valued her opinion. I went on. "Like you, I needed time away to think things over. If you haven't talked to Daniel about the breakup, who told you?"

"Sheila," Gretchen said. Whatever expression flickered across my face prompted her to say, "You're mad at her, huh?"

"Not really. I don't know. Maybe."

Our waiter came with our food, giving me a chance to consider Gretchen's words. Sheila Meyers was Jake's younger sister, and there was a lot of history between us. More than ten years before, we'd even dated for a while, when I was a high school senior and she was a freshman. But we'd been friends long before then.

"Sheila would never do anything to hurt you, Blaine," Gretchen said, reading my mind and picking up where we'd left off when the waiter was gone. "She can be impulsive and flighty, but her heart's always in the right place."

We spent a quiet few minutes eating while I thought about Daniel and Sheila. It was strange that she'd been a part of our breakup, since she'd helped get us together in the first place.

I could still remember the first time I'd seen him. My fifth-floor apartment overlooked the alley between my building and Daniel's. His apartment was first-floor rear and had a patio, where he'd created a garden. While he labored over his plants, I'd watch from my window and try to figure out a way to meet him. From a distance, I couldn't see how handsome he was. Since it was summer, he was usually dressed in nothing more than a pair of shorts and sometimes a T-shirt, so I knew that he had a good, if slender, body.

But it wasn't his looks that made me return to my window to watch him every day. I liked the graceful way he moved; the way his hands so lovingly and gently tended to his plants and flowers. I felt like I was secretly sharing in something sweet and intimate with him. Sometimes it even seemed like he knew I was there and returned my interest.

Eventually I found out that was true. A few months after I moved to New York in 1997, Sheila followed and became my roommate. Daniel had contrived to meet her so he could find out about me. They became best friends; and he became my boyfriend.

Three years later, our breakup didn't require a moving van, since our only baggage was emotional. Like Woody and Mia, we had maintained separate apartments. Unlike them, however, our rift didn't rate a mention in the tabloids, so I had no idea what was going on with Daniel. When I came back from Colorado, I noticed that his first-floor apartment stayed dark every night. Nor was he ever outside in his patio garden during the day. Even in the dead of winter, Daniel took painstaking care of his plants, using heaters, lights, and plastic to keep things alive until spring. Evidently, most of his plants had been moved inside, and I'd seen no sign of him. It had started to worry me.

"Did Sheila by any chance tell you where Daniel is?" I abruptly asked Gretchen.

"Yes," Gretchen said. "He's in L.A. in preproduction for a TV movie. Then he'll be filming."

"He got the *Lifetime* movie?" I asked, feeling a mixture of relief, happiness, and pride.

"Uh-huh."

"It wasn't too long ago that he got a better contract with his soap," I said. Daniel played America's favorite daytime villain, Angus Remington, on the daytime drama *Secret Splendor.* "I'm surprised they gave him time off so soon."

"Angus Remington is sending videotapes to terrorize the residents of Splendor Falls while he's away on a sinister mission," Gretchen said. We both laughed, considering that Daniel's *Lifetime* movie would feature him as an angel sent to help three of America's sitcom sweethearts: Meredith Baxter, Valerie Bertinelli, and Jasmine Guy. "Daniel shot the videotapes before he left. That's how they're keeping his storyline moving."

"That's great. He must have been thrilled when it all worked out." Gretchen gave me a strange look and I said, "You're surprised that I'm happy for him? Daniel deserves the best."

"I'm not surprised," she said. "You've always been supportive of him. He *had* the best. I don't understand how he let it slip away."

"I'm not sure I understand it, either," I admitted. "I don't think I realized how many problems we had until after the Maddie Awards."

Gretchen sat back to indicate that she would listen while she ate.

The Maddie Awards were held at a gala dinner and recognized people who'd done outstanding work in Manhattan advertising. I'd been nominated for a campaign I did for my advertising firm that featured Sheila as our model. Sheila's fiancé, photographer Josh Clinton, was nominated for a Prada spread he'd shot for *Ultimate Magazine*. We were all excited about the nominations and, at Daniel and Sheila's request, broke tradition and sat with one another rather than at tables with the other nominees and executives from our respective employers. When both Josh and I won our awards, the night was declared a triumph, and we partied until dawn.

During that evening, I'd experienced a vague uneasiness, but I didn't have time to analyze it because Sheila and I took an extended business trip to Europe immediately afterward. We came back to endless photographs of Sheila and Daniel looking like a radiant couple in publications like *People*, *W*, and *Variety*. When an entire paragraph of Lola Listeria's gossip column in the *Manhattan Star-Gazette* described Daniel and Sheila as the coming century's first supercouple, I hit the roof.

I agreed with Daniel when he pointed out that my work in advertising should make me understand the value of publicity, even when it was contrived or false. But I was furious about feeling used and managed to that end, reminding him that he'd not only capitalized on an event that was meant to be for Josh and me, but he'd been more than a little deceptive in how he'd turned the situation to his advantage.

After I explained all that to Gretchen, she said, "I guess I can see why you were annoyed with Sheila and Daniel. But it doesn't sound serious enough to break up over."

"It wasn't," I agreed. "There's more. Over the past year, he and I made a lot of plans for our future. The big ones were moving in together and eventually having kids. The whole package. I think as his part on *Secret Splendor* got bigger and more demands were made on him to promote the show, our goals stopped being a priority for him. I didn't get that until one night when we were already having a bad fight. He started talking about problems that I didn't even know we had. The stuff he said . . ." I looked at her. "I don't want to get into that. We both said awful things to each other. He told me it was over. I walked out. I haven't seen him or talked to him since."

"You've both been traveling," Gretchen reminded me. "Maybe when he comes back, the two of you can talk more rationally about your problems."

"I think it's beyond that, Gretchen. But I don't want it to hurt my other relationships. Like with Sheila. I hope it doesn't cause problems for you to be friends with me as well as Daniel."

"Are you kidding? You and I will always be friends," she assured me. "Who else would sit through Woody Allen movies with me? Plus you never give me unsolicited advice about my love life. You always heed my recommendations about your investments. You've given me free advertising expertise on my various Happy Hollow ventures. You're my only gay friend who doesn't tell me when my hair is a disaster. You can call me anytime. Except, of course, when *Lou Dobbs Moneyline* is on CNN."

I laughed and shifted the conversation to more neutral topics. After we split the check, we walked outside. It was no longer raining, so once I saw Gretchen into a cab, I decided to walk, hoping to exhaust myself. I'd been having trouble sleeping, which I attributed not only to the breakup with Daniel, but to a slowdown in my workload. I wasn't being challenged enough, which gave me too much time to think about the wreck my personal life had become.

I briefly considered stopping at a bar and finding someone to divert me for an hour or two. There'd been a few of those after I became single. I decided against it. Maybe if I went to bed early enough, I'd sleep in spite of myself. At least I no longer had to look down at Daniel's dark apartment and wonder where he was.

Over the next couple of weeks, cold, gray days continued to dampen my mood. True to her word, Gretchen and I talked every few days. We made tentative plans for our next Gay Day, a screening of the movie *The Women* in mid-February. Gretchen insisted it was mandatory viewing for a gay man. I ended up having to cancel on her because of a business trip. I wasn't sure I regretted missing the movie, but I definitely wasn't sorry that work was kicking into high gear as we finished getting ready for spring and summer.

My focus was all business as yet another soggy day found me boarding a flight to Baltimore with Sheila. She was behind me in line, yelling into her cell phone. I tried to ignore her conversation, but it was next to impossible. Especially when she slid into her seat next to mine.

"Bob," she said into the phone, "you're not listening to me. The point is, I'm presenting an award for best costumes on national television, and Claude Martrand called with an offer to dress me from his couture line . . . Yes, well, you can imagine my surprise when he wondered why I had ignored his invitation to be in his spring runway show . . . Oh, really? He said you were the one who ultimately declined for me, since I was under obligation to Lillith Parker and couldn't do any shows . . . You know that's not true, Bob! I don't want to hear your excuses, either. Lillith may have me on a busy schedule as her Zodiac Girl, but my contract clearly says I can do other jobs as time permits . . . Oh? You think? Well, I've got news for you, honey, I'm on my way to meet with Lillith. I'm on a plane even as we speak . . . No, I don't need you with me. Blaine Dunhill is with me . . . No! Don't call Lillith! It's a personal meeting, Bob . . . Just don't lie to me again. Bye." She closed her cell phone and tucked it into a highly polished, black leather purse.

"Rough day at the office, dear?" I asked.

"Blaine," she said, turning to me, "I swear I'm going to leave Metropole if they don't give me another agent. Bob's a fascist. He thinks he owns me or something."

"Maybe you should talk to your lawyer, Sheila," I offered. I didn't know much about the hierarchy of modeling agencies, so it was the best advice I could think of.

"Maybe you're right." I watched as she bit her lower lip. It was odd how the little overbite never corrected by braces could now earn upwards of fifteen hundred dollars an hour. "It's not even noon and I already have a headache."

"Excuse me," a woman seated across the aisle from us said. Sheila and I both turned to look at the magazine in her hands. "Is this you?"

The magazine was open to an ad for Zodiac's Aquarius line by Lillith Allure Cosmetics. Spread out over two glossy pages was a photograph of Sheila dressed as a mermaid, being carried by a buff man in a Speedo on a sandy beach.

"Gosh. Look at my hair. It's huge," Sheila pointed out.

"It looks great," I observed. "You look fantastic."

"I look like the chicken of the sea."

"Sorry, Charlie," I quipped.

"Would you sign this for me?" the woman asked. "It's for my daughter. She wants to be you when she grows up."

"Aw, that's sweet. I'd be happy to." Sheila took my Mont Blanc pen and signed the magazine. "How old is she?"

"Nine."

"When I was that age, I wanted to be Barbie," Sheila said. "Looks like I made it."

"If you start singing Barry Manilow, I'm getting off this plane," I said.

"You stay right where you are, mister," Sheila ordered. "There's no way I'm facing Lillith the wacko on my own. Besides, she wants to meet with you, too."

"I don't know why I had to cancel two days of meetings to fly to Baltimore for one meeting with her," I said. "If she could just use a phone, or e-mail, like a normal person, my life would be so much easier."

"She can," Sheila said. "Just not while Mars is interfering with her communication planets."

Lillith Parker was my number one client in my role as an advertising executive at Breslin Evans Fox and Dean. In fact, Lillith Allure Cosmetics was my only client. As Lillith Allure's Account Planner, I oversaw all packaging, product development, and promotions. There was a lot on my plate, but I thrived on it. The only hitch was dealing with Lillith's penchant for all things astrological. Her every waking moment—and possibly her dream state, as well—was guided by a series of charts, readings, and courses designed to keep her personal and business lives in harmonious balance with the universe.

Most CEOs had a personal assistant to organize their business lives. Among Ms. Parker's staff were people who read tarot cards, threw rune stones, communed with "the other side," and kept meticulous astrological charts. If there was one star or planet out of place, her life was in turmoil and an entire ad campaign might have to be reworked. During the three years I'd worked with Lillith, I'd had my aura fluffed, my palms read, and my chakras balanced. While I never felt different after these exercises in faith, and whether or not Lillith knew I was only going through the motions, she trusted me with her product line.

"Speaking of Zodiac," I said and opened my briefcase, "I have the final prints for the Taurus line."

I handed Sheila a set of color prints which featured her in a boxing ring. In the photos, she wore bright red boxing trunks, gloves, and a simple tank top. Her eyes were "bruised" with Zodiac's Taurus eye shadow as she charged her opponent in the ring with gloves raised.

"These are terrific, Blaine," Sheila praised, flipping through the pictures. "You've got a great mind for this stuff."

"See how your 'trainer' is whipping that red towel off your shoulders as you're charging into the ring?"

"So it also looks like a bullfight," Sheila observed.

"Taurus is the sign of the bull," I reminded her.

"Such a crafty ad exec, you are," Sheila continued. "I never know how these things are going to turn out when I'm posing. I just trust that you know what you're doing."

"Funny," I said, returning the photos to my briefcase, "that's exactly what Lillith always says."

"She never would've entrusted her business to you if she didn't think you were the right man for the job."

"The same could be said for you, you know. Out of hundreds of women, she picked you to represent her biggest line."

Sheila nodded thoughtfully, her silence giving me time to remember how I'd ended up with a client as bizarre as Lillith Parker. I would never have been able to handle her at the beginning of my career.

Fresh out of college, I'd been hired by Trueluck and Frost, a Wisconsin advertising firm. One of their clients was Frank Allen, the founder of Allure Cosmetics, which sold a line of products that embraced simplicity and classic beauty, yet never went beyond the drugstore and beauty supply market. I'd gotten my shot at the account because Frank wanted to change the direction of Allure Cosmetics' advertising, hoping to appeal to a younger market, and I was the youngest member of the firm. Rehashing an old idea, I launched the "Lady in Red" campaign. We repackaged his line in bright red boxes with black letters and did a series of ads featuring a model with a

Grace Kelly appeal. She had a patrician beauty, but somewhere beneath her surface, one sensed a temptress. One of the first ads featured her in a red dress, clinging to the back of a tuxedoed man on a motorcycle. She traveled in style, but she did it dangerously. She never checked a coat, only a helmet.

Allure Cosmetics' sales rose ten percent, and Frank wanted to keep me and the Lady in Red. But he'd also decided Trueluck and Frost was too provincial to deliver the kind of audience he wanted his ads to have. He was courted by Breslin Evans Fox and Dean, a powerhouse agency in Manhattan. When he signed with them, it was with the stipulation that the firm hire me.

My early days at Breslin Evans were brutal. With the move, Allure Cosmetics became a little fish in a big pond, so I wasn't much more than plankton. The competition for accounts was intense. It was only thanks to Frank's loyalty that I held on to Allure during a time when I was given every third-rate, undesirable project that my superiors—which included basically everyone, since even the administrative staff got more respect than I did—could throw at me.

Through it all, the Lady in Red never waned in popularity. But what did she smell like?

Frank had no experience with perfume, so he asked me to find a line that would mix well with his company. I would never have thought to merge Allure Cosmetics and Lillith Parker Designs if it wasn't for my then-assistant, Sharon. We'd been holed up in my office for a week with Allure samples and hundreds of bottles of perfume, trying to find a good match. My office smelled like the main floor of Bloomingdale's, and we were giddy from the fumes.

"For Pete's sake, open a window, Sharon," I barked. "It smells like my Aunt Gladys in here."

"Believe me, I would," she said, "but we're on the twenty-third floor, and the windows don't open. Where's that can of coffee? It'll cleanse your nose. Here you go." When she passed me the coffee, the can knocked over an open bottle of Halo by Lillith Parker. My desk and several Allure compacts were saturated with the smell of verbena and lilac. "No! Not the eye shadow! I was going to wear it at my bridal shower!" Sharon screamed.

"My desk! You got perfume all over my desk!" I hollered.

"Me? You got perfume in my compact!"

"Hey, wait a minute. Which perfume was that?"

"Lillith Parker's," Sharon answered. "Why?"

"She's the one with those wacky names, right? How about, *Allure Has a Halo?*"

Sharon found the file on Lillith Parker and read aloud, "Lillith Parker Designs manufactures perfumes with celestial imagery in its bottles and titles." She scanned the file. "Aura, Halo, Saturnine, Balance. You could work with these names, Blaine. They'd go well with Allure."

"I think we found it. Where is Lillith Parker located?"

"Baltimore."

"Book us on a flight tomorrow."

"I'll book a flight for you and a temp," Sharon said. "I'm getting married and moving to Connecticut, remember? You need to learn to live without me."

"Whatever, Sharon. Just do it. And send a memo to purchasing that I need a new desk. This one reeks."

Over the next few months, I'd lost Sharon, but Frank Allen gained Lillith Parker as a partner in their joint venture, Lillith Allure Cosmetics. Lillith had all the clout with Breslin Evans that Frank lacked, and she was able to see to it that Blaine Dunhill, new kid on the block, was appointed to handle their account exclusively. In some ways, my life got easier. In others, Lillith definitely was not the easiest client in the world to satisfy.

As the company grew, Lillith decided to try her hand at a subsidiary line of cosmetics based on her passion for astrology. Once Mercury was out of retrograde and it was safe to delve into new ventures, Lillith Allure launched Zodiac. Zodiac's beauty products were based on sun signs. There were twelve different "looks" to the line, which meant a full year of ad campaigns. Lillith wanted one new face to represent the whole line. The Zodiac Girl would be an "All-American," freshly scrubbed beauty transformed by Zodiac's vividly glam colors.

I didn't think about Sheila when Lillith asked me to find the Zodiac Girl. During our first months in New York, Sheila was a relative newcomer to the world of modeling, and her photogenic clock was ticking. She was twenty-two, just out of college, with a degree in liberal arts and a few letters of recommendation to some Manhattan modeling agencies. Because no one told her how impossible her dreams were, she made them come true, getting a contract with Metropole. She owed it to luck, chutzpah, and a few other assets, including flawless skin, legs that wouldn't quit, and a winning disposition. Even the most jaded people in the industry found Sheila irresistible.

In 1998, more than a year into Sheila's career, everyone wanted to be the Zodiac Girl and enjoy the kind of success Elizabeth Hurley had experienced with Estée Lauder or Cindy Crawford had found with Revlon. It wasn't until the eleventh hour that Sheila's composite card made its way to my desk among the hundreds of other faces that I'd been sifting through. Since she had every quality that Lillith had described, I included Sheila among my five choices for the face of Zodiac.

Lillith had zeroed in on Sheila's picture right off the bat. "That's her. She's the one," Lillith said, pointing a finger at Sheila's picture. Which I imagined must have been difficult for Lillith, since she was bound in a detoxifying seaweed wrap at the time of our meeting.

A star was born. Almost literally, since everything connected to Lillith Parker and the Zodiac line was fraught with cosmic significance.

I looked over at Sheila, who was staring through the window of our plane. We'd broken through the rain clouds; bright sunlight illuminated the hair surrounding her face, making her look like an angel. Since I could remember her as the gawky kid who'd tagged along after Jake and me, I sometimes forgot how beautiful she was.

Sheila turned to say, "I'm fucking tired, Blaine."

"Gee, Sheila. You sound like a teamster."

We laughed together as the seat belt lights went off, signaling that it was safe to move about the cabin of the airplane.

"I'm sorry," Sheila continued. "What I mean is—well, I'm *tired*, Blaine. I need a break from all this. I've been going nonstop for over a year now. It's finally getting to me. And I can't hold Josh off any longer."

"I understand," I said.

"It's too bad the days of hair bands are over," Sheila said. "The next logical step in my career would be to put on a bikini and writhe on the hood of a car in a rock video."

"While being hosed down," I added.

"Or licking whipped cream off my fingers and tossing my hair around."

"You could do all that while being hosed down," I said. "You're good at multitasking."

"Thanks!" Sheila said. She pointed to the woman across the aisle, who'd dozed off, and said, "I lied to that woman. When I was younger, I really wanted to be one of those rock video vixens. Maybe not when I was nine, but when I was in high school. Then the grunge thing happened, Guns and Roses broke up, and where are the video vixens now?"

"Come back to the five and dime, Tawny Kitaen, Tawny Kitaen," I mused.

Sheila laughed, then said, "It's just as well. I'm too tired and have no time. I never thought working for Zodiac would be so involved."

"So why did you rip Bob a new asshole because he turned down one fashion show for you?" I asked.

"It's the principle of the thing. I love doing runway work. If it was up to me, I'd do as many fashion shows as possible, even though the money sucks compared to what I get from Zodiac. No questions asked. And no complaints, either. I guess it doesn't matter. I have to think about Josh. I barely have enough time to spend with him as it is. Let alone get married to the poor guy."

After dating for over a year, Josh had proposed to Sheila and she'd accepted. However, the proposal came just before Sheila won the position as the Zodiac Girl. Before she knew it, she was swept into a cycle of travel between print shoots, public appearances, interviews, and commercial shoots. Her life became a "Who's That Girl" media frenzy, and she was rarely at home in Manhattan at the same time as Josh.

Working as a fashion photographer for many years made Josh sympathetic to Sheila's job. Although he freelanced occasionally, he was employed by *Ultimate Magazine* and often worked close to home. After Josh's proposal, they'd decided to marry in the summer of 1999. It hadn't happened, and he'd agreed to postpone the wedding a year because of Sheila's new job. They had both thought that Lillith Parker would want a new face for the Zodiac line after the first year was over.

They were both wrong. Lillith was drastically opposed to changing anything about how Zodiac was represented to the world. In her opinion, when people thought of Sheila Meyers, they thought of Zodiac. And vice versa. Josh began pressuring Sheila to drop the Zodiac job and help him plan their wedding.

Since Josh's main concern was that her job was limiting their time together, Sheila offered a compromise: She would move in with him into an apartment on the Upper West Side. They moved, I lost my roommate, and Sheila continued as the Zodiac Girl, certain she could squeeze in a wedding this year if she planned everything just right.

"How are the wedding plans going?" I asked.

"Josh wants to get married in June," she replied.

"What do you say?"

"I figure it can happen," she agreed, opening a PalmPilot and bringing up a calendar on its tiny screen. "There's a window of three days during the first weekend of June. If I fly into Wisconsin from—where are we shooting Zodiac's Leo ads?"

"Miami."

"If I fly to Wisconsin from Miami on Thursday night, have my shower on Friday, rehearsal and dinner on Saturday, and wedding on Sunday, I should be able to fly back to New York Sunday night to kick off the promotion for Zodiac's Cancer line after the reception."

"And Josh goes on the honeymoon by himself?" I asked.

"Blaine, you heard my schedule," Sheila said. "Unless I hire a stand-in for my own wedding, it's going to be like an Olympic event trying to fit everything into three days. I can't live my life and also be the Zodiac Girl. It's not fair to Josh. Or to me, for that matter. I'm going to ask Lillith for some time off."

"What? That's impossible."

"I knew I shouldn't have told you," Sheila said and frowned.

"Sheila, we're talking about a multimillion-dollar ad campaign. And you're it. This isn't a shift at Dairy Queen, sweetie. Unless you have a twin sister that I don't know about, there's no way you can take time off."

"I can't believe you're reacting as a businessman instead of as my friend," Sheila said, violently tossing her PalmPilot into her purse. "I hoped that since you were going to see Lillith, too, and since you're supposed to be Josh's best man, you might help me find a way to convince her to give me some time off. You'd think there would be a way to free some time for my wedding."

I sympathized with her, but she knew how Lillith operated. The woman kept every magazine that placed Zodiac's ads in a complete panic because she was determined to shoot each sun sign's photos as closely as possible to the actual dates the sign encompassed. Added to that was her horror of Mercury's capricious behavior and some nonsense about the power of the full moon on cosmetics.

"Call me selfish, but I thought, since you're one of my oldest friends as well as a business colleague, you might find a way to make this all work out," Sheila added, her voice soft, perhaps even a bit defeated.

"I am your friend. And you are selfish. I just don't see it happening," I said, and put my hand on her arm, giving it a gentle squeeze.

"It's easy for you. You're not the one running all over the world for the sake of a tube of lipstick. You're the one pulling the levers behind a curtain like the Wizard of Oz, running the show. If you want to take a break, all you have to do is say *Stop!* and everything comes to a halt. But what about me? I have to answer to you, Lillith, Bob the pig, and Metropole. I just want to get married, for gosh sake."

We both paused, listening to the white noise of the airplane as it zoomed us to Baltimore, while we sat in our seats, stuck between a rock and a hard place. A flight attendant stopped by and asked if we'd like something to drink.

"I'd love a Bloody Mary," I said.

"I'll have a diet ginger ale, please," Sheila said.

"She's being awfully difficult today. Would you add a little arsenic to her ginger ale?" I asked. "Oh, wait. This is first class. I should be able to get cyanide."

"Ignore him," Sheila said, giving the flight attendant a winning smile.

The flight attendant eyed me warily, then stared at Sheila as if noticing her for the first time. "Aren't you in those cell phone commercials?"

"Yes," Sheila said, blushing.

"I love the one where the spy is trying to break into an office, but he can't remember the alarm codes. Then you fall down from the ceiling on a cable, like in *Mission Impossible,* with a cell phone in your hand so he can call headquarters."

"But I scare the crap out of him and he ends up setting off the alarm," Sheila recalled. "That was the first ad in the series. Another one will premiere during the Oscars, but it's my last. I only signed to do five."

"That's too bad," the flight attendant said. "They were cute. I'll be right back with your drinks."

"Your fans know no altitude. We're always running into people who adore you," I said. Sheila shrugged, but said nothing. I couldn't tell if she was trying to be humble or if she was still annoyed with me, so I said, "When we were teenagers in Eau Claire, I never thought we'd turn into the two people on this plane."

Sheila started laughing and said, "You didn't? Gosh, when we were dating, I just *knew* you'd turn into a gay advertising executive and I'd be a jaded, bitter model."

"You're not jaded," I said. "You're tired. Anyway, when we were dating, even I thought I was straight. I dumped you for Sydney Kepler, after all."

"You dumped me? I think not, Mister Man. I dumped you when you slept with Sydney, my alleged friend, behind my back. And you stayed with that hag just to look good to all your dumb jock buddies and frat brothers."

"I did not," I protested. "And Sydney isn't a hag." Sheila stared at me with a bemused expression for a second, and we both burst out laughing. "Okay," I gave in. "Sydney's a bitch, but she's not a hag."

"You say tomato, I say tomahto."

"It's best that we don't speak of the extortionist," I said, using my favorite pet name for my ex-wife.

"You're the one who lets her get away with it," Sheila said. "I can't believe you fronted her the money for that gallery. As if she'd recognize a decent painting if one landed on her perfectly coifed little head."

I closed my eyes, wishing I could shut out the memory of Sydney and her paintings, about which the kindest description might be "uniquely atrocious." Sydney had started out doing the standard novice's still lifes. Bowls of fruit, flowers in a vase, sheet music resting atop a grand piano, next to a violin, in front of a picture window, beyond which could be seen a well-manicured lawn. It was what our friend Blythe called "Junior League Art," after all the women who took an art class between shuffling kids to soccer and raising money for charity.

Then one night the accident occurred. In the middle of a fight with me about the Lady in Red campaign—Sydney was positive I was having an affair with the model because our marital bed was hardly blissful and rarely busy—she flung a bottle of Allure's Ruby Red nail polish at me. It shattered on a canvas of marigolds, the glass sticking in the paint, and *art* was born. Sydney liked to give interviews in which she said she was challenging a patriarchal society's view of beauty in its traditional forms. It was all bullshit, but somehow it launched a career for her.

Unfortunately, that career didn't come with enough money to keep Sydney away from my bank account, even after our divorce. She was determined not to slither back under the thumb of her wealthy, domineering father, and I was easily intimidated by her, especially after she learned "Blaine's little secret," as she liked to call my homosexuality.

Sydney's manipulations were like a well-executed marketing campaign, and her slogan was, "Knowledge is power." Unoriginal, much like Sydney, but effective, since I'd spent so many years successfully selling the product that was Blaine Dunhill: scion of a prominent Eau Claire businessman, hero of the gridiron in my youth, the golden boy who was going places. If Sydney exposed my secrets, my trophies and awards would be yanked from the shelves faster than a tainted batch of Tylenol. Daniel's slogan for the quandary was, "The truth shall set you free." Unfortunately, that clashed with my golden-boy catchphrase, "What you don't know won't hurt you." Even if I could face a fall from grace in Eau Claire, there was still my family to consider. The truth would probably finish what remained of my relationship with my parents after my divorce.

I opened my eyes again when I heard our flight attendant say, "Here are your—"

Just then we encountered turbulence and the plane began shuddering violently. I watched as the flight attendant stumbled and our drinks flew out of his hands and onto the woman across the aisle. She woke up with a yelp when the ginger ale and ice covered her lap, then she screamed in alarm as the Bloody Mary oozed over her head.

"Ladies and gentleman, this is your captain speaking. We've run into some turbulence. Please buckle your seat belts and refrain from moving about the cabin."

"Now he tells us," I said.

"I'm so sorry," our flight attendant whimpered, while the saturated woman ignored our captain and unbuckled her safety belt. She stalked toward the rest room and the flight attendant followed, still apologizing.

"That poor woman," Sheila said.

"I hope the cyanide doesn't eat through her skirt," I said. "What were we talking about?"

"Your ex-wife. Where is the *stunning* Sydney these days?" Sheila asked, injecting the adjective with enough venom to fatally poison half of our fellow travelers.

"In Italy. Procuring artists for her gallery or some such nonsense. She'll be back in a couple of months, I think."

"Oh, no," Sheila said, obviously doing the math in her head.

"Uh-huh. While we're in Eau Claire for your wedding—"

"The hag from hell could be there, too," finished Sheila with a frown. "Doing everything in her power to make your visit the most miserable experience possible. Our best man won't be in best spirits, that's for sure. I'm sorry, Blaine. But hey, there probably won't be a wedding anyway, since I'll be too busy and Josh will be so infuriated that he'll leave me. And you won't have to worry about me, so you can focus your energy on battling Sydney, the hound from hell."

"Hag from hell," I corrected.

"You said she's a bitch, not a hag," Sheila reminded me.

"Tomato, tomahto," I responded in a singsong voice.

"Please don't say tomato or tomahto when that woman gets back from the rest room," Sheila implored. "I don't understand why Sydney's still milking you for money. From every horrifying account I hear, she has one of the most successful small galleries in Chicago."

"She enjoys making me sweat," I said. "She's just like her father; they both love power. She has a little power over me, and she luxuriates in reminding me of it."

"If you could just be honest with your parents—"

"You know why I can't," I said. "My mother."

Again I watched Sheila bite her lip. I knew what she wanted to say, and the problem was that I agreed with her. For as long as I could remember, my mother had used her health to avoid anything unpleasant. I was convinced that most of her maladies were imaginary, but she'd had a mild heart attack after my divorce from Sydney. That, at least, hadn't been faked, and my father and brothers placed the blame squarely on me. If my family found out I was gay, and anything happened to my mother . . . As estranged as I was from them all, I would never forgive myself.

"How are your brothers?" Sheila asked, seeming to read my mind.

"I think Shane is having an affair with a waitress," I said. "As for Wayne, who knows?"

Giving their sons rhyming names had been the only "cute" thing my parents had ever done. In fact, it baffled me that, as staid and unapproachable as they were, they'd managed to produce offspring. I'd always hoped that in one of the many deathbed scenes my mother enacted to her guilty and captive audience over the years, she'd confess that I was the result of some midlife indiscretion. It would explain so many things.

Both of my brothers worked for my father at Dunhill Electrical, a fate I'd managed to escape. Since I'd be twenty-eight in May, I calculated that Shane must be forty-two. Being a married father of three hadn't slowed him down any. Even though I thought his wife was shallow and self-absorbed, I found his serial adultery disgusting.

As for Wayne, he was eleven years older than me. Though I was the one they called "the accident," I tended to see Wayne in that category. Actually, I saw him as a sociopath waiting for the right moment to rain down destruction on Eau Claire. For as long as I could remember, he'd had a rifle and a Confederate flag in the back of his pickup truck, though to my knowledge, no ancestor of ours had ever been south of the Mason-Dixon Line. Wayne was a conspiracy theory buff. If they hadn't already arrested the Unabomber, I'd have been happy to turn *my* brother in for questioning. He had to be guilty of something.

"It's not easy, Blaine. I understand," Sheila said softly.

"Oh, hell, there are worse things than coming from a dysfunctional family. At least we had money. And they put me through college so I could get away from them. At any rate, you and I have been friends for a long time. I understand your frustration about your wedding plans. But this could be a bad time to ask Lillith for favors, and timing is everything. If there's anything I understand, it's when and how to pitch an idea. Trust me and be patient. Don't give up on me, or Zodiac, just yet."

Sheila turned a warm smile in my direction and said, "I won't. I'm sorry for being so demanding when you're still dealing with—" She saw me cringe and stopped herself from mentioning my breakup with Daniel. Before I could say anything, she continued, "As far as Zodiac goes, even if things don't work out my way, I'll be there for you. You know that, Blaine."

We spent the rest of our flight in silence. I assumed Sheila was brooding over Josh and their elusive wedding. I was envisioning a product called Milk of Amnesia. It could settle my stomach even as it helped me forget my ex-boyfriend.

Ex-boyfriend. That description for Daniel didn't seem real. In any case, he was still Sheila's best friend. I knew that if Daniel was in my position, he'd do whatever he could to help her work things out with Lillith so she could have her wedding. He nurtured his friends with the same painstaking care he gave the plants and flowers in his garden.

I sighed and tried to figure out a way to present Sheila's need for a leave of absence to Lillith Parker and Frank Allen. It might help me silence the Daniel voice-over in my head that was scolding me about the importance of friendship.

CHAPTER 2

Sheila's situation was uppermost on my mind while we rode to the offices of Lillith Allure Cosmetics. I also wondered why I'd been summoned to Baltimore by Ms. Parker. The message relayed to me by my executive assistant, Violet, was cryptic, to say the least.

"I don't know, Blaine," Violet had said. "All Lillith said was, 'Now is the time for removing clutter and putting things in the proper order.' Then she informed me that she needed to meet with you immediately and asked me to book you a flight to Baltimore."

I could only guess what Lillith's idea of *clutter* and *proper order* were, and what they meant to our business arrangements. Obviously it had to do with some nonsense read to her by an astrologer or a gypsy fortune-teller. However, despite the carnival of mystic charlatans traipsing in and out of her offices, Lillith Parker was a shrewd businesswoman sitting on top of a multimillion-dollar industry. I had no doubt that, all karma aside, her main interest was running the well-oiled machine that was Lillith Allure Cosmetics.

"Why do I always feel like Dorothy walking down that long corridor on her way to see the wizard whenever I come here?" Sheila said during our elevator ride to Lillith's office.

"Hey. A mere hour ago, you said I was the wizard."

"No," Sheila stated. "I said you were the man behind the curtain pulling the levers."

"Oh, great," I said. "I'm the humbug."

"You said it. Not me," she said, following her words with a giggle.

When we arrived at the eighteenth floor—the numbers one and eight added together equaled nine, which represented the number of planets in the solar system—Sheila and I departed the elevator and greeted Barbara, Lillith's assistant.

"Perfect," Barbara said, looking at her watch. "You two are right on time. I'll take you into Lillith's office, but we have to be quiet. She'll be finishing up with her last appointment."

"Maybe we should wait," I said cautiously, not wanting to upset the harmonious balance of Lillith's appointment calendar.

"Are we seeing her together?" Sheila asked.

"Yes," Barbara answered. "Follow me. It's okay."

Barbara led us into Lillith's cavernous office and quietly shut the door behind us. French doors opened to a sitting room, where Lillith was seated on a Victorian fainting couch posing for a photographer. Her dark, graying hair was twisted on top of her head in a chignon and held in place by a jeweled comb. Although her face was slightly equine, long with pronounced cheekbones and jutting chin, she had a regal beauty. Her brown eyes were accented by the shimmering brown of Zodiac's Aquarius eye shadow, and her lips were rouged in the deep red from Zodiac's Leo line.

As Lillith turned her face to the left and the photographer's shutter started clicking again, I whispered to Barbara, "Is this for a magazine?"

"No," Barbara whispered back. "She's having her aura photographed. She does it periodically to monitor changes. We can often predict how our fiscal quarters will turn out based on the color of Lillith's aura."

I could see Sheila, standing behind Barbara, suddenly bite down on her fist to keep from laughing out loud. Feeling as though I had now heard everything, I merely said, "I see," and watched as Lillith rose from the settee and thanked the photographer.

"I think she's ready for you now," Barbara said, turning to leave the office. "Good luck."

"Ah," I said, "but Barbara, you know there's no such thing as luck." She snickered softly and winked before shutting the door behind her.

"Blaine. Sheila," Lillith said, striding toward us with an outstretched hand. "It's so good of you both to cooperate with my busy schedule and see me today. I'm sorry about the short notice, but you know how it is. Please sit down." As Lillith sat behind her desk and began opening a few folders, Sheila and I situated ourselves in two ornately carved chairs, each with dragon heads protruding from the armrests. "Sheila," Lillith went on, glancing over what looked like a memo, "Barbara informs me that you have issues with your Zodiac contract."

"Yes," Sheila said somewhat meekly. "Sort of."

Lillith looked up from the memo, arched her eyebrows, and looked down her nose to where Sheila met her line of vision. "Sort of," she repeated. "That must be a business term that I've yet to encounter. Be that as it may, Sheila, I adore you as if you were my own child. I want you to know that I have your best interests at heart. I know you're well aware that I prefer to conduct my business affairs one-on-one without the interfering energies of lawyers, agents, and the like. So first of all, thank you both for bringing yourselves and nobody else."

Unsure of what to say, Sheila and I answered in unison, "You're welcome."

"I'm unclear what the dissatisfactory nature of your contract might be, Sheila," Lillith continued, dropping the memo in favor of a red stone, which she began rubbing with her fingers as she spoke. "Whatever it is, I sense that it's of a personal nature. Am I correct?"

"I guess it is," Sheila slowly agreed.

"I'm sure it is," Lillith said, smiling as she dropped the stone on her desk. "My astrologer recommends business before pleasure today. Therefore, Sheila, please allow me to conduct business with Blaine before we attend to your personal issues."

Sheila opened her mouth, perhaps to protest that her contract was indeed a business-related issue, but she sighed instead and answered, "Sure, Lillith. Should I leave while you talk with Blaine?"

"No, my dear. Our interests, our jobs, and our energies are all connected," replied Lillith. She turned her brown eyes to me and said, "Blaine, the time has come for me to remove clutter and restore balance to my company."

"Yes. My assistant relayed that message to me," I said. "But what does that have to do with me? As far as I know, things are going well for Lillith Allure and Zodiac."

"Be that as it may, for some time now, I've been wanting to make changes within our company. As Saturn has entered Virgo, it's time to remove the clutter and business will improve."

"Exactly what is this clutter that you keep referring to?" I asked, suddenly nervous.

"Breslin Evans Fox and Dean, of course," she said with a half smile. I tried to remain passive as I felt my stomach churn in horror. My hands began strangling the dragon heads on the arms of my chair as Lillith went on. "In the long run, I'll be making a move to benefit Lillith Allure. I want to cut out the middle man, so to speak. Breslin Evans Fox and Dean are getting the boot. They're the clutter."

"Who's taking over your advertising? Who are you going to find that's better than our company?"

"I think Lillith is looking to hire you," Sheila guessed.

"Exactly," Lillith said. "I'm willing to break my contract with Breslin Evans Fox and Dean, and pay whatever fee I have to, if you'll quit and work for me. I want you to run an in-house ad department. It's more cost-effective for the company, so I'm going to do it whether or not you take the job, Blaine. It's your call."

"What about Frank?" I asked. "How does he fit into this?"

"Perhaps that's what I mean when I say restore the balance. Wouldn't you say that Lillith Parker is the big number in the Lillith Allure equation?"

I stared at her, thinking of all that Frank had done for me. It would take more than the expense of my Manhattan lifestyle, not to mention the bottomless pit that was Sydney's blackmail, to make me betray the goodhearted soul of Frank Allen. Although I knew it might be professional suicide, I heard myself saying, "If you're planning to push Frank out, I'm afraid I can't be part of your team, Lillith."

She picked up her seer's stone—I flinched inwardly, remembering how Daniel loved to call it her Sears stone—and stared into it. Her face was calm, as if I hadn't rejected her offer.

"Blaine, you understand me so little, but I'm glad that I understand you so well. If you'd said anything else, I'd have been disappointed. I want your kind of loyalty. Frank has become a friend as well as my business partner over these last two years. I can't imagine going forward without either of you." I exhaled, and she finally

smiled, then continued. "After consulting with my advisors, I understand that it's best if we relocate our base of operations to Manhattan.
Frank agrees. That's going to be expensive, and we'd like to cut costs
in other areas. I can double what the agency is paying you and still
save money."

"I want to stay with you, Lillith," I said. "But I have two requests."

"Indeed?" The hand on the seer's stone became still.

"We have to stop shooting our print ads so close to deadline. It's
awful for the morale of everyone involved. It builds resentment and
jacks up our ad prices. It may be astrologically sound, but it's bad
business. And at least this year, we need to double up on the Cancer
and Leo campaigns, because Sheila needs a rest afterward. She's
hardly going to be our fresh-faced, healthy spokesmodel if we work
her half to death."

I could sense Sheila leaning forward to grip her dragon heads.

"Gracious, Sheila, why do you pay your agency twenty percent
when Blaine is doing their work?" Lillith asked. "Here I thought you
simply wanted time off for something so frivolous as your wedding."

"You knew?" Sheila asked.

"I had three of my most reliable psychics do a reading for you,
dear. Better make it July, not June. We'll shoot the Cancer, Leo, *and*
Virgo campaigns between now and then, which will give you all of
July to marry, honeymoon, and, er, rest, as Blaine says. So, do we
have a deal?"

"I thought you said it was business before pleasure today," Sheila
said, giving Lillith her most dazzling smile as she stood and held out
her hand.

Lillith took it then turned to me and asked, "Blaine?"

"I'd like to see everything on paper, but my tentative answer is
yes," I said.

"I'll leave all that to you, Frank, and the attorneys," Lillith said.
"Now if you two will excuse me, I have a shiatsu session scheduled."

I felt like we should back out of there bowing, but we managed to
leave with our dignity. At least until Barbara winked at us outside the
door and gave us a thumbs-up. Both Sheila and I laughed with nervous relief.

"Josh is going to be so happy," Sheila said. "I mean, he wanted

June, but to get the whole month of July! We can have a real wedding and a real honeymoon! Blaine, would you really have made your employment contingent on what Lillith would do for me?"

"You heard me say it," I reminded her.

She threw her arms around me and said, "I'm sorry for being so vile to you on the plane. You're my best friend in the whole world!"

She was wrong. Daniel was her best friend in the whole world, but he still had enough influence over me to make me put her happiness before my business concerns.

"Hey, would you mind flying back to New York solo?" I asked. "There are some things I'd like to take care of here. I need to see Frank."

"Not at all," she said. "I could practically fly back under my own power right now. I don't need Lillith's psychics to know I'm going to have a *great* night with Josh."

I hugged her at the elevator. When the doors closed and I could no longer see her beaming face, I glanced at my watch, sure Frank would still be in his office.

Unlike Lillith, Frank didn't keep his desk between us when his secretary Phyllis ushered me in to see him. I never had to worry about the position of the moon when meeting with Frank, who operated on a normal schedule and took Lillith's astrological beliefs with a grain of salt. The only charts Frank was interested in were net gains and customer demographics. I admired his sound business practices, but I also appreciated his amiable approach to the people who were part of his business. After several years of his support and belief in my work, I felt an almost familial connection with him.

He enthusiastically shook my hand and guided me to his leather sofa, sitting down next to me. As I always did in his presence, I felt relaxed and unworried, as if we were sitting on a porch swing drinking lemonade, while we went over the reasons why Lillith's offer was a good one for me.

"It's not as bad being in the same office with her as you might think," Frank assured me. "In fact, there's fun to be had trying to anticipate what hocus pocus might be part of any given day. And she's a damn shrewd businesswoman, with terrific ideas."

"I agree with you there," I conceded. "I just never thought you'd move to Manhattan, Frank."

"It's all been downhill since Kenosha," he said with a smile. "Baltimore, New York. Six of one, half dozen of another. Rowdy and I get back to Lake Michigan for R and R whenever we can."

Rowdy was Frank's yellow Labrador retriever and his constant companion since his wife's death a few years before. Frank seemed to be satisfied with that arrangement, although I was sure there must be women who pursued him. Not only was he a gentleman with a good sense of humor, but he wasn't bad looking for a man in his late fifties who'd lost most of his hair. In fact, I thought the bald look worked for him. But I'd never heard him mention anyone special in his life, except his son, who did something at the Pentagon, and Rowdy.

Thinking of Frank's dog reminded me of Dexter, my cat, and I made a mental note to call Violet and ask her to check on him in my absence.

"Oh," I said, "if I accept Lillith's offer, there's no way I can go anywhere without Violet. I can't function without her."

"Way ahead of you," Frank said. "Lillith and I already decided to have Violet work with our realtor to look at office space in Manhattan and coordinate the move with our people here. I'll feel better knowing she's involved."

"Good. I can give your agent a recommendation regarding moving and setting up computer equipment. A friend of mine who's based in Wisconsin has a Manhattan office, too."

"I always like to give business to someone from the Badger State," Frank said. After a pause, he added, "You said *if* you decide to take our offer. What's making you hesitate, Blaine?"

"I was thinking earlier of when I first went to Breslin Evans Fox and Dean," I said. "Except for your account, I was basically a grunt. You were the one who trusted me. They didn't. They gave me the most menial tasks on other accounts because they thought I didn't have what it takes. I used to seethe about the humiliation and think to myself, 'One day, it will be Breslin Evans Fox and *Dunhill*.' "

"What happened to Dean?" Frank asked with a laugh.

"I'll never tell where the bodies are buried," I said. I gave him a rueful smile and said, "If I leave, it's like I'll never get a chance to prove myself there. Does that sound pathetic?"

"Not pathetic. Inaccurate," Frank said. "Your creativity helped put

Allure Cosmetics in a new league and was an important part of the Lillith Parker/Allure merger. You don't have anything to prove to anyone. If you choose to come to Lillith Allure, you'll be the final authority on our advertising, reporting only to Lillith and me. That's not a step back."

"True," I said, knowing he was right.

After I left Frank, I called Violet so I could tell her that I'd decided to stay in Baltimore.

"I know; I already spoke to Sheila," Violet said. "I'll check on Dexter."

"A couple of hundred years ago, you'd have been on trial for witchcraft," I said, awed as always by her efficiency.

"A couple of hundred years ago, I wouldn't have been anywhere near your Puritan ancestors. I would have been reading chicken entrails in Cuba."

"Could you please not ever mention that to Lillith?" I begged.

Violet laughed and said, "I booked you a suite at the Harbor Court Hotel. It's got a view of the Inner Harbor, a fitness center, and a couple of restaurants. Or twenty-four-hour room service if you prefer, because I also took the liberty of booking a massage therapist—his name is Gavin—to come to your room at nine. Henry from Brooks Brothers will be delivering a couple of changes of clothes and underwear to you. Anything else?"

"Yes. Will you marry me?"

"No. The first thing you'd do is cut my salary. Have a good night, Mr. Dunhill."

"You, too, Ms. Medina. Tell Dexter I miss him."

The view from my hotel room was as pleasing as Violet had led me to believe. I decided to forgo the restaurants and fitness center, ordering from room service. While I was eating, Henry arrived with my new clothes, crisp and fresh from a detour to the cleaners. He made me try on everything to reassure himself that Violet's measurements had been accurate. Obviously he had no idea how thorough she was.

I had been through many assistants before and after the days of Sharon. Even Daniel had worked for me, until it became obvious that our relationship was getting serious and we needed to separate our personal and business lives. But no one could compare to Violet Medina, who'd initially been assigned to me on a temporary basis. After a week, I'd have given her anything, including my salary, to hold on to her.

More than a year later, I had only one reason to regret hiring her—her physical appearance. She was a dead ringer for Jennifer Lopez. In fact, building security had more than once ushered the celebrity's young fans out of the lobby when they'd followed Violet from the subway or the sidewalk. Straight men in the office tended to gather wherever she was, but she paid them little attention. My biggest fear was that she'd get married one day and leave me. I knew nothing about her personal life, but Sheila told me to relax. She was sure Violet would be with me for a long time. Since Sheila always seemed to know everything about everyone, I took her word for it. Mainly because anything else was unthinkable.

I took a quick shower and was watching CNN in the terry-cloth robe provided by the hotel when Gavin arrived. I was impressed. Violet had managed to locate a massage therapist who was not only courteous and professional, but also handsome. His curly auburn hair was clipped short and gelled off of his high forehead. His bright brown eyes matched his chatter as he set up a massage table. Once I dropped my robe and settled onto the table, he was quiet, only asking if I minded if he turned off the television to play a CD.

As soon as his hands made their first pass down my back, I knew how much I'd needed this kind of work. "Did my assistant schedule you for one or two hours?" I asked.

"One."

"You're staying for two. I hope that's not a problem."

"Not at all."

I relaxed, letting my mind drift as Gavin found knots and aches I hadn't known were there. After only a couple of minutes, I was bored thinking about work. It was obvious to everyone, including me, that I'd leave Breslin Evans and go in-house with Lillith Allure. It would be exciting to manage a staff of my own, with Violet's help, and get more creative freedom than I'd had as part of the agency. And the salary increase would be great. Of course, it was nothing compared to what Sheila was making. But Sheila's career had a short

shelf life, as she was well aware. I had decades ahead of me, and I
knew Frank was right. Going to Lillith Allure was not a step back but
a step forward.

It was weird not to call Daniel and share my good news. I wondered if Sheila would tell him. Or if he'd call to congratulate me. Or if
he'd even care.

I didn't realize I was crying until I noticed the dampness of the
cover on the face rest. I felt like an idiot and hoped Gavin couldn't
tell. He was working deep into my lower back and glutes, though, so
unless I sniffed or something . . .

"Do you need a Kleenex?" Gavin asked quietly.

"Yeah, I guess." He handed me one then went back to work.
"Sorry," I said. "It's not like you're hurting me or anything."

"It happens more often than you'd believe," Gavin said. "Sometimes this is the first chance people have to be quiet and think about
stuff that's bothering them. Don't worry about it."

In some ways, Gavin was right. My emotions about Daniel ran the
gamut from anger to hurt, but I could usually block them out. Until I
went to bed, when I'd replay the months before we broke up, trying
to figure out how it happened. I'd thought we would be together forever.

It was hard to know when the strain between us started. There
wasn't any one event; something easy to pinpoint like infidelity. Or
the usual issues that broke people up, like money worries, incom-
patibility, a drinking problem, or family crap. Nor had the magic gone
out of our relationship. Sometimes when we looked at each other,
the entire world seemed to vanish, and he still made my heart race.

There had been some tense moments because of friends, although we both got along great with Sheila, Josh, and Gretchen.
Daniel was also originally from Eau Claire, and we had mutual friends
there, including Adam Wilson, the computer genius that I'd recommended to Frank. Adam and I had become close friends, and I made
a mental note to suggest that, in addition to helping us set up our
systems at the new office, he take over Lillith Allure's Web site from
the company that presently handled many of Breslin Evans' accounts.

But Adam was part of a package deal. His boyfriend, Jeremy
Caprellian, had been Daniel's boyfriend only a few years before.

They'd salvaged a friendship out of their bitter breakup; sometimes Daniel was a little too preoccupied by Jeremy to suit me. Still, once Jeremy moved to Wisconsin to be with Adam, he wasn't always demanding Daniel's time and attention the way he once had.

It was Daniel's other friends who caused problems. For several years, he'd performed as a female impersonator, becoming something of a Manhattan celebrity. Though he'd given up the job before I met him, many of the people from those days remained part of his family of friends.

I felt as if someone was always asking Daniel for something. His time, his attention, his money. He never said no. Which was admirable, but it got tiring, especially the histrionics that accompanied breakups, cruel landlords, lost jobs, and traitorous friends—few of those whiners ever took the responsibility for their own misfortunes. I accepted that what Daniel did for them was his business, but it got annoying to live with a choir of poor-me victims singing in the background.

Likewise, Daniel had issues with some of the people from my past. Although he understood my unwillingness to confront my parents with the truth about my sexuality, he didn't always understand why I let it upset me so much. Nor did he like feeling that our relationship became invisible when we went to Eau Claire. But what he really didn't like was the way I capitulated to Sydney. He could always sense when I'd heard from her. He didn't ask for details about the money I gave her, but he found ways to silently communicate his disapproval.

In retrospect, I supposed that it wasn't what we fought about, but how we fought, that caused most of our problems. Daniel and I both tended to sit on our feelings until they exploded. By the time we got around to fighting, it was nastier than it needed to be. We could also both hold a grudge, so old issues tended to reappear during our fights, which didn't help.

In spite of that, we'd had no major problems until a few months after Daniel got his role as Angus Remington on *Secret Splendor.* I didn't notice any changes at first. I'd always worked long hours, so most of our time together came on the weekends, whether we took trips upstate, enjoyed Manhattan nightlife, or just hung out at his place or mine. It gradually began to dawn on me that not only were

Daniel and I no longer going out, but Daniel never went to Club Chaos, the nightclub where he'd once headlined as his alter ego, Princess 2Di4. Since his friends weren't seeing him there, they tended to appear at his apartment at odd hours, often interrupting our dinners, videos, and more intimate moments.

I complained, and the river of needy friends slowed to a trickle. When I finally realized that Daniel had seriously curtailed his social life, he confessed that a few of the people at his show's network had advised him to keep what they called an LGP—Low Gay Profile. Apparently soap viewers had a tendency to overidentify actors with the roles they played. Angus Remington was written as a lady-killer, and although the executives hadn't asked Daniel to step back into the closet from which he'd emerged well over a decade before, they did encourage his discretion.

It didn't really bother me. I'd never been one for trumpeting my sexual orientation to the world, especially since my family was clueless. So it was probably unattractive of me to enjoy taking an occasional shot at Daniel for his new discretion. I considered it payback for the times that he'd jokingly told people how he had to drag me kicking and screaming from the closet after Sydney and I separated. Maybe Daniel felt he had it coming, too, because he tolerated my verbal bullets.

Looking back, I could see what a toll the situation must have taken on him. He'd always lived his life with an honesty that I admired, and he was struggling with his new boundaries. *Us* magazine gave him a cover, dubbing him "Soap's Sexiest Snake," and his fans were clamoring for information about him. The press was willing to play his game as long as they had something to hook their stories on. Sheila's rising celebrity provided exactly that.

It came to a head the night Sheila and I got back from our publicity junket in Europe. In spite of the excitement we'd felt about our trip, we'd both been homesick. She missed Josh, and I missed Daniel. It was the longest he and I had ever been separated. I'd wanted to make a celebration of our return, so I asked Daniel to hire a limo and meet us at the airport with champagne and Josh. What I didn't know was that Lillith, delighted by the attention Sheila had garnered, wanted to keep the momentum going. She'd arranged for us to be met at the airport, too. By a team of reporters and photographers.

I was used to stepping away from Sheila when the media focused on her. The only thing I wanted was to feel Daniel's arms around me. But when I walked toward him, he took a step back and looked nervous. When I stopped, confused and hurt, Sheila spotted him and rushed to hug him. While the flashbulbs exploded, I met Josh's eyes. He shrugged, as if to remind me that it was all part of the game. Unfortunately, I didn't feel as resigned as he did.

This incident added to the Maddie Awards caused bad feelings to simmer between Daniel and me for days. It might have been resolved eventually, and at least half forgotten, but it was still too fresh when I found out by accident that Mrs. Lazenby was dead. In fact, had been dead for several weeks.

"Did that hurt?" Gavin asked, jolting me back to the present.

"What?" I asked.

"You made a noise. I thought I hurt you."

"No. It feels great. Sorry."

"I'm ready for you to turn over," he said.

I did, and he started working from my feet up into my quads, while I brooded about the proverbial straw that broke the camel's back. I'd just stepped out of bodyWorks, my Chelsea gym, when I heard someone call my name. I turned and saw Daniel's friend Martin Blount and our artist friend Blythe Mayfield walking down the sidewalk, their arms loaded with bags from Bed Bath & Beyond. I stopped to talk to them, awed that Blythe's hair, usually magenta, was now brilliant purple with an occasional red streak. It took me a few minutes to comprehend what they were excited about.

". . . and it was Daniel who suggested it as the perfect solution," Blythe was saying. "Now I've got light and heat and someone to make sure I'm still alive when I go off on one of my painting tangents and don't surface for days."

"Like Mrs. Lazenby," Martin said, and they laughed with guilty expressions.

"I'm sorry," I said. "What are you talking about?"

"If only I could speak with subtitles. Try to keep up this time, Blaine," Martin said. He continued, using elaborate hand gestures. "Mrs. Lazenby *died*, so obviously she didn't need the second floor of the town house. I wanted Blythe to move in, but she said the lighting sucked. Then the couple on the third floor agreed to switch apartments for a rent reduction, so now they're on the second, and Blythe will be on the third, with new skylights installed courtesy of Daniel."

There was an angry humming in my ears, and I was certain I could not have heard him correctly. The town house he was talking about had been left to Daniel by an old friend, Ken Bruckner, who'd died from AIDS a couple of years before. I'd wanted to move there with Daniel, but he hadn't wanted to displace Martin, who'd been Ken's lover. Our compromise was Daniel's assurance that if his second- or third-floor tenants ever left, we'd take the first available floor and move out of our separate Hell's Kitchen apartments to set up housekeeping together.

"This was Daniel's idea?" I asked.

"Isn't it great?" Blythe asked.

"It was a solution, yes," I agreed. "I'm sorry; I have to run. I'm late for a meeting that's long overdue."

I let myself into Daniel's apartment, doing all the things I knew he'd love, including turning on the fountain and the lights of his patio garden and timing our meal of Thai lemon chicken just right so that when he walked in, I was lighting candles on the table.

"What a nice surprise," he said, wrapping his arms around me. "I skipped lunch today because that idiot Jane-Therese kept blowing our scene. Recovery. Ha. She recovered from rehab faster than anyone I've ever known. Mmmm, you smell great. You showered at the gym?"

"Yep," I said. "Just get comfortable and let me serve you."

"You don't have to twist my arm," Daniel said, grinning with his eyebrows raised. He sat at the table and watched while I poured wine. When he bit into the chicken, he made an appreciative noise and said, "This is perfect."

"Good," I said, biting into my own chicken, which might as well have been shoe leather. "Now tell me about your day and the evil Jane-Therese."

I laughed in all the appropriate places during his story, refilling his glass from time to time. When the first candle sputtered, he seemed to realize that he'd been doing all the talking.

"I'm sorry," he said. "I didn't even ask about your day."

"Oh, you know, the usual. I'm much more concerned about you."

"Concerned? Why?"

"I heard the news, and I know how much it must have upset you. It's always hard to lose a little piece of your history."

Daniel frowned, trying to figure out what I was talking about, but obviously enjoying the evening so much that he wasn't sure he wanted to go wherever sad place I was leading him.

"History?" he asked.

"I heard about poor Mrs. Lazenby," I said. "I know how much you and Ken thought of her, so the loss must be hitting you hard." He shifted, but before he could say anything, I went on. "Please don't worry. I'm not going to hound you about moving into her apartment together when you're still reeling from the shock. Besides, I'm not sure I'm ready to do that."

"You're not?" Daniel asked, trying to conceal his relief, which might have been amusing if I hadn't wanted to fling my half-eaten chicken at his face.

"No. The more I thought about it, the more I realized it wouldn't work. I don't want to live that close to Martin."

"You don't?"

"On the floor right above him? No. Can you imagine having to listen to Britney and Cher through our floor at all hours of the day and night?"

"It would be annoying," Daniel quickly agreed.

"I have a much better idea. What if we could get that nice couple—what are their names? I never can remember. The couple on the third floor of the town house. What if we could get them to move to the second floor, then we made renovations to the third floor? I've always thought that kitchen needed to be modernized. And maybe we could have one of those whirlpool bathtubs installed. Wouldn't that be romantic?"

"Well, I—"

"Since neither of us has to give up our apartments anytime soon, we could hire someone to take down that wall between the kitchen and dining room. Make it one big room, with terrazzo tile. If you're really willing to splurge, we could have skylights put in. How great would that look?" Daniel was now on the edge of his chair. "More wine?" I asked, pouring him another glass before he could answer. "Don't you think it would be fun to redesign the place any way we wanted to before we move in? Or . . ."

"Or?" Daniel repeated faintly.

"Or would it be too crowded for us with Blythe living there, too? She does have all those canvases. And I'd be worried about Dexter drinking turpentine."

"I can explain," Daniel said and took a gulp of wine.

"Can you? You can explain how it is that Mrs. Lazenby died weeks ago, but I never heard about it? Not from Adam, who I just talked to a couple of days ago. I'm sure Blythe or Martin told him. Not from Sheila, even though she always knows everything about you, and I see her all the time. And definitely not from you. No, I had to hear about it on the fucking street from Martin and Blythe, with Martin relishing every moment of the bomb he was dropping on me. You fucker."

"They're evicting everyone from Blythe's building to turn it into co-ops—"

"If you and I had moved into the town house, we'd be leaving two empty apartments, either of which could have been sublet to Blythe."

"She can't afford—"

"And since we'd be living for practically nothing in a building you already own free and clear, I'd have been more than willing to help pay rent on whichever of our apartments Blythe wanted. Even though I've been led to understand that she not only has a rich father, but is actually solvent now that her paintings are selling."

"It isn't just the money. You know how close Martin and Blythe are."

"Yeah. So close that you arranged for her to have everything you promised would be ours when it was available. Stop making excuses. You deliberately did all this behind my back because you knew damn well I'd be furious."

"You're right," Daniel said. "You were still so pissed about the Maddie Awards that I didn't think we needed more problems."

"So deceiving me was better for our relationship than having an honest discussion about whether you were ready to live together? God, you've changed. You're such a good liar now."

"I didn't lie," he said angrily, which let me know I'd struck a nerve.

"First it was the little straight show you put on with Sheila for your job, and now this. Maybe you're right. Maybe I'm the one who's lying. To myself. About your level of commitment and your ability to have an adult relationship with anyone. Even worse, you've got my friends lying for you."

"*Your* friends? Most of them are *my* friends. You wouldn't even know them if it wasn't for me."

We were off and running for hours, rehashing every other argument we'd ever had about our friends, our living arrangements, our busy schedules, and our future. By the time I slammed out of his apartment, we both knew we'd said things we shouldn't have, things that couldn't be taken back.

I didn't care what he told our friends. Or *his* friends, as he'd pointed out to me, insisting that my life consisted of little more than my job, my business acquaintances, my gym, and my tendency to live through him. I resolved to keep my mouth shut, especially to Sheila. I was sick of performing the Blaine and Daniel Show for an audience. I'd always tried to have a real relationship with him, not some gay version of *Secret Splendor,* and I had no intention of turning it into a melodrama just because it was over.

"Do you have any idea how much tension you're holding in your jaw?" Gavin asked. "You obviously work out. Do you have a trainer? Because he—or she—could recommend some exercises or body work that would help bring down your stress level."

"I don't have a trainer," I said.

"Maybe you should. Where do you live?"

"New York. Manhattan."

"Oh, God, I miss Manhattan. I know a couple of people I could recommend, if you're interested in working with someone. You should take better care of yourself. What do you do?"

"I'm in advertising."

"Really? Maybe you've heard of my old boss. Lowell Davenport."

"Of course. He was a Madison Avenue legend. You worked for him? What did you do?"

"I started as his trainer," Gavin said. "By the time he died, I guess I was just about everything to him. It was a big scandal that he had AIDS. A lot of his old friends and colleagues abandoned him. You'd think, as gay men, we'd be beyond that after two decades, but advertising's a cutthroat world. No wonder you're so tense."

Gavin's gaydar was apparently more finely tuned than mine, since he assumed I was gay and I'd had no idea he was.

"I never met Lowell," I said, "but he was one of the people I studied. He reinvented advertising in the seventies. What kind of person was he?"

"He was a class act. I adored him. I helped him as he deteriorated physically. Cooked for him. Took care of whatever needs he had. He jokingly called me his manservant, but we were really friends, especially at the end. He took care of me, too. His fortune was pretty well depleted, but he left me the money that helped me set up my practice. But I was so tired of people dying. Sometimes you just want to run away, you know?"

"Yeah, I know."

"My family is here. Outside Baltimore. So I came home. But now that time has passed, I find myself wishing I was back in Manhattan. It's just so expensive to live there."

"You're really good. I probably seemed to be a million miles away, but it's because for the first time I felt relaxed enough to think about things I've been avoiding."

"You're going to be sore, in spite of the fact that you're in great shape. You released a lot of tension. Drink twice as much water as you usually do. Add fresh papaya and pineapple to your diet. And do think about working with a trainer."

"You're hired," I said, only half joking. Gavin laughed and handed me my robe. "Seriously, give me your card." I, in turn, took one of my business cards from my wallet when I paid him. "If you fax me your references, and you're genuinely interested in moving back to Manhattan, we can discuss it."

While Gavin took down his table, I thought it over. If Gavin sent me his references and they checked out, I could offer him a job similar to the one he'd done for Lowell Davenport. It would be helpful to have someone manage my home as efficiently as Violet managed my office. Now that Sheila had moved out of my apartment, I even had an empty room. Although there wasn't much reason for me to stay in Hell's Kitchen after breaking up with Daniel. I wasn't crazy about living in an apartment across the alley from him, where looking out my window meant looking at his garden.

Once Gavin was gone, I stared out at the harbor, feeling restless, though it was nearly midnight. I'd never be able to get to sleep after dredging up my bad memories of Daniel. I decided to get dressed and see if there might be a gay bar or club in the area. Anything was better than moping alone in a strange room.

CHAPTER 3

After pushing my way through the lobby doors, I consciously kept my pace slow and steady. I was in Baltimore, not Manhattan, so there was no reason to rush. I heard a dog barking when I rounded a corner, and I wondered how Rowdy would like living in the Big Apple. I couldn't imagine Frank turning his dog over to one of the dog walkers who stride down the sidewalks clutching a dozen leashes pulling in different directions like a willful balloon bouquet. Rowdy rarely left Frank's side, and I was sure that wouldn't change in Manhattan.

A pair of men, obviously a couple, walked toward me. They weren't holding hands, or walking with their arms around each other, but the close proximity they kept, as well as the affectionate eye contact they maintained as they spoke, indicated that they were a couple. Both men were in their late thirties and were dressed similarly in khakis, sweaters, and light jackets. I imagined the two of them in a Dockers ad in *The Advocate,* with their hands in each other's back pockets and grins on their faces.

When they passed me, I could see how attractive they were. One of the men returned my appraisal with a quick wink. I smiled, and I could see his partner give him a playful jab in the ribs to get his attention back where it belonged. After a few paces, I couldn't help but turn around to look at them. I caught them looking back as well, and they laughed and waved. I waved back.

I remembered taking long walks through Central Park with Daniel when we were still together. We'd buy coffee and donuts to take with us as we meandered through the winding paths in the park. Daniel would point out certain plants and trees to me, explaining their growth habits and blooming periods. I'd listen and nod, but Daniel knew I'd never remember what he told me. To me, horticulture was like quantum physics; I appreciated it, but knew I'd never use it.

We'd have our coffee and donuts on the terrace of Bethesda Fountain. Oftentimes we'd tell each other stories and people-watch, since the terrace was a popular tourist stop. Then we'd follow paths deep into the heart of Central Park, walking hand in hand, oblivious to anyone but each other. When we reached the Reservoir, we'd walk along the running trail, mindful of the joggers while we loped along, talking the whole way, until we'd walked the entire distance around the basin of water. Then we'd go home, to his apartment or mine, it didn't matter, and lie together on the sofa, holding each other until our breathing matched.

As I watched the khaki couple walk away, I felt a stab of jealousy deep within me. I missed being part of a couple. Standing on a sidewalk in the middle of Baltimore at night, I suddenly felt very lonely.

I noticed that I was in front of a bar that had several signs with rainbow strips of buzzing neon underneath, around, or unfurling from the names of domestic beers in the darkly tinted windows. An imposing man with several tattoos, who was dressed in camouflage pants, a black T-shirt that looked a few sizes too small for his muscular build, and heavy black boots, stood to one side of the door. I glanced at him, looking for any sign that indicated a cover, and found none. He said nothing to me, but simply raised his eyebrows once in acknowledgment of my presence. I nodded my head in response and stepped inside.

There were televisions mounted throughout the bar, playing everything from soundless performances of music videos to clips from MGM musicals and *Saturday Night Live* skits, none of which matched the music I heard from the jukebox across the room. Through a doorway to the right, I could see two well-built men, one leaning against a wall with a beer poised phallically on his groin, the other stretching over a pool table, carefully lining up his shot. There must have been several tables in the second room; although he hadn't shot, I could hear the clacking of billiard balls from other directions and the "thunk" of an occasional ball dropping into a pocket.

I walked to the bar. The bartender, a shorter version of Michael Jordan, greeted me with a smile and said, "What can I get you?"

"Sam Adams," I answered.

"You got it." He popped the top. "Glass?"

"No, thank you."

"No, thank *you*," he said as he put the change I left with the rest of his tips. "You're obviously not from here."

"People from Baltimore don't tip?"

"Not *that* much. I'd welcome you to Charm City, but I'm sure someone as cute as you has already been welcomed." That removed all doubts. I was definitely in a gay bar. He went on. "I can at least be the first to welcome you to Shenanigans."

I stopped midturn and said, "Shenanigans? That name sounds familiar. Are you famous for something?"

"Do you watch soaps?"

"No," I answered. Which was honest enough; I hadn't watched *Secret Splendor* since Daniel and I broke up.

"Our owner is a big *Days of Our Lives* fan and named this place after a bar they wrote out of their storyline in the eighties. His little homage to days of our lives gone by."

"Good times," I said, and heard him laugh as I made my way to a table. At least I could be sure *Secret Splendor* tapes wouldn't be popping up on Shenanigans' TVs, the way they did in a couple of bars in Manhattan.

I decided to put my people-watching skills to better use than nostalgia over Daniel, settling in to check out the bar's patrons. I was reminded of those beer commercials with young, vibrant, beautiful people having fun and laughing. Shenanigans was nothing like that. Everyone I saw struck me as ordinary. Perhaps I was used to Manhattan bars, the majority of which were designed to be featured in magazines as the next hot spot, only to be shut down and renamed a month later. I liked the idea of a bar that stayed around long enough to have a floor that felt a little gritty, lighting dimmed by a few burned-out bulbs, and regulars who knew I wasn't one of them but still gave off no attitude.

I saw a man come out of the poolroom and sit at a table across the room. He saw me squinting at him and raised his glass in my direction. I realized that I'd started an exchange I hadn't intended. He picked up his napkin and wrapped it around his drink, then crossed the room toward me. As he got closer, I thought of how Lillith always said, *There are no accidents.* Maybe I did mean to start an exchange with him. He was attractive, with shaggy blond hair, brown eyes, and a five o'clock shadow.

"Hey," he said. "May I join you?"

"Have a seat. I'm Blaine."

"Todd. You come here a lot?" he asked.

"No. I'm in town on business. Do you?"

"No, I'm here for work, too. Where you from?"

"I live in Manhattan, but I'm from the Midwest," I answered. "How about you?"

"Miami. I work for an import-export company. What do you do?"

"I'm in advertising."

"How long are you staying?" Todd asked.

This was the part I hated. Until Daniel and I split up, he'd been the only man I'd slept with. After we broke up, I made up for lost time, feeling like I'd spent my twenties in two dead-end relationships. I'd married Sydney because I thought it was the right thing to do. I'd been with Daniel for love. I'd quickly learned that one-night stands were about instant gratification, so I didn't see the point of forced conversations or shared histories.

"Long enough to fuck you," I answered.

He started toward my side of the table, and I turned on my barstool to face him. He nudged his way between my legs and put his arms around my waist. Without another word, we tilted our heads and pressed our lips together as I put my arms around him, bringing him closer to me.

When I opened my eyes the next morning, it took me a minute to recognize the hotel room and another minute to realize that I wasn't alone, although I couldn't remember his name. I ran through the alphabet until I got to *T.* Todd. That was it.

I did remember the previous night and how removed I felt when Todd gripped the railing on the balcony overlooking the harbor until his knuckles turned white. Physically, it had been exciting to discover a new body, and a rather nice body at that. Something was missing though. Or maybe it just felt wrong because I'd let him spend the night. Sleeping together in the same bed implied an intimacy that I didn't feel.

I rubbed my eyes and decided to take a shower to rid myself of the smell of Todd. I got up without causing him to stir, then looked back at him. I feared that in daylight, I would discover that I'd brought home a monster whose imperfections had been hidden by shadow and the dim lighting of the bar.

The blinds cast vertical lines up and down his firm body. In the slats of light, I could see that my first impression had been right. He was handsome. But I felt a shocking rush of discomfort when I realized something else. He reminded me of Daniel. A rougher and less put-together version of him, but a resemblance nonetheless. Maybe I was looking for similarities, but the end result was the same. I wanted to get him out of my bed and my life and get in the shower to wash away the night before. I almost sprinted toward the bathroom, but something squished between my toes. I looked down and saw a hastily discarded condom.

"Yuck!" I exclaimed, not meaning to say it out loud.

"What?" a sleepy voice asked from the bed.

I turned my back to him as I spoke. "Nothing. I'm just going to hop in the shower."

Todd didn't respond, and I shut the door to the bathroom and turned on the shower. As the water ran over me, I became conscious of the sore muscles in my back, neck, and legs. Gavin's warning had come true. I felt as if I'd had a brutal workout rather than a soothing massage. I twisted the nozzle to turn the spray to a pounding stream, centering my sorest muscles beneath the water. I felt like I was trying to beat out more than the stiffness.

When the soreness eased, I turned off the shower and got out quickly to towel dry. Hopefully, I would have the day to myself and not feel obligated to spend it with Todd. I wrapped the towel around my waist and stepped out of the bathroom.

My gaze fell on the bed, empty except for a hastily scribbled note lying on top of Todd's pillow. I walked over and picked it up.

> *Dear Brad,*
>
> *You've definitely made my top ten best tricks list. Sorry I had to run. I forgot I have a meeting today. Maybe some other time.*
>
> *Todd*

Brad. I rolled my eyes, offended that he couldn't even remember my name. I whipped the towel from my waist, and it fell limply on the back of the oak desk chair.

After I dressed, I did a quick sweep of the room, looking under the bed for any misplaced items or stray socks. I picked up the used condoms from the floor and flushed them down the toilet, then grabbed the garment bag and strode to the elevator.

The lobby bustled with tourists and businessmen rushing to their destinations. A slight man behind the desk smiled at me as I approached.

"Was everything satisfactory, sir?" he asked, quickly typing something into the computer after I gave him my room number.

"The suite was fine," I said.

"Do you have the Amex that was used to hold the room?"

"Yes," I said, pulling my wallet from my back pocket. As I opened it, I flushed. The five hundred dollars in cash I'd had was missing. "This is not happening," I said, clenching my wallet in my fist and trying with all my might not to launch it across the lobby.

"Is the card misplaced, sir?"

I opened my wallet and pulled out the card. "No, it's right here."

I handed him my Amex and waited while he printed out my bill, silently cursing myself for bringing a stranger into my life and leaving him alone with my wallet. Everything he'd said to me was most likely a lie. Probably even his name.

I decided there was no point in calling the police or trying to get back the money. I'd only embarrass myself in the process. I chalked it up to a five-hundred-dollar lesson and asked the hotel clerk for the name of a car service to take me to the airport. Preferably one that would accept credit cards.

When my plane touched down at LaGuardia, I finally felt at ease and indifferent about Todd, the thieving trick from hell, but I was still bitter about losing five hundred dollars. I felt stupid for carrying that much cash in my wallet. Because of my size, I'd never felt threatened or worried about being attacked on the street. However, realizing that I'd invited a thief into my bed made me think that my mind wasn't as developed as my body.

I shrugged that off and found an ATM machine to get some cash. My cell phone rang while I stood in line outside the airport, waiting for a cab.

"Hello, Mr. Dunhill."

"Hello, Ms. Medina," I said to Violet. "I trust you've—"

"Cleared your schedule for today?" she asked. "Yes, I did. You only had one appointment. It was nothing that couldn't wait until Monday, so I went ahead and postponed it."

"That wasn't what I was going to ask, Violet."

"Oh. I fed Dexter this morning. Though I needn't have bothered, since he helped himself to a loaf of bread that was on top of the refrigerator."

"That's his way of telling me to back off of carbohydrates."

"I saw a dry-cleaning stub on your counter, so I took the liberty of picking that up for you, since it was ready."

"You didn't have to do that."

"I know. You owe me fifty dollars."

"My dry cleaning bill was fifty dollars?"

"No. Your dry cleaning bill was forty dollars. You were out of cat food."

"What kind of food did you—"

"And litter."

"What did I do to deserve you? Manhattan, please. Forty-sixth Street and Ninth Avenue."

"Sounds like somebody just got a cab. You're not coming to the office today?"

"No. I'm going home."

"Good. I can cut out early and go to Barneys. I mean, I can finish typing these reports," she said, as if I would ever reprimand her for taking an afternoon off to go shopping.

The first time Violet ever took a sick day was the previous November, when she literally had to be carried out of the office on a stretcher because of stomach cramps. The pain had gotten so bad she was doubled up on the floor, clutching the itinerary for an upcoming location shoot and trying to crawl to the photocopy room. An ambulance had been called after Violet screamed out in pain when Evelyn, our office manager, tried to help her walk down the hallway to copy the itineraries so they'd go out on time. Two days after her appendix was removed, Violet called me, begging me to help bust her out of the hospital so she could get back to work.

"You're taking an afternoon off? There must be a full moon," I joked.

"You sound like Lillith," Violet said, hitting me where it hurt. "Speaking of Lillith, I suspect the reason you're not coming in today is so you can have a weekend to figure out what you're going to say to the boys upstairs about your resignation."

"If there's a Cuban version of Miss Marple, you'd be her," I stated wryly. "Which brings me back to what I was originally going to ask you. Have you typed your resignation yet?"

"If that's your clever way of asking me to jump ship and work for you at Lillith Allure, Mr. Dunhill—"

"Which it is. Yes."

"I'm not sure I can—"

"Take the bridge. Don't take the tunnel," I said to the driver. "I'm sorry, Violet. You were saying?"

"That's okay. If you had given me a little more time, I might have—"

"Do I need to give you money for the toll now? Or do I give you that at the end of the trip?" I asked the driver, who eyed me curiously, as we hadn't reached the bridge yet.

"You give it to me now. You give it to me later. It makes no difference," he said.

"Okay. I'll give it to you later," I said.

"If you interrupt me one more time, *I'm* gonna give it to you later," Violet said.

"I'm sorry, Violet. It won't happen again. What were you saying?"

"Stop playing games with me. I'm not turning you down," she said.

"Good," I said, breathing a sigh of relief. "I was running out of ways to interrupt you."

"I need more information before I can give you an answer," Violet said. "Plus I want to be wooed. Take me out to dinner, and we'll talk it over."

"Wooed? You want to be wooed? All right. Why don't we—"

"Sunday night? Eight? At Firebird? I'd love to," Violet interrupted.

"You've already made the reservations, haven't you?"

Violet confirmed my suspicions by not answering. Instead she asked, "I don't suppose you've seen the papers this morning? One paper in particular, I should say."

"No," I answered tentatively, hoping that any news about Lillith Allure hadn't been given to the press yet.

"Pick up the *Manhattan Star-Gazette* when you get home," Violet instructed.

"No," I begged. Violet knew that I only read the *New York Times* if I wanted news. The *Star-Gazette* was for entertainment news or, worse yet, when my friends and clients were hit hard in Lola Listeria's gossip column. "Maybe you should read me the highlights."

"Okay," Violet answered, and I heard the rustling of newspaper pages as she found the column. I calmed myself by looking at Manhattan's skyline as the taxi cab went over the Triboro Bridge. I was almost home.

"Ready?" Violet asked. "There's a whole section about an actress whose foot had to be cut out of a boot at a department store. I was going shoe shopping today, but now I don't think I want to."

"Just skip to whatever's relevant, please."

"If you want relevance, read the *Times*. Okay, here it is. 'Fashionista's Flight of Fury.' "

"Oh, no," I said.

Violet read on, "Saturn must have been lodged in Uranus during a flight to Baltimore when a certain model learned her agent turned down a booking for Claude Martrand's fashion show. Perhaps she was more furious because she hoped the designer would give her a free wedding dress? Or is it because our girl is too busy to get married? Lola's looking into her crystal ball, readers, and the future seems mighty cloudy. Not only for our star-crossed model, but for Metropole, too."

"Sheila will have a fit," I predicted.

"A fit has been had," Violet said. "Sheila's moved on to rage. She called me an hour ago."

"Maybe I should go see her," I mused.

"Let her cool down first," Violet advised. "She's working out her aggression in a kick-boxing class. Do you really want to see her right after that?"

"You're right, as usual. I don't. I'll call her later. We're pulling up to my building. I'll see you Sunday night, Ms. Medina."

"Good day, Mr. Dunhill."

My apartment was on the fifth floor of an old tenement building in midtown Manhattan. The neighborhood was affectionately named Hell's Kitchen. Though I'd lived there for three years, I still hadn't figured out how its name originated. I'd heard several theories from my neighbors, all of them confirming that the name had been around since the late 1800s. A woman who lived downstairs said there used to be a German restaurant named Heil's Kitchen a few blocks down from where we lived. The man who owned the dry cleaners on the corner said a *New York Times* article had named a building in the West Thirties "Hell's Kitchen" because of a multiple murder that had happened inside; the name spread to the area around it. For more than a century, the west side of Manhattan was home to the mob and street gangs. I personally thought my neighborhood got its name because there were so many restaurants in the area.

If Hell's Kitchen was still fraught with crime, I never knew it. When I first moved into my building, it was because the apartment was affordable. Now I appreciated everything about my neighborhood. I loved stopping into St. Famous Bread to grab a muffin and hear a cheery hello from the owner every morning on my way to work. I loved my deli, where I was always greeted like a cherished friend. I liked seeing familiar faces among the people on the sidewalks, even if I'd never have names or histories to go with them. If I wanted to bring work home with me, I could do it on my own terms. Everyone

I knew from the world of advertising lived on the Upper East Side, out of town on Long Island, or in New Jersey, so it was rare to run into someone from the office in my part of the city.

The minute I let myself into my apartment, Dexter was underfoot, howling to be fed. I stepped to the left, trying to avoid trampling him, and knocked over a small table, sending several days' worth of mail, my keys, and a telephone tumbling to the floor.

"Damn you, Dexter!" I shouted, and he ran through the apartment to the safety of the bathroom. He didn't fool me. I knew in five minutes he'd forget all about my temper and would come back to let me know he could see the bottom of his food dish.

I was surprised to notice that my answering machine showed no messages, until I saw that Violet had screened them all and transcribed them onto a small notepad, which I found amid the clutter of stuff that I'd knocked to the floor. The majority of the calls were business related. Except for a call from Gretchen. Figuring she was most likely working, and not wanting to go through her office's convoluted voice-mail system, I dialed her cell phone, intending to leave a message to let her know that I was back in town.

"Hi!" Gretchen exclaimed, surprising me. Before I could say a word, she said, "Hey, I have to take this. Give me a few minutes."

I could hear voices in the background when she answered my call, then I heard her walk away until the sounds of New York white noise replaced the voices. She must have stepped outside.

"Okay, I can talk now," she said. "Sorry about that."

"Are you at work? It sounds like you're outside. What did you do, step out on a ledge? Don't do it, Gretchen!"

"Accountant and window ledge jokes are about as tired as postal workers and pistols, Blaine. Besides, the market is quite bullish today. And so am I. But no, I'm not at work."

"I have a message that you called me. What's going on?" I asked.

"I saw Lola Listeria's column in the *Star-Gazette.* I tried to call Sheila, but she was at the gym or something, according to Josh. He didn't say anything about the column, and I didn't ask."

"Smart move," I commented, filling Dexter's bowl with food. He immediately came out of hiding to eat, not bothering to thank me. "I haven't talked to her yet. I'm not looking forward to it."

"I don't want to see her blow a good thing by flipping her lid. That's all," Gretchen said. "She's very lucky to be successful. Especially in a career where everything could end as quickly as it began. So I wanted to see if there's anything I could do."

"Sheila's no fool. She knows she has a good thing. One little argument with her agent won't send her life falling down like a house of cards."

Gretchen suddenly became quiet, and I could hear someone speaking to her in the background. Then she said, "I have to go, hon."

"Hon? You never call me that. Or anyone, for that matter. Gretchen, where are you, anyway?"

"Okay, bye," she said quickly and disconnected our call.

Still holding my cordless phone, I stood in the middle of my apartment, wondering why Gretchen had acted so oddly. It was almost as if she was keeping our conversation a secret from someone. She'd said she wasn't at work, where it might make sense to disguise a personal call. But since she wasn't, why would she take the call outside? Away from whomever—

Suddenly it was all too clear to me. I strode across my apartment to one of the two windows and looked down at Daniel's patio garden. There, talking with Martin and gesticulating, her cell phone still in her hand, was Gretchen. I turned on my cordless phone and started punching in numbers. When she answered, I said, "Gretchen, *hon,* when you're done down there, could you stop by my place for a minute? I've been thinking of investing in a new home. The view here sucks."

I hung up without waiting for an answer. She looked up at my window, as did Martin, who blew me a kiss. I waved, then stepped away from the window. If the only word for my reaction was petulant, the best description of my mood was pissed off. Which I knew was ridiculous. Gretchen and Martin had been friends for a long time. Even if he'd been part of my breakup with Daniel, I couldn't expect everyone else to be mad at him, too.

I supposed what was really bothering me was how seeing them at Daniel's made me feel excluded. It reminded me of the time when I'd first noticed him and tormented myself trying to figure out who he was, who his friends were and what they talked about, and what the details of his life were. It was as if Daniel was a stranger again, and I was on the outside.

The phone rang, and I took a deep breath before I answered.

"You sound strange," Violet said. "I forgot to tell you something. You received a fax today from Gavin Lewis. The massage therapist I found for you in Baltimore. What should I do with it?"

"We'll talk about it on Sunday night. Stop working!"

"Not to worry. I'm already checking out a sexy sales associate at Barneys."

"He's gay. Or in a committed relationship. Or both."

"How do you know?"

"Because I don't need for you to fall in love, get married, and leave me."

"I'll keep that in mind. Goodbye again, Mr. Dunhill."

The phone rang again as soon as I clicked off. I sighed and answered it in a more polite tone.

"Lunch tomorrow at one," Gretchen said briskly. "The Vinyl Diner."

"I'll see you then," I agreed.

Gretchen was at the restaurant before me the next day. "Hi," she said, but didn't stand to hug me. I could tell by her guarded expression that she was trying to gauge my mood.

"I apologize for being rude to you on the phone yesterday," I said. "I'm still not exactly in the best space when it comes to Daniel."

"Figuratively, or are we back to discussing apartment locations?"

"Both," I said, then paused while she considered her ordering options with the waiter. After he left, I said, "Why do I get the feeling this is not one of our regular get-togethers? What's on your mind?"

The clattering of plates made her wince, and she looked around. "I probably could have chosen a quieter place. I don't know how I feel about yelling private things about my life for an audience."

"We could walk back to my apartment after we eat," I suggested. "I'm sure Dexter would be thrilled by the possibility of another pair of hands to feed him."

Gretchen laughed, and we talked for a while about Dexter, then Sheila and Josh. I noticed the shadows under her eyes and wondered if she'd been working longer hours now that we were entering tax season, or if something was bothering her. I felt a guilty relief that someone other than me might have problems that led to sleepless nights.

After lunch, we strolled back to my apartment. There was a chill in the air, but Gretchen seemed to be in no hurry. That made me curious. It was obvious she had something she wanted to talk about, but equally apparent that she dreaded it.

While she petted Dexter and caught her breath from the five flights up, I poured glasses of wine for us, hoping that would help relax her. I didn't mind if it turned into a lazy Saturday afternoon that stretched into the evening. It seemed both of us needed a break from something in our lives.

"Where would you move?" she asked, sipping her wine as she looked around. "The rent here is great. You've got two bedrooms. You could convert Sheila's old room to an office."

"I like the apartment. I like the rent. I like the neighborhood. But it's impractical now that Daniel and I broke up. My gym is in Chelsea. My office is even farther. It would make sense to be closer to both."

"I guess. Except for the whole ordeal of finding another place, moving—"

"I may have that covered," I said, then told her about Gavin and my idea to hire him as my personal assistant.

"Are you sure?" Gretchen asked skeptically. "He's a total stranger. There are a lot of unscrupulous people out there."

"You're telling me," I said, thinking of Todd the thieving trick. "But if Gavin's references check out, why not?"

"For one thing, it sounds like his most important reference is dead," Gretchen said. "Although I probably have some clients who knew Lowell Davenport. Would you mind if I asked around about this Gavin guy?"

"Gavin Lewis. Not at all," I said, liking it that Gretchen felt protective of me. "I think moving is a good idea for several reasons. Yesterday, for example. I don't need to know when you're with Daniel."

"He's not back in town," Gretchen said quickly. "Martin and I were there to water his plants."

"He'll be back eventually. You don't need to be caught in the middle. We have other friends in the same predicament. Sheila. Josh. Adam."

Gretchen smiled and said, "Aren't you forgetting a few names?"

"No," I said. "You're the ones I want joint custody of."

"Maybe I should make you fight for me in court," she said, running her fingers through her hair. When Sheila made the same gesture, she looked girlish and flirtatious. Gretchen looked tired and exasperated.

"What's wrong?" I prodded. "What's this all about?"

"I don't know how to explain it," she admitted. "Without sounding really weird and freaking you out."

"You're usually blunt," I said. "That works for you, doesn't it?"

She narrowed her eyes, inhaled, squared her shoulders, and asked, "Have you had sex with anyone other than Daniel since you broke up?"

I nearly spewed my wine, but managed to merely choke. Gretchen thumped my back a couple of times, and I looked at her warily.

"Why would you ask me that?"

"Maybe I should back up. I'm not asking from a moral standpoint, or as Daniel's friend. But it's not idle curiosity, either. See, I want your sperm."

"Come again?"

"Odd choice of words. Your sperm. Swimmers? Semen?"

"I'm familiar with the word," I said. "I just don't understand why the words 'I want your' preceded it."

"Okay, obviously there are some requests that require backstory. I'm sure Daniel's told you about my miserable years as a lovelorn lesbian." I shrugged, still trying to recover from *I want your sperm.* "It was Ken who pointed out to me what the women of my twenties had in common."

Ken had been Gretchen's best friend, the one who'd originally introduced her to Daniel. I was glad that I'd had the chance to meet him before he died. He was not only as sane as Gretchen, but had always given Daniel flawless advice. Ken would have never let Daniel move Blythe into the town house and ignore his promise to me. Of course, if Ken were still alive, Daniel wouldn't own the town house.

I realized my thinking was going in circles and asked, "What was Ken's wisdom about your girlfriends?"

"They all had children. Even I had to admit that I liked their kids better than I liked them. Ken said it was obvious that I wanted a baby. At first I denied it. I was a lesbian who had liberated herself from her parents' old-fashioned expectations. I didn't want it all. I wanted a good woman, a good job, and a good bottom line on my financial statements. But as time went by, I had to admit that Ken was right. Sometimes having a child was all I could think about. Then it would pass, and I'd think it was some kind of hormonal thing. But it always came back."

"Uh-huh."

"Ken and I joked about it. He said that if I reached the age when the alarm of my biological clock started clanging too loudly, we'd do the whole turkey baster thing."

"You always did like to spend Thanksgiving together," I teased.

"I don't eat turkey," she shot back. "It was only partly a joke. I knew if that's what I wanted, Ken would do it. Of course, the virus caught up with us, and it became a moot point."

"Because they can't centrifuge HIV out of sperm samples," I said.

"Right. All they can do is store the samples for six months to ensure that they're not HIV-infected. So I could safely go to a sperm bank. But that's not the way I want to do it. If I'm going to have a child, I want to know the father. Even have a father who's a part of my child's life, if he's willing to be."

"I'd have thought Daniel would be your first choice."

Gretchen laughed and said, "Blaine, you know Daniel. He does more processing and analyzing than any lesbian I know. By the time he made a decision, I'd be postmenopausal. Besides, you told me Daniel had reconsidered some of his decisions about the future, including having a family."

I nodded and said, "It came as a total shock when he said he wasn't ready. Actually, what he said was that *we* weren't ready. He said our careers kept us too busy, and he didn't intend to raise a child by proxy. When I argued that we could make changes to accommodate a baby, he gave me a list of reasons why I shouldn't take the plunge into fatherhood, including my inflexibility and my need to control everything."

"I don't always agree with Daniel," Gretchen said slowly, and I could tell she was trying to be honest without sounding disloyal. "I think you'd be a great father. Both of you would be. But I definitely got the message that it isn't something Daniel wants right now. You do. So do I."

"Tell me more about your desire to have a baby," I urged. "Knowing you, you've considered it from every angle."

"I have," she agreed. "It's not because I don't feel complete without a child. This is the best time of my life. I'm not in a relationship, but I'm okay with that. My career is solid, but not all-consuming the way it once was. I've learned to relax. I've made peace with my family. I have a great life. So great that I'd like to share it. I know I'd be a good mother."

"Have you considered adoption?"

"Of course. When Ken found out he was positive, that was something he and I talked about. He knew how much raising a child meant to me, and he wanted to be around to see it happen. I've been trying to adopt for six years, Blaine. It's not easy when you're a single lesbian. I've come very close to getting a child three times. But it always fell through. Yet here I am, perfectly capable of conceiving and giving birth. Physically, emotionally, and financially. I've got so much to offer."

"All you're missing is sperm. And you don't want an anonymous donor, so you're turning to your friends."

"Geez, Blaine, it's not like I'm going through my address book, and I'm up to the *D* section. I came to you first."

I was touched by her words. Even flattered, considering how highly I regarded her ability to make good choices. But I had to be honest with her. "You know that Daniel and I were monogamous."

"Yes. I also know that the two of you get tested regularly. I don't mean to sound cold-blooded, but we're talking about people's lives, including a baby's. So I have to be rational about my decisions."

"I agree. But honestly, there has been someone else since Daniel and I broke up. A stranger. Okay, a few strangers. I'm always safe, but how can anyone be sure they're safe enough to take that kind of chance?"

Gretchen frowned and said, "So even if you donated sperm right now, I'd have to wait six months to be sure. Which is not that long, but of course, I don't know how long it will take to get pregnant. The longer I wait . . . I'm thirty-eight. I don't have the luxury of a lot of time."

I decided to level with her, saying, "I still have to consider all the ramifications of this, but if I decide to do it, you don't have to wait six months."

"But you just said—"

"Last year, Daniel and I got our HIV tests right after we came back from a trip to Wisconsin. While we were there, we spent a lot of time with his sister Mary Kate's kids. That's when we started talking about what it would be like to have a child. Daniel said he'd given up the idea years ago, because he didn't want to do it alone. But one of the reasons I married Sydney was because I fully intended to have a family. Which would have been a disaster. Not only because I was living a lie, but if Sydney ever decides to reproduce, someone should call the EPA. Or the ASPCA."

Gretchen laughed but said nothing as I went to the kitchen and came back with the rest of the wine. I refilled our glasses, and Dexter, disgusted that my trip had netted him nothing, jumped from Gretchen's lap and ran to the back of the apartment.

"Anyway," I went on, "once Daniel knew it was something I wanted, we started talking more seriously about it. Although our relationship was exclusive, we knew things can happen. Circumstances can change. Since we were both healthy and had just gotten negative HIV tests, we went together to a lab and put—What did you call them? Our swimmers?—on ice. A reserve for the future, if we ever decided to go for it. Somewhere along the way, Daniel changed his mind. But my point is, I have a perfectly healthy, viable sample in storage."

Gretchen's expression had gradually brightened with joy, and she said, "Would you be willing to let me have it?"

"I can't give you an answer right now," I said. "You said you'd want the father to be involved. I'd want that, too. I'm not just talking about birthdays and holidays. I mean I'd expect to play an active role in raising a child. You and I would have to agree on what that means."

"We can talk about everything, Blaine. Any concerns you have. We can draw up legal documents if you need them to feel like you're making the right decision. But please promise me you'll consider it!"

"If I wasn't considering it, I wouldn't have told you about my sample," I said. "But you just sprung it on me. I need some time to think about it before I give you an answer."

"Just let me know when you've decided, okay? Say maybe by to-morrow?" We both laughed.

"I'll see what I can do," I assured her.

I was able to think about little else over the weekend. I felt as if Gretchen was throwing me a lifeline. My instincts told me to grab it, but it seemed like a decision that shouldn't be made on impulse. Especially when I was already dealing with other changes: the end of my relationship, a shift in my career, and the possibility of moving.

Violet helped alleviate some of that anxiety when I met her for dinner Sunday night, proving not to be a hard sell about changing jobs. I wanted to think that she couldn't resist the allure of working for me, but her fear of remaining behind with Evelyn, the Gargoyle of Breslin Evans, and her gaggle of goons, had probably cinched the deal. I privately decided that I was going to build a bonus plan into her compensation package. She was worth every dollar we would spend on her.

She also agreed to do a background check on Gavin. If I decided to hire him, she assured me that she could help bring him up to speed on my needs. And between the two of them, they could make my search for an apartment easier if I decided to move.

If Gretchen and I had a baby, I'd need a bigger place. After I went home, I entered "artificial insemination" into my computer's search engine and maneuvered my way through lesbian stories of bringing up baby. Until Debi and Dora's detailed account of getting pregnant, including pictures, made me back away from the computer and go to bed.

A few nights later, the phone was ringing when I got home from the gym. I managed to evade Dexter's best efforts to trip me, grab-bing it before the machine could.

"Hey, it's Adam. You sound breathless. Did I interrupt something steamy that would require full and immediate disclosure?"

"I did just leave the steam room at bodyWorks. All your boyfriends were asking where my big, dumb jock friend is," I joked. Although Adam was a member of my gym and worked out there whenever he was in the city, neither of us, to my knowledge, had ever tricked with anyone from there.

"Damn. If you'd only known I was flying in this afternoon, you could have arranged an orgy for us."

"Yeah? What would Jeremy do? Film it for your Web site?"

Adam laughed and said, "I'm here on business, so Jeremy didn't come. Seriously, wanna get together?"

"Sure, that sounds great," I said, hoping this wasn't going to be Adam's opportunity to offer me advice about Daniel. Adam and Jeremy were the poster couple for marital bliss.

"Hmm, either you're the worst actor around, or you've had one hell of a day, because your tone tells me that it'd be anything but great."

"Pay no attention to my moodiness. I'll snap out of it."

"Maybe it's something in the stars."

"Please," I implored, "no astrological references."

Adam laughed, knowing what my relationship with Lillith was like. "Actually, I'm in Manhattan to accompany one of my clients to a stone and gem convention. I thought maybe you'd want to go, considering it might give you an edge with Lillith."

"The National Gemological Society meeting?"

"Yeah!" Adam exclaimed. "At the Hilton in Midtown. How did you know that? Are you already going?"

"No, but I read about it. It might be interesting."

"If you're open tomorrow, why don't you meet me there?"

"Sure," I replied. "What's a good time for you?"

"I should be there all morning," Adam answered. "If you can make it, why don't we meet in the lobby around eight?"

I agreed, and after we hung up, I thought about how much I'd missed him. Since I was sure that Jeremy had heard all the details about the breakup from Daniel and shared them with Adam, maybe we wouldn't have to talk about it. Regardless, like I'd told Gretchen, Adam was one of the friends I didn't intend to lose in the divorce.

CHAPTER 4

The next morning, I entered the Hilton and saw Adam strategically seated so that he could see the lobby doors. He was working on his laptop and seemed oblivious to the admiring glances cast his way. His fingers traced his firm jaw, while his blue eyes remained riveted to his computer screen. Not only did Adam teach computer courses at the University of Wisconsin, but he also ran his own Internet consulting business out of his home in Eau Claire.

Although we'd grown up in the same hometown, we hadn't become friends until the previous year. Adam often joked about how he'd come to New York to "find himself." Instead, he found several new clients and friends, and fell in love with Daniel's ex-boyfriend. Although he and Jeremy lived in Eau Claire, Adam flew to New York at least once a month to maintain ties with his East Coast clients. We would often get together to work out, go out for dinner to talk, or meet Gretchen for drinks so we could all complain about our business lives. I always insisted that we go out. Adam maintained a room in Martin's apartment in Daniel's town house, and I'd never chosen to hang out with Martin, even during the best of times in my relationship with Daniel.

Adam glanced up as I approached him, snapped his computer shut, and stood to give me a quick hug. "I'm glad you could make it. Have you eaten?"

"No. I was hoping I could join you."

We made small talk over breakfast in the hotel café. Jeremy was doing well. Adam was working like a dog, as if he knew another way. His mother was organizing her PFLAG chapter's march in the

Madison Gay Pride Parade. He'd seen Sheila the day before, and she'd updated him about her wedding plans and the ongoing assaults from gossip columnist Lola Listeria.

Adam was at the convention to meet one of his clients, Bonnie Seaforth-Wilkes. I'd met her before, at functions that Daniel and I had attended, since she was not only an executive producer of *Secret Splendor*, but one of her company's products, Fiberforth, was the primary sponsor of the show. I could still hear the ad that always made Daniel and me laugh. *Fiberforth: Because sometimes nature needs a little helper.* I didn't know if Bonnie would remember me, but it didn't matter one way or the other to me.

After breakfast, we made our way to the Hilton ballroom, where Adam found Bonnie standing alone as if she was Nefertiti awaiting a barge. Every time I'd seen her, she'd been wearing the same Egyptian-inspired garb, though she apparently had her outfits made in a million different colors and fabrics. I wouldn't have been surprised to see that her purse was actually a canopic jar. Adam reintroduced us, then we wandered through the maze of exhibitors. Bonnie was probably looking for some jewel worth more than my annual salary.

Behind me, I heard a commanding voice say, "Blaine."

I turned to find I was face-to-face with Lillith Parker. "Lillith! What are you doing here?"

"I could ask you the same question, but instead I'll answer yours. My gemstone therapist tells me that it's a good time to surround myself with aquamarines, so I'm here to find some. It's not my stone of choice, as it's a bit too watery for my taste. But then, I only eat broccoli because it's good for me."

"I guess I can't argue with that," I said.

"You could, but it would be a mistake. Taurus is supposed to watch his step with superiors today."

I wasn't sure what to say to that, so I was glad when Adam turned to see who had my attention. I introduced them and Adam said, "Nice to meet you."

Lillith shook his hand saying, "Gemini. Nice energy."

"How did you know that?" he asked.

"How could I not?" she answered.

He looked befuddled. Bonnie, who'd been hovering over a table of stones with a jeweler's loupe in her eye, turned around. The loupe dropped from her hand and dangled from a chain around her neck.

Adam said, "Bonnie, this is—"

"Lillith," Bonnie said.

"Bonnie," Lillith countered.

Neither woman extended a hand, or any warmth, to each other. I glanced nervously at them, wondering what would warrant such a chilly greeting.

"I'm not surprised to see you here. You never could keep your hands off valuable stones," Lillith said.

"You're not still harping on that, I hope," Bonnie said. "You stole that amulet while my family was mammoth hunting and yours was cowering in caves."

"So you say. Our tribal leaders made an even trade. You had no right to take it from my sarcophagus because it was shiny and pretty."

"You promised my grandfather you'd never sell me at the Athens slave auction," Bonnie snapped. "You betrayed—"

"You want to talk about betrayal? You slit my throat."

"That was in the fourteenth century!"

"Be that as it may, it still hurt my feelings," Lillith answered, lifting her chin and looking down her nose at Bonnie. "You duped my father into believing you were going to marry me just to get the amulet back."

"And two hundred years later, you traded me, your own *child*, to a band of gypsies to get it. Then you claimed it was lost," Bonnie accused.

"No, I claimed it was stolen. I'm sure we both know who was responsible for that. Lifetime after lifetime, and you're still pillaging."

They subsided into icy silence. Adam and I exchanged a look, and he mouthed, *Meet me in the lobby later.*

I nodded. I wasn't sure what shocked me more, that I took Lillith's arm or that she allowed me to lead her away. When we were a safe distance from Bonnie and Adam, she seemed to recollect herself.

"Aquamarines," she said, as if the confrontation had never occurred.

I followed her when she approached a semiprecious gem dealer called Facet Expressions. The booth was small, its back panel encrusted with small garnets, amethysts, aquamarines, and citrines. The woman inside the booth introduced herself to Lillith, who almost immediately began to haggle over the price of a small group of aquamarines that she wanted delivered to her hotel room.

After Lillith struck a deal without making the vendor cry, I tentatively repeated the suggestion I'd made to Frank of hiring Adam to oversee the IT aspect of the company's move, then suggested that he also take over our Web site.

"Despite his affiliation with Bonnie Seaforth-Wilkes, I trust him because of your apparent confidence in his abilities," Lillith said. "I leave these details in Frank's hands. I have an appointment at a spa in SoHo."

I watched as she floated through the throngs of people untouched and without any further altercations. When I reconnected with Adam, he greeted me with a look of disbelief.

"Apparently, those two have been at odds for centuries," Adam said, looking around nervously.

"Lillith didn't seem to want to talk about it, so I didn't dare ask questions," I said. "What are you looking for?"

"Bonnie," he replied. "Or Lillith. And I half expect Shirley MacLaine to show up, too. Bonnie found what she came for: a necklace with a rock the size of my hand. I guess she hitched a ride with the armored car that's delivering it to her apartment, so I seem to be free for a while. Want to get out of here?"

"Let's go back to my place," I answered, already leading the way out of the hotel. "I have to change before I go to my office for a meeting."

Outside on the sidewalk, we began winding our way through pedestrians toward my neighborhood. "I miss this," Adam said with a broad grin.

"Miss what?"

"Every time I go home, it's too quiet now," Adam replied, dodging a messenger on a bike who raced past us while blowing on a whistle.

"You were the one who gave up city living for a farmhouse in the country," I stated. "Why don't you and Jeremy live here? You've already got the clients. Not to mention all the contacts you'd ever need."

"And I have friends here," Adam said, gesturing to me.

I remembered Daniel's angry accusation that I only had my friends because I was dating him, as if our friends couldn't make up their own minds. Although Adam had known Daniel first, he was such an affable person that I was sure he could stay friends with both of us. I hoped that was what he wanted. Although I appreciated my friendships with Gretchen and Sheila, as well as with Jake and Josh, I'd grown accustomed to the camaraderie of my gay male friends. When I began to accept my sexuality, it was a relief to learn that there were other men who could relate to me in a way that was uniquely ours.

"Look out!" Adam barked.

I felt his hand on my shoulder, pulling me back to the curb. A gust of wind rushed over my face as a truck resembling a huge box on wheels zoomed by, inches from my nose. I held my breath and stood frozen until it rattled and rumbled down the street. Then I stared in shock at an enlarged image of Sheila on a building mural across the street. She was in her mermaid garb, reclining on her back with a fin in the air and applying lipstick.

"Holy buckets, that was close! Are you okay?" Adam asked, still holding my shoulder.

"Yeah. I think so," I replied, shaken. "Thanks."

"I've probably been saving your ass for centuries," Adam joked.

"Then you must owe me an enormous karmic debt," I said, affecting Lillith's imperious tone. "Let's get moving." This time, I looked both ways before crossing the street. Even though the traffic could only go one way.

"Although Jeremy's family is here," Adam went on, continuing our previous conversation, "and regardless of everything else I mentioned, we're happy where we are. He just got his teaching credential and has a chance at a part-time instructor's position at the university. He doesn't have the advanced degree that they wanted, but I guess they took his experience on stage and television into account. People still remember him from the sitcom he was on. He even gets asked for his autograph."

"Good for him," I said, meaning it. I liked Jeremy. Admittedly, I liked him better after he got over Daniel and became Adam's boyfriend, but I'd always wished him well.

"Plus my father would never let him go," Adam went on. "Jeremy's the only one who can get my mother to back down when she gets going on one of her rants. She says she's no match for a boy with beautiful eyes. I can't argue with that. Or his ass. Anyway, I like things as they are."

Once inside my apartment, I went into my bedroom after telling Adam to help himself to something to drink. I changed from slacks and a sweater into a navy Armani suit, then packed a bag with work-out clothes, all the while thinking about my brush with the truck, gemstones, past lives, friends, change, and the future.

I returned to the living room to see Adam staring out the window while drinking from a bottle of Poland Spring water.

"Looking for someone?" I asked, knotting my tie.

Startled, Adam turned around and replied, "No. Not really."

"Daniel's still out of town shooting his *Lifetime* movie. If that's what you're wondering," I offered.

"No," Adam said coolly. "That's not what I was wondering. I was wondering what you've done with Sheila's old room. But now I'm wondering why you're suddenly bringing up Daniel."

"Oh," I said, sliding my Mont Blanc pen into my shirt pocket. "I haven't done anything with Sheila's room yet. I was thinking about turning it into a nursery."

With the bottle of water still poised on his lips, Adam's eyes bulged as he tried to swallow a gulp of water without choking. "A what?" he asked, after he regained his composure.

"Made you forget about that Daniel comment, huh?"

"I'll say," Adam agreed. "What's going on, Blaine?"

I sat down and explained Gretchen's proposal that I father her child through artificial insemination. Adam's face remained passive while he listened to me, though he kept running a finger over his lips. I didn't know what that meant.

"What do you think?" I finally asked.

"If you haven't decided whether or not to do it, I don't think I should state my opinion on the subject," Adam said. "In fact, either way, a good friend would say, *That's great,* and stay out of it."

"Let me piss you off then, so you'll give me a real answer," I said, growing frustrated. "Are you not answering my question because of Daniel?"

"What does Daniel have to do with this?" Adam asked.

"Nothing, as far as I'm concerned. I've just spent several weeks wondering about people's loyalties."

"What the hell are you talking about?"

"I'm talking about how Daniel moved your best friend, Blythe, into the town house so he and I wouldn't have to move in together. Then swore all of our friends to secrecy so I wouldn't find out. Of course, I did. I don't know how he could've thought I wouldn't. Especially with Martin running loose in the city."

"Blaine," Adam began slowly, almost cautiously, "I didn't know anything about that until after it happened. Blythe sent me an e-mail about it *after* she'd moved in. I'm pretty sure she had no idea you wanted to move into the town house with Daniel."

I walked up to Adam and stared hard into his eyes. He returned my gaze, not moving his head or darting his eyes away, but obviously wondering what I was doing. I relaxed and said, "I believe you."

"Good," Adam said. "I didn't want to have to beat some sense into you if you didn't."

"I'd like to see you try," I said, raising my fist and lightly punching his jaw before I gave him a fraternal hug. I released him and went to the kitchen to feed Dexter before I left for the office. "You don't think it's a good idea, do you?" I asked as I opened a can of Fancy Feast. Dexter immediately appeared out of nowhere so he could try to trip me while I moved around the kitchen.

"Fathering Gretchen's child?" Adam clarified. "Honestly? It's not something I would do, no. There are way too many complications. Emotionally, financially, and mentally. And that's just now, while Gretchen is trying to get pregnant. What about the future? Gretchen's single, right?"

"Yes."

"What about when she gets involved with someone? That's one more person involved in how your child is raised. And what legal recourse will you have if something goes wrong in your friendship with Gretchen?"

"I hadn't thought about that," I said, still holding Dexter's bowl of food.

"Don't hate me for pointing this out," Adam began, "but what if there's a chance that you and Daniel can work things out? Will this spoil that? Or if that's not an option, what about other guys? I don't know too many gay men who'd jump at the chance to get involved with someone who not only has a kid, but also a lesbian coparent to boot."

I stared into space, digesting Adam's advice. Dexter, digesting nothing and hating me for it, reached up and sank a claw into my leg. "Ow!" I exclaimed, kicking him off and setting his bowl on the floor. "Thanks for giving me your input, Adam."

"You asked for it," Adam said, and flashed me a weak smile. He looked at his watch and said, "Are we okay? Because I have to go to Jersey to have dinner with a client, and I'd better get back to Martin's to change."

"Martin," I growled. "I'd like to wring that little fucker's neck."

"Leave me out of it," Adam said. "I'll call you before I go back to Eau Claire."

My afternoon meeting was with Josh Clinton. One of the perks of being in charge of Lillith Allure's advertising was being able to occasionally employ Josh to photograph Zodiac's print ads when his schedule permitted. It gave him and Sheila extra time to be together.

Violet wasn't behind her desk when I arrived at work. I walked into my office and found her and Josh seated at my desk with the sound of artillery fire emanating from my computer.

"Go for the tank! Get the tank!" Josh screamed.

"I can't!" Violet shrieked. "The helicopter is—"

"I'll get the helicopter. You worry about the tank," Josh commanded.

I audibly cleared my throat. Josh and Violet looked up guiltily. There was a loud noise from the computer, as what I assumed was either a tank or a helicopter exploded.

"Am I that late?" I asked.

Violet clicked a few keys on the keyboard, stood up, and said, "I wasn't—uh—I mean, I was just leaving."

Josh moved to the chair in front of my desk and said, "I forced her to entertain me until you got here."

"I didn't even know there were games on this thing," I said, pointing at the computer.

"It's hidden in the financial logs," Violet confessed. "It's on the network. We were playing against the mail room. I'll be at my desk if you need me."

"Thanks, Violet," I said.

"Yeah," Josh said with an impish grin. "Tanks." With his expressive brown eyes and shaggy brown hair, Josh always looked adorable, but he was even more irresistible when he was being funny.

Once we were alone, I asked, "How are the wedding plans going?"

"Not bad," Josh assessed. "So far, Sheila has bought every bridal magazine and book in publication. I've been wracking my brain to put together the guest list, which isn't as easy as I thought it would be. We initially wanted to have a small wedding, but every day there's someone else who Sheila remembers to add to the list. Some distant aunt or friend whose fragile ego will be shattered if they're not invited."

"And just think, you've only just begun," I said.

"Thank you. You just reminded me of last night's trauma," Josh said wryly. "In the middle of the night, Sheila woke me up, frantic, because she wanted to know what our song was."

"Your song?" I asked.

"Actually, that's what I said. 'Your Song,' by Elton John, because I sang it to her at Gretchen's retreat when we took our first vacation together. But Sheila insisted it was 'We've Only Just Begun.' Apparently that was playing in the background when we first met."

"Wait," I said. "I thought you and Sheila met at a photo session. You play the Carpenters during your photo sessions?"

"No," Josh insisted, shuddering. "Technically we met at a photo shoot. But it was all business. The next day, we ran into each other at the dentist. I was leaving from having a cavity filled, and she was arriving to have her teeth bleached."

"How romantic," I lied.

"Yeah, right," Josh protested. "How could Sheila resist me? I was drooling all over myself with cotton stuffed in my cheek. Despite that, I asked her out."

"And the Muzak version of 'We've Only Just Begun' was playing in the dentist's office," I surmised. "Leave it to Sheila to remember that."

"Leave it to Sheila to remember that at two in the morning," Josh complained. "Anyway, tomorrow we're going on a tour of every bakery in Manhattan to find the perfect wedding cake."

"If I'm not mistaken, they have bakeries in Eau Claire."

"We have to find it *now,*" Josh said, obviously imitating Sheila. "What if we don't like any of the cakes in Eau Claire? How can the cakes there be better than the ones here? What if we get to Eau Claire and they can't make it in time for the wedding?"

"Who's *they?*" I wondered.

"That's what I asked," Josh said. "I slept on the couch. If I had known that I'd be woken up and quizzed about our musical history, I'd have slept there last night, too." We both laughed. "This wedding is making her neurotic but, boy, do I love her," Josh said, sounding surprised.

"Good," I said. "You deserve each other."

"Speaking of good partnerships, I heard about that offer from Lillith Allure. Did you accept it?"

"I had no choice," I said. "If I hadn't, I'd have lost my only client and probably gotten fired anyway. I like the tax bracket I'm in. I'm far too comfortable to start eating Ramen noodles and have my phone turned off every other month."

"There's no way that would happen," Josh said. "Every ad agency in the country would be calling with job offers."

"Not if my phone was turned off. I'm guessing the transition will take place quickly, so we can start work on the next ads as soon as possible. I've got a lot of work ahead of me in the next few months. I don't know how I'm going to have time to sleep, let alone impregnate Gretchen."

"What?" Josh asked.

Thinking about moving into a new office, streamlining four months of work into two months, and the impending nuptials of Zodiac's star model had made my mind wander. Especially after nearly getting hit by a truck and my conversation with Adam. I'd completely forgotten Josh was in the room and didn't realize I was using my "out loud" voice.

"Impregnate Gretchen?" Josh repeated.

"No. I said, 'That ingrate, Gretchen.' I referred Lillith to her and Gretchen won't take on any new clients. That ingrate. Geez." Josh stared at me, frowning silently, so I asked, "What?"

"I was waiting for you to say, 'Yeah. That's the ticket.' What's the story, Blaine?"

"First of all, I know she's your fiancée, but you can't tell Sheila.

This is very personal, and I shouldn't even tell you, but I'm trying to make a decision, and I need to hear myself talk about it, I guess."

"Okay," Josh agreed. "My lips are sealed."

"Gretchen has asked me to be a sperm donor so she can have a child. However, if I do it, I want to be more than just a donor. I want to be a diaper-changing, baby-burping, boo-boo-kissing, PTA-joining parent. The works. And she's fine with that. More than fine, actually. She's all for it."

"So what's the problem?" Josh asked.

"You tell me," I said, waiting for the inevitable cautionary advice.

"I think it's great," he said.

I was skeptical, remembering how Adam had said a good friend would stay out of it and say, *That's great.*

"I know it's going to change my life," I said. "A heck of a lot more than changing employers will. I always wanted kids. I figured the circumstances would be a little different."

I trailed off, and Josh caught my train of thought. "You thought you'd be a parent with someone like Daniel, maybe?"

"Yeah," I said. "It seems more normal, doesn't it?"

"A lot of people would tell you otherwise," Josh said, smiling.

"A lot of people can go to hell. I only meant that when Daniel and I were a couple, we discussed raising a child together. When he signed for three more years on *Secret Splendor,* it was as if he forgot all about it. He was suddenly the best thing in daytime drama, so he had no time for fatherhood. Well, I didn't forget about it. Then he sabotaged our plans to move in together by moving Blythe into the town house. Obviously our relationship wasn't stable enough to even think of bringing a child into it."

"It's no wonder you're becoming a lesbian," Josh joked.

"I'd rather be a lesbian any day than a back-stabbing liar. I'm still angry just thinking about what Daniel did to us."

"Sheila feels like you're angry at her, too."

"I know she was in an uncomfortable position. And I know it wasn't her place to tell me Daniel's plans for the town house. But it still feels like a betrayal. That's why I think it's best if she and I don't discuss Daniel. She won't be in that position again."

"She wonders if things will ever be the same between you and her. But Sheila's not the only one affected," Josh said. "Because of the tension, you and I haven't gotten together as much as we used to."

"I know. That's my fault. I avoided everybody for a while. I don't want my problems with Sheila to change my friendship with you. Anyway, she and I have too much history not to work this out eventually."

We both sat quietly, lost in thought, until Josh asked, "So, are you gonna do it?"

"Yes," I said, annoyed because I hated to repeat myself. "I said Sheila and I have been friends for years. We'll work it out. We just need a little space right now."

"No," Josh said with a laugh. "I meant are you going to have a baby with Gretchen?"

"Oh, right. In all likelihood, I think it's going to happen. I just need to think about it a little longer. In fact, maybe over a game of racquetball?"

"Is that an invite?" Josh asked. His eyes lit up because he loved my gym. Sheila was a member of the Reebok Sports Club on the Upper West Side. Not only did it provide every piece of exercise equipment and workout class known to man, but it was a private, almost windowless facility with a steep membership fee. Which made it seem like an elitist day spa-cum-fortress. Whereas my gym was listed in magazines as being a cross between a gym and a nightclub. There was a regular rotation of deejays spinning club music, colorful lighting from a theatrical grid on the ceiling, and a membership application that required a headshot. Josh loved going there with me, not only for the ambiance, but because of his illicit sense that he was being unfaithful to Sheila's gym.

After a game of racquetball, a free-weight session, and a chamomile-infused steam bath, Josh and I went our separate ways. Still sipping my strawberry-banana protein smoothie from BodyWorks, I tossed my gym bag in my hall closet and hung up my Armani jacket. I decided to listen to my messages while I changed clothes.

The first message was from Violet, calling to tell me my itinerary for the next day and to let me know she'd finished her background check on Gavin, finding no reason why I shouldn't hire him.

It was the next message that made me start nervously winding my tie in my hands.

"Blaine? This is Shane. I don't know what it is this time, but Mom blew a gasket and is in the hospital. Well, the gasket in her heart. Valve. Some valve. Maybe you should call Dad. He knows more about it than I do. I'm going to the hospital now, but they wanted me to call you before I left. Later."

Not knowing what to expect, especially after my brother's inarticulate assessment of our mother's health, I tried calling home. Of course there was no answer, which I assumed meant my mother had been taken to the hospital, as Shane had alluded. So I called my father's cell phone and learned that my mother was scheduled to have an operation after complaining about pains in her chest.

"If you want to come home, it's up to you," my father said.

"Is it serious?" I asked.

"Open heart surgery is usually serious, Blaine," my father said, sounding annoyed.

"They have to open her heart?"

"I'm pretty sure that's where the valve is. They said it's a bad valve in her heart. So I doubt they're going to open up her foot. But I'm not a doctor. I could be wrong."

"Oh for the love of"—I broke off to take a deep breath. "I'll be there as soon as I can, Dad."

"Okay," he said. "Take your time. We all know what a busy and important man you are. I have to go fill out insurance paperwork."

Before I could start yelling, my father disconnected our call. I stared in disbelief at the receiver in my hand then dropped it on the floor before I lost control and threw it from my bedroom window.

Although my relationship with my father could never have been called warm, it had at least been civil while I was growing up. In his eyes, my triumphs as an athlete and a student were attributable to his good genes. My breakup with Sheila had been met with wary silence from both my parents. The news that I was engaged to Sydney seemed to elicit relief, and they joined the Keplers in giving us an expensive wedding, then left us to our own devices. Which, according to my father, had been why my marriage failed. I was obviously incapable of good judgment.

Jake thought my father's attitude was based on resentment. Unlike my parents, I'd refused to be trapped in a bad marriage. Nor was I content to stay safely in Wisconsin and use the reputation and connections of the Dunhills or the Keplers to get ahead in business. In some ways, I agreed with Jake. Being successful on my own terms, in a business my father knew nothing about, cheated him out of taking credit for my accomplishments.

Since I'd spent most of my life trying to win his approval, I couldn't pretend his biting comments didn't upset me. I'd finally decided the best reaction was not to respond. I was afraid if our animosity ever escalated, my temper would get the best of me and I'd say things I never intended to say. At least not in anger.

I shrugged off the conversation and picked up the phone. "Hi, Adam. It's Blaine. When are you going back to Wisconsin?"

At least flying with Adam meant I had a ride from the airport to Eau Claire. After he dropped me at the hospital, I let him take my luggage to his place. I hadn't stayed at my parents' house in years, since my disastrous divorce from Sydney. And I no longer had the option of staying with the Stephensons now that Daniel and I had broken up. I told Adam I could rent a car and stay at a motel, but he wouldn't hear of it. I knew I'd be comfortable at his renovated farmhouse, although this would be my first opportunity to see Jeremy since Daniel and I had broken up. I wondered if that would make things different between us. Maybe we could form a Daniel's Ex-Boyfriends Club.

I found my oldest brother, Shane, flirting with a couple of nurses near the cardiac care unit. As usual, I felt a chill pass over me when I saw him. If I stopped working out and let my muscles get soft, then added a few cocktails to every afternoon, in a few years I'd be him. It was hard to believe that Shane, like me, had once been an award-winning high school athlete. Unfortunately for his wife, he still thought of himself as Eau Claire's hottest ladies' man.

Until I showed up, the nurses seemed to think so, too. He was none too pleased to see their attention shift to a younger, healthier version of himself, so he hurried me to a waiting area to fill me in on my mother's situation.

"She was just having the usual heart flutters she complains about," he said, "but Dad got tired of being paged every day and hearing that she was having a heart attack. He finally convinced her to get a complete checkup. Her mitral valve wasn't working right, so they're repairing it. She'll be in the hospital a few days, then she'll do rehab as an outpatient. I guess you have to rebuild your strength slowly. I don't know. Anyway, this surgeon says he's done over a hundred of these operations and her prognosis is good. He tells us she's in great physical condition other than the valve problem."

"Did he tell her that, too?" I asked.

"Oh, yeah. Naturally she told us later that he's just being positive so we won't be too worried about her. Oh, and that since he's only treating her heart condition, he really has no understanding of the many physical problems she's dealing with."

"She'll outlive all of us. Where's Dad?"

"He had to oversee a wiring job at a new bank."

I wasn't surprised. Whenever there was any crisis, my father was always at work. He'd come in later and make some grand gesture with flowers and brisk cheer that my mother would probably be too drugged to know about. Not that it mattered. He wasn't doing it for her, but so everyone else would know what a great husband he was.

As if reading my mind, Shane said, "Don't be too hard on the old man. You know what it's like to listen to her day and night. You moved all the way to New York. Work is his only escape from her."

"What if something goes wrong? Any surgery is risky, no matter how many times the surgeon has done it. Dad should be here."

"He'll be here later. He's only as far away as his cell phone."

"Whatever," I said.

I walked to the window and stared out, swept by a longing for Daniel that took me by surprise. For so long he'd been my refuge from Dunhill drama and disappointment. Even though he could never be with me on the rare occasions that I saw my family, the comfort of knowing I'd be going back to him had made my visits to Eau Claire endurable.

The worst part of visiting Wisconsin and being around my family was that I felt like I reverted to an identity I'd tried to outgrow. I always found myself hoping my parents would suddenly start acting like Jake and Sheila's parents. That if I presented myself to them as a happy, successful adult, they'd not only approve of me, but it would somehow fix their relationship.

It had taken me a long time to figure out why I never enjoyed sitcoms. A part of me longed for happy endings to any family crisis, but I knew my family was not the Huxtables or the Tanners. I'd have been satisfied with the thirty-second relief offered by commercials. The right product could fix anything from split ends to excruciating pain. I'd tried in vain to be the cure for my parents' miserable marriage, like the kid version of Bufferin.

Maybe it would have worked if they'd ever fought, but the displeasure in our house was silent, leaving me helpless to fix it. The best I could offer was listening to my mother complain about her health or giving my father no reason to extend his disappointment with her to me.

"Oh, geez," I said, catching sight of a pickup truck wheeling into a parking space outside. I knew by the Rebel flag in the back window that my brother Wayne had arrived. I turned back to Shane and asked, "How's Beverly doing? And the kids?"

"Great. Beverly's managing the Clinique counter at Drayden's now. All she's done is boost me into a higher tax bracket, but it makes her happy, so what the hell. You know Tony graduates this year. He got a football scholarship to Nebraska. Looks like we got another jock hero in the family. Pretty soon Dad'll be taking your pictures out of the lobby at Dunhill Electrical and replacing them with Tony's."

"That's fine with me," I said. "Life goes on. How are the twins?"

"Chuck made All State in track. And Nicky—well, he's just weird. He stays in his room listening to music or surfing the Internet all the time."

I didn't blame him. It had to be tough being the gawky kid in a family with two self-absorbed parents and two overachieving brothers. I could only hope that if being gay was hereditary, the gene had bypassed Nicky. He already had enough strikes against him due to his lack of athletic prowess and his propensity to listen to Marilyn Manson and Eminem.

"Yeehaw," Shane muttered as Wayne ambled into the waiting room in faded jeans, his orange T-shirt covered by a denim jacket. He was wearing a "gimme" cap with the Dunhill Electrical logo. Unlike Shane and me, Wayne had always been wiry, but he shared our green eyes and brown hair, although his fell in lanky strands over his collar. I knew if he took off the cap, I'd see a mullet cut.

"Hey, Blaine," Wayne said. He looked at Shane and asked, "Any news on Mom yet?"

"No," Shane said. "We're waiting."

"Dad should be along soon. We just finished at the bank. I still think this whole thing is bogus."

"What do you mean?" I asked.

"Aw, hell, it ain't nothing but a heart murmur. This valve story is a plot between the doctors and the insurance companies to make money. They hit paydirt with a hypochondriac like Mom."

"Wayne, I don't think they do heart surgery on a whim," I said.

"Well, at least they let me and Shane donate blood for her. I damn sure wouldn't take any stranger's blood, with all the diseases out there. You can't trust anybody but family. You think if Mom got some fag's blood, she'd flirt with Miss Comensky and move to San Francisco?"

Miss Comensky had once been a girls' PE teacher, and though I was pretty sure she had no Sapphic leanings, such rumors had always swirled around her spinsterish state.

But it wasn't Miss Comensky I wanted to defend as Wayne's words replayed in my head: *some fag's blood.* I thought about Ken, and his sad, premature death. I remembered Adam's mother angrily talking about the ban on gay men donating blood. If my brothers knew the truth about me, they'd consider me unfit to offer what they had to our mother, as if my very nature tainted me or they were somehow purer than I was, no matter who they had sex with, as long as it wasn't with *some fag.*

I heard with shock the words coming out of my mouth. "I'm gay."

When Wayne and I didn't join Shane's outburst of laughter, he broke off abruptly and stared at me. "That's nothing to joke about, Blaine."

"I wasn't joking," I said, refusing to take the out he'd given me.

"Well, that's just great," Wayne muttered. "Why don't you tell Mom that and finish her off?"

"You can't be gay," Shane said angrily. "You played football."

"I don't think one has anything to do with the other," I said.

"But you were married," Shane said, refusing to give up.

"That would explain why Sydney divorced him," Wayne said.

"Sydney didn't divorce me. I divorced her."

"How the hell could you turn gay? What's wrong with you?"

Shane's face was getting redder, and I suspected he was itching to hit me.

"I didn't turn gay. It's the way I've been for as long as I can remember. It's not my intention to tell the folks. At least not now. So I'd appreciate it if you keep it to yourselves."

"I'm sure not telling them," Shane said. "I'm getting coffee. Do you want any?"

Both Wayne and I shook our heads, and Shane left us. I met my brother's gaze, determined not to back down now that I'd gotten this far.

"Well, hell," Wayne finally said. "I'll tell you what it is. It's nobody's business. You know there are people in the government who'd like to round all of you up and stick you in a camp somewhere. You'd better be careful who you share that information with."

I knew that in his own way, he was trying to offer brotherly advice, but I said, "Wayne, could you give the conspiracy theories a rest? If anybody's involved with fringe groups that the government is watching, it's you."

He ignored that to ask, "Does Jake Meyers know you're a—that you're gay?"

"He's my best friend. Of course he knows."

"He's not one, too, is he?"

"No," I said wearily. "Maybe we could have this heart-to-heart another time?"

"Suits me," Wayne said. "You're not sick, are you?"

"No."

"That's good. You be careful and keep it that way."

I was surprised and touched, and my mind wandered as he began to expound his theory about the origin of AIDS, which was, predictably, that it was another government conspiracy. In that respect, I was sure Wayne could find bosom buddies among some of the more virulent AIDS activists.

Since my brothers were so much older than me, we'd never been kids together. Although Shane had been the athletic one, it was Wayne who took the time to throw a football to me in the backyard. It was also Wayne who made sure I got to and from practice when I was older, since my father was always working and my mother said driving made her nervous. She had never gone to any of my games, nor could I remember Shane being there. My father always sat among his cronies in the press box, but Wayne stood on the other side of the fence behind the bench, sometimes yelling praise after I made a good play, or looking unconcerned if I'd blown one. I could never have confided all my teenage anxieties to him, but he did at least make me feel like someone in my family felt affection for me.

My father's arrival brought an end to Wayne's rambling. After a chilly greeting to me, he went to find Shane and, hopefully, a doctor who could tell us what was happening with my mother. I was sure that my father didn't want to sit in a waiting room, forced to make small talk with me, any longer than necessary. I didn't see how our relationship could deteriorate any further, even if he found out I was gay. But I was afraid he'd find a way to take it out on my mother, and her life seemed to hold little enough joy as it was.

I was relieved to hear that she was being taken from recovery to cardiac intensive care. We were only allowed a few minutes each to visit her. She was still too groggy to know what was going on. It bothered me more than I'd expected to see her looking so small and helpless in a hospital bed hooked up to monitors and IV tubes.

I was able to leave the hospital after offering a "staying with a friend" story without any uncomfortable questions. I reminded my father that I had my cell phone if he needed to reach me. I was sure my brothers didn't want to know into what den of homo iniquity I was taking myself, and my father probably assumed I was staying with Jake.

As I walked outside the hospital to call Adam on my cell phone, I heard a woman call my name. I turned and saw Gwendy Stephenson heading my way. I immediately imagined her in a Marlboro or Harley-Davidson ad, since she was wearing cowboy boots, blue jeans, and a cream turtleneck, over which was a brown leather coat with shearling lining. Her mousy blond hair wasn't styled, but swung healthily around her shoulders. Although she was Daniel's least favorite of his three sisters, I'd always liked her. Despite her feminine assets, she had broad shoulders and an androgynous look. Not to mention a wry sense of humor. In high school, Gwendy had been captain of the field hockey team and was known by the nickname "Dinty Moore," like the hearty beef stew. There was something blunt and honest about her that reminded me of someone else . . .

Before I could complete the thought, she was giving me a big hug and saying, "I thought it was you. What are you doing in town?"

"My mother had surgery," I said. "Were you visiting someone at the hospital?"

"Just delivering a power of attorney to a client," she said. "Is your mother okay?" When I nodded, she went on. "It's great to see you. I was sorry to hear that you and Daniel are having problems. Has that gotten better?"

"We broke up," I said, unsure of what she knew.

"You'll get back together. You two are meant for each other," she said casually. "How long will you be in town? Where are you staying? At your family's house?"

"No. With Adam Wilson. I was just about to call him to pick me up."

"Don't do that. I'll give you a ride. It'll give us a chance to talk." She caught me up on Stephenson family news as I walked with her to her red Jeep Cherokee.

"New wheels, huh?" I asked, sliding into the passenger seat.

"I promised myself the first thing I'd do when I got a job was get rid of that piece of crap I had since high school."

"I can't believe that Gremlin didn't explode years ago. Congratulations on the job. Daniel was surprised that you took their offer. He figured you'd go with a larger firm in Minneapolis or Milwaukee."

"It suited my needs. Bigger fish in a little pond."

"That's the same thing I did when I started out. In advertising, of course, not law. Do you like it? Are you happy where you are?"

"For now. Hey, I heard about Sheila's wedding. It's going to be quite an event, isn't it?"

"All I know is that they've set the date in July. She's probably got Daniel right in the middle of making plans though, huh?"

Gwendy gave me a funny look and said, "It's so strange to think of you two apart. Okay, I'll shut up. Sheila has decided on a theme wedding. They've hired a full orchestra to play big band songs, and she wants everyone, even the guests, to dress in vintage forties clothes. Or at least reproductions. She wants it to be like a set from some old

Cary Grant or Fred Astaire movie. You know, the men all in tuxes and tails, the women in silk and chiffon."

"Leave it to Sheila," I said, trying to picture either the sturdy Gretchen or the kaleidoscopically coifed Blythe in chiffon and fuck-me pumps jitterbugging to Glenn Miller. Or whatever dances they did in the forties. With Sheila's penchant for theme parties, no doubt we were all expected to take dance lessons before July.

I lost the thread of Gwendy's conversation as I pictured Daniel and me dancing across a ballroom floor in tails, with some great old Cole Porter classic being played in the background: "You're the Top," "Easy to Love," "You Do Something to Me."

I rolled my eyes, thinking it was more likely that the two of us would glower at each other from across the room while the band played "Don't Fence Me In" or "After You, Who?"

"Is anybody home?" Gwendy asked, pulling into Adam's circular drive.

"If they aren't, I know where the key is hidden," I said. "Thanks for the ride."

"Do you know how long you'll be in town?"

"Just a couple of days. I have to get back; I've got a lot going on at work."

"I hope everything goes well with your mother."

"Thanks. Give my best to your family." I hugged her and got out of the car.

Just before she pulled away, she rolled down her window and called, "Don't forget what I said. You two are meant to be together!"

I shook my head and waved goodbye.

CHAPTER 5

When no one came to Adam's door after I knocked, I walked around back. Adam had recently installed a new deck, and Jeremy was propped on a railing, his legs wrapped around Adam's waist as Adam rested his arms on Jeremy's shoulders while they kissed. With the snow-dusted trees and fields behind them, they looked like a gay travel brochure. I had to admit that they were a good-looking couple. But it was Jeremy that I studied momentarily as I thought about the common ground between us. We were both ex-boyfriends of Daniel Stephenson.

The similarities ended there. He was an actor and a teacher; I was a businessman. He was inclined to be expressive and emotional; my feelings ran deeply, but I tended to keep them to myself. On the other hand, although Jeremy had a good sense of humor, sometimes he couldn't laugh at himself, and I considered that ability to be one of my virtues.

Physically, I was muscular, with dark hair and green eyes. Jeremy was about my height, but had a swimmer's build, with an angular jaw and the fair, light-haired attributes he'd inherited from his northern Italian family.

"You two can stop that crap right now," I said. "I'm in no mood for love."

Adam laughed and pulled away. Jeremy jumped down from his perch and met me at the top step with a hug. "Believe me, nobody understands how you feel better than I do," he said.

"Totally different situation," I said.

"Yeah, last time I was the idiot. This time Daniel is. All right, that's my last word on the subject."

"For ten minutes," Adam said, ruffling Jeremy's blond hair. "How's your mother?"

"Well sedated. I'm jealous. She came through the surgery fine."

"That's good. Your stuff is in your room. We're on country hours here, so dinner will be at six. How'd you get home?"

"I ran into Gwendy Stephenson. She gave me a ride."

"Huh," Jeremy said.

"You promised," I reminded him.

"I didn't say anything!"

We walked inside as Adam said, "I invited Jake to dinner. I figured he'd help stifle any Daniel discussions."

"Thanks," I said. "I haven't seen him since our Christmas ski trip. And now, Jeremy, I'll make your vow of silence easier and clean up before dinner."

After Jake arrived, he and Adam began their usual litany of sports chat. When they got into a heated discussion about the basketball playoffs, Jeremy fled to the kitchen faster than you could say "jump shot." I made myself another drink, content to sit back and pretend to listen. My interest in sports had waned when I graduated from high school and no longer needed them to gain acceptance. I wasn't worried that I'd be forced to join their conversation. Adam would never give me a chance to remind him that I'd broken all the high school football records he'd set five years ahead of me.

While they talked, I scrutinized Jake, wondering why he was still single. He'd definitely be a catch for anyone, man or woman. He was the male version of Sheila—tall, blond, wholesome, and straight. I liked him for all the same reasons I liked Josh. He accepted people for who they were, and was himself no matter what company he was in.

Jake had been the first person I'd told that I was gay, and I only did that when Sheila came to live with me, so he wouldn't think I was taking advantage of his little sister. I remembered how tense that time had been.

Sheila had turned up at my Hell's Kitchen apartment without warning, expecting to see Sydney with me. No one knew we were separated, because Sydney was afraid if her father found out, he would make her move back home. I made up a story for Sheila about how Sydney had been accepted to an art school in Chicago, and we commuted to see each other. Sheila didn't need much convincing. Not only did she and Sydney no longer get along, but Sheila was afraid of how her family would react to her taking off without telling them. She wanted me as an ally. As soon as I realized what she'd done, I made her call home to let them know where she was. Her parents were furious.

The day after Sheila's arrival, the Breslin Evans receptionist, Mitzi, buzzed me to tell me that Jake Meyers was there to see me. My relief that it wasn't Sheila's father dissipated when I saw Jake's expression. I left orders not to be disturbed and closed my office door with trepidation.

"My parents sent me to get Sheila, but I don't know how to find her," Jake said. "What the hell is going on, Blaine? You dumped my sister years ago to marry Sydney, and now Sheila's here, and Sydney isn't? You've got five minutes to tell me why I shouldn't deck you."

"It's not how it looks. I had no idea Sheila was coming. But she's twenty-two years old, Jake, and capable of making her own decisions. Not one of which, I promise, has anything to do with me. I'm just a port in a storm. If you drag her back home, she'll leave again. At least with me, she's safe."

"You're a married man. She can't stay here with you."

"Nobody knows this, and I'm only telling you because I know you'll keep it to yourself, but Sydney and I are separated."

Jake glared at me and said, "That's supposed to make it better?"

"There's nothing going on between Sheila and me. There won't be."

"Right. She's a beautiful young woman who's been in love with you since she was what, eleven? How stupid do you think I am?"

I knew I had to diffuse his anger. I could think of only one sure way, and I decided to do it even if it cost me his friendship. "Jake, I'm not going to take advantage of Sheila. I'm gay."

He blinked at me and finally said, "You're not lying, are you?"

"No," I said. He sat down as if the wind had been knocked out of him and stared at me for a few minutes. "Go ahead and say whatever's on your mind. I've had this conversation with you in my head a thousand times, and it never turns out good."

"Jesus, Blaine. You're my best friend. What do you think I'm going to say?"

"I honestly don't know."

"Sit down. Talk to me."

It had been such a relief to admit the truth to someone else, and Jake listened in silence while I described how long and hard I'd fought this essential fact about myself. It helped that I didn't have to explain why Sydney and my parents couldn't know. It also helped that Jake had other gay friends and didn't ask me stupid questions that I probably couldn't have answered anyway.

Telling Jake had ended up being one of the most liberating experiences of my life. We'd even been able to laugh about some of the awkward situations my secret had created for me. By the time I rode with him to the airport that night, after a good dinner and a few drinks, Jake was sure he'd be able to handle his parents.

And he had. Sheila never found out he'd been there. Jake kept my secrets. All of them. Even from his sister.

I realized that Adam and Jake were staring at me.

"What?" I asked.

"How's the Apple Dunhill Gang?" Jake repeated.

I filled him in on my mother's condition. He knew better than to ask questions about my father or brothers. Nor did he put me on the spot about Daniel. He already knew my perspective on things, since he'd been the only person I'd felt like I could talk to after the breakup. Since then, I figured Sheila had given him her side of the story, which meant he probably knew more about how Daniel was taking things than I did. The same was true of Adam and Jeremy, but at least with Jake, there was no question of divided loyalties. It might be interesting to hear what Sheila had told him. But definitely not when Jeremy was around.

It was Jeremy, however, who gave me a little surprise while we were eating dinner. I asked him some questions about how his work was going, and I watched his expressive face as he seemed to go through some kind of inner struggle before reaching a decision.

"You know part of my program involves outreach to the public schools," Jeremy said. "Using acting to help teens express some of the stuff they're working through."

"Yes."

"One of your nephews recently joined my group. Nicky."

"Really? He *is* the problem child, so I guess I'm not surprised. I would have thought he was too bashful to get into acting, though."

Jeremy shrugged and said, "He's a good kid. He seems to really enjoy himself."

Later that evening, when Adam ever-so-tactfully said he had a Web project to work on, and Jeremy a little less tactfully made himself scarce, Jake and I sat in front of the fireplace and caught up. He shook his head when I told him about my brothers' reactions to the little bomb I'd dropped on them.

"Typical, huh? Shane takes it personally, and Wayne just wants to build a bomb shelter and stick you in it."

"I know he's going to make newspaper headlines someday," I said.

"He's harmless," Jake assured me. "We've all got one in our families."

"Yeah? Who's yours? Sheila?"

We laughed, then his face grew serious. "Sheila says Daniel's torn up about this, Blaine. It's been, what, nearly three months since you broke up? Have you talked to him yet?"

"No. I've thought about it. I'm not as angry as I was. But it's hard to forget the things we said the last time we spoke. I know if we could get past that, it would make things easier on our friends. But I guess that's not my biggest priority right now."

"Your friends will survive," Jake said with a shrug. "You'll know when the time is right." After a long silence, he asked, "What is your biggest priority right now? It's obvious you've got something on your mind."

I laughed and said, "I'm worse than a teenage girl asking all her friends for advice." I told him about Gretchen's proposition and what Adam and Josh had to say on the subject.

I barely had time to take a breath before Jake said, "Do it."

"You don't even have to think about it?" I asked.

"Blaine, I've known you all our lives. You've always wanted kids, and it's obvious you and Gretchen care about and trust each other. I don't know why you're hesitating."

"It bothers me that Adam thinks it's a bad idea," I said. "I respect him, so his opinion matters to me."

"Adam said *he* wouldn't do it. He's not you. He's happy with his life the way it is."

"It's my family," I finally admitted. "It's not like I had good role models. What if I end up like my parents? I wouldn't want to make a child feel unloved."

Jake shook his head and said, "Haven't you figured out what's wrong in your family? It's not that they don't love you."

"It's not?" I asked.

"No. It's that they never let you love them. You've got so much to give. You'll be a great father."

"Thank you," I said, impressed as always by the way Jake could say the right thing.

After he was gone, I called the hospital and checked on my mother, then sat in front of the television in a stupor. It had been a long day. I dozed off; when I opened my eyes, Jeremy was standing in front of me with a glass of water in his hand.

"I was about to go to bed," he said. "Can I get you anything?"

"No, I'm good. I just need to haul myself upstairs."

I was too tired to think about the times Daniel and I had shared the guest room. I must have fallen asleep as soon as my head hit the pillow. But sometime later, I awoke, feeling disoriented. After I remembered where I was, I could hear muffled voices from Adam's room.

I turned over and pulled a pillow over my head. The sounds of lovemaking couldn't have made me feel anywhere near as jealous as the comfortable intimacy of a couple talking just before they fell asleep. My need of Daniel gnawed at me, and I finally uncovered my head and fumbled in the dark until I found my cell phone. Gretchen answered a little sleepily on the third ring.

"I know it's late, and I'm sure I woke you. But we have to talk."

"It's okay," she said, sounding a bit more alert.

I told her about my day, focusing on the emotional turmoil my family caused me. "You might want to reconsider the gene pool you're diving into," I finally said.

"Are you telling me yes?" Gretchen asked.

I realized that I'd been asking myself that same question for days. Whether I was at work, the gym, home in New York, or revisiting my past in Wisconsin, I was constantly looking at my life and the world through a father's eyes, wondering if having a child with Gretchen was the right thing for me to do. My head, heart, and gut all pointed to the same answer. I took a deep breath and said, "I am telling you yes. Yes. It just feels right. Does that make sense?" She didn't say anything, and I thought I heard her sniff. "Are you crying?"

"A little. With relief. I was worried you might say no, even though I had a feeling you'd say yes," Gretchen said. "Can I just tell you how happy you've made me? We'll talk about all the details when you get back to Manhattan."

"Okay. I'm sorry I woke you up."

"I'm not," she said with a laugh. "The bars are still open. I'm going out to get hammered."

"Isn't it kind of late? Don't you have to work tomorrow?"

"So? It could be years before I can get drunk again. I want to get it in while there's still time."

"If we were talking about contraception, that could be the new slogan for—"

"The sponge: because I want to get it in while there's still time," Gretchen interrupted, her voice serene and breathy like Sheila's in the Autumn Dusk commercials she'd done early in her modeling career. She'd forbidden her friends to mention the douche product in her presence, which provoked a puerile desire in us to bring it up whenever we could.

After Gretchen and I stopped laughing, I said, "You'll have other chances to drink. I won't be home for a few days. Insemination isn't like sex. It doesn't work over the phone."

"Neither does sex. I mean, I've heard. Good night, Blaine."

I intended to leave early for the hospital the next morning, since Adam's office was in his home and I wanted to stay out of everyone's way. But after my shower, I found Jeremy in my room. He'd made my bed and was sitting in the middle of it, his chin on his knees, appearing lost in thought.

"This can't be good," I said. "Did you not assure me last night that you were done with advice and wisdom on the topic of Daniel?"

"That was before Adam told me the plan you and Gretchen have hatched."

"Good choice of words," I commented.

"It was hard for me to give up my dreams of a life with Daniel,"

Jeremy said. "I was so frustrated with him, and I made mistakes I couldn't undo."

"Ancient history," I said.

"Would you let me talk? I know you stonewalled Sheila and Adam on the subject of Daniel. Well, I'm not intimidated by you. If you don't value your friendship with me enough to hear me out, then I obviously don't have much to lose by saying what I have to say anyway."

"Fair enough," I said.

"I started making peace with my mistakes after I saw how happy Daniel was with you. He'd moved on. It was obvious I had no choice but to do likewise. I know you got tired of me while Daniel and I were reinventing our relationship. But the thing is, though Daniel can be a frustrating lover, nobody could ever ask for a better friend. I can't imagine my life without him in it."

"So you're telling me that one day Daniel and I will be friends?"

"I'm telling you his friendships are forged in something that's rare and irreplaceable. He doesn't turn his back on the people he loves. Even the ones who piss you off, like Martin. Hell, Blaine, you know how little Martin and I like each other. But what I do like is that Daniel has never failed his friend. Even now, when Martin is part of something that's hurting you, and your relationship with Daniel, do you really expect Daniel to piss away years of friendship because you didn't get your way? Get over it. If you don't appreciate his loyalty, then you don't deserve him."

"You're entitled to your opinion. But you know what they say. Nobody but the two people involved really know what's going on in a relationship. Maybe you'll have to live with the fact that you don't know everything," I said, starting to get annoyed with him.

"That's fine, and you don't owe me any explanations. But there's another relationship at stake here. One that's older than Daniel's and Martin's, older than Daniel's and mine. His friendship with Gretchen. If you understand Daniel at all, and the emotions he invests in his friends, then I can't help but wonder if this isn't a great way to strike back at him. That's just wrong, Blaine."

"First of all, I didn't go to Gretchen with this plan. She came to me. I'm sure she took everything you're saying into consideration before she did. Since she's okay with it, maybe she has insight into

Daniel that you don't. I understand why Adam told you. But now you need to stay out of it. It's up to Gretchen to talk to Daniel about any decision that she and I make."

"If you decide to go through with it, will she talk to him *before* you do it? And if she won't, will you? Please?"

"I don't know what Gretchen will do. But as for me, no. Daniel made it clear that he expects me to go on with my life, just as he intends to, with the understanding that we're done. I don't know what the hell Daniel's telling all of you, but let me set you straight on something. I didn't just have a big temper tantrum and walk out on him. He wasn't begging me to reconsider. He hasn't picked up the fucking phone and said, 'This is wrong. Let's work it out.' The decisions I make about my life and my future don't have to take Daniel into consideration anymore. And vice versa. As for Gretchen, she's a big girl. She can negotiate her relationship with Daniel on her own terms. I value my friendship with Adam. I know you're part of the package, and I have no problem with that. But stay out of my personal life, because it no longer involves your friend Daniel. I'm sure he would agree with me."

"Okay, this needs to stop," Adam said from the doorway. "Everybody's caught in the middle of something, because we're all too connected. It's like everybody's broken up, and it hurts. My advice, for what it's worth, is that we focus on those things that pull us together. Like Sheila and Josh's wedding. Or supporting Blaine through a family crisis. And respecting the boundaries and loyalties of our various relationships, whether those are with Daniel, Gretchen, Sheila, Martin, Blythe, or whoever. Blaine, you are always welcome in our home. And it is *our* home, not the place where Jeremy happens to live with me. He's not a piece of furniture you have to tolerate just because it's my room and I put it there."

"I'm sorry if I gave that impression," I said.

"Jeremy, Blaine is my friend and our guest. He already made it clear that he doesn't want to talk about Daniel. If you force it—"

"I've said what I had to say," Jeremy interrupted. He left the bed and tried to go through the door, but Adam caught him and put his arms around him.

"Don't break your heart over this," Adam said gently. "It's all going to work out, one way or another."

Jeremy's brown eyes were brilliant with tears when he looked at me over Adam's shoulder.

"I'm sorry, Jeremy," I said. "I know your intentions are good. It's just too raw right now, okay?"

"I'm sorry, too," he said.

"I need to get to the hospital. Dinner tonight?"

"Yes. You can take my truck," Adam said.

My mother was still out of it, but when I went to the hospital the day after that, mere hours before I was scheduled to fly back to New York, they'd moved her from cardiac intensive care into her own room. They'd also assured us that the damage to the valve was less serious than they'd thought. The doctors felt she would make a full and quick recovery.

My father and brothers were not at the hospital, and although I was glad to see my mother in her own room, she still looked small and frail to me. When I walked in, she turned her head slowly toward the door. She lifted her hand in my direction, seeming to use all her strength to do so. Her eyes were at half-mast as she weakly asked, "Is it Blaine?"

"Yes, Mom. It's me. How you doing?"

"Not too well. I guess they've told you that it won't be long now."

I chose to ignore her ominous prophecy and changed the subject, saying, "Wow, look at all the flowers. Makes you know how many friends you have, doesn't it?"

"I don't even know some of these people," she said, sounding more normal after she realized I wasn't playing Race to Death with her. "Who is Adam Wilson?"

"Dad knows him. His company, Adam AdVentures, has contracted Dunhill Electrical on some jobs. Adam's a friend of mine. In fact, I'm staying at his house while I'm in town."

"I see." She gestured toward an arrangement by the window and said, "Gwendy and the Stephenson family? Who is that?"

I felt my throat constrict. It would be so nice to have a mother like Adam's. To drop my head on the bed next to her and bawl over Daniel, knowing she'd smooth my hair down and tell me everything was going to be okay.

"It's Daniel Stephenson's family. Daniel is a close friend of Sheila's and mine. He lives in New York, too. Maybe Sheila told him about your surgery. Gwendy's his sister."

"It's nice of them to send flowers. The Meyers sent the basket by the door. They signed Sheila's and Jake's names, too. Jake was by this morning, right after they moved me into my room. That large arrangement in the corner. Will you give me the card?" When I did, she opened the envelope and handed me the card.

> *So sorry to hear you've been ill. Hope to see you up and about when I get home from Italy.*
>
> *Love,*
> *Sydney*

I might have known that my mother, even after heart surgery, would be eager to fire the first salvo in our ongoing war about my divorce.

"Nice of her," I said, refusing to fight back.

"She's always had the most impeccable manners," my mother said. "Could you find some paper and start making a list for me? I'll be writing a lot of thank-you notes if I get out of here."

"When you get out of here," I corrected.

"There are always so many complications that can set in after surgery," she said. "I'm sure they moved me out of intensive care too soon. I suppose I should be grateful they aren't sending me home. With health plans being what they are, no one is allowed to recover properly anymore. It's amazing that they don't drive you straight from the hospital to the mortuary. These days, after a woman has a baby, they send her home the next day!"

I indulged myself in a fantasy of bringing a new grandchild to Eau Claire.

Mom, Dad, this is my baby, little Civil Liberty. Liberty's mommy, Gretchen Schmidt, of the Pennsylvania Schmidts, and her lesbian lover, Susan B. Hillary Rodham Roosevelt. And this is my longtime companion, Todd. What does Todd do? He's in currency exchange.

I knew I had to get back to New York before I lost my mind.

I saw proof of the old maxim that there's a first time for everything when Violet's mouth dropped open in shock after I finished a Monday morning meeting with a final request.

"Blaine—"

"I don't care how you do it," I said. "But after Wednesday, I have to be out of the office for a week."

"You just took a trip to Wisconsin!" She leaned over and tapped one perfectly manicured nail on my computer screen. "Look at your calendar. You have meetings with Gavin Lewis, an apartment locator, the real estate people for Lillith Allure, Lillith herself, Frank, and a whole set of West Coast distributors who are expecting to be wined and dined with Sheila on Friday. Blaine, do you hate me? Did I give Dexter the wrong cat food? Was your coffee too cold? Your office too hot? Why are you doing this to me?"

"As far as I'm concerned, you can make the decision about Gavin. Make sure he's not allergic to cats. Find out what I should be paying, draw up some kind of privacy agreement for him to sign, and hire him. The apartment locator can wait until I get back, unless you want to meet with him. You know what I'm looking for. In fact, you pretty much manage the Allure account in spite of me. You could probably take the meetings with the real estate people, Lillith, and Frank. As for the West Coast—"

"Is that it? I'm too efficient? You feel useless? Blaine, nobody reschedules Lillith Parker. You know how meticulously her people chart her every move." She stopped, as if struck by a thought. She came around my desk and toggled the screen from my calendar to a search engine, her fingers flying over the keys. I sat back, waiting, as her eyes darted over one site after another. Finally she breathed a sigh of relief and said, "Solar flares."

"Excuse me?"

"Over the next few days, we're having solar flares."

"Was it something we ate?"

"Some people think solar flares can affect—oh, you don't care, do you? It's a good thing for you that Barbara owes me one."

"Barbara?"

"Lillith's assistant," she said impatiently. "Don't ask questions. You're better off not knowing."

"You two conspire against us all the time, don't you?" I asked suspiciously.

"Blaine, if I pull this off and reschedule everything for next week, and you flake on me again—"

"Remind me, which one of us is the boss here?"

"Can *you* put off Lillith and the West Coast?" she asked.

"All right. Thank you for working miracles for me."

"Where are you going? Where can I reach you?" she asked, picking up her ever-present PalmPilot.

"You can reach my cell phone. And I'll take a laptop with me to check e-mail."

She left my office with an air of surrender.

Surrender: the new fragrance from Lillith Allure Cosmetics, I thought and laughed, then dialed Gretchen's office number.

"I have Thursday free," I said, knowing better than to waste her time with small talk.

"Great. Our first appointment is at two. Then we go back at two on Friday."

"Isn't it fortunate for us that you ovulate in time to take a four-day weekend, since you're supposed to stay in bed?"

"In bed, yes. But my god, you wouldn't believe the amount of work I have to do. Why are we doing this during tax season?"

"It's worse than you know," I said. "I don't want to hear any objections. Farm out your work however you have to. From Thursday until next Wednesday, you won't be available."

She laughed and asked, "Are you crazy? I can work from home over the weekend, but Monday morning—"

"Gretchen, I'm putting my foot down. Thursday night, I'm staying at your place with you. Friday evening, I'm taking you to Happy Hollow. We'll be back Wednesday night."

"There's no way I can leave now!"

"Remember what you said? That you've gotten to a point in your life where you have time for motherhood? Motherhood begins at two o'clock on Thursday. If you get yourself exhausted and stressed out trying to save financial empires, we may have to go through this again in a month, which will be April. You know you'll be up to your neck in tax laws and receipts scribbled on napkins by then. This is our only window of ovulation opportunity until May. Besides, if you think you're busy now, wait until the baby comes. From what little I know of kids, they'll change your definition of busy."

"Seven days without working?"

"Consider it a rehearsal for maternity leave," I said.

"What about you? Your schedule can't be any easier to rearrange than mine. Besides, you don't really have to do all this with me. Your lab is sending the sample to my clinic; your work was done the day you spilled your seed into a cup. Or whatever you used."

I laughed and said, "We've already been over this. Years from now, I want to be able to tell, er, whoever, that this wasn't as clinical and impersonal as it could have been."

"Fine. You win," she said, and I envisioned her looking a little like Violet had when she left my office.

On Thursday, while we waited, Gretchen placed a clammy hand over mine, and we exchanged a sympathetic glance. She looked as daunted as I was by the clinical surroundings.

"It's not too late to back out," she said in a small voice. "If you're having second thoughts."

"Are you?"

"No." She paused, then said, "Maybe. I've read so much about this. I know it's going to hurt more than the nurse implied when she described the procedure. If they use benign words like 'discomfort' for 'pain,' what else aren't they telling us? And what if it doesn't work? What if we have to keep coming back?"

"Then we'll keep coming back," I assured her, sounding more matter-of-fact than I felt. "Just remember, we're not one of those desperate couples struggling to balance marriage with infertility issues. This could be the only time we have to go through this part of it."

"Which takes me back to what I said. This may be your last chance to back out."

"I don't want to back out."

They let me stay with her through the entire procedure, which was done by a dyke who reminded me of one of the Gibb brothers. I wasn't sure if I was thinking of Maurice or Robin, but thankfully it was the one without a beard. As Gretchen was maneuvered into a position that I assumed had been perfected during the Spanish Inquisition, I kept hearing the tune to "How Deep Is Your Love" in my head.

Smiling, the doctor held up the sperm sample and said, "I feel very good about this."

"So did I, when I . . ." I trailed off when I realized they were both looking at me with revulsion. "That's all you use?"

"Honey, this little cc contains twenty million sperm. You just know one of them is planning to get lucky. And if not, there'll be a scrappier one tomorrow afternoon."

I liked thinking of my sperm as scrappy, and I began to feel downright giddy. Gretchen, on the other hand, looked very pale and had a death grip on my hand.

"Don't let go, Rose," I said. She laughed and eased up.

"You've already heard all the statistics and scary facts," the doctor said. "So I'm only going to give you one warning."

"Another one?" Gretchen asked from between clenched teeth.

The doctor winked at me and said, "There are no refunds if my aim is off and you get a straight kid. All I can promise you is a male or female who's happy, healthy, and will keep you awake every night for the rest of your lives."

I totally loved her, even if I knew that for as long as I would remember her, I'd never be able to call her anything but "Dr. Gibb." Ten minutes later she was gone, and Gretchen spent the next half-hour with her hips elevated as we tried to remember the words to Bee Gees' songs.

"You really don't have to stay," Gretchen said as I tucked her into bed that night.

"I'll be fine on your sofa."

"Blaine?"

"Yes?"

"Do you think you could sleep with me? I'm sorry. I'm feeling very vulnerable all of a sudden. It's a new sensation for me."

I undressed and crawled in next to her. It had been a long time since I'd shared a bed with a woman, but I'd never felt as relaxed with Sydney as I did with Gretchen.

I left her the next morning to pick up our rental car. I'd chosen a Ford Excursion so she could lie down in the backseat when we drove upstate. After our second rendezvous with "Dr. Gibb," we were on our way, since I'd loaded our luggage before we went to the clinic. I kept the radio low and checked in with Violet on my cell phone while Gretchen dozed behind me. As I'd expected, Violet had everything under control at the office. Lillith had been particularly grateful about dodging the solar flare issue.

As I started up the winding road to the old Victorian hotel that Gretchen and her colleagues had transformed into a cozy resort, I heard Gretchen yawn and sit up.

"We're almost there," I said.

"There's something I forgot to tell you," she said. "This past week, a group used Happy Hollow for a retreat. Something about healing through the colors of nature."

I shuddered and said, "Please don't tell me I'm going to be stuck with a bunch of New Age nuts over the weekend. I thought I'd escaped that by rescheduling my meeting with Lillith."

"Only one," she said. "You know him. Ethan Whitecrow. He led the retreat and wanted to stay a few days by himself after the others left."

I felt a sinking sensation. Though I barely knew Ethan, and he'd always seemed like a nice person, we had one disturbing connection. For a time, he'd dated Martin Blount, and they were still friends. The last thing I wanted was for Gretchen and me to become fodder for Martin's wicked tongue. We might as well call Lola Listeria at the *Manhattan Star-Gazette* and give her the whole story.

"We'll just have to be careful what we say around him," I commented. "Or you know—"

"It will get back to Martin?" she interrupted. "I don't think so. Ethan's a stand-up guy."

"Umm," I said noncommittally.

At the very least, he was an invisible guy. It felt like we were all alone as I unloaded the SUV. Gretchen had directed her housekeeping staff to prepare the room next to hers for me, which was a relief. It meant I didn't have a fireplace, but at least I wouldn't be moping around the room I'd always shared with Daniel.

"Are you hungry?" I asked Gretchen after getting her settled in her room.

"Not really. I'm sleepy. I don't know why I can't hold my eyes open."

"Because you rarely ever stop," I said. "That's why I knew I had to get you out of the city. I'll leave you alone so you can rest. If you want anything later, just let me know. I don't want you running up and down the stairs."

She grinned and said, "I've always wanted to say this. I'm not an invalid, Blaine. I'm just pregnant."

"Wow, you're psychic, too, huh? You always knew that a man named Blaine would come along and—"

"Get out of my room before I had to throw something at him, yes," she said.

"Sweet dreams, Mommie dearest."

"You're evil."

I laughed and went downstairs. I was starving, and no kitchen was as well stocked as the one at Happy Hollow. Gretchen always made sure her guests could eat anything their appetites demanded. I was just finishing a huge omelet and two slices of ham when Ethan joined me in the kitchen.

"Hi," he said, brushing back his long black hair with one hand as he looked at me with surprise. "I didn't realize that you and Daniel were spending the weekend here."

I was astounded that Martin had missed a page in his address book when he spread the news about the big breakup. "Actually, it's just Gretchen and me. It was sort of a last-minute idea to come here. She was tired and went to bed. How was your retreat?"

He cast a sideways look at me from the refrigerator and said, "Please. I know what you think about my *sorcery*."

"Martin talks too much," I muttered. After a pause, I added, "Actually, sometimes he doesn't talk enough. Daniel and I broke up."

"I'm sorry to hear that. And surprised, to tell you the truth. The last time I saw Daniel, on the set of *Secret Splendor,* we talked about you. Was it a sudden thing?"

I'd forgotten that Ethan was a favored spiritual advisor to Bonnie Seaforth-Wilkes. No doubt she'd had him smudge the soap's set with cedar and sage incense because the ratings had dropped, or some such nonsense.

"Somewhat," I said tersely. "It was a mutual decision. I'm really tired of it being a delicious drama for people like Martin to savor."

Ethan set down a container of orange juice and said, "Look, I know you don't think highly of what I do. And I realize you're not a big fan of Martin's. But could you lower the volume on your hostility? I've done nothing to you."

"I'm just hoping to head off any well-intentioned advice about my love life. Or lack thereof," I said.

"I wouldn't presume," Ethan said. He poured a glass of orange juice and drank it without dropping his eyes from mine. He walked past me to put his glass in the sink. "If you tell me what room you're in, I'll build your fire while you clean up your mess. It's supposed to drop into the twenties tonight."

"I don't have a fireplace in my room," I said.

He stopped a few inches from me and said, "I have one in mine. And the fire's already burning."

I abandoned the dishes and followed Ethan up the stairs. As soon as he closed the door behind us, I reached for him.

"No," he said. "I don't do angry sex."

"I don't need spiritual counseling."

"What you need is to stop thinking you call all the shots." He slid a couple of fingers under the waist of my jeans and pulled me toward the fire. "In fact, what you need is to stop thinking and follow your instincts. Isn't that your usual style?"

"What's your usual style?"

"You're about to find out," he said.

I tried to unbutton Ethan's jeans, but he stepped away from me with a reproachful stare, yet smiled at the same time. Keeping me at arm's length, he slowly undressed in front of me. Even when he pulled his shirt over his head, his eyes never left mine. I stood in place, watching him and drinking in the sight of his body as, bit by bit, it was teasingly revealed to me. He was sinewy and toned, most likely from hours of yoga. The firelight danced over his bronze skin. I was aroused just looking at him.

After he'd undressed, he stepped toward me and lightly ran his hand over my cheek. "Your skin is so soft," he said.

I brushed his hair over his shoulder and traced a line from his collarbone to his hand. He brought my hand to his mouth and kissed my palm. My breath caught for a moment as I became aware of a charge of energy running down my arm.

Ethan folded his arms around me and pressed his body into mine. He kissed my neck while I ran my hand down his back, enjoying the warmth of his skin and the feeling of his naked body through my clothes. Still kissing my neck, Ethan tugged my shirt free from my jeans and ran his hands over my back.

I let go of his waist and tried to unbutton my shirt, but Ethan took my hands away and began to do it himself. "Let me undress you," he said. "Relax."

"I trust you," I said.

Ethan tossed my shirt aside and looked into my eyes while he lightly ran his fingers over my chest. "Good," he whispered. "I get off on giving pleasure, Blaine. If you enjoy it, I'll enjoy it. It's as simple as that."

I couldn't argue with that logic and smiled as Ethan knelt to take off my shoes. When my feet were bare, he kissed them and ran a hand under the leg of my jeans, caressing my calf. Still kneeling in front of me, he unbuttoned my jeans and slowly slid them down my legs, holding them for me as I stepped out of them.

I ran my hands through his hair as he gazed up at me from the floor, taking in the sight of my body. While I watched, he began to slowly stroke himself, running a tongue over his lips and breathing deeply. I bent down and lifted his face to mine, kissing his full lips. Our tongues met and Ethan's breath quickened, a soft moan escaping his lips between kisses.

Without saying a word, he walked over to a duffel bag by his bed and began rummaging around inside it. When he found what he was looking for, he sat on the bed and motioned me over. I stood next to him and watched him roll a condom onto me.

"Lie down, please," he instructed, and I did as he asked.

For once in my life I let go of everything that kept me grounded and gave in to Ethan's authority. It felt good not to be the one making decisions and maintaining control. Perhaps because of my deviation from the script of my normal behavior, the Daniel voice-over in my head was silent. Instead, I listened to Ethan as he whispered exotic words into my ear.

We lay together afterward, not needing to speak. I stretched out on my stomach while Ethan lightly traced his fingernails across my back, humming a low melody that lulled me to sleep.

CHAPTER 6

When I awoke, the sky outside was gray, and I wondered if it was going to snow. I propped myself on one arm and stared at Ethan. He looked beautiful asleep. His mouth was so tempting that I almost woke him, but I knew if I did, I wouldn't get back to my room anytime soon. I'd never been one to analyze things too much, so what I really wanted was to hold the memory of the night before somewhere inside me without having to talk about it. To Ethan or to Gretchen.

I shivered after I slid out of bed, but that gave me an idea. As quietly as I could, I added logs to his fire, stirring the coals and watching the wood catch. I hoped he would understand that even though I'd left while he was sleeping, I'd been thinking of his comfort and I had no regrets about our night together.

I put on my jeans but carried the rest of my clothes back to my room. After taking a shower and dressing in a pair of jeans and several layers of shirts, I slipped through the adjoining door into Gretchen's room. Her quiet, even breathing reassured me that she was asleep, so I went downstairs to the kitchen. It took a while to clean up my mess from the night before. After that, I made myself breakfast, then prepared a tray for Gretchen.

This time I knocked, and heard her call, "Come in."

She was awake and sitting up, bathed in the warm glow of a lamp, but staring toward the window. "I think it may snow," she said. "I hope we don't get snowed in."

"If it does snow, it'll be light," I predicted. "Are you hungry? I remembered that you like French toast."

"I'm starving," she said. "I can't believe you're bringing me break-fast in bed. It's like a honeymoon. But a honeymoon in some twisted, *Twilight Zone* kind of way."

"If this was your honeymoon, you got robbed," I said, grinning at her and trying not to look too satiated. While she drank her juice, I said, "You're planning to take it easy, right?"

"If I had my way, I'd never get out of bed," she said. "It's been years since I spoiled myself this way. Usually when I come up here, I'm busy hosting."

"You don't have to do that this time. I've got my laptop if I want to work. I brought a book if I want to read. But what I'd really like to do is spend time outside. Clear out some cobwebs."

She rolled her eyes with pleasure as she bit into the French toast. "It's perfect," she said. "Why couldn't you be a dyke?" I laughed, re-membering Josh's joke that I was turning into a lesbian. She went on. "I made arrangements for someone to cook dinners for us, so you won't be trapped in the kitchen. We'll be on our own for breakfast and lunch every day."

"Just tell me what you want," I said. "I don't want to bug you, but I won't neglect you, either. Whenever you want company, all you have to do is say so."

She nodded, then finished her breakfast while I rebuilt her fire as I had Ethan's.

It was still overcast when I went outside later. I brought in more logs, then went for a walk, enjoying the sound of the ground crunch-ing under my boots. It didn't bother me to visit some of Daniel's fa-vorite places on the property. There was something dreamlike and safe about the weekend. I didn't know if it was because of Gretchen's uncharacteristic lassitude or the energy Ethan gave off, but I felt bet-ter than I had in months.

When I went inside later, Ethan was downstairs doing yoga in front of the fire. Although he had to have heard me come in, he seemed very much inside himself. I went back to the kitchen and heated water for tea. I was leaning against the counter drinking a cup when Ethan joined me.

"Come here," he said. "I want to show you something." I followed him, and we stared through the beveled glass of the front door at the lightly falling snow. "Over there," he said.

I looked where he pointed and saw a fox moving near the trees. Ethan put his arms around me from behind, resting his chin on my shoulder, and we watched until it disappeared into the woods.

"Last night," he said, "was exactly what I needed."

"Me, too," I said. "In fact—"

"I'll race you there," Ethan said with a laugh, reading my mind.

The fire was still burning in his room, making it so warm that I quickly began to shed my layers of clothes. Unlike he had the night before, Ethan didn't stop me. He undressed as eagerly as I did, and we tumbled on the bed together with a desire that demanded immediate satisfaction. I discovered that sex with Ethan had the same effect when it was fast and passionate as it did when it was slow and sensual. It left me feeling contented, calm, and comfortable.

Later, lying on blankets and pillows in front of the fireplace, I said, "This is the first time I've really relaxed since December."

"That's when you broke up?"

"Yeah." After a pause, I said, "Maybe I'm regressing. I should pay someone to sing lullabies to me until I fall asleep every night."

"Is that what did it?" Ethan asked. "Damn. I thought it was my sexual prowess." The expression on my face was all the compliment he needed, and he smiled, then said in a more serious tone, "You've had trouble sleeping? That can definitely take its toll after a while."

"Tell me about it. Do you have a little voice in your head that's always nagging, questioning, or criticizing you?"

"Not really," Ethan said. "But I know what you're talking about."

"Daniel has one. He calls it his inner voice and treats it like it has its own personality separate from him. I think he inflicted one on me by the power of suggestion. I use an advertising term for mine. It's the Daniel voice-over, because it sounds like him. I mean it sounds like his voice. He never said the things to me the voice-over says; he's not a mean person."

"The voice-over is mean?"

"It's a bastard, and it kicks in when things get quiet, especially when I'm trying to sleep."

"But not last night?" When I shook my head, he said, "Does your voice-over usually involve your relationship with Daniel?"

"It sounds off about everything," I said. "Lately, its favorite topic is Sheila."

"Sheila Meyers?"

"Yes. We've been friends since we were kids. Now she's Daniel's best friend. After he and I got together, we were always careful not to put her in the middle."

"Is that where she is since you broke up?"

"Not really. It's more complicated. It all started with a stupid publicity stunt that Sheila and Daniel pulled." After I told him about the Maddie Awards and everything that happened afterward, I said, "The publicity machine that successfully ran our careers malfunctioned and wreaked havoc in our personal lives. Josh and Sheila appear to have fended it off. But Daniel and I had other problems. He made some decisions that affected me, and our relationship, without telling me. I'm sure Sheila knew about them. But she didn't tell me, either."

"So you feel betrayed," Ethan surmised. "It can't help that you and Sheila work together."

"She's worked hard to shift public focus to her and Josh. Which means they've had to sacrifice the privacy they wanted for their wedding. She and I are able to get along because we don't talk about Daniel. But I miss my friend. If circumstances were different, she'd be the one I'd turn to. I think Daniel probably does."

"Do you resent that?"

"Of course I do."

"What sign are you?" Ethan asked.

"Please don't. I hate that shit."

"I'm guessing Scorpio or Taurus."

"Taurus," I admitted. "I already know what you're going to say. We're placid creatures, but very territorial. When provoked, we paw the ground and charge. But I don't believe in astrology. I get enough of that at work." I thought over my last words. "That sort of sums up a lot of things. I make women think a twenty-five-dollar tube of lipstick is going to give them the life of Supermodel Sheila. In fact, it's not much different from a three-dollar lipstick at any drugstore. That's work. At home, what I want is a real person, without artifice. Somewhere along the way, that got lost."

"It's a good thing I don't wear lipstick," Ethan said. I laughed and leaned over to kiss him. We stared at the fire awhile, then he said, "I think it's good that you and Sheila have to spend time together because of your work. In the long run, that will help you iron out your differences. Avoiding someone is rarely a good way to work things out."

I nodded, recognizing the wisdom of his words, particularly since they could also be applied to Daniel and me and our past three months apart.

If Gretchen realized that my weekend was punctuated by sexual interludes with Ethan, she didn't say anything. Nor did Ethan and I feel the need to analyze it. We seemed to share an understanding that this wasn't the beginning of anything more than a new, somewhat unusual, but definitely fulfilling friendship. He'd been right to tell me to follow my instincts, because I knew that we were meeting each other's needs without looking for any complications.

I wasn't sure if Ethan changed his plans because of what was happening between us, but I found that by the time Monday afternoon rolled around and he'd shown no sign of leaving, I was hoping he would stay as long as Gretchen and I did. Especially when I came in from a long walk to find the two of them relaxing downstairs next to a roaring fire.

"Since most of my clients are big Democrats," Gretchen was saying, "I just hinted that I was spending a few days planning strategy with a new and important New Yorker who had the potential to be a very powerful influence in my life. Can I help it if they assumed I was talking about Hillary and her Senate campaign?"

Ethan burst out laughing and said, "Very clever."

"I thought so." Gretchen saw me and said, "Did you have a nice walk? I was just regaling Ethan with our adventures in artificial insemination."

"Ah," I said, trying to read his expression.

"You know, it might not be the conventional method, but I don't think of it as artificial," Ethan said. "I like the other term for it. Alternative fertilization. We're already comfortable with the idea of being alternative, and fertilization sounds more life-affirming."

I sat next to Gretchen on the sofa to take off my hiking boots. While Ethan was talking, he reached over to test my socks for dampness. Apparently satisfied, he kept his hands on my feet and began lightly massaging them. I saw Gretchen take it all in and draw the obvious conclusions, but she merely gave me a Mona Lisa smile and moved her gaze back to Ethan.

"When will you know if it worked?" Ethan asked.

"They do a test after two weeks. If I don't start my period in the meantime. I'm not even allowing myself to think about it until after the test. I don't want to be disappointed."

She shifted and put her feet on my lap, and I absently rubbed them in imitation of the way Ethan was rubbing mine. I was glad she'd told someone what we'd done. I'd felt guilty for telling Adam and Josh that we were thinking about it.

Our conversation flowed into more intimate disclosures about our respective pasts. I gained a new respect for Ethan, who had overcome drug addiction and made a name for himself as one of the country's preeminent voices on the New Age lecture and workshop circuit. He'd also spearheaded programs working with at-risk teens, including the one that Jeremy was associated with in Eau Claire. I shared what Jeremy had told me about my nephew Nicky being part of Jeremy's group, and Ethan and I exchanged a smile at that coincidental connection between us.

"If I am pregnant, Blaine and I agreed to wait awhile before telling people," Gretchen said, returning the conversation to what was uppermost on her mind.

"I won't say anything to anyone," Ethan said. "Especially Martin, if that's what you're worried about."

"Telling Martin would be like—"

"I brought videos," I rudely interrupted Gretchen. "Who's up for a Rock Hudson–Doris Day film fest?"

"Blaine, I'm so proud," Gretchen said. "It's almost like you've graduated and been accepted to Queer College."

Ethan and I kept Gretchen entertained with imitations of Rock's Rex Stetson character from *Pillow Talk* over the following days. By the time Wednesday arrived, with a bright blue sky and a calming warmth that hinted of spring's arrival, I was ready to fall back into the caffeine-fueled, work-dominated buoyancy of New York City. My mind felt clearer and better able to undertake the hectic schedule that Violet warned me about in an e-mail that I read while I drank my morning coffee. The cozy sounds of Gretchen and Ethan cooking breakfast and laughing in the kitchen were a strange accompaniment to the busy world asserting itself through Violet's words.

Violet also gave me an update about Gavin. At first, she'd thought that Gavin might not accept the offer to become my personal assistant, the salary being somewhat low by New York City standards. But when he was assured that he would have enough free time to supplement his income with out-call massage clients, and that his weekends would usually be free, he accepted. I agreed to pick him up at the airport on Sunday, amazed that he was able to orchestrate his move from Baltimore so quickly. I decided that in terms of efficiency, he could be the male version of Violet.

Ethan had to leave earlier than us, since he wasn't driving back to Manhattan. He was speaking at a weekend retreat somewhere in rural Vermont. I helped him load numerous boxes of whatever New Age materials his various activities demanded.

"You folks should just use your psychic powers to communicate with each other and save trees," I commented, grunting as I loaded the last of the boxes into his rented minivan.

Ethan laughed and handed me a book titled *Shamanic Dance.* I noticed that he was the author, but before I could open it to see if he'd signed it for me, he said, "Don't read the inscription in front of me. That always makes me feel stupid."

"I'm at a loss for words myself," I said.

"No words necessary," he said. "It's been a great week. I feel recharged."

"That's exactly how I feel," I agreed, and we hugged goodbye. After he drove away, I opened the book.

Blaine, he'd written, *thank you for helping me remember to lighten up. And especially for discovering, with me, that friendship grows in unexpected places. With deep affection, Ethan.*

I smiled, thinking how perfectly he'd expressed my thoughts.

Gretchen slept most of the way back to Manhattan. After dropping her at her loft, I went directly to my office at Breslin Evans to catch up on anything I might have missed. Since Violet had practically done my job as well as hers in my absence, there were only a few contracts to sign and bills to approve. Once those were out of the way, I looked through a folder labeled REAL ESTATE PROSPECTS, which Violet had left to keep me up to speed on the office properties Lillith Allure was considering. As I read through the listings, I stumbled upon the one office that I knew would be the perfect space. I only hoped that Lillith and Frank would like it, too.

Owing to the increasingly rapid drop-off of Internet businesses, valuable office space was popping up left and right. One of the larger, but now diminishing, companies had moved to a smaller office on the Lower East Side. They had vacated two floors at the top of an office building in Chelsea, which had a view of the Hudson River from a terrace that surrounded the building. Because the walls were made entirely of glass, there was light from every angle during the day.

I set the commercial listings aside and riffled through another folder Violet had made of residential listings. My heart sank at the prospects. Even though I'd only lived in Manhattan for three years, I noticed a marked increase in property values for co-ops and condos. I'd learned to shudder at the words "cozy," which meant cramped; "charming," which meant inefficiently designed; and "unique," which translated to, *You would never want to live here if it was the last apartment available in Manhattan.*

Despite the view of my ex-boyfriend's garden, my rent stabilized, two-bedroom dive of an apartment was a dream in comparison to some of the cramped quarters that I'd heard about from my coworkers. But I felt like it was time to own a place that I could redesign any way that I wanted. Even though I'd originally imagined undertaking that with Daniel, there was no reason I couldn't do it on my own. Especially with Gavin's calm reason and Violet's enthusiastic input to guide me.

The following morning began with a surprise visit from Lillith, who strode into my office wearing black from the collar of her coat to the tip of her boots. Her hair was pulled into a tight knot, and a stone, suspended from a long chain around her neck, swung back and forth as she walked. The grim look of determination on her face made me wonder if she intended to take off her necklace and beat me with it.

"Good morning, Lillith," I said tentatively. "I wasn't expecting you."

"Of course you weren't. We don't have an appointment. But I'm free of toxins, and there's a small window of time when it's safe to talk about new projects today."

"I have to be honest, Lillith, I have quite a lot on my pl—"

She cut me off before I could finish, raising her silver-ringed left hand in the air and causing her many bracelets to slide down her arm in a cacophony of clanging. "I feel that there is an entire market we're missing out on. I need you to come up with a concept for a line of men's products. This is not your first priority. Keep it in mind until we're caught up with the Zodiac campaign," she said, then stopped short. Her eyes fixed on the sheet of paper which detailed the space in Chelsea. She picked it up and quickly scanned it, then looked at me with a broad smile replacing the tension on her face.

"We want this space, Blaine. Tell Violet the decision has been made. I have a meeting with an art dealer uptown, so we'll catch up later." She whirled around to make an exit, but stopped short and turned back to me. "By the way, it's too bad you aren't trying to have a child right now, because the next two weeks are excellent for the houses dominating conception."

I shivered inwardly as she walked out of the room. I figured that she would eventually stop shocking me with her eerie accuracy. But her words gave me pause for thought. I picked up the phone, intending to test Lillith's prophecy by calling Gretchen and asking her to take a home pregnancy test, but quickly dropped the phone back in its cradle. Not only would the test be unreliable—it was still too early—but even entertaining the idea would be giving credence to Lillith's beliefs. The thought made me cringe.

I told Violet that Lillith wanted the Chelsea space and had her set up meetings for me to look at apartments. Still reeling from Lillith's visit, I put the idea of a men's product line out of my head, worrying that visions of pendulous rocks would distract me from devising a masculine line of colognes, shaving lotions, and balms.

On Sunday, I picked up Gavin at JFK. During our drive back to the city, I told him what was going on and what I would require of him. I gave him a PalmPilot with all of my pertinent numbers and addresses already downloaded, as well as lists of my favorite restaurants, clubs, car services, cleaners, gym, and grocery store. He was very professional and seemed to retain every word I said.

"I don't expect you to remember everything I've said, Gavin. I understand how taxing a move can be," I said.

"No, I'm fine," he assured me, sitting on the leather sofa in my living room with a bottle of Poland Spring water. "Ever since Violet called with your offer, I've been excited to return to the city. You're right; change can be daunting. But only if you let it. I guess I knew that my time in Baltimore was only temporary. My horoscope even said I could expect a new job prospect. Then the universe offered me a new path, so I thought, why not take it?"

For a moment, I was unsure about my decision to bring Gavin into my life. I didn't really know much about him, other than what was on his résumé. His personality seemed to lie somewhere between Ethan's New Age philosophies and Lillith's astrological extremism. As long as he leaned toward the former and not the latter, I figured things would be fine between us.

"Change is in the air," I agreed. "I'm about to change companies. My new employers are relocating to Manhattan, too. Let me show you your room." I lifted the case that held his massage table. Gavin recapped his water bottle, picked up his bags, and followed me to the second bedroom. "This used to be my friend Sheila's room. She left a few months ago to move in with her fiancé, Josh. She didn't take the furniture, because she wanted new stuff. If you don't like any of it, just let me know, and we'll replace it."

"I'm sure it'll be fine," Gavin said, dropping his bags by the door and sitting on the bed. "The mattress feels firm. As long as my spine is supported, I'll be okay."

"I'm thinking about moving," I said, grateful for his easygoing nature. "So don't get too comfortable. My financial advisor, Gretchen, assures me that investing in my own home will only benefit me in the long run. I'm looking into it. I could use your help."

"Not a problem," Gavin assured me. "Whatever agency you use, give the realtors my cell number and have them call me if you aren't available. I can always check out any apartment they have and tell them to hold on to it until you have time to see it. We'll work it out. Are you hungry? I am. Point me in the direction of the nearest grocery store, and I'll make whatever you want for dinner."

"Gavin, I meant it when I said you can relax. We'll order takeout or something."

"I won't hear of it," Gavin said, holding up his hands. "Not only is takeout food a waste of money, but if I cook, it'll be healthier. And it'll give me a chance to get used to your kitchen. Plus, I'll admit, I'm a little nervous being in a strange place. If I'm doing something, I'll relax."

Later, he made me grilled chicken on a bed of saffron rice with steamed asparagus. After one bite, I knew that hiring Gavin ranked up there with hiring Violet as among the best decisions I'd ever made.

The next morning, I woke up to the aroma of freshly brewed coffee. I followed the smell to the kitchen and was pushed to the table by Gavin, who offered me crepes with fruit, orange juice, coffee, and the paper.

I stared at my plate, and Gavin asked, "Is everything okay? Do you need protein, too? I can do a quick steak if you want."

"No, everything looks great. I'm just waiting for a voice-over by Rod Serling. I feel like I'm in a parallel universe. But I like it."

"Good," Gavin said. When I began eating, he slipped behind my chair and stage-whispered, "Submitted for your perusal. We've secretly replaced Blaine Dunhill's regular coffee with dilithium crystals. Let's see if he goes into warp speed."

After I finally managed to swallow my crepes through my laughter, I said, "I'm going to take you around the neighborhood this morning and show you all the places that make my life run from day to day. I guess we can cross the grocery store off the list. But I'll show you where Whole Foods is later. That's where I get all the healthy stuff. I should call Violet to remind her that I'm coming in late today."

I dialed Violet at home, and she picked up on the second ring. "Hi, Blaine," she said.

"Good morning, Violet. I'm sorry to bother you at home."

"That's okay. Don't forget that you're coming in late today, so you can show Gavin around."

"I was wondering why I called you. Thanks."

"Don't mention it. I logged in to the office e-mail from home this morning. We already have an e-mail from the broker regarding the Chelsea offices."

"That was fast," I said. "What's the word?"

"I think it's in the bag. Show Gavin the dry cleaners first, because you always get there after they close."

"I swear they see me coming and lock the doors," I grumbled.

Following Violet's advice, our first stop was the dry cleaners, where I introduced Gavin to Mrs. Chan, who gave a polite nod and a smile.

"It is nice to meet you," she said to Gavin. To me she said, "I have not seen you for a very long time."

"I can never seem to get here before you close," I said sheepishly.

"We close at four. Every day. But where is that nice lady friend of yours who picks up your cleaning? Violet?"

"Gavin will be taking care of my cleaning from now on."

"Oh. That's a shame. She is such a nice lady. I will miss her very much. But I will look forward to seeing you again soon, Gavin."

Next, I showed Gavin the only deli in my neighborhood that I trusted to get everything right.

"Hey, Mr. Blaine! How are you?" the man behind the counter shouted as if I was deaf.

"I'm great, Amir. I wanted to show my friend, Gavin, your deli. I was just telling him that it's the best in town."

"Such kindness, my friend! But where is your sexy Violet today? I have not seen her in so long that my heart grows heavy."

"I'll tell her, Amir. And I'll tell her you wish to marry her and take her home to your country, where she'll live like a princess."

"A man can dream, no? Can I make you a sandwich, Mr. Blaine?"

"Not today, thank you."

We continued our tour so I could point out the closest restaurants that I found palatable and the laundry where I dropped off everything that didn't get dry-cleaned. Then I took him to Barneys to introduce him to Nathan, the sales associate who I entrusted to pick out my suits.

"Gavin will pick up any items I buy over the phone," I explained.

"What happened to Violet?" Nathan asked with a look of concern. "You didn't fire her, did you?"

"No. Nothing like that. Her work will be limited to the office from now on. Don't worry. I'm sure her love of shoes will bring her in to see you."

"Good. I just love her," Nathan said.

"Is Isaac in today?" I asked, then explained to Gavin, "Isaac is the best tailor in Barneys."

"He is in," Nathan answered. "Speaking of Violet, you should go see him. Isaac's son is having his bar mitzvah, and he wanted to invite Violet. You could hand-deliver the invitation."

After leaving Barneys, we took a cab down to Chelsea, where I took Gavin on a tour of my gym and added him to my membership.

"Thanks, Blaine," Gavin said. "There weren't any gyms like this in Baltimore. I usually just went to the weight room in my building."

We left the gym and walked to Whole Foods on Seventh Avenue. I explained to Gavin that I liked to shop there after my workouts. We wandered up and down the aisles so I could show him the kinds of foods that I liked to keep stocked in the apartment. As we passed a large display of a new cereal called Eighth Wonder Grains, I heard a familiar voice say, "Get your zucchini away from me."

With my heart pounding, I rounded the corner into the produce section, where I came face-to-face with Daniel. A hand extended from behind the cereal display, brandishing a very large zucchini in his direction, like a sword. As the hand dropped out of sight, I heard a voice I didn't recognize answer, "I've never heard you complain about my zucchini before."

Daniel's beautiful blue eyes stared at mine, and his face flushed bright red. I finally broke the silence to say, "I didn't realize you were back from L.A. Congratulations on the *Lifetime* movie."

"Thanks," he said. "Congratulations on your new job."

Gavin came to my side and looked toward Daniel. Daniel's gaze moved from me to Gavin, and I felt my heart drop to my stomach when he grabbed the handles of a shopping cart and disappeared among the rows of fruits, vegetables, and nut dispensers. I didn't get to see the face behind the voice of the stranger he was with, but assumed he was spending a lazy day shopping with a new lover.

I took a deep breath and reminded myself that his companion could have been one of his friends. He'd always had too many for me to keep track of. Of course, there was that zucchini joke . . . Then it occurred to me that Daniel might have made the same assumption—that I was with a new lover—when he looked at Gavin.

"Are you okay?" Gavin asked.

"Yes," I answered. I felt like I was on autopilot. "He was the reason for my breakdown on the massage table."

"You're kidding," Gavin said, sounding shocked. I half expected him to shove me while screaming, "Get out!" like Elaine on *Seinfeld*.

"Nope, not kidding."

"Your ex is Angus Remington?"

"No," I protested. "My ex is Daniel Stephenson."

"I'm sorry. I think I'm in shock. It's not every day that I see a celebrity. And it's not every day that I see one of my favorite soap stars in person."

"You watch *Secret Splendor?*" I asked. I wanted to throw up, but didn't think Whole Foods would take kindly to me vomiting in a bushel of tomatoes.

"Yeah. I never miss a day. Well, I guess I missed today. But that's okay," he said, then seemed to notice the grim look on my face. "I'm being so insensitive. I'm sorry, Blaine. He was your lover, not a soap star. Was that the first time you've seen him since you broke up?"

"Yes."

"Do you think you'll get back together? Would you want to?"

"I don't think that's an option anymore," I said, wanting to cut the conversation short.

"So, what kinds of vegetables do you like?" Gavin asked.

"Anything but zucchini," I said, grateful for the topic switch, and rattled off what I would eat as he made notes on his PalmPilot.

I shoved the incident out of my mind until late that night, when I endured an attack of insomnia brought on by running into Daniel. For some reason, the shock of his being with someone else had faded. What I couldn't get out of my mind was how good he looked. When I'd seen Daniel every day, I'd probably taken his appearance for granted. Instead of sleeping, I found myself scrutinizing every detail of my mental picture of him.

He'd always kept his fine blond hair cut short, and now he seemed to be growing it out. Since that wasn't really his style, I wondered if it had something to do with the show. From time to time, they changed Daniel's hairstyle to reflect the different aspects of his character's personality. The longer cut gave him a softer image, and I wondered if the evil Angus was about to get a love story. That would be a new twist, since Angus was the most hated person in Splendor Falls, USA. Maybe I should have guessed, since Daniel played Angus to such perfection, that his own nature was not without its cruelty.

"Oh, come on, Blaine," I muttered, turning my pillow over to the cool side.

Although some of Daniel's actions had been thoughtless, only his words had been cruel, and those were spoken in the heat of anger.

It surprised me how many feelings had passed between us in a few seconds at Whole Foods. Shock, love, fear, resentment, desire, anger, anxiety . . . all underscored by what I could only describe as yearning. I remembered that one from the early days of our acquaintance, when we'd kept each other at arm's length because of our boss/employee relationship.

I smiled, thinking of those hours at Breslin Evans when I'd forced myself to ignore an endless and illogical list of reasons for him to come into my office, or for me to pass by his desk, just so I could look at him. I'd fantasized about him constantly, and any reference to his personal life had made me crazy because I felt excluded.

Excluded. That word again. I remembered how I'd felt the day I glanced from my window to see Gretchen talking to Martin in Daniel's garden. It took me right back to my first months in New York, when I'd struggled with all the fears that came from finally admitting to myself that I was gay.

Not that my admission had changed the way I lived. Until I saw Daniel five floors below me, my life was all about work. I was too scared, even in Manhattan, to explore what being gay meant. In time, as I got to know Daniel, I learned not only how to accept who I was, but to build a life for myself that included everything I'd feared I would never have. Especially love. Which was the hard truth that was keeping me awake. Regardless of the hurt, anger, and disappointment, I was as deeply in love with Daniel as I'd ever been. If I'd thought it was challenging to make a life with him, I finally realized that it was going to be agonizing to make a life without him.

It was a relief to get up after a few hours of fitful sleep and find

Gavin already awake and cooking breakfast. It made me happy when he sat down with his cup of tea while I attacked my Southwestern omelet. I felt like he was getting more comfortable with me.

"What's on today's agenda?" he asked.

"First we have to go to Refined Felines and pick up Dexter," I said. "After a few days at the kitty spa, he'll probably be a little aloof. I'm never sure if he's punishing me, or if he thinks he's too upscale for the likes of me after his little vacations."

Gavin was staring at me with the same patient expression that I suspected was often on my face whenever Lillith began talking about astral travel or pyramid power. I figured he'd learn soon enough that I was not one of those people who gushed over my cat. Dexter and I appreciated our creature comforts, but I thought we were pretty low-maintenance overall.

"After that," I said, "we're looking at apartments."

When we walked into Refined Felines, the receptionist gave me a blank stare. "May I help you?" he asked.

"I'm here to pick up Dexter," I said. I did a sidestep to avoid the shells a parrot was dropping on the floor while he ate his breakfast on the counter. When the receptionist looked warily from me to Gavin, I repeated, "Dexter. Dexter Dunhill?"

"I'm sorry, I can't release Dexter to anyone but Violet Medina." His tone clearly indicated that Gavin and I looked like sinister cat-nappers. Even the parrot stopped eating to stare at me.

"I'm Blaine Dunhill. Dexter's my cat."

"Excuse me." He crossed the room to a woman sitting behind another counter, and the two of them spoke in low whispers while they cast strange glances our way.

I looked at the parrot and said, "Polly want a cracker?"

The parrot bobbed its head and said, "Asshole."

Gavin and I stared at each other, then I said, "Did I hear that correctly? Did you hear that, too?"

Gavin looked at the parrot and softly said, "You'd look even prettier on a spit over a low flame."

The parrot laid its head on the counter, winked at Gavin, and said, "Pretty boy."

"Maybe it's just you," Gavin said to me.

I rolled my eyes and turned to see the woman disappear behind a door. When she returned, I saw that she was carrying a file folder instead of Dexter's cardboard carrier. "Mr. Dunhill?" she asked, looking at me over the tops of her reading glasses. "I'm Tabitha Katz."

I heard Gavin cough to cover up his laugh. She heard it, too, and frowned at him. No doubt she'd endured every possible reaction to her name, but I had to wonder why anyone who could be called *Tabby Katz* would want to work where she was working.

"This is my assistant, Gavin Lewis," I said. "I'd like to add his name to Dexter's file, since he'll often be the one dropping him off or picking him up."

"But Mr. Dunhill, *your* name isn't even in Dexter's file." She glanced down at it and said, "Violet Medina. Sheila Meyers. Daniel Stephenson."

"I'm the one who filled out the paperwork," I said, starting to get annoyed. "Not to mention the one who pays the bills."

Before she could answer, Gavin held up a hand and whipped out his cell phone, hitting a preprogrammed number. "Violet. Gavin Lewis. Could you call . . ." He paused to look at the receptionist.

"Darnell."

"—Darnell at Refined Felines and explain that it's okay for Blaine to pick up Dexter?"

"Oh, just hand me your phone," Darnell said, and Gavin gave it to him. "Vi? Sweetie, Mr. Dunhill is not listed in Dexter's file . . . Yes, so he told us, but so many of our little clients come from broken homes, and you wouldn't believe what irate ex-spouses will do. We can't be too careful with young Dexter, you know . . . A little under six feet tall. Brown hair, green eyes. Frowning. Turning crimson . . . Okay, I'll add him to the file. Is it okay for us to add Mr. Lewis, as well? Thank you, dear. Oh, and thank you, also, for that lovely gift basket."

While Darnell continued to chat with Violet, Ms. Katz motioned us over to her counter. "If you'll both just show me your drivers' licenses, I'll update the file," she said. She took mine without comment, but Gavin's Maryland license gave her pause. After another measuring glance at him, she shrugged as if the entire situation was out of her hands.

She used an intercom to ask for a handler to bring Dexter to us, then added our information to the file. Just as Darnell returned Gavin's phone, the handler came from the back with Dexter in his carrier. She was one of those perky teenagers, but as soon as she saw me, her face fell.

"I was expecting Violet," she said.

"Violet!" the parrot screamed.

"He says Dexter's his cat," Darnell said, nodding toward me.

The handler looked as if she was being forced to give me her grandmother's wedding ring, and when I passed the carrier to Gavin so Darnell could total my bill and run my debit card, I could have sworn she had tears in her eyes as she turned away.

When we were finally outside Refined Felines, Gavin and I exchanged a disbelieving look, then burst out laughing.

"Is this cat made out of gold?" he asked.

"You'd think so," I answered, waving my invoice at him. "Good grief."

"After the last two days," Gavin said, "the only thing that surprises me is that when we ran into your ex at Whole Foods, he didn't look at me and wail, 'Where's Violet?' "

I laughed again and said, "You got lucky. In all the time Violet's worked for me, she and Daniel never actually met. They only talked on the phone."

"I'm beginning to be afraid of her," Gavin said.

"Me, too!"

When we got back to my apartment, Gavin released Dexter, who seemed as suspicious of us as all his protectors had been.

"He just wants his Fancy Feast," I said. "God knows what kind of gourmet crap they give him at Refined Felines." I dished it out while Dexter attempted his usual Let's Make Blaine Fall Down feat. I saw that Gavin was giving him an odd stare. "You do get along with cats, I hope. I specifically told Violet—"

"Oh, yeah, I love cats," Gavin said, collecting himself. After a pause, he added, "He's just . . . so . . . Blaine, that cat is ugly!"

"Isn't he?" I agreed. As far as I was concerned, Gavin had passed his final test. Anyone who thought the mottled Dexter was a handsome cat was certifiable. Or qualified to work at Refined Felines.

Later, Gavin and I got into the car Violet had hired to take us to various apartments. First, we stopped at the office to pick her up.

She got into the back of the car next to me, only briefly glancing at Gavin. I couldn't interpret the expression on her face, but when I introduced the two of them, I noticed that Gavin looked somewhat uncomfortable.

"Is there something I don't know?" I asked.

Gavin blushed, and after a pause, Violet said, "We actually met several years ago through a mutual friend. That's how I knew to book Gavin in Baltimore. I didn't know he'd end up working for you."

"That's fine," I said. "I don't mind if you two are friends. Did you think I'd feel like this was a conspiracy if I found out?"

"We weren't actually friends," Gavin said.

"Now you can be," I said. "Just don't start bossing me around like she does."

Violet flashed me a weak smile then gave the first address to the driver. We went to a building on the Upper East Side, entering a grand lobby that had a high ceiling and was decorated in dark woods with light gold accents. As we walked down a burgundy carpet to the elevator, a group of older women, dressed in obviously expensive clothing, breezed past us speaking in affected voices.

We took the elevator to the tenth floor and exited into a small hallway with four doors, one of which was slightly ajar. The broker, Lanie, was already inside. The apartment was open and airy, with large windows that had a sliver of a Central Park view. It was obvious that the seller was wealthy, as all of the furniture was antique. Lanie gave us a tour of the updated kitchen, large master bedroom, and guest room. It was an exquisite space and the price was not as exorbitant as I imagined it would be. After the tour was over, Violet and Gavin turned to me excitedly. The smiles ran from their faces as they looked at mine.

"What's wrong?" Violet asked.

"I'd feel like I was living in a nursing home," I said, remembering the group of women who'd passed us in the lobby.

"But look at this place, Blaine. You can't beat it, especially for the price." It was hard for Gavin to hide his excitement at the prospect of living there.

"You know, I've never really liked the Upper East Side," I said.

Not another word was spoken on the subject as we all filed back into our car. Violet looked at her PalmPilot and gave the driver the next address, which was on the Upper West Side, almost directly opposite the last apartment.

The apartment was in a fifteen-story Art Deco building, with a concierge in the marble lobby. The agent, Wendell, was waiting for us there, and whisked us to the elevator with the efficiency of a border collie.

As soon as he opened the door of the apartment, Violet and Gavin were drawn to the oversized, double-paned windows that looked toward the park. Wendell apologetically took a call on his cell phone, and I wandered through the apartment, admiring the high ceilings, the black marble fireplace with its gas logs, and the spacious closets.

As much as I appreciated the two bathrooms, I knew I was going to have to disappoint Violet once again. What I didn't know how to convey was why I needed three bedrooms. If I tried to explain the third room as office space, she'd look at me like I was crazy, because both apartments we'd viewed were spacious enough to allow me a work area. Both buildings had also installed high-speed Internet access lines. They were beautiful and I could probably swing the payments, but they wouldn't accommodate a nursery, and I fully intended to have a separate room to allow overnight visits from my child.

"Can you believe these hardwoods?" Violet asked in a low voice. "I know it's a little pricier, but—"

"I wish I could find something where the bedrooms aren't in such close proximity to each other. I need to feel like I have privacy. You know what would be great is one of those brownstone apartments that has two levels. That way, Gavin could be downstairs, and I'd have more work space upstairs."

I could tell by her expression that there was nothing like my description in her PalmPilot. "I'm not sure any of the places we're supposed to see meet that requirement," she said.

"We may as well keep the appointments. I'm not that hard to please. I'm sure one of them will be suitable."

When I went by to see Gretchen that night, she laughed until tears streamed down her face as I described my day. She hadn't fully recovered from the Dexter story when I detailed my rejection of each apartment and Violet's exasperation with me.

"One had a rude doorman. Another's entrance was too close to a subway stop. The closets were too small in one. I developed an instant dislike for one of the brokers and insisted that he'd be too difficult to negotiate with. The apartment she was the most in love with had pastel walls. I pretended not to be able to visualize how it would look with some color. But it was the last one that defeated her. I told her it smelled like Old Spice. It was the agent's aftershave, of course, but I kept walking around sniffing, and she dropped her PalmPilot in her purse and said she'd start over tomorrow."

"Asshole," Gretchen squawked, and I glared at her. "Poor Violet. I'd have resigned on the spot."

"She loves a challenge. Anyway, I figured Gavin was starting to wonder what he'd gotten himself into, so I told them I was having dinner with a friend and let them take the car without me."

"I've probably got a two-year-old Lean Cuisine in the freezer," Gretchen offered.

"That's tempting. But I'll just grab something on my way home. Are you not eating tonight?"

"My stomach's a little queasy, and I've been craving oatmeal."

"Should we take those as signs?"

"Hopefully not signs of PMS," she said. "It's way too early to know if I'm pregnant. Blaine, sooner or later, you'll have to tell Violet you want three bedrooms."

"I will, once we're sure you're pregnant. Like you said, it's too early."

"So other than the fact that you are now allowed to take your own cat out of daycare, did you accomplish anything today?"

"Absolutely. I went by Breslin Evans for my exit interview with Mr. Fox. He wasn't happy. Which isn't about losing me; it's about losing the Lillith Allure account. But he knows I have no control over that. Nobody changes Lillith Parker's mind once it's made up."

"Violet could," Gretchen disagreed.

"Violet could make Cardinal O'Connor give his blessing to Dykes on Bikes leading the St. Patrick's Day Parade," I said.

"You are going to owe her big time for what you're putting her through."

"I already owe her for more than I can ever repay," I said. "I'm an awful boss."

"You don't deserve her," Gretchen concurred.

I left her with her tax codes and a stack of paperwork and ate dinner alone in a small Italian restaurant. When I stepped outside to
catch a cab, it struck me that I didn't particularly want to go home to
face a second sleepless night being depressed about Daniel.

What I needed to bolster my spirits was another blue-eyed
blonde, but of the female variety. I looked at my watch to reassure
myself that it wouldn't be totally rude to drop in uninvited and without warning.

CHAPTER 7

As I walked along the quiet street, I realized where I'd gotten the idea to ask Violet to find me a brownstone apartment. Although the apartment Sheila and Josh lived in wasn't on two levels, as I'd described to my assistant, it did have the charm that I envisioned when I thought of Manhattan's early-twentieth-century residences. It was squeezed into a row of similar buildings, but because the area was midway between Central Park and Riverside Park, the streets were quietly romantic. The trees along the sidewalks would be budding soon, adding to the tranquillity of the neighborhood.

I waited at the door for a bit after Sheila buzzed me into the brownstone's common foyer. I could hear footsteps racing back and forth inside. Something fell to the floor, and I pictured Sheila and Josh frantically throwing on clothes after untangling themselves. I looked at my watch again and wondered if I'd made a poor decision by arriving unannounced.

The door opened, and I was greeted by Sheila in her robe, her face entirely green with one of Zodiac's cleansing and moisturizing masks, and her hair held captive by what seemed to be hundreds of pink sponge curlers. Without a word, she grabbed my arm and pulled me into the apartment, slamming the door behind me.

"What are you doing?" I asked with a laugh.

"I was about to leave to go to the bank," she replied sarcastically. "What does it look like I'm doing?"

"I just thought—"

"If you can believe it," she cut me off, whirling around and flying down the hall toward the kitchen, looking like Sister Bertrille escaping from a day spa, "we finally decided on a cake from Johann's Bakery in Eau Claire. I called to place the order, and they told me they don't make that cake anymore."

"I'm sure that—"

"Then Patti—my best friend from home, do you remember her?—called and told me that she can't be at the bridal tea."

"You can always—"

"I still have to meet with the designer for the dress. And Josh has been no help whatsoever. We discussed other cakes, and when we agreed again, we called Johann's. They gave us some song and dance about how they couldn't make the one we wanted with the custard filling that was in the first cake they don't make anymore. Now I ask you, what difference should it make what the cake looks like? Shouldn't we be able to get it filled with whatever we want? I should be able to decorate it with chocolate coins wrapped in foil if I want to." I laughed at this comment, and she glared at me.

"Where's Josh?" I asked.

"He's doing a shoot tonight using the Brooklyn Bridge as a backdrop for something or other. He said he'd be late."

"I'm sure he'd help with anything you wanted."

"Men have no idea what kind of preparation a wedding requires. It would take me so long to explain anything that by the time I finished, I could have done it myself. When any of this stuff starts to happen, he says, 'Just tell me what to wear, and when and where to show up.'" While she was talking, she'd taken down two wineglasses and opened a bottle. "My mother has definite ideas how she wants this wedding to look, and none of them coincide with what *we* want. If she had her way, I'd be dressed like Little Bo Peep. She wants to have the reception at the church hall, and I can't imagine anything less elegant. It would be like a high school dance. We can't make up our minds where to have it, and the location keeps changing depending on how many people are coming on any given day, but I'm not having it in a church hall."

"Have you thought about—"

"Neither of us even wanted a big wedding. Now we find that by the time we invite all of the necessary business contacts, between the two of us, we're up to over five hundred people. And that doesn't include our friends and family. All we need now is to have the printed napkins come to us announcing, 'Happy Bat Mitzvah, Eunice,' two days before the wedding." She took a sip of her wine, leaving part of the green mask on the rim of the wineglass, and grimaced as she swallowed some of the mask with her first sip of Merlot. "Ugh! I can't believe you let me do that. I gotta get this stuff off my face. I'll be right back."

"I saw Daniel," I said, finally able to get a word in.

She froze, then turned and looked at me. She measured my face for my reaction to the statement I'd just made. When she saw nothing, she said, "You want to hold that thought for a minute?"

I nodded and went into the living room to wait for her. She returned, her face scrubbed clean, but still in robe and curlers. She set the bottle of wine on the table close to my glass, then curled up next to me on the overstuffed sofa.

"So," she said and stared at me. "The forbidden topic, huh? Where'd you see him?"

"At Whole Foods. I was showing Gavin around—"

"Gavin would be?"

"My personal assistant."

"What happened to Violet?" Sheila asked.

"Violet's my assistant at work. I don't expect her to run my personal life."

"Since when? And who is Gavin, anyway? Where did you meet him? Is this someone *you* hired?"

I looked at her, exasperated, and asked, "Where is all this suspicion coming from? Are you the same person who invited a total stranger into our apartment a few years ago, just because he proffered flowers from his patio garden?"

"Look how that turned out," she said.

We considered her words, both of us evidently trying to determine what regrets we might be feeling about Daniel's effect on our lives. I decided I wasn't ready to explore that, with or without Sheila's wisdom on the subject.

I explained how I'd met Gavin and decided to hire him, finishing by saying, "I'm sure you'll meet him soon. He's great."

"He must be if he's willing to live in that apartment with you," she said. "I can't believe you have live-in help in a tiny Hell's Kitchen apartment. That's so weird."

"I'm planning to get a bigger place," I said. "Without cracks in the ceiling and a deranged opera singer next door."

"Valencia is a wonderful person," Sheila said. "I'll bet she misses my casseroles."

"I'm sure she does. She hasn't sounded the same since you left. Anyway, I was taking Gavin to all the places that I go to, you know, for shopping and the cleaners and stuff like that."

"You don't go to places like that. Violet does all that for you."

"More than even I was aware." I shared the same story with Sheila that I had with Gretchen earlier, half hoping it would divert her from asking more about Daniel, but half counting on the idea that she'd bring us back around to the subject. We both laughed about the reaction of the people at Dexter's version of Club Med, and at Gavin's reaction to Dexter.

"He is ugly, but you can't help but love him," Sheila said. After a pause, she asked, "How'd he look?"

"He was as scruffy as ever," I said, pretending to misunderstand her. "I think he has a rash on his ass."

Sheila nearly dropped her wine and said, "How'd you see his ass?"

"He's always shoving it in my face, and I think he's losing some of his fur there."

She let out a peal of laughter and said, "Not Dexter. Daniel. How'd *he* look?"

"He was with someone," I said after I'd stopped laughing.

"Oh?"

"Yeah. I didn't see him."

"Daniel?"

"No, the man he was with."

"He was with someone that you couldn't see?" She looked at me quizzically and moved my wineglass out of my reach.

I laughed and retrieved the glass, taking a slug from it. "I didn't say that I couldn't see him; I said I didn't see him. It's not that he was invisible; he was behind a cereal display."

"Oh. Did Daniel see you?"

"Yeah."

"How was that?"

"It was strange to see him with a new boyfriend."

"Daniel has a boyfriend?" Sheila gave me an odd look.

"Doesn't he?" I asked.

"Not that I know of," she answered. "I mean, I have been busy lately, but I think that's something Daniel would have told me."

"It sure seemed that way to me."

"Did you introduce him to Gavin?"

"No."

"How do you know he didn't think the same thing about Gavin? Maybe Daniel was with his personal assistant, too."

"Daniel has a personal assistant?" I asked.

"Not that I know of, but I didn't know about yours until five minutes ago. So what did you say to each other?"

"I congratulated him on his movie. He congratulated me on my job. Then he walked away." I let her digest that, then added, "I guess it bothered me more than it bothered him. Unless you're only pretending that he didn't tell you about it."

"I didn't even know he was back from L.A. But if he'd told me, why would I pretend otherwise?"

"Daniel tells you everything. Probably because you're good at keeping his secrets."

"If you're talking about your breakup, he's told me the same thing you have. Nothing."

"Gosh, things have changed," I said.

She looked confused and said, "Not really. I've never been in the middle of your relationship."

"The middle? No. In fact, you were front and center for the cameras, weren't you?"

Sheila blushed and said, "I was stupid. I had no idea getting a little publicity for Zodiac and *Secret Splendor* was going to get so out of control."

"If I'd been handling things, it wouldn't have. There's good publicity and bad publicity. Your job is to promote Zodiac, not that fucking soap opera. I've since learned that Lillith and Bonnie Seaforth-Wilkes—you do remember who that is?"

"*Secret Splendor*'s sponsor. The Fiberforth woman."

"Right. Lillith and Bonnie can't even be in the same century without going for each other's throats. You're lucky that whole thing didn't backfire on you."

"It did!" she said. "Josh and I nearly broke up over it."

"Excuse me for my lack of sympathy, but Daniel and I *did* break up."

"About that?" Sheila asked, horrified.

"Don't play dumb."

"I'm not playing!"

"You know we fought because Daniel failed to mention that Blythe was moving into the town house. Are you going to pretend you didn't know about that before I did?"

"I knew he was thinking about it. So what?" I was speechless, and my expression made her scoot toward the opposite end of the sofa. "You live in the town house; you live somewhere else. What's the difference?"

"I wanted to live with Daniel."

"What made you change your mind?"

"I didn't—what?"

"So it wasn't going to be the town house," Sheila finally said. "Why couldn't the two of you live somewhere else?"

"I'm sure if I was willing to wait a few years for Daniel to *process* the idea of living together—"

"What made you think he wasn't ready? Did he tell you that?"

I stared at her a minute, then said, "Did he tell you he was?" She looked uncomfortable and took a drink of her wine. "Sheila, if you have some information that you're not sharing, I can arrange for you to go over Niagara Falls in a barrel in the next Zodiac ad."

"I told you, I've never been in the middle of your relationship. I'm not going there now, either."

"The barrel is optional," I warned. Sheila took a large breath of air and bulged out her cheeks so that she looked like a bullfrog. "What are you doing?"

She exhaled audibly and said, "Learning how to hold my breath for long periods of time. I'm not talking about this stuff with you. These are things you should be discussing with him."

I shook my head and said, "It doesn't matter. It's over."

"Maybe it wouldn't be if the two of you talked it out."

"Too much damage has been done," I said.

"Damage can be fixed. You know how when you're a kid and you accidentally break some porcelain statue or something? And you have to glue it back together if you can? When it gets put back together, it doesn't look the same. But you mend it so that the spirit of why it was bought in the first place, the beauty of the piece, the sentimental value, can live on. It might have a chip, but it still has meaning. If it's worth putting back together, that is."

"I didn't break it," I said.

We heard the front door open and shut, then Josh walked into the living room, loaded down with photography paraphernalia. "Hey, you two!" he said, dropping the bags to the floor where he stood. I could sense that Sheila was regarding the mess he was leaving with annoyance. In fact, I realized that their apartment was oddly uncluttered, which was unusual for Sheila. She generally left mayhem in her wake, all the while looking as if she'd emerged from one of our print ads. Now the apartment was orderly and Sheila was a mess.

"Hi," we chorused solemnly.

Josh froze. "Something wrong? Am I interrupting?"

"No," I said, getting up. "I was just about to leave. It's been a longer day than I thought."

"Sheila, do you remember where I put those wrist weights that I wanted to show Blaine?" Josh asked.

We both stared at him as if he'd suddenly started speaking Japanese. Considering the workouts I inflicted on myself at the gym, wrist weights would be like attaching a couple of sparrows to my arms. I wasn't sure what Sheila's expression indicated.

"I do have my ovarian tracking device in; let me look for them," Sheila said.

After she stomped out of the room, Josh hissed at me, "Did you just tell her?"

"Tell her what?" I whispered back.

"The pregnancy thing. Gretchen."

"Oh. No," I said. "She's in a mood because we were talking about Daniel."

"Okay. Please warn me before you drop the baby bomb on her, okay?"

I couldn't ask him why he sounded so ominous, because Sheila returned with the wrist weights. Josh and I embarked on a completely inane discussion of their merits, while Sheila stared at us with obvious suspicion until she'd had enough.

"What's going on here?"

"She caught us," I said, giving Josh a guilty look. "I swear, Sheila, there won't be any strippers or women jumping out of cakes."

"You're planning a bachelor party? Considering our guest list, it might be more exciting to have a man jump out of the cake."

"I told you she'd try to organize that, too," I said, sacrificing myself on the altar of Sheila's nuptial madness. "The bachelor party is for Josh. Not all your gay friends."

"We'll see," Sheila said. She followed me to the door. "Can we finish our conversation later?" she asked, fidgeting with my collar as an excuse to give me a piercing look.

"Let's not talk about Daniel anymore," I implored. "I feel like we cleared the air between us. That was more important to me."

"You!' she said. "I was beginning to fear for my life."

"I'll admit I've been annoyed about you and Daniel, but I've never threatened your life," I protested.

"The danger of a Zodiac shoot is directly proportional to your dissatisfaction with your personal life," Sheila insisted. "Remember last year, when you had me stringing a garland of flowers around that bull's neck for Taurus? I think you and Daniel were arguing about vacation plans."

"Not true," I disagreed. "And this year's Taurus ad required nothing more than boxing gloves."

"Excuse me. Pisces? In a tank with a shark?"

"Six inches of Plexiglas between you," I reminded her.

"Aries. Head to head with that goat."

"It was a ram," I said, laughing.

"It smelled like a goat. Now you're talking about barrels and Niagara Falls—"

"Your safety always comes first," I insisted with finality. "Our insurance company demands it."

She smiled and said, "Blaine? I need for things to be okay between us. I've loved you all my life. Maybe I don't always handle things the best way with you and Daniel. But I never meant to hurt you, and I'm sorry."

I hugged her and said, "It's okay. I love you, too. That won't ever change."

After she shut the door, I paused on the stoop for a moment, thinking about the question she'd asked earlier that I hadn't answered.

How'd he look?

"Beautiful," I whispered to myself.

That night, though I fell asleep quickly, my Daniel voice-over evidently silenced by my reconciliation with Sheila, I had a dream that left me puzzled when I woke up. I stepped into the bathroom to shave and shower. Afterward, I donned a charcoal gray Hugo Boss suit and combed my hair, all the while trying to remember the details of my dream. Martin had been telling Daniel how boring I was, Sheila had been miffed that I'd given my sperm to Gretchen, and Daniel had watched me with sad eyes.

While I ate my breakfast, I couldn't get Daniel's expression out of my mind. Maybe we hadn't really tried to resolve things. Maybe we'd taken the easy way out and let it all crumble to nothing. Or maybe I was just nervous about how Daniel would react if Gretchen and I had a child.

I considered the range of possibilities. He might feel like I'd preempted his relationship with Gretchen, somewhat the way I felt like he'd taken Sheila from me. Or maybe he would wonder why Gretchen had chosen me instead of him to be her child's father. Or he could simply resent being out of the loop, especially if anyone else found out before he did. Even worse, what if he thought I'd be a lousy father?

I looked at Gavin and said, "If I don't leave soon, I'll be late for a meeting downtown. I have no idea what time I'll get home tonight, so just do something like a chicken Caesar salad that I can eat cold. Could you call Violet for me? I want to put apartment hunting on hold for a while. I have too much going on at work to worry about that right now."

"No problem," Gavin said. "Anything else?"

"Do something fun tonight. Reconnect with old friends. I've been monopolizing your time."

"I've only been here a few days."

"And I've barely let you catch your breath." When I tried to take my dishes to the sink, he took them from my hands. I grabbed my keys, then dropped them and picked up the phone, walking to the window to glance down at Daniel's patio garden. I dialed his number without letting myself think about what I was going to say.

"Hi, this is Daniel. If you're a friend, I'm on location. If you're planning to break into my apartment, bring a couple of raw T-bones. The rottweilers are hungry."

I smiled, realizing he'd forgotten to change his greeting, which was unlike him. I hung up without leaving a message, since I wasn't sure what I wanted to say.

Over the next few days, I had to work twelve- and fourteen-hour stretches, arranging to shoot Sheila's three ad layouts back to back. I relocated the Cancer shoot from L.A. to Colorado, timing things so I could make a quick stop in Wisconsin to check on my mother. I scheduled both the Leo and Virgo shoots for Miami, saving time by hiring one crew to do both.

Over the weekend, I participated in a seemingly endless round of conference calls with Lillith, Frank, and Adam, who'd agreed to fly in the following week to go over our networking needs in the new office space. I didn't mind working over the weekend, however, since it made the time go by quickly. Monday was the big day when Gretchen and I would find out the results of the insemination.

While clasping her hand in the waiting room, I stared at a gold-framed illustration of a long, pink flower. I shuddered, thinking of those Georgia O'Keeffe paintings that resembled vaginas. I wondered if the flower was meant to bring luck to the women who came to the fertility clinic.

Gretchen and I could have passed for any of the married couples who also waited in tense silence for their names to be called by the nurse. The door from the doctors' offices opened as a young couple came through the waiting room, their faces depicting the news they'd received. The woman had tears forming in her eyes, while the man gently held her arm with one hand and caressed her hair with the other. Seeing the disappointment on their faces made me feel sympathetic. It also filled me with anxiety that our own results would be negative.

I must have begun to squeeze Gretchen's hand tighter, because she emitted a quiet yelp. "Watch it, Hercules. I may be a tough cookie, but I'm not made of steel," she whispered.

"Sorry. I'm more nervous than I thought I'd be."

"That makes two of us," she admitted. "I'm optimistic, though. Aunt Rose hasn't been to visit me yet." It took me a second to remember what Aunt Rose was a euphemism for. I felt only slightly more at ease, though.

The nurse behind the desk let her thick, black glasses slide down her nose as she stood up and leaned over the counter to call out the next name on her list.

"Schmidt? You're next."

Gretchen and I looked at each other as we stood up. We both took a deep breath and proceeded to the door. A buzzer sounded as my hand reached out to take the knob. I opened the door and looked down the hall toward the doctor's office, desperately searching my memory banks for her real name. Just as I'd predicted, the only name that came to mind was "Dr. Gibb."

The walk to her office seemed longer than I remembered. "Come in!" called the familiar voice when Gretchen knocked.

We stepped into her small office, sitting across from her while she pushed away folders and opened the one I presumed was ours.

"It's so good to see you two again," she said. Just then, the red light on her telephone began to pulse urgently. "I'm sorry. Excuse me for one second."

She picked up the phone and greeted the person on the other end. She riffled through the stack of folders she'd pushed aside, found the one she wanted, and opened it. She made a few notes, periodically glancing at Gretchen and me with an apologetic smile. I wanted to jump up and grab the phone out of her hand. I felt even tenser than when I'd waited for the results of my HIV tests.

"Now then," the doctor said, placing the telephone back in the cradle, "where were we? Oh, yes, the results." She opened our folder again and skimmed through a few pages. "It looks like you two are going to be parents."

Neither Gretchen nor I spoke immediately. We turned to each other and stared for a second before Gretchen's face was split by the brightest smile I'd ever seen. We fell into each other's arms and hugged. When we separated and faced the doctor again, she, too, was smiling. She obviously enjoyed doling out good news.

"This is incredible! I can't believe I'm pregnant. I spent the last couple of weeks preparing myself for the worst. I was willing to keep trying, if we had to, but I didn't really want to go through this again. I mean, it's an election year, so now isn't the time for frivolous spending. Not that this is frivolous, but you know what I mean," Gretchen gushed.

"I think what she's trying to say is thank you," I said.

"Yes!" Gretchen exclaimed. "Thank you so much!"

"Don't thank me," the doctor said. "Thank Blaine's tough little sperm and your egg for being willing. All I did was introduce them. There are a few things I need to tell you." She gave Gretchen advice about prenatal care, then said, "Your OB/GYN may give you a different date, but I've calculated your due date as December fourteenth. It's not an exact science though, and can be affected by several variables."

"Thank God neither of us works in retail," Gretchen commented.

"You can basically live life as normal," the doctor went on. "On your way out, the nurse will give you the book that we give to all of our successful candidates. It'll walk you through what to expect throughout your pregnancy. Congratulations to both of you!"

When we stepped out of the clinic into the cool, early spring air, I hailed a cab and gave the driver the address of Gretchen's Tribeca loft. I wished I could spend the next few days with her, as I had done after the insemination procedure, but the sadistic timetable for the upcoming Zodiac ads wouldn't allow me that luxury. But I could see her home and spend an hour with her to rejoice in our good fortune.

I wanted to share the good news with everyone we knew, but most of the books we'd been reading advised waiting until after the first trimester to tell people, especially in high-risk pregnancies. Gretchen was considered high risk because she was experiencing her first pregnancy at age thirty-eight.

When I turned to look at her, she was absolutely aglow. She grinned at me and said, "I know you didn't know him very well, but I wish Ken was here. I could tell him, and the news would go no further. I wish there was someone else we could tell."

"There is," I said excitedly. Gretchen looked at me with a quizzical expression, and I said, "Ethan."

After the cab let us off on Greenwich Street, Gretchen and I bolted past the ancient doorman of her building and took the freight elevator, both of us silent as it creaked upward. When she unlocked her door, I followed her down the four steps into her living room. I stood on the rectangular white carpet that lay over a deeply stained hardwood floor, and looked around with new eyes. This was where my child would live.

The sofa and chair were soft leather contemporary pieces with chrome legs. A flat-screen television faced the sofa, chair, and marble-topped coffee table. Gretchen's taste in decorating was simple, yet elegant, and bent toward trendy. There was no room for clutter, and everything was efficiently designed. Beyond the living room lay a den which she used as her office, two bedrooms, and two bathrooms. She also had the luxury of a tiny laundry room off the kitchen. I wasn't sure whether or not she sent her laundry out, but I knew that her washer and dryer would be convenient once the baby came.

Her windows were northern, and the late afternoon light made the loft look warm and comfortable, especially the hardwood floors. I glanced down at my feet.

"I'm thinking this white carpet—"

"I know," she said, looking around with a smile. "A lot of things are going to change here over the next nine months."

I walked to the telephone and brought out my PalmPilot, looking up Ethan's phone number. Gretchen stood beside me, pushing her head close to mine. I was disappointed when Ethan's machine picked up. I didn't want to leave our news on a machine, so I asked him to call us. Just as I was about to hang up, Ethan answered, sounding out of breath when he said, "Wait; I'm here."

"Hi, Ethan, it's Blaine and Gretchen."

"I heard. How are you? I just got home from a lecture."

"We have some exciting news," Gretchen said, butting in.

"Guess what?" I asked.

"We're going to be parents!" Gretchen exclaimed.

"That's great! I'm so happy for you both."

We talked for a few minutes before hanging up, then Gretchen and I looked though the maternity handbook the clinic had given us. As the initial excitement faded slightly, Gretchen said, "If we wait twelve weeks to tell our other friends, that will be mid-June."

"Actually, I was wondering if we could do it after Sheila's wedding.

Remember when she tried to announce her engagement, and everyone else had big news and kept upstaging her? I don't want to steal her thunder again. If we do it after the first trimester, that's just a couple of weeks before the wedding. Can we delay the announcement until afterward?"

"I guess," Gretchen said, giving me a measuring look.

"What?" I asked. "Too long to wait?"

"If it's Daniel you're worried about, I don't think our news will affect him as much as you fear," Gretchen said. "This probably isn't the best time to tell you, but Daniel's been seeing someone else."

I sat quietly for a minute, trying to figure out exactly how that made me feel. In spite of having known he was with someone the day I saw him in Whole Foods, I'd been encouraged by Sheila's assurance that she knew of no new lover in his life. In any case, I didn't want it to spoil the momentous news that Gretchen and I had just received.

"I don't want to talk about it," I said.

"I don't know how serious it is, but I felt you should know," Gretchen explained.

"I'm glad you told me, but I really don't want to talk about it. I need to go."

"Blaine, I'm sorry. Please don't leave upset."

"I'll admit that I've been on a seesaw about Daniel lately. But that's not why I'm leaving. I have to get ready for my trip. I'll call you from Colorado," I promised. Remembering her favorite way to relax at the end of the day, I added, "And no wine for you."

"So it begins! You haven't even known I'm pregnant for an hour, and you're acting like an oppressive male," Gretchen teased. "I'll be good. Just think, in a few days, tax season will be over and I'll be a woman of leisure again."

"Again? Tell it to someone who doesn't know you."

When I was back on the sidewalk, I felt torn between rapture and depression. I went to the only place other than the gym that I knew would help me clear my head.

I wanted to pack my office before leaving for Colorado, but when I arrived at Breslin Evans, I was surprised to find boxes sitting outside my door. They were labeled with my name and Lillith Allure's new

Chelsea address. Violet wasn't at her desk. The door to my office was open, and Charlie, the maintenance man, was removing my nameplate from the door.

"Hi, Charlie," I said.

Charlie's hand slipped from the chisel he was using to pull the plate from the adhesive and wood of the door. He cursed under his breath and removed his glasses as he turned to me.

"Hello, Mr. Dunhill. I sure am sad to see you going."

"In a way, so am I. It's for the best, though. Have you seen Violet?"

"I haven't seen her in a half hour."

I walked into my office for what would be the last time. I opened the drawers of my desk to make sure nothing had been overlooked. When I opened the lower left drawer, I saw a piece of paper wedged between the bottom and the side. It was from the phone message pads that had been phased out of use in the office two years before, when nearly everything became electronic. I flipped it over and couldn't help but laugh. It read, "Mrs. Dunhill called."

I recalled the awkward moment when Daniel had taken the message after speaking to Sydney for the first time. That had been before he and I started dating, and my confession about my doomed marriage to Sydney had helped break down barriers between us. It seemed like a lifetime ago.

Daniel's been seeing someone else . . .

"Why the hell did I hang on to that?" I asked. I crumpled the message and tossed it over my shoulder, not caring where it landed.

I looked out the window. I felt very little actual sadness about leaving. I categorized the moment as a stepping-stone in my career. It was time to move on. I said a silent goodbye to the bare walls, then walked out the office door, which no longer held my nameplate. I strode down the hall toward the elevator. Just as I reached the glass doors that would let me out of the suite, I heard someone call my name. I turned around to see Mitzi, the receptionist, standing behind her counter and waving at me. She had an envelope in her hand.

"Blaine Dunhill, come here," Mitzi ordered. She took her ever-present wad of gum from her mouth and dropped it into her wastebasket. By the time I reached her, she'd taken off her headset and walked around her counter.

"What's wrong?" I asked.

She threw her arms around me and wailed, "You're leaving!"

"I didn't know you cared," I said, trying to keep my face passive as I extricated myself from her hug.

"You're taking Violet," she blubbered.

"Oh, geez," I muttered. "Mitzi, dry your eyes. You and Violet can always get together after work."

"It won't be the same," she sniffed. "She's already gone. She asked me to give you this envelope."

"Thanks," I said. "Okay, then, I'm out of here."

"Tell Daniel hello," Mitzi called as I made it to the doors again. This time I didn't turn around, just waved my hand and kept going. While I waited for the elevator, I opened the envelope to find a clipping of Lola Listeria's latest column. I groaned and started reading.

"Start spreading the news! There's a new kid in town!" If this was going to be an entire column of song lyrics . . . I read on, exasperated. "The always alluring—get it?—Lillith Parker will be relocating Lillith Allure's offices from that drab old building in Baltimore to lavish digs in our own Chelsea. Guess the glam face of Sheila Meyers is keeping them in the black, huh? Speaking of black, word has it that our fave supermodel is being considered for a role in the sequel to *Men in Black*. But she'll be wearing white come July, when she walks down the aisle to yummy photographer Josh Clinton. Or will she? Why do those rumors about Ms. Meyers and luscious suds star Daniel Stephenson keep bubbling up? The latest is that our gal refused to go on Howard Stern's show after his comment that Daniel is one Angus—get it?—who should be sent to the slaughterhouse posthaste. Surely the blond beauty knew the shock jock was talking about the soap character, not her longtime 'friend,' Danny Boy."

I rolled my eyes, fearing that the trip to Colorado with an angry model was not going to be, as Lola herself might have said, a Rocky Mountain high.

CHAPTER 8

I parked my rental car in the driveway of my parents' house, checking under the flowerpot where they kept the extra house key. Even though I was sure my mother was at home, I didn't know if she was mobile enough to answer the door.

I let myself in quietly, then looked around. I hadn't been in the house since my divorce from Sydney, but not much had changed. It was a great old house, five stories if I counted the basement and attic. It had been built in the 1920s, but my parents had made numerous upgrades in the forty-five years since they'd bought it as newlyweds. My bedroom, as well as my brothers', had been on the third floor. My parents' room and the guest room, along with a study and my mother's sitting room, were on the second floor. The first floor had a den, formal living and dining rooms, and an enormous kitchen with a breakfast nook and oversized pantries. After growing accustomed to the small residences of Manhattan, it amazed me that only two people inhabited so much space. I assumed my father thought the location, size, and maintenance of the house were signs of his success. Even though my mother had always had a maid, I knew she probably still supervised the housekeeping with her exacting demands for cleanliness and order.

I thought about the time Gretchen had rented *Mommie Dearest* for us to watch, and the way Daniel had snickered through Joan Crawford's obsessive cleaning scenes. He might not have found it so amusing if he'd grown up with it.

I wandered through the rooms, trying to find any sense of warmth in the expensive, tasteful furnishings, but all I felt was sadness. The house had never felt like a home, even during the days when my parents hadn't been disappointed in me. My brothers had been too much older to provide a sense of camaraderie; my father had been distant when he was home; and my mother had always treated me like she expected me to break something. At school, I'd never lacked for friends or dates. But every time I came through the back door, I felt like the entire weight of the house rested on my shoulders. Which was probably why I spent every moment I could at the Meyers house. Though Jake's parents were strict, they'd provided a fun, loving environment for him and Sheila, and they'd treated me like one of their own.

I turned from the custom-built cabinets where my mother's Wedgewood dishes were displayed when I heard someone coming from the kitchen. I wasn't sure who was more surprised, me or the woman who stopped short at the sight of a strange man in the house.

"I'm sorry," I said quickly. "I didn't mean to startle you. I'm Blaine Dunhill."

She smoothed her gray hair then said, "Grace Fields. You're Mrs. Dunhill's son?"

"Yes, and you're . . ."

"Her home healthcare worker. I should have recognized you. You look like your brother, Shane."

"How's my mother?" I asked.

"She's doing well. She's probably awake; shall I tell her you're here?"

"Yes, please. I guess it's not a good idea to surprise someone who's just had heart surgery, is it?"

She didn't crack a smile, and I decided she and my mother must share the same lack of a sense of humor. It promised to be a fun visit. I waited downstairs until Grace returned.

"Your mother asked if you could give her about ten minutes," she said, and I nodded. When she went back to the kitchen, I took the stairs to the third floor to look at my old bedroom.

Nothing was the same. My mother had a tendency to redecorate about every five years. The changes to my room started as soon as I went away to college, when my father had moved my sports trophies, ribbons, and awards to the display case at Dunhill Electrical.

I'd never felt like that had much to do with his pride in my accomplishments, even though excelling in sports had been my way to seek his approval. Instead, my mementos provided conversation starters with prospective business associates and offered proof that he'd sired a "real" man. I wondered if, in the deepest recesses of his mind, my father suspected that I was gay, and that was why he had a need to authenticate that I'd actually been involved in what he saw as manly pursuits. Certainly I'd never gone hunting with him, as Wayne had, and I wasn't a chip off the old block, like Shane.

I thought about Shane's serial adultery, wondering if that was another way he was like my father. I'd never heard any rumors that my father was unfaithful. My mother wouldn't have acknowledged such a thing, much less discussed it with any of her sons.

I frowned; the last thing I wanted to think about was my parents' sex life, or lack thereof.

After one last look around to establish for myself that there really was nothing of mine left in the room, I went down one flight of stairs and knocked on my parents' bedroom door, walking in when I heard my mother's voice.

She was sitting up in bed, several books scattered around her. I kept my face blank as I bent to give her an awkward hug, noticing the titles: *Managing Chronic Pain, Mayo Clinic Family Handbook, Complete Home Medical Guide, The Pill Book, Everything You Need to Know Before You Call the Doctor.*

I'd once attempted to explain my mother to Daniel, and he was a lot more sympathetic than I was. He saw hypochondria as my mother's terror about illness and aging. I tried to understand, but I had too many memories of the way she'd used her imaginary illnesses to avoid things. Not just disagreeable things, like arguments, but even those things that might have given us pleasure as a family, like holidays.

"This is a surprise," my mother said, her tone making it sound like it wasn't a particularly welcome one, either.

"I'm on my way to Colorado for business. I wanted to see how you're doing," I explained in a cheerful tone that I hoped didn't sound as forced as it was. I pulled a chair over and sat next to the bed, trying not to be too obvious as I scrutinized her. She didn't look like she'd had heart surgery only a few weeks before. In fact, she looked like the picture of good health and much younger than sixty-three.

"I suppose I'm as well as can be expected for someone in the shape I'm in. It's nice of you to show an interest." I didn't know what to say to that, so I didn't answer. After a few moments, she said, "Your visit is timely. After the scare I've had, your father and I decided to make a few changes to our estate plan."

"Mom, I don't need to know—"

"Of course, you still have your trust," she went on, ignoring my interruption. "Your father has always kept that up for all three of you. If I predecease him, which seems likely, naturally everything goes to him. But we've made some changes to our bequests should both of us die."

"You've cut me out of the will?" I asked, trying not to sound sarcastic.

"The business will go to your two brothers. Since you've never been part of it, your father is sure you'll understand why you won't have a third interest in it. We've set up our insurance policies so that money will go into trusts for the grandchildren. Of course, if you and Sydney had stayed married . . ."

I fought my urge to tell her that she was going to be a grandmother again. Gretchen and I were more than capable of providing financial security, and though it might be fun to watch my parents squirm over the details of the conception, I already felt protective of my baby. I could not foresee any circumstances that would cause me to bring the disparate parts of my life together.

"What about the house? The stuff that's in it?" I asked.

"That will be divided equally between Shane and Wayne."

I gave a little laugh and said, "So you really have disinherited me. This is all because of my divorce?"

"You'll have your trust. It's not insubstantial. It's not as though you want the house. And you've never expressed any interest in our valuables. Your brothers have stayed in Eau Claire and helped your father's business thrive. A lot of what he and I have is because of their hard work. It only seems fair that they should be rewarded."

"I'm not arguing with you, Mom. It's your money. Your stuff. Your business. Do whatever you want with it." She shifted impatiently, and *The Pill Book* landed on the floor at my feet. I picked it up and decided to change the subject. "After your surgery, I started thinking about how many years you've suffered through so many illnesses. It doesn't seem like modern medicine has offered you much in the way of relief."

"I've learned to live with it," she answered in her stoic tone.

"Maybe you should try something different. In fact, I could get you all kinds of information from my boss. She's an expert on alternative healthcare," I said, thinking that Lillith would faint from happiness if I asked her to help me gather information for my mother.

"I've been to an acupuncturist," my mother said, her voice dropping as if she was confessing something shameful.

"Oh, that's just the surface," I assured her. I found the idea of my mother delving into alternative healthcare very satisfying. She could probably spend a small fortune chasing down one remedy or another, which would make my father insane. But she also might find a little more compassion and acceptance than she had from the medical community.

"I liked the man who did the acupuncture," my mother admitted. "I just don't think it was very effective."

"I think those treatments have to be ongoing," I said. "It's not a one-visit-fixes-all thing."

"It's a shame you couldn't have been here yesterday," she said, changing the subject. "But I suppose if this is just a detour on your business trip—"

"It's not just a . . ." I stopped myself, knowing it was pointless. "Why? What happened yesterday?"

"Sydney spent the afternoon with me."

"Sydney?" I blurted. "I thought she was in Europe."

"She's back. She came here, instead of going straight to Chicago, because she said she was worried about me."

"Oh, please," I muttered.

"I can't tell you how much I appreciate it," my mother said, pretending she hadn't heard me, "that she makes such an effort to visit me. I remember when the two of you were married. She was like the daughter I never had. She treated me better than my own children ever did."

I shut off my brain. Berating her children to me as if I was an uninvolved stranger was one of my mother's habits that upset me the most. I had long ago learned that there was no useful way to react. Assuring her of my love was as futile as arguing with her. All I could do was wait it out.

"She was like a breath of fresh air," my mother went on. "Full of amusing stories about her travels. But I could tell something was troubling her. Other than my health, I mean. I finally convinced her to admit that she's having financial worries with her gallery. You know her own parents think it's a money pit, so I'm sure they won't help her. But I admire her for trying to be successful. I even offered to help her out, but she wouldn't hear of it."

"Uh-huh," I said, sure that it was only a matter of time until I got a call from Sydney asking me to bail her out again. Her visit to my mother was meant to remind me of the power she had over me.

"She's a courageous young woman. Not at all like most young people these days." When I didn't respond, too wrapped up in trying to figure out how long I could dodge my ex-wife, my mother went on. "I guess it's our own fault. After our parents came through the Depression and a World War, they taught us to be frugal and responsible. We foolishly tried to protect our children from harsh realities and raised a selfish, careless generation who thinks only of its own pleasure."

Before I could stop myself, I snapped, "Selfish? I can't speak for an entire generation, just my friends. We have a good time, and we probably do spend a lot of money to have comfortable lives, but I wouldn't say we think only of our own pleasure. My friend Daniel spent over ten years raising money for AIDS groups, even though he could barely make ends meet. Nobody bankrolled him. He took a break from that, but he still volunteers his time to Parks and Recreation in Manhattan, helping maintain green space in the city. Jake has been a Big Brother to a single-parent kid for six years. Sheila donates ten percent of her earnings to the American Foundation for AIDS Research. Another friend, Andy, volunteers his time and uses his nightclub to help raise money for Gay Men's Health Crisis. My friend Blythe pulls shifts every week for a group called God's Love We Deliver. She helps prepare and package foods for people with AIDS."

I took a breath and stood up, refusing to look at her so that I couldn't see her reaction to what I'd said or if she was hearing everything that was remaining unsaid. Then I went on.

"Adam Wilson, the computer guy who contracts Dunhill Electrical on jobs? Most of the Web sites he designs donate valuable advertising space to not-for-profits of all kinds. A couple of other friends, Jeremy and Ethan, do community outreach to at-risk teens, trying to keep kids alive, off drugs, and out of gangs. And my friend Gretchen is amazing. There's nothing she won't do to help kids. From letting children impacted by AIDS use a resort she owns for summer camps, to donating her business expertise to pediatric AIDS groups, to rocking crack babies and AIDS babies in hospitals. One of her best friends, a television producer, did a documentary about women like Gretchen that aired on cable. It generated millions of dollars in donations. I don't know, Mom, call me crazy, but none of that sounds selfish to me."

I finally looked at her. Her eyes were a little glazed over as she stared beyond me. I waited, wondering which of my comments had gotten through to her. I wanted her to ask questions. For the first time in my life, I was ready to give her honest answers.

"Thank goodness for our strong churches in the Midwest," she finally said. "Not only do they help people, but they instill values to prevent some of those problems you mentioned."

"Right," I said. "I'm sorry this has to be such a short visit, but I have a plane to catch."

Which was pure fiction, since I wasn't flying out until the following morning. But I knew I had to get out of there before I started using my honesty as a weapon to hurt her.

Our parting was as civil as I could make it. I replaced the house key, then sat in my rental car for a few minutes, trying to get control of my emotions. It was as close as I'd ever come to telling her the truth, and I was positive she didn't want to hear it. I figured we would go back to the way things had been ever since my divorce, with minimal contact between my family and me, and certainly no more visits to the Dunhill mausoleum.

I considered getting in touch with Adam, Jeremy, or Jake, but it wasn't even noon when I made my getaway. I was sure all of them were working. Without letting myself consider the ramifications, I turned my car toward the Stephensons' house, wondering if a visit with Daniel's mother could help me forget the reunion I'd just endured.

Joyce Stephenson gave me a startled look when she opened her front door. She was wearing an apron and hastily wiped her flour-smeared hands on it before she reached to give me a warm hug.

"What a nice surprise, Blaine! I had no idea you were in town. You've just caught us in the middle of—come in, goodness, where is my head?" She practically dragged me into the house toward the kitchen.

"I know I should have called but—"

"You are *always* welcome here," she said. I understood that she was trying to convey more than just the message that I didn't have to stand on ceremony. She meant that I was welcome even though Daniel and I were no longer together. I suddenly felt lighter, as if I'd let go of some fear or hurt that had been dragging my heart down. "But be prepared. We're going to put you to work!"

There were a half-dozen other women in the middle of frantic activity in the large, farmhouse kitchen. One of them broke away from the group when she saw me.

"Blaine Dunhill!" Adam Wilson's mother, Aggie, said, flashing me an ear-to-ear grin. "Just in time to give us another pair of hands."

She, too, hugged me, and I looked around with curiosity. "What are you all doing?"

"We're giving a little PFLAG soiree tonight," Aggie said. "For teens. Adam and Jeremy will be there, and we'd love to have you join us."

I looked at Joyce and said, "You joined PFLAG? What does Daniel think about that?"

"It was Daniel who introduced me to Aggie," Joyce said. "Louis joined, too. He and Adam's father are setting up things in the church basement now, for our get-together tonight."

"*Your* church?" I asked, feeling like I'd walked into someone else's surreal dream.

"Heavens no, they're not ready for this," Joyce said.

"Yet," Aggie said, then winked at me. "Here, make yourself useful and help me with the sandwiches. You will come tonight, won't you?"

"I'm flying out tomorrow, so I'd planned to—"

"You can spend the night here," Joyce said. "In your old room."

Although Daniel's parents had taken a long time to deal with his being gay, by the time I'd come along, they were able to accept their son's boyfriend. But they'd always put us in separate rooms, which I'd never had a problem with. Even though Daniel groused about it, I reminded him that they would probably do the same thing with his sisters' boyfriends if they stayed there, and he'd had to admit that I was right.

"I don't know if Daniel—"

"Daniel is not here. You are. Case closed," Joyce said, then started introducing me to the other women in the kitchen.

While I murmured polite hellos, I couldn't stop watching Daniel's mother. She'd been transformed from the somewhat reserved woman struggling to understand her son into . . . I wasn't sure. Maybe into a moderate version of Aggie Wilson, who not only accepted but embraced Adam and treated Jeremy like another son. In either case, they were both galaxies away from my own mother, and it felt good to be with them after my ordeal with her.

I took the loaf of bread Aggie was pushing at me and sat at the table to begin making sandwiches while the women chattered around me. All of a sudden one of the women looked at her watch, gasped, and said, "Joyce! It's time!"

Joyce grabbed a remote from the counter and flicked on the television. I stifled a groan when I saw the opening montage of *Secret Splendor* flash across the screen. Of course Daniel's mother would be addicted to the damned soap opera. Her son was the star.

"Do you really think it's going to happen?" one of the women asked. "If he pulls this off . . ."

She trailed off, as mesmerized as I was by the sight that greeted us. There was Daniel—or rather, Angus Remington—standing at the end of a long aisle, the "Wedding March" sounding more ominous than celebratory. I couldn't believe my eyes. The last time I'd seen the show, Angus wasn't even dating anyone. Since the storylines of *Secret Splendor* moved at a snail's pace, I didn't know how it was possible that he was actually standing at an altar about to be married. But most of all, I couldn't believe how sexy Daniel looked in his tuxedo. I wanted to crawl through the screen and devour him.

"Who's he marrying?" I asked.

"Oh, my gosh, you haven't been watching?" Joyce asked. "He's marrying Cressida."

My mouth dropped open. Cressida was played by Jane-Therese

Pennick, the cocaine-snorting bimbo who was the only person I'd ever heard Daniel say he hated. Any love scenes between them would require every ounce of his acting skill.

"The last time I saw this, Cressida was convinced he was responsible for her father's death," I said.

"She still thinks that. She hopes to get information by marrying him," Aggie explained.

"What about Angus? What's his angle?" I asked, glad I was sitting down, with my crotch well hidden, when the camera moved in for a tight shot on Daniel's gorgeous face as he watched his bride from hell walk down the aisle toward him.

"He wants control of Porterhouse Industries," Joyce said.

I'd always thought the *Secret Splendor* writers were obsessed with the beef industry, considering the names they gave their characters. Cressida Porterhouse had inherited her father's business when his car went over Splendor Falls after the bridge collapsed.

The look that Daniel—or Angus—gave Jane-Therese as she finally reached him could have melted an iceberg and saved the *Titanic*. I didn't know about Cressida, but I'd have signed over my inheritance on the spot.

Each time the soap switched back from other storylines or commercials to focus on Angus and Cressida, I sensed Joyce and Aggie casting sidelong glances at me. I didn't even try to act like I wasn't mesmerized by Daniel. It wouldn't fool them, and I realized that I needed the support that they could offer me.

When the women were ready to take the refreshments to the church, I asked Joyce if she minded if I drove myself later. I wanted to rest, take a shower, and change clothes. She gave me an understanding look and insisted that I make myself at home, even going upstairs to put out clean towels for me while I helped the women load their cars.

After they were all gone, I went to Daniel's boyhood room, closed the door gently behind me, and looked around, especially at the photos. I loved the ones from his high school plays. He and Adam had been five years ahead of me in school, so I hadn't known them then. Though Adam had been popular, Daniel had been shy and unsure of himself. Being in plays had provided relief from his unhappy adolescence. I thought of the kids PFLAG would be hosting that night. It was hard to say how Daniel's life might have been different if he'd had something like that when he was a kid. Maybe he would never have fled to New York to make a name for himself.

I knew that when I was a teenager, I wouldn't have taken advantage of the support PFLAG offered. I was too determined not to be gay to find any group that would help me come to terms with it. Unlike Adam, Daniel and I had both had to move away to figure out how to be ourselves. I hadn't done as well as Daniel had, until I met him.

I turned to look at the lone photo on the back of his door, where he was dressed as his alter ego, Princess 2Di4. I'd gotten to know him after his drag years, which was a good thing. I'd been way too closeted to handle that.

Finally, I lay down on his bed, burying my face in the pillows and surrendering to the big, gulping sobs that I'd been fighting since seeing my mother. I wasn't sure if I was crying about my family or about Daniel. Probably both.

After it was over, I felt a lot better. Nothing had really changed. My parents had never been, and never would be, what I needed. But there were other people in my life, like my friends' parents, who could help soften the hurt of that. It meant so much to me that Daniel's mother wasn't going to cut me off just because he and I had broken up. I was sure his father would be just as friendly when I saw him later.

As for Daniel . . . Maybe he was, as Gretchen said, dating someone else. Maybe things were really over between us. But I also remembered the things Jeremy had said. If he and Daniel could salvage a friendship from their bad breakup, there was no reason why Daniel and I wouldn't eventually do the same. In time, the hurt and anger would fade. Maybe the love and need would, too, and I'd find something with him that would be just as strong and sustaining.

In any case, I needed to stop ruminating about the past and start thinking about the future. I had a great career, and I was going to have a child in a few months. I'd be too busy with both to worry about things that would never be.

By the time I followed the directions Joyce had given me and walked into the church basement, I felt immeasurably better, as if I'd made some kind of peace with myself. My eyes immediately found Adam in the crowd of people, and I crossed the room to him.

"There you are," Adam said. "My mother told me you were coming." I prolonged our hug a little longer than was necessary for a greeting, and he pulled back to look at me. "You okay?"

"I'm a lot better than I have been," I said cheerfully. "It's been quite a day."

"I'm glad I got to see you, since you'll be traveling when I go to Manhattan in a few days. Now where did Jeremy get to?" He looked around, as did I. Adam spotted him first and said, "Let's go say hello."

The smile I'd plastered on my face in preparation for Jeremy froze as my eyes went past him to the kid he was standing with: my nephew, Nicky. He was listening to someone else, so I got to check him out before he became aware of me.

He'd grown at least a foot since I last saw him, which made him appear even more gangly. But his skin was clear, and his eyes seemed happy in a way they'd never been on those occasions when I'd seen him with his parents. He was dressed in black from head to toe, gothlike, and his hair was a little long and messy. As he reached up to push a strand behind his ear, I saw that he was wearing about ten black bracelets and that he had a small, black onyx in his earlobe. Thoughts of his father flashed through my head, especially when I saw the black polish on his fingernails. There was no way Shane could know his son was out in public looking like this.

As Nicky laughed in response to whatever was being said, his eyes shifted, he saw me, and it was like someone had dropped a mask over his face. He looked stunned, almost terrified.

"Uncle Blaine?"

"Nicky," I said. I saw him flinch when I moved toward him, and even when I gave him a quick hug, his body remained rigid. To give him some recovery time, I turned to embrace Jeremy.

"This is big for him," Jeremy whispered, so that only I could hear him.

"I'm sure," I said as quietly, then turned back to Nicky with a smile. "I guess you're as surprised as I am, huh?"

"Uncle Blaine, are you—" He broke off, as if saying the word might bring down my wrath.

"Gay? Yeah. I am. Come over here; let's talk." He followed me a few feet from the others. "You?"

"I don't know," he said and shrugged. "I mean, I'm sort of confused."

"I felt that way, too, when I was your age," I said. "You've got time to figure it out. In any case, I sure never had the balls to wear nail polish."

He gave me a glance that let me know I was too ancient to even conceive of his chosen style of dress and said, "Lots of kids dress this way. Including straight ones."

"What do your brothers think of that?" I asked, not daring to mention his parents.

"Who cares," he answered with bravado that didn't fool me for a minute.

"Your dad and Wayne would probably have beaten me up," I said.

"Does Dad know you're gay?"

I nodded and said, "I told him recently. He probably would have liked to beat me up then, too, except he knows I could kick his ass."

"That clears up a couple of things," Nicky said.

"Yeah? Like what?"

"Nothing. It doesn't matter."

"Did he say something about me?"

"Not to me. I heard him tell Mom if they didn't do something, I was going to end up like you. It didn't make much sense to me at the time," Nicky said, giving my crew-necked sweater and jeans an appraising stare that showed I was the last person in the world he expected to grow into.

"You could do worse," I said, with mock hurt, and his eyes darted back to mine.

"You're just—"

"Hopelessly uncool?" I asked.

"I didn't mean—"

"Relax, Nicky, I'm on your side. Even if you're not gay, you're all right."

"I need to go talk to my friends," he said, the wariness returning to his eyes.

"Hey, Nicky, hold on," I said, taking out my wallet to give him my card. "If you ever need to talk, here's my work and cell numbers. You can call, anytime, collect if you need to. Okay?"

"Yeah, okay," he said, jamming the card into his pocket.

While I watched him walk away, Jeremy joined me. "How'd that go?"

"A little tense," I said.

"I wanted to tell you the last time I saw you, but it wasn't my place," Jeremy said. "He's a great kid, Blaine. I know he's going through a struggle at home, but he's got a lot of support in my group. And from people like Adam's mother."

"He says he doesn't know if he's gay," I said, clinging to a shred of hope that he'd be spared some of what I'd gone through.

Jeremy laughed and said, "They all say that at first. Some of them aren't. But Nicky? He must have gotten the same gene you did. The sooner you come to terms with it, the easier it'll be for him to turn to you if he needs to."

"Great, Jeremy, it's a huge fucking step that *I'm* at a PFLAG meeting in my hometown. I'm not exactly the ideal role model."

"I think you're a great role model," Jeremy said. "You're way too hard on yourself, Blaine."

"Thanks, *Daniel,*" I answered.

"What can I say? Sometimes Daniel is right. And sometimes," he stopped and gave my shoulder a little shake, "Daniel is wrong."

I was overwhelmed and exhausted by the time I went to bed at the Stephensons' house that night. The next morning, Daniel's parents served me a hearty breakfast, keeping our conversation neutral. When they walked me outside, they repeated their assurances that I was always welcome there.

By the time Sheila joined me in Colorado a couple of days later, everything was in place for our shoot. She seemed a bit subdued, which I attributed to her preoccupation with her wedding. Josh couldn't join us, since he was photographing a producer's apartment for *Ultimate Magazine,* but the photographer that I'd hired for the Cancer shoot was just as likable. I had to wonder if the stress of wedding planning had necessitated a small break from each other, owing to Sheila's obvious need to let off a little steam.

"Cancer's the sign of the crab, right?" she asked when she arrived at our location, a rocky area on the side of a mountain with a panoramic view of the valley below. "Will I be scratching myself furiously in the pictures?" The production staff laughed as she began vigorously rubbing her crotch while pretending to apply lipstick with an aggrieved expression.

"No," I said, leading her to the makeup and wardrobe trailer. "Cancers are free spirits, who explore the world with passion, smiling in the face of adversity. We're not going to be too literal, like with the Aquarian mermaid costume. All I need is for you to be your natural, vivacious self today."

An hour later, Sheila emerged from the trailer in a strapless yellow evening dress, which clung to her torso but flowed around her legs with diaphanous layers of fabric. Her hair was swept up and secured into an elegant mass of curls, and her face was highlighted with Zodiac's natural but shimmering Cancer line.

I introduced Sheila to Colin, the dark-haired, youthful, tuxedoed hunk she'd be posing with in the pictures. After shaking his hand, she said to me, "Colin and I look like we're on our way to the opera. Why are we on a mountain? And why aren't we wearing shoes?"

Her questions were answered when we were taken to the location of the photo shoot. A river ran down the side of a precipice opposite us, creating a massive waterfall.

"I don't like where this is going," Sheila said. She looked at Colin and asked, "You don't see a barrel around here anywhere, do you?"

"Surely we're not going over there," he said to me.

"To the waterfall? No," I assured them. "It just provides our scenic backdrop. We'll start with the two of you on that ledge, then we'll use the crane to get some more shots with Sheila suspended over the valley."

"I hate you, Blaine," Sheila muttered, but she gathered up her long gown and marched off to the ledge.

The shoot was exquisite. The photographer captured striking images while I barked directions to Sheila and Colin through a megaphone. For the final shots, Sheila was strapped into a harness that was hidden by yards of yellow fabric, then dangled from the crane like a human wrecking ball. With her arms outstretched and an exuberant smile on her face, it looked as if she was flying right in front of the waterfall.

I left the location breakdown to the crew, and we took a flight to Miami the next morning. Sheila slept most of the way, and I tried unsuccessfully to read a novel to keep from brooding about Daniel or worrying about my nephew. I wondered if Nicky had told his parents he'd seen me. I suspected that they knew very little about his social life. Shane had told me that Nicky spent a lot of time surfing the Internet. Since my e-mail address was on the card I'd given him, I hoped he would contact me. It might be easier for him to open up in that medium than in person or on the phone. Then again, for all I knew, his parents monitored his e-mail. Somehow I doubted it. They'd always seemed too wrapped up in themselves and their other sons. Nicky was more of an afterthought.

I smiled, staring from the window at the clouds. That gave us something else in common. It hadn't taken me long, as a kid, to figure out that my parents hadn't planned on having any more children after Shane and Wayne. It hadn't made me feel unwanted, exactly. But it had made me want to be the perfect kid, so they wouldn't be sorry I'd been born. That effort had peaked with my marriage to Sydney. She was their idea of the perfect wife.

I looked at the unconscious Sheila, grateful that I hadn't made a huge mess of her life by marrying her. She'd been hurt by our breakup, especially since, unbeknownst to anyone but the two of us, I'd been the boy who took the gift of her virginity. But we'd settled all that between us years before, and she admitted that it would have been devastating if I'd tried to live a lie with her. I'd never wanted to hurt Sheila, and not just because of my friendship with Jake and the Meyers family.

She opened her eyes, realized I was staring at her, and asked, "What?"

"Do you think I'm stubborn, too demanding, and that I bulldoze people into giving me my way?" I asked.

Sheila sat up and shot a desperate glance at our fight attendant, who immediately responded with a smile and two fresh drinks.

"I think," Sheila said, "that the words people use when they fight are best forgotten."

"That isn't an answer," I said.

Sheila took a long look at me and drew a deep breath. "I think you're very good at what you do, and you've always been good at anything you tried."

"Uh-huh." I let my pause communicate that I was waiting for her to continue.

"I think you're used to getting your way when you really want something. And I think," she continued, when it became clear that I expected her to elaborate, "when you have an idea about how something is supposed to be, you can have trouble considering different options. There's usually more than one way to reach the same end, but sometimes you only see your way."

"So you *do* think I'm a stubborn, demanding bulldozer," I said.

"That's not what I said."

"Not in so few words, but I get the bigger picture."

"Blaine, you have a million wonderful qualities. You're creative, and you are incredibly visionary. You're sweet and thoughtful and protective of everyone you care about. You're unbelievably committed to those people and things you believe in. Maybe that's why some people might think you're stubborn. You're not easily swayed. But that's not always a bad thing."

I thought about what she'd said and how it compared to my final fight with Daniel. Her words seemed like a softer version of his accusations.

You lay down the law and state your wishes, and the rest of us are supposed to follow orders and make them come true . . . I am not *your employee.*

Sometimes it seemed like Daniel had understood me better when he *was* my employee. He'd known that projecting an image of authority, and the confidence and determination that went along with it, was how I survived in a competitive environment and how I compensated for my rivals' doubts about my age and inexperience. Maybe I'd had trouble leaving the attitude at the office. If that was true, leaving Breslin Evans would probably help me tone down my approach. I felt like I already had with Violet and Gavin. It was possible I needed to be more careful about it with my friends.

"Blaine? As long as I'm being honest, I'll tell you something else."

"Okay, but remember, I had you dangling from a crane over a gorge. If I don't like what you have to say, I can do worse."

Sheila laughed and said, "You just spoiled the impact of what I was going to say."

"Say it anyway."

"You have to lighten up, Blaine. Find the same balance in your personal life that you have at work."

"Balance? This is starting to sound like a Lillith speech." I didn't add that she also sounded like Ethan, for whom the words *lighten up* were a mantra.

"Perfect example. You know how to balance Lillith's unusual notions with the seriousness of a multimillion-dollar account. Your ads are fun. Whimsical. You need to inject some of that into your personal life. You're doing the same thing I am with the wedding."

"What do you mean?"

"I'm so bogged down in the details of arranging the perfect wedding that I'm not having any fun. How wrong is that? Just because you don't talk about Daniel or your breakup doesn't mean you aren't consumed by it. There's no fun in your life anymore. Remember when we lived together . . ." She broke off with a gasp.

"What?" I asked, startled.

She put a finger to her lips, signaling me to keep quiet, then undid her seat belt and quietly turned in her seat, bringing her knees under her. She slowly rose up, peering over the seatback to see who was behind us. I heard a newspaper fold and a man's voice say, "Can I help you?"

"Me? No. I was just . . ." I could tell she was fumbling for words. ". . . stretching. Mmmmm." She raised her arms over her head in a big stretch, then turned around in her seat and buckled her seat belt. I could hear the newspaper being rattled back into a readable shape.

"What was that all about?" I asked.

She whispered, "I didn't want our whole conversation to end up on Page Six. Before I went on and on about living with you, I wanted to make sure no one was sitting behind us taking notes." We both laughed, and the conversation lulled into a comfortable quiet, until she broke it by saying, "Blaine? Are you ever going to call Daniel?"

"I've already tried. There was no answer, and I didn't leave a message. I would have, but I don't know if he's ready to talk to me."

"You'll see him at the wedding, you know."

"I hope to speak to him before the wedding. There's no reason we can't be civil on your big day, and I want to make that clear to him. At least that's going to be my position."

"I guess if civility is the best I can hope for . . ."

Thinking of Daniel at a wedding reminded me of how handsome he'd looked on TV, and where I'd seen the show. I told Sheila about seeing the Stephensons and how welcome they'd made me feel.

"You'll never believe this. Daniel's mom was helping Aggie Wilson organize a PFLAG event. Next thing you know, she'll be doing print for Virginia Slims. 'You've come a long way, baby.' "

Sheila smiled, perhaps at the idea of Joyce Stephenson reclining with a cigarette, and said, "Everything's an ad to you."

"Blaine Michael Dunhill. The Ultimate Advertising Machine."

Sheila rolled her eyes at my parody of the BMW tagline. "How was it? Oh, I guess you didn't go to the actual event, huh?" I could tell she was dancing around another of the issues that Daniel I used to fight about: my not being out in Eau Claire.

"As a matter of fact, I did go." I smirked at her with self-satisfaction, finally acknowledging that it had felt good to be publicly honest about myself in our hometown.

"And?" she queried.

"It was pretty cool. Of course, it was mainly for kids and families dealing with them." My thoughts turned again to Nicky. I had the nagging feeling that I should call him and offer him support, but I thought about the insight Sheila had given me earlier. Maybe Nicky's situation was one in which I should let someone else determine the outcome. I needed to stop trying to control everything.

Sheila dozed again until we landed in Miami. As we stepped around people waiting to greet loved ones at the gate, I took my cell phone out of my pocket and turned it on. It beeped to let me know that I had a message. Sheila waited while I listened.

"Uh . . . Hi, Uncle Blaine, it's Nick. I just . . . uh . . . You gave me your card, and Mom and Dad aren't home, so . . . Well, later." *Click.*

"To repeat your message, press one—" I cut off the computerized voice with the press of a button to save the message. Now that he'd given me an opening, I intended to call him later, when I could give him my full attention.

CHAPTER 9

Sheila and I were both dazzled by the blindingly white Fontainebleau Hilton. I missed Manhattan, a city with the balls to put its grit and grime out there for everyone to see. I suspected that anything so pristine must have evil lurking somewhere. I'd chosen the hotel because it was close to the following day's shoot, but also because of its reputation for hosting celebrities. I was sure Sheila could be pampered without worrying about intruders like Lola Listeria leaping out from behind tropical plants to record her every move.

"You know what this place looks like?" Sheila asked. "Remember when we were kids, and you'd come over to watch cartoons with Jake and me? Doesn't this look like the Hall of Justice on *Superfriends?*"

I laughed, although I shouldn't have been surprised that Sheila's analogy reflected my sense that the Legion of Doom was out there. Daniel and I had always sworn she could read our minds.

"I'm amazed that you remember that, since it was on opposite *The Smurfs*. You'd cry for the whole half hour because we wouldn't let you watch those little blue freaks," I said.

"Twenty years later, and you still think you're running my life," she said and strode into the hotel.

I hung back to pay and tip our driver while he transferred our bags to the care of the bellman. As I put my wallet back in my pocket, I heard her shriek inside the lobby. I smiled, knowing my plan had worked, then sauntered inside. I almost shrieked, too. I'd just located the evil lurking within—acres of red and green tropically patterned carpet in the lobby.

Sheila was in Josh's arms, the two of them rocking back and forth in a warm embrace. After they kissed, Sheila turned and looked at me. "Did you do this?"

"This carpet? I had nothing to do with it."

Sheila looked down, blanched, and looked back at me with a shudder. "Not that. Josh."

"Guilty," I answered as Josh grinned.

"We got away with it, huh?" he asked.

"Looks that way," I said.

"What are you doing here? What is he doing here?" she asked me, not waiting for an answer from her fiancé.

"There's not much sense having a photo shoot without a photographer, is there? Let's have a drink before we go to our rooms."

Inside the Garden Lobby Bar, we chose a table near a glass wall that provided a sweeping view of the lobby, ordered our drinks, and sat back. Despite the frustration of planning their wedding, Sheila looked radiant because she was with Josh. I was happy that she no longer looked exhausted, for her own good as well as for the sake of our ads.

"You'll never guess who I saw a couple of days ago in New York," Josh said.

"Adam?" Sheila asked.

"Someone told you!" Josh gave me a knowing look. "Yes, Adam. We had a good time. Went out to dinner and had a couple of beers."

"When the cat's away . . ." Sheila began.

"The mice go bar-hopping," Josh said and laughed. "He came up with a great idea. I know you and I haven't discussed this, but I think you'll love it when you hear it."

"Uh-huh," Sheila said, sounding wary.

"I told him how frustrated you've been trying to find the right place for the ceremony and reception. We wracked our brains thinking of places that would be special. And large. Then Adam had his idea." I could tell Josh was a little nervous about her reaction when he raced through his explanation. "Adam suggested having our wedding at his place. He has room for tons of people. The property's big enough to accommodate one of those wedding tents. He said we could have the wedding and the reception there. I thought it was a great idea, but there's more."

"Go on." Sheila seemed to be thinking it over.

"We went to Daniel's to knock some ideas around, and the three of us came up with an even better plan."

"Yeah? What's that?" Sheila's curiosity was starting to get the best of her. I was just grateful the mention of Daniel's name hadn't prompted stricken looks my way.

"We decided to have two tents. One for the wedding, and the other for the reception. Doesn't that make sense?"

"I guess it does," Sheila answered.

"Daniel is going to take care of the plants and the decorations and stuff, or at least the design aspect. Adam said he'd follow through on whatever Daniel says to do. He'll also arrange security."

I realized that I was holding my breath, just as Josh seemed to be. We'd both been subjected to Sheila's recent unpredictable and volatile moods. After a pause, she threw her arms around him, exclaiming, "I'm so lucky to be marrying you! I love you so much."

Josh beamed, hugging his bride-to-be and giving her a big kiss. "You don't mind that we took some of this stuff over?"

"Are you kidding? We both know what we want. Besides, you're the creative one in this outfit. I'm just the pretty one." She laughed, knowing how untrue that statement was. Josh was pretty, too.

Josh turned to me and said, "I almost forgot. Adam and I were talking about the progress that's been made toward setting up Lillith Allure's new offices. That same afternoon, I got the invitation in the mail for the opening gala. Pretty snazzy; they must have cost a fortune. It looks like it'll be a great party. I hope Sheila and I can make it."

We laughed at the idea of the company's spokesmodel being a no-show. I was certain Lillith had gone to great lengths to make sure the event would not be star-crossed.

Later, after Sheila and Josh went to their suite, I settled into my room, running over my mental list of all that would have to be done to complete the next two photo shoots and the television spots I'd set up. I jumped when my cell phone rang and flipped it open.

"Lions?" Lillith asked. *"Lions?"*

"Lillith? *Lillith?*"

She laughed, and I was relieved. She didn't always handle her business with a sense of humor.

"I think you should know, in 40 A.D., Bonnie—she was a centurion, then—had me thrown to the lions. But not before she snatched my amulet from around my neck. Be that as it may, Frank approved it, so I suppose it's too late now. Proceed."

She hung up without another word. As I snapped my phone shut, I remembered my message and looked up my brother's number.

"Hello?"

"Nicky?" I asked.

"Chuck," he said. I panicked, wondering how I was going to explain a call to Nicky. But I didn't have to, since I heard Chuck drop the phone and yell Nicky's name. Apparently phone etiquette was a thing of the past. After a pause, Nicky picked up the phone.

"Nicky, it's Blaine. I'm returning your call."

"You didn't have to. Did you tell Chuck it was you?"

"No. What's up?"

"Nothing."

"You must have called for a reason. Did you need to talk about something?"

"No."

I suppressed my sigh, trying to remember what it was like to be a teenager. Which didn't work, because I felt like Nicky, at fifteen, was braver than I'd been at twenty-five. After a moment, a solution presented itself. I tried to imagine Daniel at fifteen.

"Did something happen at school?"

"Yeah," Nicky said, and I felt grateful for Daniel's diatribes about his troubled youth.

"Do you want to talk about it?"

"All right," Nicky said. "We have to choose our classes for next year. Should I take drawing or photography?"

I almost felt disappointed. I was not staying in the Hall of Justice, after all. I was in the Hall of Guidance Counselors. While we talked about his schedule, he asked me several questions about the advertising business, which seemed to explain why he'd called me. But as our conversation wound down, he surprised me with a question.

"Uncle Blaine, do you have a boyfriend?"

"I did. We broke up."

"Why?"

"Do you have a boyfriend?" I asked, hoping to change the subject.

"Why do people always change the subject when they get a tough question?"

"There's no easy answer," I said. It dawned on me that, regardless of his age, trust was something that had to work both ways. "Relationships are complicated. I can't narrow it down to one pat answer. But I can say that we wanted different things."

"So it was easier to break up than work it out?"

I held the phone away from myself and briefly took on the appearance of a mime screaming loud enough to shatter glass. "Something like that, I guess," I said, wondering why I was the one who felt like I was fifteen. *Do* you have a boyfriend?"

"Nope. My mom's home. I have to go."

"Do you have an e-mail address?" I asked.

"Yes."

"You've got mine. You can call or e-mail me anytime."

"Yeah, okay," he said and hung up.

I stared at the phone, thinking I had two choices. I could either dispatch Violet to teach phone manners to everyone who called me, or I could do what I really wanted to do. I dialed the phone and waited through the customary three rings.

"Hello?"

"I think my nephew is gay," I said.

"That's an opening," Daniel said.

"Original?"

"No, you're the third one today."

"The reason I'm calling is because rumor says that we're going to be attending the same wedding."

"I need to call Demi Moore and tell her to keep her kids off the phone," Daniel said.

It took me a few seconds to figure that one out, then I laughed. "I was wondering if we could agree to be civil. For Sheila and Josh."

"I don't want to talk about that yet. Let's get back to the nephew thing."

I must have been thinking about Nicky's question, because I heard myself ask, "Do you have a boyfriend?"

"Your nephew's too young for me. Is this the hunky one that plays football?"

"No, and he's too young for you, too. This is the formerly geeky twin."

"Nicky?"

"Right." I told him what had been going on with Nicky, finishing with my doubts about whether I'd been any help, or could be.

"He called you, Blaine. You must be doing something right." I'd forgotten how supportive Daniel could be. "And the answers are yes. And no."

"Yes, you have a boyfriend?"

"Yes, we can be civil at the wedding. No, I have a boyfriend."

"Wait, does that mean yes or no?"

I could almost hear Daniel count to ten before he said, "I have no boyfriend."

"But you're seeing someone?"

"That was just a friend with me at Whole Foods."

"Gretchen told me you're seeing someone."

"Gretchen was misinformed." There was a long pause. "By me."

"Because?"

"Can we talk about the nephew thing again?"

"Daniel . . ."

"Because I thought *you* had a boyfriend. I was being petty and in-secure. Then Sheila told me he's your personal assistant."

I'd also forgotten how honest Daniel could be. I decided to be as honest. "I've dreaded making this call. But it hasn't gone too badly, has it?"

"No. See? We can be civil."

"I'm glad."

"Me, too," Daniel said, and added, "The next one might be easier."

That sounded promising, and I figured we should quit while we were ahead. "I have to get back to work. I'll—"

"Don't say you'll call me," Daniel said, and I felt my heart turn over. He'd said that to me after the first time we'd had sex.

"You remember that?" I asked.

"Of course I remember. I told you to say, 'See ya.' "

"And I did."

"Then *I* said, 'I'll call you.' And I will, Blaine."

"Okay."

I assessed myself for damage after we hung up, but I only felt good. Our conversation had consisted of none of the drama and re-crimination I'd feared it would. And Daniel didn't have a boyfriend. And he said he'd call me.

* * *

I was amazed at how well the work in Miami went. I examined the contact sheets while I rode to my apartment. There could have been any number of problems, since we'd used real lions for the Leo shoot. I was sure Sheila had visions of being mauled. On the other hand, I'd had visions of the lions not wanting to be photographed, or not sitting still long enough for Josh to get the shots I wanted.

Sheila was dressed as a ringmaster, her hair styled to give her a leonine appearance. She was seated in the bleachers, her booted legs resting on one of the five male and female lions that surrounded her. They were indifferent to the popcorn scattered around them, their eyes riveted to the circus act: buff, hot men in leopard-print squarecuts jumping through hoops, perching on stools, and leaping on barrels.

Sheila had proved to be the most glamorous lion tamer anyone had ever seen. She professed not to be too concerned about the risk I was taking with her million-dollar overbite, since several animal trainers were on hand to make sure nothing went awry. In fact, she'd been a real sport, considering that in the past week I'd had her dangling from a cliff then surrounded by potentially dangerous animals.

If anything, she was less enthralled by the Virgo ads. When she heard that she would be dressed as Marie Antoinette, she was sure my plan involved a guillotine. Just to prove that I wasn't always jeopardizing her life, the worst thing I inflicted on her was two hours in a corset, repeating the line, "The revolution was written in the stars by Zodiac," for the taped ads.

I was exhausted from traveling and didn't need an astrologer to tell me that a hot shower and a massage from the healing hands of Gavin were in my future. When I finally got to my apartment, my keys jingling as I started to unlock the door, it flew open and I was nearly bowled over by Violet.

"Welcome home," Gavin said. "Violet was just showing me what she thinks I could wear to the Lillith Allure party."

"I'm also here to drop off the contact sheets from the shoot in Colorado. They're in the FedEx envelope on the kitchen counter. Gotta run." Violet waved at Gavin, then me, and whooshed down the hall.

I walked inside and decided that my massage would have to wait.

I found the envelope and pulled out the contact sheets, losing myself in my work.

Two weeks later, our limo pulled up to the entrance of Lillith Allure Cosmetics' new location on Twenty-sixth Street. I was gratified by the turnout of reporters and photographers lining the red carpet leading into the lobby. It felt more like a movie premiere than an office's grand opening because we'd strategically leaked the names of celebrities who would be making appearances—Sheila not among the least famous.

The driver opened the door to let us out. I looked at Sheila and Josh, wondering which of us should exit first. Sheila gave me a soft boot with her left foot. I stood, helped Gavin out, then we waited for Sheila and Josh before making our way to the door. We paused occasionally, just long enough to be blinded by the flashes of photographers leaning over velvet ropes to get shots for the society and style sections of their papers or magazines. As we headed for the door, Sheila worked the carpet like a seasoned pro, trailing behind to answer questions in ad-libbed sound bites.

"Who are you wearing?"

"My fiancé, Josh Clinton," she said, which garnered laughter from the paparazzi. "Dolce and Gabbana. They design all my clothes for the Zodiac ads."

"Is it true that you're leaving Metropole?"

"I'm also wearing Gemini, by Zodiac. Which means I'm unpredictable."

"How do you feel about Lillith Allure moving their headquarters to New York? Is this a sign of better things to come?"

"It'll certainly cut down on my commuting time to the office," Sheila joked. "Our demographic research shows us that New York women love the Zodiac line. So it's like coming home."

"Did you pitch snake oil in your last life?" I murmured.

"You'd have to ask Lillith," Sheila said, with one last brilliant smile for the cameras before we went inside.

When we reached our floor, one of the security guards ushered us to the back entrance, which led to a VIP lounge that was lined with plush sofas and velvet upholstered chairs. We had a stunning view of upper Manhattan and the Hudson River.

Lillith and Frank greeted us warmly and introduced us to a few of the other people in the lounge. Almost the entire cast of a popular sitcom sat around a small table, chatting and laughing. They had come because the four women on the show used Zodiac products during taping.

"I think I'll find Violet. Hopefully she isn't working," I said to no one in particular.

I was excused with nods as the others headed for the bar. I found Violet listening to the lighting designer explain how he'd gotten his light show to work. The ceiling of the office had been transformed into a nighttime sky with projectors and lasers. Twelve constellations traveled in a circular pattern around the room.

"Isn't this amazing?" Violet asked, staring into "space."

"You did a fantastic job organizing it," I said, truly pleased with how everything looked. The caterers were dressed in tuxedos and bustled about refilling drinks and carrying trays of delectable hors d'oeuvres.

I offered my arm to Violet, determined to make her relax. I stopped a passing server and ordered her a drink. Just then, something out of place caught my eye.

"Who's that?" I asked, pointing to a woman I didn't recognize.

"Between Lillith's, Frank's, and your invitee list, I can't possibly put a face to every name. I have no idea," Violet said.

The woman in question had long, curly blond hair framing her triangular face. She wore wire-rimmed glasses and lipstick too dark for her pale complexion. I identified it as Aries; she needed Libra. Lillith would not be pleased. The woman's black dress fell clumsily over her plump body and spilled onto the floor in a pool of sequins and lace.

"Let me go introduce myself. Care to join me?" I asked, trusting that Violet's photographic memory would recall the name and ascertain whether or not the woman was a party crasher.

Our quarry held a cosmopolitan, which she passed back and forth between her hands. She was standing outside a circle of men and women who were chatting joyfully, not seeming to notice her as she shifted in her obviously uncomfortable shoes. I saw her gaze dart toward us as we approached.

"Hello," I said cheerfully, not wanting to scare her if she happened to be an acquaintance of Frank's or Lillith's. "Are you enjoying yourself this evening?"

"Yes, I am. It's a magnificent event. You're Blaine Dunhill, aren't you?" she asked in a Spanish accent. This only made me more suspicious, and judging from the look on Violet's face, she was ready to pounce.

"Yes. May I introduce my assistant, Violet Medina, Ms.—?" I paused for a response, which came a second too late for my liking.

"Mrs. Vallejo. Regina Vallejo."

Violet's face lit up, a smile breaking from ear to ear as she launched into a flow of quickly moving Spanish.

The woman stared at Violet blankly, and as she tossed her blond hair over her right shoulder, I saw something that looked like a wire leading into her black sequined handbag. Violet's Spanish litany came to an abrupt end with an injection of English.

". . . no recording devices."

Violet reached out and yanked the handbag from the woman's shoulder, which caused the wire to rip out the side seam of her dress, sending sequins flying. The woman dropped her cosmo and attempted to reclaim her bag, but ended up tripping on her hem. She caught herself before falling, and her wig shifted to reveal a shock of bright red hair. I recognized her immediately.

"If it isn't our favorite gossip columnist, Lola Listeria," I said with a smile and waved Gavin over. "Please escort this woman off the premises and confiscate all contraband cameras and recording devices."

"Sure," Gavin said in a deep, don't-fuck-with-me voice. Lola glared at Violet as Gavin led her away.

"I knew that wasn't Mrs. Vallejo," Violet said. "Mr. and Mrs. Vallejo are in Buenos Aires and sent their regrets. That stupid bitch, thinking she could fool me with her fake Spanish accent."

"Good work, Jackie Brown. Let's get back to the real guests." I turned as I felt a hand on my shoulder.

"What was that about?" Frank asked.

"That was Lola Listeria, party crasher," I said.

"I'm glad you got her out of here before Sheila spotted her. Our model might have learned a thing or two from those lions."

"Believe me, those lions were docile compared to Sheila on a rampage," I said, bending to scratch Rowdy's ears. "How's this one liking Manhattan?"

"He prefers Riverside Park, but Washington Square Park is closer to the office, so he's adjusting. Have you found a new apartment yet?" I was surprised that he remembered I'd been thinking of moving, and shook my head. Violet made a strange noise. Frank looked at her and said, "What was that?"

"Nothing," Violet answered and added, "Excuse me."

"She never stops working," I said as we watched her walk away.

"Like her boss," Frank said. "Now that you're a couple of months ahead of schedule, I hope you're planning to take some time off."

"Men's line," Lillith spoke behind us. Rowdy whimpered, expressing the feeling that must have shown on my face. "It's deplorable that you've trained that dog to react to me this way."

"I swear it's his genuine response," Frank said, trying not to smile.

"Hmmm," Lillith answered. "It's not as if I'm asking you to create the products, Blaine, the way Frank did before the merger. You only have to develop a brilliant ad campaign. In two weeks." My mouth dropped open, and she whinnied with laughter. "Mercury goes retrograde in June, so your window of opportunity will be between mid-July and mid-October. I expect to be advertising before the end of the year."

"Perfect," Frank said. "After Sheila's wedding, you can use my cabin at Lake Geneva for a working vacation and please both of your bosses."

I decided not to blurt out the first words that came to mind: Lyme disease. I had two months to find a plausible way out of an adventure in the great Wisconsin outdoors.

"It sounds perfectly dreadful to me," Lillith said. "Be that as it may, I came over here to steal Frank. *Entertainment Tonight* wants to interview us with Sheila. Excuse us, Blaine."

They walked away, and I was left alone. From my vantage point, I could see Lillith and Frank being positioned in front of a display of Zodiac products while lights were adjusted around them. Sheila was introducing Josh to the *ET* correspondent in front of TV cameras.

I scanned the crowd of guests and saw Gavin and Violet on the opposite side of the room. Gavin plucked a glass of champagne from the tray of a passing waiter and handed it to Violet. She laughed at whatever he said to her, tucking her hair behind her ear when it fell into her face. The gesture was light and carefree. I was glad she was finally loosening up and having fun. A photographer stopped to take a picture of her, and I smiled when I saw her point to the bar, where the real Jennifer Lopez stood.

I went to the men's room, relieved to be away from the frenzy of the party. I opened my cell phone and hit a button.

"You can't be bored already," Gretchen said when she answered.

"I have no witty rejoinder, so I must be," I said. "What are you doing?"

"I'm looking at my ankles. I think they're beginning to swell."

"You're not even six weeks pregnant. It's not possible."

"I know my body. We've been cursed with each other for years. Wanna come over and watch Barbara Stanwyck movies with me?"

"That sounds more like Dyke Night than Gay Day. Try again."

"Wanna come over and watch my ankles swell?"

I laughed and said, "I thought you'd never ask. I hope it's not wrong of me to skip out of my party."

"You don't own the company. It's not your party," Gretchen said. "Besides, what's a work-related function for, but to slip out early?"

"It's a cool party. But . . ." I stopped to properly word what I was thinking. "Is it stupid of me to say that ever since we got pregnant, I've been realizing how superficial my job can be?"

"It's not stupid," Gretchen assured me. "It's sweet, actually. I'm discovering that the whole world is pretty damn superficial when you get pregnant. My ankles, however, are not superficial. You're really missing out. Get over here."

When I arrived at Gretchen's, I was surprised that her "mother gene" had kicked in at full force so quickly. She took my coat, offered me tea, and practically forced me to sit down, all within a matter of minutes, despite my protests that she should relax and let me fend for myself. Of course she got her way, but we met halfway once we sat down with a cup of chamomile. Gretchen lay back on her sofa, and I sat down on the floor next to her, not caring about my tuxedo. She caught me staring at her and said, "You want to touch my belly, don't you?"

"I know it's silly, but—"

"It's not. But for someone with body issues, the idea of everyone wanting to touch your stomach . . ." She shuddered and cringed, wrinkling her face like a child who was just offered Brussels sprouts. "However, I guess I have to get used to the idea. Go ahead."

She stared at the ceiling, which I took as my cue to put my hand on her stomach. Physically, I felt nothing, of course. But inside, my emotions were milling around and colliding like bumper cars. I looked up at Gretchen and found her staring at me with an expectant gaze.

"This is incredible," I said. "I feel so excited. Not to mention scared, thrilled, proud, and kind of nauseated."

"You should feel it from this side," Gretchen said. She put her hand over mine and added, "But it's going to be good. I know this isn't the way either of us planned on becoming a parent."

"We've been over this," I said.

"I know," she said. "But . . ."

"It's going to be good," I echoed, with an inward sigh of contentment when I realized that I meant it. She patted my hand then sipped at her tea. I knocked lightly on her stomach and said, "Is everything okay in there, son?"

"Daughter," Gretchen contended. She released my hand and sat up, adding, "Just for that, you're not allowed to touch me again until she kicks."

A few days later, Gretchen gave me the excuse I needed to decline Frank's invitation to use his Lake Geneva cabin after the wedding. I'd invited her to lunch so I could show off my new office, which I loved. It was easily three times the size of the space I'd had at Breslin Evans. Violet and Adam had gone all out to give me separate areas for the different kinds of work I did. My desk was uncluttered and angled toward the window to provide me a panoramic view of the Manhattan skyline. It was a place where I could sit and daydream, which was how my advertising ideas were born. Across the room was a bank of computers that were networked with the copywriters, illustrators, and storyboard, layout, and graphic artists who brought my ideas to fruition. At the other end of my new office was an area where I could have meetings, either on leather sofas or around a small conference table. There were phones located conveniently in each of the work areas. In essence, I could do every part of my job without leaving my office.

"Of course," I said to Gretchen, "Lillith brought in a feng shui expert to arrange everything in a harmonious balance."

"Om," Gretchen chanted.

"And someone came in with sage sticks to smudge the room."

"Is that how they did that on the walls? I thought they used sponges."

"That's not faux marble," I said, frowning at her. "It's real. She also had a priest come in to bless it."

"I guess if it had been faux marble, an altar boy would have sufficed. I love all the windows. You have a great view."

"I know. I hope I'm as lucky when I find a new apartment."

"You're still determined to move?"

"Not until after the wedding. I figured I can use moving as a way out of a vacation Frank has planned for me."

After I told her the details about Lake Geneva, Gretchen said, "By then, we'll be telling everyone our news. You can always pretend you're having expectant father jitters and you don't want to travel until after the baby's born."

"You're a genius," I said. "Are you up for lunch?"

"Isn't that why I'm here?"

"I wasn't sure if you were having nausea yet."

"I'm still working. I don't have time for nausea. My appetite's voracious."

"Are you having any cravings?"

"There was this blonde on the subway—"

"I was thinking Le Madri," I said.

Frank was waiting for the elevator when we left the office. I didn't know if it was because Rowdy wasn't with him, but he looked a little lost to me. I introduced him to Gretchen, then asked, "Where's Rowdy? Don't you usually grab lunch while you're walking him?"

"Rowdy is my yellow Lab," Frank explained to Gretchen. "He's at the groomer."

Gretchen surprised me by saying, "If you don't have other plans, why don't you join us?"

"I don't want to intrude."

"We'd love to have you," I insisted. It occurred to me that Frank had to be lonely in a new city where, as far as I knew, Lillith and his employees were the only people he was acquainted with.

"If you're sure you don't mind," Frank said, looking happier.

"Not at all."

When we got into the elevator, Gretchen took the opportunity to smile at me, and I knew she'd picked up the same vibe I had. It touched me that she'd forgo one of her few opportunities to discuss our baby to share lunch with a lonely stranger. She also knew how to go straight to his heart, asking him questions about Rowdy. I let them carry the conversation until we arrived at Le Madri, where Frank looked with appreciation at the cheerfully appointed tables and beautifully finished wood floors.

While we stood in line waiting to be seated, Gretchen stifled a laugh, and I followed the direction of her eyes. Ahead of us, I could see a woman's heavily jeweled hand gesturing to her companions with a cigarette holder which held an unlit cigarette.

"Get her," Gretchen whispered.

I smiled absently, then I suddenly focused. There was no way it could be. But it had to be—

"Daniel?" I asked loudly, and a man standing next to the woman turned to look at me.

After we exchanged stunned gazes for a few seconds, his face broke into a smile so warm that it made my heart turn over. He said nothing to his Aunt Jen when he stepped toward me, nor did he seem to notice Gretchen and Frank standing beside me.

As we stood staring wordlessly at each other, I felt like I was having some kind of out-of-body experience. Lillith would have been proud. I was dimly aware of our two groups merging and introductions being exchanged, then we were moved toward our table. The turning of heads and whispering provided my first dose of reality; Daniel had obviously been recognized by some fans. By the time I snapped to, I realized that he was sitting directly across from me, flanked by Gretchen and his aunt. Daniel's sister Gwendy was on my right, and Frank was on my left. I could barely remember being seated at the table covered by a starched white cloth, but as I smoothed the matching napkin over my lap, I figured I must have been managing coherent speech, because no one was casting strange looks my way.

Gretchen did, however, catch my eye, inclining her head toward Gwendy, and I remembered my manners.

"Is this your first trip to New York?" I asked, trying to catch up with the conversation.

"Yes. I love it! There's so much to do here, and the people are wonderful. I can't believe Daniel kept it a secret all these years."

Daniel made a disparaging noise and said, "That's the way we New Yorkers are. We don't want a lot of tourists cluttering up the place and spending their money, so we never let our city be featured in any books, television shows, or movies."

"Hush," Gwendy said. "You know what I mean. Everybody talks about New York like it's dirty and unfriendly and awful. But frankly, I'm dazzled."

"Yes, and she bought one of those dreadful tourist books and intends to traipse over the entire city in a week," Aunt Jen said with a shudder. "Dragging me with her, I might add."

"I keep telling you that I can sightsee alone," Gwendy assured her.

"Aunt Jen doesn't believe in young females exploring the city unescorted," Daniel explained to Frank. "Fortunately, I've had some time off."

"That's why we planned the trip for now," Gwendy said.

Everyone paused to order. I thought Gretchen seemed abnormally subdued; she didn't even harangue the waiter about the best vegetarian choices. I decided she might feel strange sitting with Daniel and me, considering everything that had happened. Or maybe it was just difficult for her to be in his presence when he didn't know about our baby.

Daniel, on the other hand, could have been my mirror. Instead of feeling like things were awkward between us, I had a giddy sense of happiness just sitting across from him. I could tell by the way his eyes danced every time he looked at me that he felt the same. It almost seemed like we were sharing a tantalizing secret that no one else knew.

"I notice neither of you has complained about being chauffeured around after you've walked your silly feet off all day," Aunt Jen finally said to her niece and nephew.

"I'm new to the city, too," Frank said. "I've been intending to see some of the sights, but it's not much fun alone."

"You wouldn't say that if you had to do it with two people who act like they're heading to the gas chamber every morning," Gwendy assured him.

"Perhaps with a charming companion like you, instead of my headstrong niece, I might enjoy a spot of sight-seeing, too," Aunt Jen said, flashing a brilliant smile Frank's way.

I met Daniel's eyes and mouthed, *She's flirting with him.*

"I confess," Frank said. "I'm a hopeless sucker for any tourist trap. We should consider making a couple of days of it. I'll be your escort in return for the pleasure of your company."

"How gallant," Aunt Jen murmured.

"You don't have to do that," Gwendy demurred, shooting an exasperated glance at her aunt.

"Everything's running so smoothly in our new office that I'm useless there," Frank vowed. "It's a great time for me to explore my new home, especially in such pleasant company."

I looked at Daniel, who stared pointedly at Frank. Then he mimed taking a large bite of food to communicate, *He's eating it up.*

Conversation halted again as our salads were set before us, then Frank asked Aunt Jen, "Are you from Wisconsin, too?"

"Originally. I still maintain a home in Eau Claire, but I also have apartments in Tampa and San Diego. You?"

"Kenosha," Frank said.

"Really? Perhaps you know my dear friends, Edward and Anita Oliver?"

"I've spent many a Sunday on the links with Ed Oliver," Frank said.

This propelled them on a mission of discovering other mutual acquaintances. Gwendy sighed and asked in a low voice, "Is your boss loaded?"

"He doesn't usually drink this early in the day," I said, pretending to misunderstand her.

"I'm just giving you fair warning. That old termagant could be your future boss-in-law."

"Behave, or she'll write you out of the will," Daniel said softly, after making sure his aunt was still engrossed in her conversation with Frank.

"Oh, you've got it made. You're leaving for Hawaii tomorrow," Gwendy said.

"You are?" I asked Daniel. "Vacation?"

"No. In spite of the expense, the show has decided to shoot my latest storyline on location. Picture it. Weeks in Hawaii with the delightful Jane-Therese Pennick. The plus side is, she's getting shoved into a supposedly extinct volcano."

"Jane-Therese or her character, Cressida?" I asked.

"That remains to be seen," Daniel said, assuming Angus Remington's best menacing look.

"Weeks?" Gretchen asked. "How many weeks? What about the wedding?"

"Oh, God, you don't think I'd screw that up," Daniel said. "Sheila would have a breakdown. In fact, when I get back from taping in Hawaii, I'll be on vacation. I'm spending it in Wisconsin so I can help get everything ready for the big day."

"Oh, good," Gretchen said.

Not good, I silently disagreed. We seemed to be experiencing a mutual return of our fascination with each other, and it was disheartening to know that it would be nearly two months before I saw him again.

Gwendy stared at her aunt, who was glowing as she flirted with Frank, and said, "I can see how the rest of my vacation will go after Daniel abandons me. I'll be like an unpaid companion to her. At this rate, I wonder who's chaperoning whom?"

"Make Daniel give you all our numbers," I urged her. "I'm sure Sheila and I can rescue you."

"Are you the attorney or the social worker?" Gretchen asked Gwendy, obviously unable to sort through Daniel's array of sisters.

"The attorney. Family law," Gwendy said.

"If you don't mind mixing business with pleasure, I'm supposed to attend an interesting discussion group tomorrow night on pediatric AIDS and the Family Leave Act," Gretchen said. "You can meet some brilliant professionals, and it might be of use to you in your work someday. I'll treat you to dinner and drinks afterward, at some place a little livelier than your aunt might enjoy."

"I'd love to," Gwendy said. "That's so nice of you."

"Women's networks helped build my career," Gretchen said. "We have to look out for each other."

"Networks," I said to Daniel, doing air quotes around the word.

"Yeah, what is it Rush Limbaugh calls them?" Daniel asked.

"Don't even go there," Gwendy warned him, while Gretchen jabbed him in the ribs.

"Congratulations," Aunt Jen said, and I realized she was talking to me. When I gave her a quizzical look, she said, "Frank just told me about your new position as Creative Director. I always knew you'd be tremendously successful."

Maybe it was paranoia, but I could have sworn the expression on her face communicated, *Whatever the cost.* When she cast a doting look on Daniel, I was sure I'd read her correctly. Whether or not she knew any of the details of our breakup, she was, as always, squarely in her nephew's corner. It didn't bother me. I wouldn't mind being in his corner, myself. Or in his bed, his shower, his garden, his arms . . .

I cleared my mind of those kinds of thoughts. Maybe when I wasn't actually in his presence, I'd regain my equilibrium.

Later that afternoon, as I stared from my office window, my senses were still full of him. When our accidental lunch had ended—there was no haggling over the check, as Aunt Jen was completely willing to let Frank be the gentleman he was, and cover it—and we'd all walked outside, Daniel's group to climb into their limo, mine to hail a cab, he'd given me a quick hug.

"You and I," he said, "need to make time in Eau Claire for a serious talk. Although I can't say I feel all that serious at the moment."

"Me, either," I admitted.

"I'll call—"

"See ya," I interrupted, and heard him laugh just before the driver closed the door between us.

I jumped when my cell phone rang. Maybe he hadn't been kidding. "Blaine Dunhill," I said, my heart pounding.

"That was an amazing lunch," Gretchen said. "What with Daniel's aunt ogling Frank, and you and Daniel doing whatever you were doing."

"I thought we behaved very well," I said. "No fighting, no nasty names—"

"I thought about suggesting that the two of you get a room," she interrupted.

"I don't know what you're talking about."

"Blaine," she said after a long pause, "do you ever wonder how it

will affect things with our child if one of us gets involved with someone else? We've gotten accustomed to spending what little leisure
time we have with each other. What if—"

"Daniel and I were just making the best of an awkward situation,"
I lied, not wanting to go down the Daniel and Blaine path in case it
ended up leading nowhere. "I don't see being in a relationship again
for a long, long time. And no matter what, I'll be there for you and
Civil Liberty."

"Would you stop calling her that?" Gretchen demanded.

"You're right. It's not really a boy's name," I said.

"Girl."

"Mmmm. We'll see."

We hung up, and I returned my gaze to the window. Sheila's
words came back to me: *There's usually more than one way to
reach the same end, but sometimes you only see your way.*

I was learning. When my plan for fatherhood had been thwarted
by the breakup with Daniel, I'd accepted another option from
Gretchen. I'd stepped back from the situation with my nephew, letting Nicky call the shots. I had to do the same thing with Daniel and
allow him to make the next move.

CHAPTER 10

I unlaced my hands from behind my head and swung my feet over the side of the bed. Adam had placed one of his old computers, "old" being a relative term, on the desk in his guest room. Naturally, he had it fitted with the latest in high-speed Internet access. I signed on to my remote office server, and found a new e-mail from a name that I hadn't seen before with "It's me—Nick" in the subject line.

> *Hi, Uncle Blaine, it's Nick. Thought I would write and tell you that I heard my parents talking about how Aunt Sydney has been hanging out at Grandma's. For someone who walks around like she has a lot of money, she sure whines a lot about not having any. That's what my dad says. Anyway, last time we talked on the phone you asked if I had an e-mail address. So now you have it. If you want to answer this, all you have to do is hit the button that says "Reply." Later.*

After I read the e-mail a couple of times, I realized that one of the first things I needed to do, if I intended to get closer to my nephew, was to stop calling him "Nicky." He obviously preferred "Nick." I also recalled one of my earlier revelations involving him, which was that trust was a two-way street. It wasn't right to expect him, at his age, to open up to an uncle he barely knew just because I felt like he should.

I found myself wishing I'd made more of an effort with my nephews over the years. I could remember liking them when they were babies, and being amused when they started showing their own personalities. I'd probably let my feelings for Shane keep me away from them after he started turning Tony and Chuck into carbon copies of himself. And once I didn't have to spend time with my family, I didn't. Sydney had made it easier. Not only was she ill at ease around kids, but she'd aspired to a more pretentious lifestyle, so we usually spent our holidays somewhere trendy instead of with family. I wrote checks so my nephews could buy what they wanted for their birthdays or Christmas, as I had no insight into their interests.

Now I regretted my distance from them. I hadn't offered even the minimal support that Wayne had given me. And in Nicky's case, I'd developed nothing we could use as a starting point in a relationship.

I figured he would probably respond if I opened up first, but I didn't want to do that in an impersonal e-mail. That seemed more like the way my father would treat me, and probably was how Shane treated Nicky. *Nick,* I reminded myself.

> *Hi Nick. Thanks for the note. And thanks for the hot tip about hitting the "reply" button—don't know how I ever got along without you. (kidding) I'm actually in Eau Claire for a wedding. I should be in town for a while. If you want, maybe I can take you to dinner or something? Coffee? You pick the spot.*
>
> *Sydney has been over to my mother's, huh? I guess that's fine. Last time I was here, I spent some time with your grandmother after her surgery, but I haven't talked to her lately. As for Sydney, I don't really see her anymore.*
>
> *But I would like to see you, so think about my dinner offer. Like I said, I'll be in town for at least another week. Let me know what you want to do. Talk to you soon.*
> *Uncle Blaine*

I clicked "Send"—without any input from Nick—and watched as the note to my nephew disappeared into cyberspace. I was about to sign off when I heard footsteps coming up the stairs.

"Hey," Adam said, peeking his head around the door frame. "Did you have a good nap?"

"Nah. I just sort of lay there, thinking."

"I hope you got to relax a little," Adam said.

"Sometimes it can be just as relaxing to lie around and be alone with your thoughts, you know?"

"I remember naps," Adam said. "But that was before I had Jeremy and my mother competing for my attention. The rest of my time is usually taken up by work. Sometimes I'd give anything for just a half hour by myself."

"To take a nap?" I asked.

"Who cares about naps? I'd rather masturbate," he said.

I laughed in surprise, and asked, "Why? You've got Jeremy. Or is the honeymoon over?"

"Not by a long shot. It's like you said, Blaine. Sometimes a guy needs to be alone with his thoughts." Adam winked at me before he turned from the doorway.

"Adam?" I called after him.

"Yeah?" He stuck his head back inside the door.

"I was wondering," I started, "when everyone else gets into town for the wedding . . ."

"Yeah?"

"Where are they all staying?"

Adam laughed and said, "Don't worry. You're the only one who's staying here. Daniel's been at his parents' house for a couple of weeks. Everyone else will be at the Hampton Inn. It's close enough that people can get here without much trouble, but they won't be underfoot while we're getting everything ready for the wedding."

"Is there anything you don't think of?"

"Oh," he said, "except for Martin."

I groaned. "I try not to think of him, either. So much for relaxing."

"Don't worry. He's staying with my parents." When I breathed a sigh of relief, he gave me a commiserating look. "My work here is done. What do you want for dinner?"

"Whatever. I'm easy."

"I've heard that about you," Adam teased.

"Hey!" I exclaimed, and mimed picking up the computer and heaving it at his head.

"Your assistant sent me an e-mail detailing your every dietary need," Adam said. His enjoyment when I flinched with embarrassment was evident in his smile. "I'll pick something especially yummy from the list. Maybe something from page three."

"You'd think since I'm not in the office, Violet would take a day or two off," I grumbled.

"She had an accomplice. It was signed from Violet and Gavin," Adam said before he walked down the hall.

Gavin had stayed in New York to take care of Dexter, and Violet would be handling everything at the office. Both of them knew how to reach me by phone and e-mail, but I didn't anticipate any problems. I'd worked my ass off before coming to Eau Claire so that I'd be able to relax and forget work. I still didn't want to take Frank up on his offer of the Lake Geneva cabin, but I did intend to enjoy a well-deserved vacation.

I hadn't come up with anything solid for the men's line that Lillith had dropped in my lap. I didn't know when Neptune passed by Venus again, or whatever astral-babble meant I could take another stab at it if I missed my deadline. But missing a deadline was not in my nature. For weeks I'd been trying to devise something.

It hadn't been nearly as hard when I was first visualizing the ads for the Zodiac line. Back then, Daniel would lie in bed next to me and listen while I brainstormed ideas. We'd usually end up laughing when we talked about Lillith's bizarre astrological quirks, but sometimes even those moments led me to fresh concepts. With that in mind, I'd turned to Gretchen, since these days, ours were the conversations that usually left me laughing.

When I'd called her one night to talk about the challenge of the men's line, I could hear her shuffling papers and assumed she was sitting at her desk.

"I want to keep it separate from the Zodiac line, but somewhat related," I explained. "Know what I mean?"

"Uh-huh." More paper shuffling, now underscored by the unmistakable sound of a ten-key.

I occasionally felt that her mind was somewhere else when we talked. I assumed her distraction had to do with the baby. I decided to test my theory that she hadn't heard a word I'd said.

"I think I'll run an ad campaign that focuses entirely on gay sex. In one of the ads, one guy can say, 'What's that you're wearing?' And the other guy can say, 'Come To Me,' and the first guy can say, 'Funny, it doesn't smell like cum to me.' "

Gretchen took a deep breath before addressing me. "Just because I'm not right in front of you, and I throw in the occasional *uh-huh,* doesn't mean I'm not listening."

"Good god, we're starting to sound married."

"Tell me about your ad campaign, dear," she said sweetly.

"I was thinking about a line of products that centered around the characters of the Chinese calendar."

"So you'd only have to do one ad each year?"

I laughed. "No, but it would be an interesting correlation to the Zodiac line."

"Yeah, I can see it now. *Cock: the new fragrance from Lillith Allure.*" We both roared with laughter.

"I guess 'Rooster' doesn't bring about a much more positive image, does it?" I asked.

"Not unless you want to smell like a chicken coop. Not to mention 'Rat,' 'Dog,' and 'Pig.' Now that I think about it, at least your idea is fairly accurate."

"Don't forget, this dog gave you the sperm that got you pregnant. If you're not careful, you might find yourself having puppies."

"I wonder if I'd still have to childproof the loft, or if installing a doggie door would suffice?"

"Definitely stick with the childproofing," I answered.

The more I thought about my idea for the men's line, the more I realized what a ridiculous concept it was. I was glad that I'd shared it with Gretchen rather than Daniel during the one phone call he'd made to me while he was still in Hawaii. It was the first time we'd spoken since our group lunch in New York. My cell phone rang on my way home from the gym after a long day.

"Hello?" I answered, after fishing the phone out of my gym bag and nearly running into a trash can.

"I think my aunt is dating your boss."

"That's an opening," I responded.

"Original?" Daniel laughed as we replayed the conversation we'd had about my nephew when I was in Miami.

"Third one today," I said on cue. "How are you?"

"Well, I'm in Hawaii, where I've always wanted to be, with Jane-

Therese, the last person I want to be with. I'm good, but I could be better. How about you?"

"I'm not in Hawaii, where I've always wanted to be, but I don't have to work with Jane-Therese, which is a bonus. I guess about the same as you." We both laughed. "What makes you think Aunt Jen and Frank are dating? Isn't it possible they're just friends? It might be nice for your Aunt Jen to have someone her age to pal around with."

"Blaine, they're not a hundred. It's not like she has to find someone to take her to Tapioca Night at Shady Pines. She's a lively woman. But he's younger than her. And rich, I might add. I've seen how this plays out."

"He's probably only five years younger," I countered. "And she's rich, too. I think they can both take care of themselves."

Daniel seemed willing to let it go as a topic of conversation, but it was obvious from his tone that he was as reluctant as I was to get into the "us" discussion that we intended to have in Eau Claire. Instead, he turned the conversation to Sheila, asking if I'd been reading "The Lo-Down."

"I try not to, but for some reason, Violet's always shoving it in my face," I said. "I think Lola Listeria is obsessed with Sheila."

"Maybe that's why she's so hopeful the wedding won't happen," Daniel said. "She wants Sheila."

"She seems to think *you're* the reason the wedding won't happen," I disagreed. "I think my favorite was when she said Sheila would be dining at the Angus Steak House on her honeymoon."

"That's just disgusting," Daniel said.

"Beef. It's what's for dinner," I said.

Daniel ignored that, saying, "I thought it was more clever when she said Sheila would choose 'Acute Daniel over Obtuse Josh in her oblique love triangle.' "

"That's not even good math," I said.

"Is Sheila really going to be the next Bond girl? Or is that another rumor like the *Men in Black* sequel?"

"You'll probably read it in 'The Lo-Down' before I know about it," I said.

Our call had ended before we could discuss anything more personal. I knew Daniel had come to Eau Claire directly from Hawaii, but since I'd just arrived myself, I hadn't seen anyone other than

Adam and Jeremy. I wasn't sure if Sheila and Josh knew about all the publicity Lola Listeria was giving them. But Adam was aware of it, and Jeremy had attributed Daniel's heightened celebrity to broadcasts about *Secret Splendor*'s location shoot by several networks on their entertainment shows.

I wondered if there were reporters stationed at the Stephensons' house, and how Daniel's parents were reacting to that. Adam said the persistent group camped out where his driveway met the road had been there ever since the two tents were erected. Jeremy noted that Sheila's wedding was getting more publicity than the Gore campaign.

After we ate a fantastic meal prepared by the team of Jeremy and Adam, the three of us slumped on the plump couch in Adam's den to watch television. I felt like I hadn't watched an entire program in years. Truth be told, I always honed in on the commercials to see what other ad companies were doing. I sneered as an ad from one of my former rivals came onto the screen.

"Wow, why the ugly face?" Jeremy asked, turning his head toward me as he sat up.

"It's this ad. It's so ridiculous, yet it won three awards." I watched as tiny babies in cartoon diapers floated across the screen in an ad for Plumpies Diapers.

"It isn't that bad," Adam jumped in. "Let me guess. It's an ad by the competition that beat you out of an award." I blushed at how easily Adam was able to read me. As I was about to explain the acrimonious relationship I had with Plumpies' ad agency, the phone rang. "Hold that thought; it's probably my mother wondering if we've starved to death yet." Adam leaped up from the couch, obviously not as weighed down by dinner as I was. I heard him mumbling in the kitchen, then he called out, "Blaine? It's for you."

I turned my head to look over the back of the couch when Adam came in. He was holding the phone toward me as if it was going to bite off his hand. I gave him a questioning glance, and he mouthed something that I couldn't understand. I took the phone, wondering who would be calling me at Adam's, other than Sheila, Violet, or Gavin, none of whom would elicit such a strange reaction from Adam.

"Hello?"

"Blaine?"

A chill ran up my spine as I heard the voice. "How did you get this number, Sydney?"

"I have my ways," she replied smugly.

"The phone book?"

She ignored me as she continued, "I want to meet with you. Tonight." Her tone was stern, yet somehow unsure. It was typical of her.

"You expect me to drop my plans just because you say jump?"

"As far as I can hear, Blaine Dunhill, you're watching television. And don't try to tell me you're doing something later. We both know that nothing happens around here after 9 P.M. Unless you're going to a bar."

"Fine. Where do you want to meet? And why?"

"Meet me at Drayden's department store at nine. As for why, just come." She hung up without letting me get in another word.

Sydney had always been spoiled and accustomed to getting her way when she issued commands. But it hadn't always been bad times with Sydney. When we were first dating, and then married, she had shed some of the snobbery that she'd developed over the years. She'd had dreams of becoming an artist—the next Mary Cassat. She had worked hard to convince her parents that art school would be a logical step for her. It still baffled me that they hadn't given in. They'd had no real aspirations for her except to meet a rich man who would take care of her the way they had.

Once I began bringing home larger paychecks, Sydney became a terror. She demanded an allowance in addition to the money that I'd been shelling out to have a famous artist take her under his wing. Late into our marriage, it dawned on me how much I resented her. At first I thought it was because she was constantly in need of a new outfit, or trying to find any way she could to spend my salary. But eventually, I had to admit to myself that my resentment was not over the way she squandered money. Regardless of how much she spent, I always had money left over. I just wasn't being honest about what I truly wanted. A man. Once I accepted that, my marriage was doomed, even if Sydney hadn't known it at the time.

When I got to Drayden's, I found my ex-wife standing in the window, knee-deep in fake grass, holding up a papier-mâché tree, the leaves of which were replaced with bikini tops and bottoms. I couldn't help but smile while I watched her struggle to make the tree stand upright.

"Let me help you with that," I said, steadying the tree before it could fall on her.

She swung her bright red hair over her shoulder, her steely eyes turning on me as if they were razors. "I don't need help from you."

"Fine," I said, letting go of the tree.

Sydney let out a yelp as she fell into the fake grass. She grumbled as she stood up, picking green plastic strands from her hair and removing a bikini top that dangled from her arm.

"You prick. How could you let that happen?" I stood back and tried to muffle my laugh. She glared at me, then stepped down from the window box. "Let's get to the point. I was going to try to be civil, but that obviously doesn't work with you."

"I was being perfectly gentlemanly; you've turned into a raving psycho. What are you doing working here, anyway?"

"My family owns the store now, and my mother thinks I do better work on the windows than the girl they brought in from Milwaukee. Besides, I need money, Blaine. I have a show going up in London, but I have to pay to have it shipped there. Or rather, you do."

"Sydney, you do realize this is blackmail."

She stepped closer to me, her eyes narrowed and her jaw clenched. "You wouldn't want your family to find out about your little secret, would you?"

My first thought was that I had to protect my baby, then I realized she was referring to my sexuality. "Why are you doing this, Sydney? You were a decent person at one time."

"That person is gone. You can blame yourself for that. Walking around like a god who can just point his finger and people will fall in line."

I felt a surge of anger at hearing one of Daniel's accusations spewing out of her mouth. If I hadn't taken it from him, I sure as hell wasn't taking it from her.

"Do you know why I give you money, Sydney? Because I feel sorry for you. Your parents never cared enough about you to let you do what you want. Or maybe they knew just how third-rate your talent is and didn't want you to make the family image as garish as your paint-

188 Timothy James Beck

ings. The one person who ever admired you was Sheila, and you repaid her by stealing her boyfriend and gloating about it. As for me, I don't blame you for making every minute of our marriage miserable. You couldn't help it that you were born without a soul, much less a cock." She flinched, but I couldn't stop myself. "As for not using the brain, heart, and spine that you do have, I should never have subsidized that. You're right. I am to blame. You've gotten your last payment from me."

"If you think that I won't tell—"

I held up a hand to silence her, looking past her into the accessories department. She whipped her head around to see the cluster of employees and customers who gaped at us, obviously drawn by my raised voice.

"Go ahead," I said. "Tell them." When she looked back at me, trying to see if I was bluffing, I loudly said, "Attention, Drayden's shoppers. I'm gay!"

A mother put her hands over her daughter's ears and led her away, and an elderly man turned to the woman with him and said, "Who's Ray?"

"Not Ray. *Gay.*"

"Oh, Gay. Nice woman. I thought she died."

The rest of the group laughed nervously when I did, except for one man in front, who asked, "Are you single?"

"Uh, I think he's her husband," one of the employees said.

"Figures," he whined, turning away. "The hottest gay men are always straight."

When the group dispersed, I looked at a shell-shocked Sydney and said, "Tell whoever you want. My parents, your parents, the whole goddamned town can know I'm gay. I really don't care."

I was exhilarated as I strode back to my rental car, but when I unlocked the door, I was hit by the magnitude of what I'd done. I felt like my knees were going to buckle, and I quickly slid into my seat, trying to assess my reaction. Then I smiled. I could hear myself telling the story to Daniel, and I knew what he'd say: *But how did you* feel, *Blaine?*

I felt scared and anxious and . . . free. I didn't feel regret. I felt a strange sense of power.

I was struck by a flash of brilliance. My muddled ideas about work fell into place. I knew what the concept for the men's line from Lillith Allure would be: an entire line based on the ruling male gods of mythology—Zeus, Osiris, Thor. I was so excited that I needed to get back to Adam's to write it all out. I looked back at the store window, where Sydney remained as motionless as a mannequin next to the papier-mâché tree.

"Thanks, Sydney," I said as I sped out of the parking lot.

When I turned into the driveway at Adam and Jeremy's house and stopped at the security checkpoint, I was momentarily blinded by flashes from cameras when the lurking reporters rushed to my car. They were pushed aside by two of the security guards, who didn't have to use much force when the reporters realized it was only me. One of the security guards tapped on my window. I lowered it and said, "Hi. Can I get through, please?"

"We'll need to see your ID, sir," he said stonily.

"It's me, Blaine Dunhill. I've driven through here twice since I got here this morning, and you were on duty both times," I said.

"That may be, sir, but I'll still need to see your ID," he insisted.

"I'll bet Thor never had these problems," I muttered as I fished my wallet out of my back pocket.

When I finally reached the house, I found a note from Jeremy letting me know that Josh had called while I was out. I returned his call, and he gave me an address where I was supposed to be the next day.

"Just meet me there. I'll fill you in then. I hate to be rude, but I've got a ton of things to do," Josh said.

"That's okay," I assured him.

"I'm at my future in-laws' house. Sheila's back in raving lunatic mode. And Nora is worse," he said.

"Sheila's mother? I can't believe that. Mrs. Meyers is always such a calm woman."

"That's just it," Josh said. "She's a nervous wreck, worrying constantly, and keeps knocking things over or dropping anything in her hands. She's like the eye of a hurricane. On the outside, she's cool as a cucumber. But she leaves mass destruction in her wake." I laughed, but was left with dead air after he said, "Shit. I gotta go. Nora just walked by with a crystal punch bowl."

The next day I arrived at the appointed address to find Josh and Jake waiting for me in front of a building downtown.

"Look!" Jake exclaimed, pointing at me. "It's your best man."

Josh was on his cell phone and finished up his call while Jake gave me a bear hug. "It's not a crisis, Sheila. I swear. It'll be fine . . . Okay. I'll see you soon," Josh said. He flipped his phone closed, and said, "It's another crisis. Sheila and Nora were at a fitting for the wedding dress. Apparently, Nora somehow managed to rip out an entire seam in the dress. They're not sure if it can be mended in time. Is it too late to elope?"

"Yes," I said, patting him on the shoulder. Josh rested his head on my shoulder and sighed audibly. "This will all be over in a few days. Then you can whisk that lovely bride of yours away to . . ."

"Los Angeles," Josh said.

"What kind of honeymoon is that?" I asked.

"It's only for a day or two. I have a shoot I couldn't reschedule. And Sheila has a screen test." Jake and I quickly glanced at each other, but before we could question him, Josh added, "I can't say what it's about, so don't ask."

"Okay. Where are we? What are we doing here?" I asked instead.

"Isn't this one of those places where they have estate sales?" Jake asked.

"Yes. One of your mother's friends has a friend whose husband died, and this is where most of the estate ended up. Nora's friend has it on good authority that there are several vintage tuxedos inside."

"Cool. When the reporters ask me who I'm wearing, I can say, 'Urban Legend,' " I said.

"It's a retro-chic wedding," Josh said, "and none of the vintage shops here had anything from the forties. We've got reproductions as a backup, but Sheila insists it's better if we can find the real thing."

"Hey, guys. Hope I'm not too late," Daniel said, walking up to us from the street. His sudden appearance startled me, even though I knew he was one of Josh's groomsmen. It was completely logical that he'd be there to find a tuxedo, but seeing him caught me off guard and made me feel vulnerable. He brushed his fine blond hair off his forehead in a harried manner, and said, "I can't believe I never realized that my stupid driver's license had expired. Talk about humiliating. For two weeks, I've been at the mercy of my sisters, or my parents, to drive me around. Being back here without a car is just like sixteen all over again."

The sound of a horn made us all turn around, and we saw Gwendy pulling away from the curb in her Jeep. We all waved, except for Daniel, who flipped up his middle finger at her. She returned the gesture, thrusting her hand through the sunroof and waving it frantically as she drove away.

"That's my kind of woman," Jake said.

"She could've joined us," I said.

"She's pissed off because she had to pick me up and drive me over here on her lunch break," Daniel said. "Bitch."

Inside the store, we met the manager, who'd set aside fifteen different suits and tuxedos, ten of which were said to be from the forties. We took his word for it and took turns trying on the formal wear in a room off the showroom. Josh and I had the hardest time of it, as his arms were longer than most of the jackets', and mine were big. But we finally found suits that were big enough to be scaled down to our size.

"You boys lucked out," the manager assured us. "Most authentic articles of clothing from that time period are considerably small."

"It's a good thing we're not wearing hats, Blaine," Jake said, nudging me with his elbow. "You'd be hard pressed to find one that would fit that big melon head of yours."

"Hats!" the manager exclaimed. "I think we have some upstairs. Excuse me."

While he ran off, Daniel emerged from the room we'd commandeered for our fittings. He was tugging at the cuffs of an Arrow collar shirt, arranging them just so under his tuxedo jacket. He said, "I wish we had cufflinks, so I'd know how this will look on the big day."

Daniel's tuxedo fit his lean physique perfectly. His shaggy blond hair graced the collar of his silver shirt and black jacket. Daniel's penchant for the latest trend in clothing often caused him to look like he'd stepped out of a fashion magazine or department store catalog. On him, the vintage tuxedo looked like it was new and about to be revived on a Paris runway as the hot look for fall.

He caught me looking at him and said, "With a couple of alterations, that tux will look great on you, Blaine."

"You don't look so shabby yourself," I offered, wishing I could be alone with him.

Daniel dropped his eyes and blushed momentarily before turning to a mirror alongside Jake, who was frowning at his reflection.

"I look like an undertaker," Jake said.

Josh's cell phone rang again and, judging from his side of the conversation, it was Sheila.

"Don't worry. I think we're done here . . . Yes, we all found tuxes . . . Mine? It's real sharp. It has tails . . . No, tails. Not quails. Why would I have quails? Where are you? I can hear that you're outside. I mean, where are you going now?"

The door to the showroom burst open and Sheila walked in, still talking on her cell phone. "I'm here. I ditched Mother," she said, walking toward us. "She managed to somehow set a display on fire at the flower shop. Don't ask. I didn't even want to know how she did it. So I sent her home." She stood in front of us, still holding her phone to her ear, and said, "Oh, you guys look so good! I think I'm gonna cry. Josh, your pants need hemming."

Sheila dropped to her knees and began fussing with Josh's pant legs, cursing when her cell phone slid from between her ear and shoulder.

"Sheila, breathe," Josh ordered, pulling her up by her shoulders.

Jake leaned toward my ear and said, "She's losing it."

I almost had to agree. While Daniel retrieved Sheila's cell phone and flipped it shut to disconnect the call, Josh began speaking to her in a calm, soothing voice about how everything was under control. Now that we had our tuxedos, all we had to do was get them altered, walk through the rehearsal for the wedding, attend the rehearsal dinner, then show up for the actual ceremony.

"I'll make sure nothing goes wrong, Sheila," he assured her. "All I need for you to do is relax and enjoy yourself. From here on out, it's a piece of cake."

"The cake!" Sheila shrieked. She grabbed her phone from Daniel and began punching in numbers.

"Bad choice of words, man," Jake said to Josh.

After Sheila checked on the cake, which we learned was the third time that day, Josh dropped five thousand dollars on our tuxedos. I wondered how much it would've cost if we'd taken the hats the manager offered, too. We visited a tailor on our way home, leaving our tuxedos to be altered. Sheila went that far with us, then left for the florist with Daniel before he and I could talk.

I was equally frustrated in my attempt to meet with my nephew, who sent a short e-mail to explain that his family would be on a trip until the day before the wedding, when I knew I'd be too busy to see him.

A few nights later, I got a call from Gretchen, who'd just checked in at the Hampton Inn.

"I'm fine," she said when I asked how she and the baby were feeling. "I'm not thrilled about this forties theme wedding, though. Do you know what women wore in the 1940s, Blaine?"

"Not really. What?"

"Very fitted waists, that's what. Fabric was rationed then, so all the women wore these tiny outfits and dresses."

"As I learned a few days ago, that's because they were tiny people back then. So what are you wearing during the ceremony?"

"Sheila's only stipulation for her bridal party was for us to wear purple dresses in the dreaded forties style," Gretchen explained. "I briefly considered showing up in a purple zoot suit, but knew that wouldn't go over too well. My assistant found a fabulous vintage shop in the garment district, and they had a purple dress that I bought. I had to have it let out a lot, though, which is so embarrassing. But it has these cute little sleeves that cover my upper arms. As it is, I'll look like an eggplant."

"I think Josh said that Jake is your escort. He thinks he looks like an undertaker, so you'll be a great match."

"Whatever. I found a shawl to wear, and I think we'll be carrying flowers, so maybe people won't notice my stomach," Gretchen said.

"We'll find out tomorrow at the rehearsal," I said. "Are you bored? Do you want me to come keep you company?"

"No," she said quickly. "I'm going right to bed. I mean, thanks, but I'm—"

"Going to bed," I finished for her, wondering why she sounded so flustered.

When several different cars started driving through the security post at the end of the driveway the next day, the reporters began to suspect that the wedding day was drawing near. While Adam greeted his guests as they arrived for the rehearsal, Jeremy and I stood on the front steps with a pair of binoculars, watching the security team as they tried to push the reporters back.

"They're relentless," Jeremy observed. "They just don't give up. Uh-oh."

"What?" I asked.

"They're all on cell phones. I suspect they're calling for reinforcements. I'm going to call the security company and make sure we can handle it if more reporters show up today. Just in case."

"I wonder where Lola Listeria is," I mused. "Everywhere I go, I expect her to jump out at me with that shocking red hair. But I haven't even seen her hanging around the entrance to this place."

"Maybe the *Manhattan Star-Gazette* doesn't have a big enough budget to send her here," Jeremy said. "Judging from the way she fabricates stories, she doesn't actually go to the events she writes about."

"Maybe," I said, feeling a twinge of anxiety. I would've preferred to have the enemy where I could see her.

When Jeremy went inside, I walked around to the back of the house, where Adam was directing people to park their cars on a side lawn. Jake waved to me as he got out of his car and walked around to the trunk. He unlocked it, and Sheila and Josh crawled out.

"Good grief," I said to them. "Don't you think that's a bit drastic?"

"It was kind of fun," Josh said.

"Like sneaking into a drive-in," Sheila said with a laugh.

Gretchen arrived next and enveloped me in her arms after she parked her rental car. "Is it over yet?"

"Sorry," I said. "Not yet."

"You look great," she said.

"I've been sleeping a lot better," I said, realizing that it was true. It had been a while since the Daniel voice-over kept me awake at night. Maybe because the real Daniel and I were talking again.

Gretchen drew back from me, and my eyes quickly scanned her body. She was wearing a blue Scotch plaid flannel shirt with the sleeves rolled up, and a pair of faded blue jeans. The outfit cleverly concealed her stomach, and I was certain nobody would suspect that she was pregnant.

Gretchen must have noticed my scrutiny, because she said in a low voice, "Blaine, I'm not even four months pregnant. I may think I look puffy, but I doubt anyone else will."

"You're right. I'm just being paranoid," I said.

"I know we agreed not to let the cat out of the bag until after Sheila's wedding, but you're making me think you don't want anyone to ever know about it. Are you ashamed or something?" she asked huffily.

"No," I said immediately. "That's not it at all. Your stomach may not be showing, but your hormones sure are. Let's go inside, okay?"

Just as I put my arm around her shoulders to lead her inside, another car pulled up the driveway and off to the side lawn. We watched as Nora and William Meyers got out of their car and waved to us. Sheila's friend from high school, Patricia Hunt, emerged from the backseat and strode toward me with outstretched arms.

"Blaine Dunhill, is that you?" she shrieked, and before I knew it, my face was smothered in big, frizzy brown hair. She hadn't changed at all since high school. Her heart-shaped face was obscured by a pair of horn-rimmed glasses. She still wore beat-up Converse All Stars and a cardigan sweater over her denim overalls. Patricia released me and continued, "I haven't seen you in years! You look amazing. Is this your wife? Hi, I'm Patti."

Gretchen shook Patti's hand and said, "Hello, I'm Gretchen Schmidt. I'm a lesbian."

"You are? Well, I guess you two aren't married, huh?" Patti said and broke into a gale of laughter, punctuated at the end with a loud snort. "I'm going to find Sheila. I'll see you both later," she said and walked briskly to the house.

Gretchen gave me a dry look and said, "This is why I hate weddings, Blaine. I don't ever want to have to do this again."

Sheila's parents, Nora and William, walked over and I introduced them to Gretchen. "Nora's a concert violinist," I said to Gretchen. "And William is an architect."

"Oh, Blaine. You flatter me," Nora said, and one of her hands fluttered up to her mouth. "I haven't performed professionally in ages. I'm just a teacher now, giving private lessons."

William put his arm around his wife, drew her close to his strong

Nordic frame, and said, "Don't let Nora fool you. She still does guest performances with the Minneapolis Symphony Orchestra now and then."

Nora glanced up at her husband and rolled her eyes, one of her trademark self-deprecating gestures.

"Why don't we go inside? Everyone's here, so I'm sure they want to get the rehearsal under way," I said. "Wait a minute. Daniel's not here yet."

William Meyers smacked his forehead and said, "*Uff da!* I completely forgot." He hurried to the car, fished his keys out of his pocket, and unlocked the trunk.

"I was beginning to feel like a spare tire," Daniel said as he crawled out of the trunk and dusted himself off before giving Gretchen a hug. He smiled at me over her shoulder and we exchanged a little eye play.

"Isn't it funny?" Nora Meyers asked me. "It's just like when Cressida Porterhouse hired T-Bone Reynolds to kidnap Angus Remington. He was locked in that trunk for weeks."

"It was only two days in soap time," Daniel said. "Good thing he'd left that box of Fiberforth bars in the trunk. Shall we go rehearse?"

The wedding party gathered under the main tent in the large field behind Adam's house, and the minister guided us through the steps we'd take during the actual ceremony. Afterward, we socialized with cocktails inside Adam's house.

Later that night, we reconvened for the rehearsal dinner. We drove five miles out of the city to the Fanny Hill Inn. Sheila and Josh had rented the whole facility for the evening to ensure their privacy. A few of the reporters followed and leaped out at us as we went inside, but the rest of the night was quiet and relaxed. Josh's parents had flown in that afternoon, as well as both his and Sheila's grandparents, who all joined us.

Faizah Harris, Sheila's friend, fellow Metropole model, and maid of honor, had also arrived from Paris. She shared my table at dinner, along with Sheila, Josh, Daniel, and Gretchen. Faizah, in addition to traveling the globe because of her modeling career, was in her third year at Columbia University's school of law.

"I'm just cashing in on my good genes so I can go to law school,"

Faizah explained to Daniel, who had asked about her career plans. "The minute my looks start to fade, I'm going to hang out my shingle. Or maybe go into politics. Pass Faizah the salt, baby. Thanks. Of course, being an African-American, my looks won't fade for a long time to come." Nobody said anything, and Faizah looked around the table for a reaction. Finally, she cut into her veal and said, "I throw out a perfectly good generalization, and nobody even challenges me on it. Then again, I am in the whitest state in America."

"Actually," Gretchen said, "I think South Dakota currently holds that title. Or is it North Dakota? I get the two mixed up."

"No. You want to know the whitest place in the U.S.? Maine," Faizah said emphatically. "I grew up in this little town in Maine. Not even on most of the state maps. Faizah grew up with her own title: *The Black Girl.* I even listed that as my nickname in my senior yearbook in high school. My mother wasn't amused. And you want shock? Try growing up thinking other African-Americans are like the people on *The Cosby Show,* then move to Harlem at eighteen. Talk about a rude awakening. Anyway, I can't wait to get into politics. I'm going to run for mayor of New York City someday."

"You've got my vote," Daniel said, and Faizah smiled.

"No offense, but with a gift of gab like yours, you'd be a perfect politician," Gretchen said.

"Gretchen!" Sheila gasped, her Nordic heritage obviously kicking in and fearing conflict.

"It's all right, honey. I'll be the first to admit Faizah's got a big mouth," Faizah assured Sheila. She turned to Gretchen and said, "I like you. You're honest. Tell me, if it's not too personal, are you voting for Hillary?"

When Gretchen told Faizah that the First Lady did indeed have her vote, the topic at the table turned to politics. Although Daniel was one of the most politically aware people I knew, he stayed out of the conversation, his focus mainly on Faizah and Gretchen as they tag-teamed Sheila and Josh during a heated debate regarding the Senate race. I wondered what he was thinking as his gaze volleyed between the two women and when we'd have time alone to talk about us. Both of us had been too busy; he with his family and the open curiosity of the other guests about his burgeoning fame, and I with running errands left and right for the bride and groom. As well as keeping tabs on Lillith Allure and assembling my thoughts on paper for the men's line.

When the political discussion waned, Gretchen speared a stalk of broccoli and gesticulated with it as she said, "Speaking of the approaching elections, now that your returns have all been filed, I need to tell you about something." I froze, afraid that she was about to tell the table about our baby. My fears were put to rest when she said, "I won't go into all the technicalities, but whenever there's an election, the stock market tends to go haywire. Most likely, stocks will plummet. I'm going to take a look at your portfolios and start moving a lot of numbers so you'll all be covered. I just wanted to warn you ahead of time, and I hope you'll trust that I know what I'm doing."

As we all assured Gretchen that we had faith in her abilities, I noticed that Daniel looked a bit uncomfortable. His eyes darted from his plate, to Sheila, the wall, anywhere but in Gretchen's direction. Which she didn't notice, because she was too busy eating the last of her broccoli. I knew financial planning didn't interest Daniel in the least. He would rather focus his energy on his creative outlets. As long as he had an agent to represent him, lawyers to read the fine print of his contracts, and financial wizards like Gretchen to handle his money, he thought there was no reason to concern himself with those things.

It was a part of his personality that always frustrated me. I'd try to get him to see the importance of understanding how the financial world operated, but he'd roll his eyes and tell me his way of doing things seemed to be working just fine. I'd point out articles in the newspaper about crooked lawyers and insider trading on Wall Street, but he'd wave me away, telling me I should have more faith in humanity. He'd known his lawyer for years, and certainly Gretchen would never betray him.

Gretchen flagged down a passing waiter and said, "This broccoli is amazing. Can I have some more?" The waiter nodded and walked away. Gretchen eyed the half-eaten veal on Faizah's plate and asked, "Are you gonna eat that?"

Faizah said, "No. Go for it. I'm stuffed. And I have to fit in that dress. Whoever heard of a purple dress on black skin? Faizah's going to look like a goddamned bruise."

Gretchen stabbed the cutlet with her fork and began to cut it into little pieces immediately. She popped a piece into her mouth, began chewing, then said, "Oh, my god, this is so good." Sheila's mouth hung open. Daniel stared at Gretchen like she was a complete stranger. Gretchen noticed their expressions and asked, "What? What are you staring at?"

"You're eating meat. Veal, even," Daniel said.

Gretchen looked stricken for a moment, but regained her cool composure and said, "I guess my body needs protein. Or iron. I was feeling a little light-headed earlier. Anyway, it doesn't mean anything. Just shut up."

Daniel and Sheila looked at each other skeptically. Much to my relief, and most likely Gretchen's as well, Daniel's cell phone rang. I was startled. Daniel had been one of the last great holdouts to join the cellular age.

"Excuse me," Daniel said, getting up from the table to take the call.

As he walked away, Faizah said, "So, Josh, when's your bachelor party?"

"If I'm not mistaken, it's tomorrow night," Josh said. "Right, Blaine?"

"Yes, tomorrow. I didn't forget," I said.

"I hope you didn't plan anything distasteful," Sheila said to me. "No strippers, lap dancers with tassels, or anything like that."

"Of course not," I said. "It's going to be at Adam's house. Men only. Totally stag."

"How about us, Sheila?" asked Faizah. "What'll we be doing while the men are doing their stag thing?"

"You didn't plan anything for me?" Sheila teased, knowing Faizah couldn't have, since she'd been in Paris for the last week. Faizah looked miffed, so Sheila continued, "I'm just kidding. We'll have a party of our own, trust me."

"Will there be strippers?" Gretchen asked hopefully. "Lap dancers with tassels?"

Daniel returned to the table and announced, "Martin has landed."

"On the moon, I hope," I said.

"We were just discussing my bachelor party," Josh said. "Is Martin coming, too?"

"I'm not certain," Daniel answered, glancing briefly at me. I could feel my face twitching.

"Call him back and tell him to be at Adam's tomorrow," Josh begged Daniel. "I haven't seen him in a while. It'll be fun to have him there."

"Okay," Daniel said weakly.

After the rehearsal dinner, we all went home. On the way back to Adam's, I stopped at a drugstore to buy some Pepto-Bismol. I hadn't anticipated spending much time with Martin during the wedding. I figured since he would be staying with Adam's parents, the distance from the altar to wherever he sat during the ceremony would be enough to bear, and during the reception, it wouldn't be difficult to maintain a similar distance. It had never occurred to me that he might be at the bachelor party. But it should have. He probably would've crashed the party if he wasn't invited.

An hour into the bachelor party the following night, I began to think I'd done a lot of needless worrying. Adam's living room was filled with Josh's friends who had come to Eau Claire for the weekend, along with a few of Adam and Jeremy's friends, as well as Jake and Daniel's, but Martin hadn't shown up. I'd hired the same caterer that was being used for the wedding to set up food in the dining room, as well as a bartender. There were two poker games going on in the den, but most of the guys were standing around the living room talking. It was a perfectly respectable party, just as I'd intended.

"Great party, Blaine," Adam said, leaning on a wall in the living room next to me. "When do the strippers arrive?"

"I promised Sheila a PG party," I said. "Thanks again for letting me have it here."

"No sweat. It's not every day that I get to have thirty or forty men in my house," he said.

"Oh? Weren't you just saying a few days ago that you wanted some time for yourself?"

Adam laughed, then said, "That'll be tomorrow, after everything's over and the men are all gone. I'll have this to reflect on while I—"

"Okay," I interrupted. "I get the picture. Besides, all these guys are straight."

Adam smiled at me and said, "Not *all* of you are, Blaine." Despite the fact that the lights were dimmed, Adam must have seen me blush, because he gestured with the beer in his hand and said, "I'm sorry. Alcohol makes me flirt."

"I'll remember that," I said with a quick grin before I walked away.

I poked my head in the den just as Josh threw down a winning hand and yelled, "Yes! Come to Papa!" He swept the chips toward him and said, "Now I can pay for a real honeymoon!"

While the other guys laughed, I turned around and ran into Daniel. "Oh! Sorry," I said.

"I'm not," he responded. "We haven't been able to talk. How are you?"

"Honest answer?"

"Yes, but leave the brutality on the side, please," Daniel said.

I motioned for him to follow me to a quiet corner in the hall, next to a coat closet and a small table with a lamp. "What's going on with us?" I asked. "I like that we're talking again."

"Knowing us," Daniel said, "it could be the calm before the storm."

I thought about the baby bomb that Gretchen and I were about to drop and inwardly cringed. I had no idea how Daniel would react to the news. Even if he and I couldn't get back together, I still wanted to save our friendship.

"I've missed you," I said. I reached out and touched his arm, felt a shiver run up my back, and added, "I miss my friend."

Daniel stepped toward me and took my drink out of my hand. He set it on the table then wrapped his arms around me, resting his chin on my shoulder. "So do I," he said. "Sometimes I still get angry, though, when I think back on our arguments."

"Me, too," I admitted.

"The question is," Daniel began, pulling back just enough to look me in the eye, "do we want to work through this? Together?"

I was about to answer when someone said, "Excuse me."

"Oh. Sorry," Daniel said, moving out of the way as the bartender walked by pushing an oversized cake on a small hand truck. He wheeled it into the living room, and we heard everyone whooping and calling Josh into the room.

"What the hell was that thing?" I asked. "I didn't order that."

I went into the living room to see Josh being dragged in from the den. His eyes widened in surprise at the enormous cake, and he said, "Oh, no. Guys, I hope this isn't what I think it is."

Just as someone cranked up the volume knob on the stereo, the top of the cake flew open and a woman popped out, flinging confetti and glitter everywhere. The men cheered and hollered as she was helped down and began dancing to a Whitney Houston dance mix. She was wearing high heels, long gloves, and a tight dress. As she let down her long, blond hair and shook it out over her shoulders, I looked on in horror as I realized she was Martin Blount in drag.

"It's Martin," I growled.

Daniel was standing beside me and said, "Yes." He was laughing while he watched Martin take off a glove and run it across Josh's cheek, but covered his mouth with his fingertips when he saw my scowl.

"Miss Houston is wrong," I said. "This is neither right, nor is it even remotely okay. How could he do this? That fucker."

"Blaine, please," Daniel scoffed. "Look, Josh is enjoying it. Everyone is."

"Not all these guys are from New York, Daniel," I said. "Not everyone is open-minded, you know. Not everyone loves a drag queen."

"That's a clown. Everyone loves a clown," Daniel said, his irritation with me evident by his frown. "Martin is not a drag queen. He's a performer, and sometimes a female impersonator. An actor."

"Oh, an actor. I see," I said. "I should have known you'd stick up for him. You always do. Then again, you didn't bat an eye when that cake was wheeled by us. You knew all about this, didn't you?" Daniel bit his bottom lip for a second and turned back to watch the show, his silence the answer to my question. "I knew it," I said. I left and headed for the dining room, where the bartender had resumed his post. "Vodka with an essence of tonic. Make it a double."

After another double, I could finally unclench my jaw. I wandered into the den and started flicking poker chips across the room. I could hear hooting and hollering in the other room and figured Martin was still entertaining. The door opened and Adam walked in. He saw me and shook a finger at me.

"You're not having fun," he said.

"Sure I am," I said. "This is just my poker face."

Adam rolled his eyes, then stepped in front of me. He reached down, grabbed the leg of my chair, and yanked it so I was facing him. The quick movement nearly made me fall over, since I was feeling light-headed, but I managed to stay seated. Adam sat down directly opposite of me, and pulled me forward in my chair until our knees were touching.

"What's going on in there, Blaine?" he asked, reaching over to tap my forehead with his finger.

I batted his hand away and said, "Nothing. I hate Martin."

"Oh," Adam said. He plucked his beer off the table, took a pull, then said, "That old song and dance."

"Yeah, that's just it. Song and dance. I'm sick of Martin butting in to everything I do and fucking it all up," I said loudly.

Adam quickly set down his beer and stood up, pulling me with him. He folded his arms around me and rubbed a hand between my shoulder blades. "Just calm down, okay?" he said slowly. Then he started laughing and said, "It's not right, but it's okay."

His giddiness was contagious, and before I knew what was happening, we were laughing together and holding each other up. When I could breathe again, I said, "I'm sorry. He's your stupid friend, too. I should know better than to insult that idiot in front of you."

"It's okay, Blaine," Adam said.

I left the room and went back to the bar. I ordered another double and noticed that people were walking around again. I saw Jake and pulled him aside, asking, "Is the Martin Show over?"

"Yeah," Jake said. "Sheila's mentioned him, but I never knew he was so entertaining. I'm going to grab a beer. Do you want anything?"

I held up my drink as an answer and turned away, muttering, "Entertaining. I've had gas more entertaining than Martin Fucking Blount."

I wandered into the living room, where a large number of men were still crowded around Martin, asking him questions about New York, his part in *Cabaret,* and his past as a female impersonator. After a few minutes, Martin broke away from the phalanx of men and walked by me on his way to the dining room. He was still in his dress, wig, and heels, but the gloves were off.

"Hey there, Paul Bunyon," he said as he breezed by me. "Fancy seeing you here." I turned and followed him into the hall, then grabbed his arm and dragged him after me. "What the hell are you doing?" he exclaimed. "Let go of me!"

I slammed my drink down on the small table, then grabbed both of his arms and pinned him against the closet door.

"Ow! Look, Blaine," he said, his voice shaking. "I know you've had a thing for me for a long time, but I think this is hardly the time or place to—"

"Shut up," I hissed. "You and your big mouth are getting on my last nerve. I didn't want you here. I'm sick of you popping up and sticking your nose where it doesn't belong. If you know what's good for you, you'll keep a healthy distance from me the rest of the weekend. Got it?"

"Blaine, are you drunk?" Martin asked. "They say if you don't have anything nice to say, don't say anything at all."

"What good advice," I said. Martin yelped as I spun him around and opened the closet door. "Obviously, I'm not making myself clear." I pushed Martin into the closet and slammed the door shut behind him. Two feet from me was a small ladder-back chair, which I wedged under the doorknob so he couldn't get out. I picked up my drink and staggered back to the living room.

To the right of the room, I saw Adam come in from the den. He leaned against the door frame, lifted his chin toward me, and smiled. Daniel was sitting on a sofa, talking to Josh and Jeremy. He saw me, momentarily frowned, then resumed his conversation. I walked into the room, watching him until he looked at me again. As soon as I was sure his curious gaze was following me, I went to Adam and latched on to him, pulling him to me and kissing him.

I felt Adam's entire body go rigid, and I leaned back to see that after a fleeting look of shock, his brilliant blue eyes were suddenly brimming with amusement.

"What a coincidence," I said. "Alcohol makes me flirt, too. Let me help you with your next fantasy."

When I leaned in for another kiss, I found his mouth open and ready, and our tongues met and lingered as his arms tightened around my waist.

CHAPTER II

Before I surfaced to consciousness, Daniel became part of my dreams. I could almost feel his warm, smooth flesh against mine, and the way his body hair tickled my skin when he stirred from our spooning position. It was so easy to fall back into memories of our years together and think of the many times and ways we woke up and made love.

It had never gotten old for me. Never felt predictable. There were things I'd done with him that I knew I would never do with another man. If anyone gave a thought to our relationship, considering our appearances and the differences in how we worked and maintained our bodies, they'd probably never believe the pleasure I took in being fucked by Daniel. Not just because of the physical satisfaction he could give me. He helped me understand what he already knew: the emotional strength it took to be vulnerable and trusting enough to allow myself to be taken that way. I couldn't imagine letting that happen with any other man. Only Daniel could have that part of me . . .

I wanted him so much that I could almost smell him. No matter what shampoo, soap, or other scents he used, they could never compete with the tantalizing natural odors of his skin and hair. He'd always laughed at the way I sniffed him, and been mad that I could tell when he'd sneaked one of his occasional cigarettes. But I couldn't help myself. When he was near me, I had to breathe in the smell that went to my head like liquor.

I moaned, finally awake enough for dismay about my behavior at Josh's bachelor party to seep into my thoughts. I knew better than to drink too much. Whenever I did, I made an ass of myself. In fact, I'd nearly derailed any hope of a romance with Daniel because of my drunken, boorish behavior the first time we'd ever been alone with each other. In the three years we'd been together, there were maybe five occasions when I'd had too much to drink, and Daniel always knew exactly when to swoop in and save me from myself, taking me home and putting me to bed before I could commit any grave social errors.

That woke me up. Had I really thrown myself at Adam Wilson? I had the dimmest memory of the way he'd returned my kiss—was he nuts?—before he broke it off with a laugh.

Time to get you to bed, big guy . . .

Shit. In front of all our friends. In front of Jeremy. In front of Daniel. Not only was I the second biggest asshole on the planet—Martin being the first—but I had to stand in front of hundreds of people later, trying not to look hungover, miserable, and guilty. At least Sheila hadn't been there and wouldn't know what a jerk I'd been. For her sake, I was sure all of us would pretend everything was okay. But it was a long way from okay. I dreaded having to face Jeremy's hurt, Daniel's contempt, Adam's good-natured forgiveness, Josh's and Jake's discomfort, and Martin's cattiness.

Then again, it was possible Martin didn't know. After all, I'd trapped him in the closet—

Oh, God, I'd trapped him in the closet. For all I knew, he was still there.

I was in morning-after hell. There was no way to dodge it, and I knew I should open my eyes, face the day, and try to find an effective blend of medication to ease my throbbing head and screaming conscience. I slowly cracked my eyes, bracing myself for the brilliant July sunlight that was sure to be pouring into the room.

The wooden blinds were closed, sparing me that first assault. In spite of how lousy I felt, one corner of my mouth twitched in a grateful smile. In the old days, Daniel would have made sure I awoke in a dark room. He'd have had coffee ready. And sometimes he'd even hold me gently, knowing that if he lightly stroked my neck and scalp, he could help ease my transition from blissful unawareness to shrieking hangover.

I released my death grip on the pillow and slowly began uncurling my body from the fetal position. As I moved, the hair on my legs tingled with that sensation that came just before I bumped against someone else. I froze.

Adam had not . . . Adam would not . . .

I turned over to face the blue eyes that were watching me fondly—fondly?—from the next pillow and made a noise of relief when Daniel said, "You were expecting someone else?"

"Daniel, thank you. I don't care why you did it, and I know I'm an asshole, but thank you. Is Jeremy pissed at me?"

Daniel reached over to lightly caress my scalp and said, "Honestly? Judging by what I could hear last night, I'd say your little show with Adam turned him on. It *was* pretty, in a kind of Rod and Bob Jackson-Paris way. But remember, sweetie, Rod and Bob broke up. Two gods together are too much for the rest of us mortals."

"Everybody breaks up," I said, wishing he'd never take his hands away. "You and I broke up." His hands stopped, and I begged, "Please keep doing that."

"Selfish prick," he said, making it sound like an endearment. He kept massaging my scalp. "Breaking up with you was not one of the more brilliant moves of my relationship history."

"I broke up with you," I disagreed.

He laughed and said, "Even now. Such a control freak. By the way, not that you've asked, but in spite of Jeremy's assurance that the closet would be comfortable, Josh did spring Martin and take him to Aggie Wilson's house. Promise me that you're not going to drink today."

"I don't ever want to drink again," I moaned. "Daniel, I know that we—"

His hands moved quickly from my scalp to cover my mouth and he said, "This is not your father's Oldsmobile." I shot him a questioning look, so he went on. "You're about to do what you do best, and I want to save you the trouble."

I jerked my head away from his muzzling hand, causing a thousand points of pain to explode behind my eyes. "What are you talking about?" I asked, trying my best not to whine.

"You're going to pitch me an old product in a new way. It's your great talent. Like your Lady in Red campaign. Give it a new look, sell it a new way, and—bam!—success. It's how you told me to approach taking over the role of Angus Remington, remember? When they supposedly killed off the character, everybody in America who watched the show—all twenty of them—hated Angus and rejoiced in his demise. When they brought him back, you told me to make them love to hate him. Now we've got three million viewers, and Fiberforth's sales have skyrocketed. People all over America are regular."

"Uh-huh," I moaned, grateful that if he was going to analyze everything, as usual, at least he was doing it in a quiet voice.

"I see the signs," he went on. "You're about to sell me a new and improved Blaine. You don't have to. I was fine with the original."

"I was afraid I bored you."

"*Bored* me?" I flinched, and he dropped his voice. "Volatile, stubborn, possessive . . ."

"I'm hungover," I reminded him with a whimper.

"All qualities that go along with being exciting, strong, and passionate. Trust me, Blaine. From the bedroom to the boardroom, your imaginative tendencies are anything but boring."

I closed my eyes, smiled, and said, "Tell me more. You know how thick I can be."

His free hand traveled down my body under the sheet as he said, "Yet another of your attributes." He felt my immediate reaction to his touch and warned, "We've got a wedding to get ready for."

"Cock tease."

Apparently, explosive make-up sex was the cure for the common hangover, because by the time we shared a shower, I felt almost human again. While Daniel began his painstaking grooming ritual, I toweled off, watching him in the mirror.

"Reassure me about what just happened. That it wasn't only a matter of opportunity."

Daniel turned around and opened his arms to me. I inhaled deep breaths of him, and he said, "I love you. We'll have plenty of time to talk about all this later. For now, just believe that I want us to be together. I've missed you so much."

"Me, too. I love you. I feel like it's *my* wedding day," I said, relief sweeping through me that my stupid behavior of the night before hadn't destroyed a possible reconciliation.

As we silently held each other, I realized how much I'd missed this. Daniel and I could connect in a way that made everything else seem trivial. He had a talent for making me feel like wherever I found myself, as long as I was with him, I was exactly where I was supposed to be. Central Park, the office, either of our apartments, a bar, a museum, a restaurant, the woods at Happy Hollow, even Eau Claire . . . I could remember a thousand places, but they were just the background for him, for *us*. I had missed us.

Maybe a great relationship wasn't about the big moments: the battles, reconciliations, events, sacrifices, celebrations, breathtaking sex. It was in the fragments of time when I caught his scent, felt his smooth skin beneath my chin, or when our fingers melted into each other's muscles. It was how the sound of his laugh, the flash of humor in his eyes, or the way he'd turn his head away for a few seconds when something touched him, resonated inside me, as if we'd merged into one person.

Sometimes when he worked in his garden, I'd hear him unconsciously humming, and I'd wonder, *What put that song in his head?* Then I would realize that the lyrics contained a phrase I'd used in conversation hours before, almost as if he'd continued a dialogue with me in his mind.

I remembered a day that I'd played hooky from Breslin Evans not long after Daniel and I became a couple. I'd had one of those frustrating mornings when it seemed like nothing I did pleased anyone, and I'd fabricated an afternoon appointment away from the office just so I could get out of there. I'd gone to an exhibit—in fact, it had been a retrospective of the work of Lowell Davenport, Gavin's old boss—and consoled myself with the promise that one day, my name would be as well known in the advertising world as his.

I was leaving the gallery when I spotted Daniel across the street. He didn't see me, and I followed him for several blocks, my stealth providing a guilty pleasure. He stopped in Washington Square Park, and I sneaked up behind him, intending to surprise him. When I was a couple of feet away, he whipped around so quickly that I stepped back.

"Did you think I wouldn't feel you?" he asked.

It was the first time I'd ever lost my inhibition about showing him affection in public, surrendering myself to a prolonged embrace just like the one we were sharing now. I loved him so much it left me dazed.

After a while, he moved away, turned back to the mirror, and brought me back to reality when he said, "Is make-up sex better than it used to be? Or have you learned a few new things?"

I met his eyes in the mirror, swallowed, and said, "Do you want details?"

"Nope. Did you play safe?"

"Of course. You?" I asked.

"I didn't play." He shook his head when he saw the guilt on my face and said, "Come here." I walked to him, and he put his arms around me again. I rested my forehead against his bare shoulder. "You don't need to give me explanations, okay? If I were you, I'd have done the same thing. I just knew from experience that it wouldn't be what I wanted. More like a temporary fix, since what I really wanted was you. Us."

"Yes," I said.

He pulled back so he could see my face and said, "I owe you an apology, Blaine. I let things get totally out of hand that night when we fought. I felt ambushed and misunderstood, and I wanted to punish you."

"I wish I could take back some of the things I said."

"I wish I could, too. You and I always trusted each other. I expected you to trust me, even though I didn't tell you everything I should have."

"You mean about Blythe and the town house?"

"Right. I didn't want to live in the same place as Martin, and I knew you didn't. What I should have told you was that I'd been looking for another place. One that we could buy together. That didn't have any history. Or Martin. You were already mad at me because of the stuff with Sheila. I wanted to move in with you, and part of me hoped that if I made a big gesture, presenting a new place as a done deal, you'd stop being mad at me. That was wrong."

I grimaced and said, "Daniel, why didn't you tell me that night? As soon as I started in on you about the town house?"

"I was mad. Then we started fighting about other things. It was obvious we had more problems than I'd realized. We still have a lot—"

He broke off when we heard our bedroom door open and Adam's voice saying, "Guys?"

"We're getting ready," I called. I tucked my towel around my waist, then kissed Daniel like we had all the time in the world.

"Daniel, I brought your tux and your luggage up here," Adam said, keeping his voice loud so we'd know he was approaching the bathroom door. We didn't break our embrace, and Adam grinned when he saw us. "You're going to make Sheila a very happy bride. Or am I getting ahead of myself?"

"Everything's going to be fine," Daniel assured him.

Adam's eyes raked my body, and he said, "I love the smell of testosterone in the morning." His gaze rested on my stomach, then he frowned and lifted his T-shirt. "Whose abs are better, mine or Blaine's?"

"Blaine's," Daniel said.

"Liar," Adam and I said simultaneously, and he grinned at me and dropped his T-shirt.

It always amused me when Adam's competitive streak manifested itself. Since he seemed to be in a good mood, I felt bold enough to say, "About last night."

"Not a problem," Adam said. "You're a great kisser."

"He is," Daniel agreed, laughing at the way Adam's words made me wince. "Stop worrying about it."

"Is Jeremy—"

"Jeremy's a great kisser, too," Adam said and winked at me. "He's getting ready. I need to do the same. There are already caterers and security people all over the place. Martin is getting in everyone's way. Daniel, can you rein him in? And you"—he pointed at me—"need to get yourself together. Josh has been asking for his best man."

After he left, I gave Daniel a rueful look and said, "Life beckons."

"It's okay," Daniel said. "Let's get Sheila and Josh married and on their honeymoon. Then you and I can start working on us. Oh, one other thing. About Gretchen."

"What?" I asked nervously.

"I know the two of you have become closer since we broke up. Could you not mention the thing about me buying another place?"

"I won't say anything, but what difference does it make?"

"She resisted the idea. Strongly. Probably because of that election year stuff she was talking about at the rehearsal dinner. She has no idea that I sold it. I ended up taking less than the property is worth so Martin could—"

"You sold Martin the town house? Are you nuts?" I asked. His expression warned me to back off, and I decided to let it drop for the moment. It was just one more thing we'd have to work out. But we *would* work it out, because I wasn't going to let anything spoil our reconciliation. Then another thought occurred to me. "When did you approach Gretchen about selling the town house? Before or after we broke up?"

"After." He caught on. "Oh, I see why you're asking. None of our friends knew anything before we broke up, Blaine. I wouldn't have put them, or you, in that position. Once Gretchen knows all the details, I'm sure she'll be okay with it. Like I said, we have a lot to talk about. We're still the same two people who fought that night. But I promise that I'll be more honest with you. With the intention of working things out, not winning a fight."

I nodded my agreement, relieved that no one knew about the baby. I'd be able to tell Daniel first, as soon as we got the wedding out of the way.

We finished getting dressed, admired each other in our vintage tuxedos, and after another lingering hug, walked to the bedroom door.

"Wait," Daniel said, looking back at the rumpled bed with a wistful expression. "It would have been nice to stay there all day. One of the things I missed most is talking to you in bed."

"Uh-huh," I said, pulling him to me. "The loneliest part for me was that time just before I fell asleep."

"I don't know if I can promise you much sleep tonight," Daniel warned.

"Yeah, we do have a lot to *talk* about," I said, giving him my best dumb look.

"That, too," he said with a grin, giving me another passionate kiss before we went downstairs.

We found Adam's mother in the kitchen with Jeremy. While she fussed over a bagel for Daniel, I took a deep breath and walked to Jeremy.

"Last night," I began.

Jeremy rested his hands on my shoulders and quietly said, "Thank you so much."

"For what?" I asked, shocked.

"For locking Martin in that closet. You're my new best friend."

"But Jeremy—"

"For God's sake, Blaine, you were drunk. Do you think I'm going to hold that kiss against you? After all, think of the number of times I've kissed *your* boyfriend."

"Do I have to? Wait; who said he's my boyfriend?"

"Funny thing. I woke up this morning not deaf."

"Oh," I said, embarrassed.

He laughed at me and said, "Get something to eat. It's going to be a long day."

"I don't want food," I moaned.

"Hungover?" Aggie asked sympathetically. "I've got just the thing."

She poured me a smoothie from the blender, and I had to admit it was exactly what I needed. I didn't dare ask what was in it.

"Okay, here's the plan," Jeremy said. "We have a hospitality room set up at the hotel, and we're shuttling the guests over in vans. We have three trailers set up behind the tents. One is for the bride and her attendants. I advise you all to stay as far away from it as possible. One is for the groom. That's where you need to go, Blaine."

"What's the third one?" I asked, shuddering as I saw Daniel move on from his bagel to a banana that Aggie handed him.

"There are four hairdressers in it. Anyone in the wedding party, or any of the guests, can go there if they want to get more forties-looking hairstyles."

"What a great idea," I commented.

"Thanks. It was mine," Jeremy said.

Aggie added, "Cater waiters are mingling with trays of juices and coffee, and there's a bar set up if anyone wants mimosas, bellinis, or Bloody Marys."

"Except you," Daniel and Jeremy said to me in unison. They laughed as I dropped my head.

"If you see anything suspicious," Jeremy went on, "all the security guys look like Secret Service agents. In other words, their suits are modern and navy and they're wearing the standard sunglasses. Any person who acts like a reporter or who has a camera should be wearing passes like this." He held one up. "I doubt that anyone can get through Adam's security, but you never know."

"Seems like overkill to me," Aggie said.

"There will be several celebrities here, Aggie," Jeremy said. "Not to mention a few closet cases. Sheila and Josh want their guests to feel at ease, and nobody wants to see pictures of the bride on tabloid covers."

"Is the briefing over?" I asked. "You're starting to scare me. It's like the beginning of *The Godfather.*"

Jeremy and Daniel exchanged a look and, again in unison, croaked their Marlon Brando impressions: *What have I ever done to make you treat me so disrespectfully?*

"Freaking actors," I muttered and heard them laughing as I stepped out the back door. I nearly tripped over Blythe, who was sitting cross-legged on the deck, drawing furiously in a sketch book. "What are you doing?"

She shifted so I could see that she was sketching a group of people standing about twenty yards from us. I sat down on the top step, marveling that for once, her brown hair was stripped of its magenta streaks and combed down into something resembling a bob, which I guessed was about as forties as she could get.

"It's a wedding gift that Adam and I are working on," she explained, flipping through a few pages so I could see some other sketches.

"It looks like a storyboard."

"Exactly," she said. "We're doing a Web site that makes it seem like this whole event was a movie. Look out there. Doesn't it look like a set from sixty years ago?"

She was right. I could see members of the orchestra in white dinner jackets heading for the reception tent. The guests who'd already arrived were dressed, as requested, in forties attire. I saw more than one World War II uniform and figured the folks from Wisconsin, at least, had been digging in their attics. The few cars that were allowed onto the property were leases from a company that specialized in vintage cars. It really did look like the first *Godfather* movie.

"It's kind of amazing, isn't it?" I asked.

"It's wonderful. Sheila is so smart. Being in costume equalizes everyone. The celebrities are indistinguishable from her other friends and family. That'll make everyone more comfortable. Now go away. I'm working, and Josh probably needs you."

I tried not to do a double take as I saw Faizah, who looked nothing like a bruise, holding a bellini while she laughed with Tina Fey and Sandra Bernhard. I wished I could hear that conversation, but I resisted the urge and headed for the trailers. I didn't heed Jeremy's warning, however, choosing to go first to Sheila's trailer, where I found her standing in a white silk robe amid a maelstrom of feminine chaos. Her expression was pure panic when she heard the door open, but once she saw me, she relaxed.

"I was afraid you were my mother," she said. "I can't handle any more accidents."

"Blaine Dunhill, you get out of here," Patti ordered.

I returned the disapproving stares I was getting from her and Gretchen and asked, "Why is Faizah the only one dressed?"

"Because I forgot to get something borrowed," Sheila explained, dropping her robe so that I saw her in all her lingeried glory. "We sent her on a mission to find something, and she never came back."

"She's drinking and yakking up your guests," I said. "Probably soliciting votes for Election 2008." I reached in my pocket and pulled out a twenty-dollar bill, tucking it into the top of her white bustier. "I expect to get that back. I love you."

"Thank you," Sheila said, hugging me. "I love you, too."

"Now go away," Gretchen ordered. "You might be used to seeing Sheila half naked, but the rest of us would like a little privacy."

I laughed as I stepped outside the door, remembering Gretchen in stirrups at the behest of "Dr. Gibb."

"Good grief, we do all look like gangsters," I said when I went inside Josh's trailer. "What can I do for you?"

"Do you have the rings?" Josh asked, and I patted my coat pocket with a nod.

"Is my mother being restrained somewhere?" Jake asked. "She's giving Sheila fits."

"Everything's under control," I promised.

"Why? Did you find another closet for Martin?" Jake asked.

"I'm sorry about last night," I said. "Josh, what the hell are you doing to that tie?"

"I don't know. I hate it," Josh answered, ripping it off in frustration and hurling it across the trailer.

I retrieved it and put it around his neck, trying not to laugh at the wild look in his eyes. "Be still. Let me do it. Has anyone given you the facts-of-life talk?"

"Jo, Blair, Tootie, and Natalie are the only people who haven't tried to traipse through here," Josh muttered.

"But I might have seen Mrs. Garrett with George Clooney at the bar," Jake said.

"Then they're crashing. Call security," Josh answered. "Ow, that's too tight!"

"Much like Blaine was last night," Jake said.

"I can't tell you how gratifying it is that I've given you all a moment to celebrate over your General Foods Suisse Mocha in years to come."

"He never forgets a product," Daniel said as he joined us.

"But did you remember the rings?" Josh asked, panic returning to his eyes.

Jake turned away to hide his smile when I said, "They're right here in my pocket. Do you want to see them?"

"No, I trust you," Josh said. "Daniel looks better than I do."

"Daniel looks better than everybody does," I said. "It's in his contract."

"What can I say; I've got a good agent. Who tied that tie?" Daniel asked, frowning at Josh.

"Why? What's wrong with it?" Josh groaned.

"It's perfect," Daniel said. I raised my hand, and he nodded knowingly. "You were always good at tying—"

"I don't wanna know," Jake begged.

"—ties," Daniel finished. "Have you ever noticed that heterosexuals think of nothing but sex?"

"It's how I stay in business," I said. "Now about tonight, Josh."

"I just want to get through this wedding," Josh said. "Have you—"

"I've got the rings. Everything is fine."

And it was. I was dazzled by the inside of the tent when I stood looking out from the altar. It had a gardenlike quality, the greenery twinkling with subtle white lights that duplicated the candles flickering on the altar. I leaned across Jake to say to Daniel, "This has sure changed since the rehearsal. It's fantastic. You designed all this?"

"Yes," Daniel said.

"Okay, let me fix this," Jake said. He stepped back and moved Daniel next to me, then stood where Daniel had been.

"No," Daniel said. "You're Sheila's brother. She wants you behind the best man."

"If Sheila still has the capacity to notice anything, she'll be thrilled to see the two of you standing side by side," Jake argued. "Plus this means you'll be escorting Gretchen back down the aisle, Daniel, which seems right. Haven't you two been friends forever? And I'll escort Patti, to try to redeem myself."

"Redeem yourself?" Daniel asked.

"Christmas pageant. Fifth grade," I said.

"Patti was only in the second grade," Jake said. "I was supposed to walk her off the stage. I tripped and pulled her down with me. Knocked out both of her front teeth."

"Ouch," Daniel said.

"They were just baby teeth," Jake defended himself.

Daniel's shoulder pressed against mine as we both looked out at the guests. I saw his sisters sitting in a row next to his parents and smiled at them. Mary Kate wasn't looking. Gwendy pretended not to see me. And Lydia waved frantically.

"Your sisters look so pretty," I said.

"Promise me you'll dance with Lydia. She's been bitching at me about you for seven months. Tell her I'm not a monster."

Grandparents were escorted to their seats while the woodwind quintet—friends of Nora Meyers—played. As I scanned the guests, I let out a little grunt of dismay.

"You don't have them, do you?" Josh spoke the first words I'd heard out of him since we gathered on the altar.

"Josh, I swear I have the rings," I said. I turned my head toward Daniel and said, "Two o'clock. Sixth row. The couple that looks like they have pokers up their asses? My parents."

I didn't know why I was surprised to see them. Not only had my father and William Meyers done business together for years, but our mothers were friends, too. Neither of them was looking at me. They were watching Gretchen walk up the aisle. If they only knew she was carrying their grandchild.

I'd had my doubts about how the bridesmaids would look in different outfits that could have been clashing shades of purple, but somehow it worked. Gretchen had worried needlessly. She not only looked trim, but I was going to get a lot of leverage out of lipstick lesbian jokes. When she took her place across from Daniel, I heard him tell her that she was beautiful. It was the first time I'd ever seen her blush.

Her eyes moved to me and a flicker of understanding passed between us. Sydney could do her worst with her hateful tongue. Whatever rituals the straight world denied us, not only did we have bonds of friendship most of them would never understand, but Gretchen and I shared something no one could take away from us. The tension I'd felt since seeing my parents melted. I was standing next to the man I loved, and the mother of my child was smiling at both of us.

There was a stir as Faizah came up the aisle. Even if years of runway work hadn't taught her how to command attention, her height was imposing. As she took her place across from me, she said, "If this was really the forties, Faizah would be in the kitchen wearing an apron."

Josh's nervous guffaw was cut off as we saw Sheila move to the doorway between her parents. We all held our breath as they glided under the ceiling fans with their crystal fixtures, probably expecting the curse of Nora to bring the tent down on us.

"I think I'm going to cry," Daniel said, looking at Sheila.

I had tears in my eyes, too. She had all the glamour of Rita Hayworth and the other pinup girls of a bygone era. Her dress was tightly sleek, making the most of her slender, leggy beauty. Once she had left her parents and joined us at the altar, she hugged each of her bridesmaids, then turned to us. I wasn't sure what she said to Jake, but I heard her whisper to Daniel, "You made up, didn't you?" After he nodded, she turned to me with that dazzling, million-dollar overbite and said, "That's the best wedding present I've gotten."

Then she was Josh's. Vows were repeated, rings were exchanged—I'd never been as happy to get rid of anything—then came the kiss that meant we'd done it. More than a year of planning had finally ended, and it was time to relax. Once the guests had been ushered from the wedding tent to the reception tent, we were brought back in for the pictures, all of us giddy with relief that it was over without any disasters.

Sheila had chosen not to have a receiving line since there were too many guests, so I mingled, making contact with editors from various fashion magazines I'd worked with on ad campaigns. Wherever we were, Daniel and I occasionally caught each other's eyes before we moved on. As night fell, I stored away mental snapshots to talk about with him later. Josh and Sheila dancing. People laughing appreciatively at my toast, although I couldn't remember a word I'd said. Blythe and Kate Hudson giggling hysterically about something. Models watching enviously as people stuffed themselves in that good old Midwestern way. Sheila laughingly switching partners with Rebecca Stamos, since people often confused the two supermodels. Gretchen and Gwendy Stephenson engaging in a deep discussion which I suspected was political and steered clear of.

My favorite moment came when I was standing next to a table of hors d'oeuvres. I'd just been listening to Frank and Lillith comment on the unusual assortment of friends Sheila and Josh had made over the years while I watched Mr. T pluck something from a silver platter.

"I pity the fool," Faizah said, sweeping down on him, "who takes Faizah's last mushroom cap."

He handed it over and she popped it in her mouth with an ecstatic expression. I was still laughing when Lydia Stephenson appeared before me.

"I was told you were going to dance with me," Daniel's youngest sister said.

"I'd love to." We moved onto the dance floor while the orchestra played "Sentimental Journey."

"This is the best wedding I've ever been to," Lydia said. "Is it always like this with the rich and—oh, my god, I love Garbage."

"Good. You can help clean up later," I said.

"No, silly. That's Shirley Manson over there! She sings with the band Garbage."

"Oh," I said, chastened.

As we drifted close to an opening in the tent, I heard her say, "Now!"

An arm reached in and pulled me outside. Daniel embraced me and continued the dance Lydia had started.

"So sneaky," I said with admiration.

"It's private, and the song is perfect. You are my sentimental journey home. I love you, Blaine."

"I love you, too, Daniel."

We stayed together through two more slow songs, then he sighed and said, "I guess we have to go our separate ways again."

"Only for a little while," I reminded him, but neither of us let go for a long time. Finally we kissed, and I stepped inside the tent. I saw Sheila and Lydia standing together, so I walked to them.

"Josh and I are about to change," Sheila said. "May I have one last dance with our best man?"

We were quiet while we danced, until I finally said, "I can't believe you're the little girl I used to torment."

"Don't make me cry again," she begged. "Thank you so much for everything you did to help Josh and me pull this together. I'm so happy, Blaine."

"Good. Now give me back my twenty." She threw her head back with a laugh and discreetly dug it out. After I put it in my pocket, I led her to Josh and asked if they needed any help. They assured me they'd gotten quite adept at getting each other in and out of clothes, and I watched as they left the tent without drawing undue attention to themselves.

"So help me, if you start crying, you're going to see my hormones go into overdrive," Gretchen warned from beside me. "I'd kill for a drink."

"Feeling emotional, are you?" I asked.

"It's this dress. I think it's haunted."

"After Sheila and Josh leave, the vans will continue to shuttle people out of here. Our little group will hang around, of course. If you need me to send someone to the hotel for a change of clothes—"

"No, I have what I came in. I'll change after the happy couple is gone."

It was a small group that settled around a few tables later while the cleaning crew came in and went to work under the unnecessary but determined supervision of Aggie Wilson and Joyce Stephenson.

Even after Adam reminded us that we'd probably be more comfortable in his house, nobody moved. Like me, most of the guys had shucked their coats and ties. Adam and Jake flanked me at our table; Louis Stephenson and Hank Wilson were a few chairs down. I'd lost track of Daniel and Jeremy.

Martin stayed as far away from me as possible, which I appreciated. He sat next to Lillith at a table with Josh's and Sheila's parents. I shuddered to think what he might be saying, since now and then a burst of laughter came from their group. Once Gwendy sat down with them, I stopped worrying. She was a practical woman who would know how to stifle Martin should the need arise.

Aunt Jen went to the bride's trailer with Blythe, Patti, and Gretchen so they could change into jeans and she could "make use of the facilities," as she put it, having shunned the portable toilets. No one had seen Faizah for a while.

Frank retrieved Rowdy from Adam's house and sat across from me, sharing fishing stories with Louis and Hank. Lydia sank to the ground to pet Rowdy. Watching everyone's parents reminded me that I hadn't seen mine at the reception. They'd probably left right after the wedding. No doubt my mother had experienced one of her fainting spells.

When the women returned, they had Faizah and Mr. T in tow. He seemed to be getting a big kick out of Aunt Jen, who was wildly waving her trademark cigarette holder as she told him a story. Gretchen sat down next to Frank, but everyone else stood next to our table as Daniel and Jeremy wheeled up a cart with champagne. Jeremy poured, and Daniel distributed glasses among us. He handed me one with a stern look, which I ignored. I wasn't going to drink more than the obligatory sip if toasts were made. Which seemed likely, since everyone got quiet as if waiting for someone to say something.

When Daniel set a glass in front of Gretchen, Aunt Jen said, "Don't you have anything nonalcoholic, Daniel? She shouldn't be drinking."

Daniel looked at his aunt and said, "Why not? Gretchen loves champagne."

"When is your baby due, dear?" Aunt Jen asked Gretchen.

Even the cleanup crew seemed to be locked in silence as Gretchen looked at Jen and said calmly, "December fourteenth."

At our table, no one moved except Adam and Jeremy, who swung shocked faces my way. Their movement caught Daniel's bewildered eye, and he turned to look at me, too.

"Uh-oh," Mr. T said. Our group suddenly got smaller as several people followed in his wake when he made a quick exit.

"You actually took my advice?" I heard Lillith ask. Apparently she was able to count backwards from December faster than anyone else. "I told you March favored your houses of conception."

Blythe slid to the ground next to Lydia. Both of them seemed to be trying to make themselves invisible. Gwendy said, "Gretchen, my car is parked on the road. If you need a ride, I can drive you back to the Hampton Inn."

"Nobody move," Daniel said, his gaze still locked with mine. "Blaine?"

"Yes," I said, making it a statement, not a question.

He stared at me a few seconds more, then looked at Gretchen, who resolutely met his eyes. He shook his head, turned around, and walked out of the tent.

Martin moved as if to follow him, but Jeremy quickly caught his arm and said, "Not this time," then looked at me and said, "Go. Now."

I found Daniel in our bedroom. He was furiously throwing things in his suitcase and ignored me when I walked in.

"Stop," I said. "Don't do this."

"I can't talk to you right now," Daniel said, retrieving his shaving kit from the bathroom. "I realize that you have the upper hand. You have information. I don't. You have transportation. I don't. Since you apparently don't fucking know me at all, take my advice. Leave me alone. I'll talk to you when I'm ready."

"Daniel—"

"No, Blaine!"

Louis and Joyce Stephenson came through the open door of our bedroom. Louis made a hand gesture that seemed to be a sympathetic warning, then he picked up Daniel's suitcase.

"Come on, honey, our car is here," Joyce said. Daniel strode out of the bedroom without another word or look for me, and Louis followed him. Joyce paused a moment to softly say, "Don't force it, Blaine. Give him some time."

When I was alone, I sat on the bed and absently twisted the tangled sheets with one hand. It seemed ridiculous that just a few hours before, Daniel and I had made love in this bed, and now he'd left without giving me a chance to say anything.

"Not pretty, huh?" Gretchen asked from the doorway.

"Not anything," I said. "Being Daniel, he wouldn't discuss it."

"Are you surprised?"

"Only because we came so close to making up," I said. I shrugged. "At least we had a few good hours."

"I don't know how Daniel's aunt figured it out," Gretchen said. "Maybe when I was changing clothes in the trailer, she could tell. I didn't want Daniel to find out this way. I had it all planned. I was going to talk to you both together and explain everything."

"Explain what?"

"How I meant for the baby to make things better. You and I would have the child we want, but Daniel wouldn't feel like it was a burden to the two of you or your life together."

"Come here, please." She sat next to me on the bed. "I'm sorry, too. I'm sorry that Daniel couldn't get a piece of news without over-reacting and making it all about him. I'm sorry that we weren't able to share good news in our own way. But I'm not sorry that everyone knows. I'm definitely not sorry about the baby. This has been the most surreal week. I feel like I finally had the guts to be me. I dealt with Sydney. I didn't try to smooth things over with my parents today. I let myself be just as annoyed and obnoxious with Martin as I wanted to be. I celebrated a great moment in the lives of two people I love. And I apologized to Daniel about the past and let him know how much I love him."

"And you met Mr. T."

"Yeah, I was getting to that," I said and put my arm around her. "The most real moment I had was looking at you today and feeling in my heart that we've done this incredible thing. I know any two idiots can make a baby. But in our case, there are millions of idiots who think we shouldn't. And I don't care. Protecting C.L. from that kind of crap is my top priority now."

"Calling her by her initials won't make her a boy," Gretchen said, and her arm slid around my waist. "Thank you for telling me that. Dammit. I'm getting hormonal again."

"Do you want me to drive you back to the hotel?"

"No. I have a ride. If it's any comfort, Martin left with Adam's parents. I think most everyone else is gone, too. Are you sure you're okay? I can stay."

"No. I'm fine. How are your ankles, by the way?"

"Large."

I walked her downstairs and smiled at Gwendy, who wrinkled her nose at me, which I figured was her way of saying, *You fucked up, but I still think you're okay.*

It seemed like the house was empty, so I decided to go back to the tent and see if Adam needed any help. But when I walked around back, I found Frank standing alone on the lawn, staring into the darkness toward the trees between Adam's house and the stream that ran through his property.

"Hi," I said. "I figured you were gone."

"I thought I'd stick around awhile," he said.

"Where's Rowdy?"

"When I let him off his lead, he took off for those trees. I think he's hunting."

I laughed and said, "Maybe he's treed Lola Listeria."

"He's a retriever, not a raccoon hound," Frank said. We stood for a while in silence, then he cleared his throat. "I'm assuming from what happened earlier that you and Gretchen are with child?"

"Yes, sir," I said, a little leery of where this was going. There was no telling what Aunt Jen had said about me after I followed Daniel from the tent.

"It's a good thing, being a father," Frank said. "In spite of my business success, it's Seth I'm proudest of. You do the best you can, not really knowing what the hell you're doing, and sometimes it seems like everything turns out okay in spite of you. I've known you for what, five years now?"

"That sounds right."

He lit a cigar, and I could tell he was buying time. Finally he said, "You've changed a lot over those years. I feel like I helped you grow up. Hell, what I'm trying to say, Blaine, is that you're like a son to me. I think you'll be a good father. If there's ever anything I can do to help you out, just tell me."

When I turned to look at him, he hugged me the way I'd always wished my father would. He didn't pull away until Rowdy loped up and nudged his way between us.

"Thank you, Frank. You know, if it's okay with you, I think I'd like to use your place at Lake Geneva after all. A week to myself sounds good."

"You got it," Frank said. "Stop by the hotel tomorrow, and I'll give you the key and the directions."

After he and Rowdy left, I went upstairs. Like Gretchen, I felt like I was on hormone overload. I undressed, turned off the lights, and crawled into sheets that still smelled like Daniel. I heard Adam and Jeremy when they came upstairs and hesitated outside my door, then walked on to their bedroom.

I thought about Sheila and Josh and how glad I was that they'd left before the Plumpies hit the fan. I thought about how different my reaction to Daniel was from what I would have expected. A few months before, I'd have vacillated between being furious and devastated. Instead, I felt fatalistic. Either he would learn to live with it, or he wouldn't. If he wanted to be angry with Gretchen and me, he'd be cheating all of us, but that was his decision to make.

I didn't think about work, other than the gratitude I felt toward Frank. Because what I really thought about was fathers and sons. I didn't know how the hell I would raise a daughter, but I knew how I would not raise a son. I would not be my father.

Sometime near dawn, I knew what I had to do. I slept a couple of hours, then got up, showered, packed, and slipped out of the house without disturbing Adam or Jeremy, intending to send them an e-mail later to explain things. I drove my rental car to my brother Shane's house, determined to be there before he and Beverly could start their usual busy, dysfunctional days.

Beverly gave me a weird look when she opened the door, saying, "What's wrong? Is your mother sick again?"

"I don't know. I want to talk to you and Shane."

"His tee time is at—"

"Now," I said firmly.

Her eyes widened, but she left me at the kitchen table to go upstairs and get him. When he came back with her, he looked less than happy to see me. I waited until they both filled their cups and sat down.

"I know you don't want to hear this, but I have a few things to say. You'll make your golf date," I assured my brother. "Beverly, Shane probably told you what I shared with him while our mother was in surgery. I'm gay. I've been gay as long as I can remember. Nobody made me that way. I didn't ask for it. Nobody came to me when I was nine or twelve or fifteen and gave me a choice. I did my best to fight it until I was twenty-five. I tried to do things your way. I got married with the intention of starting a family and living the life our parents wanted me to live. I couldn't do it, because it was a lie. Maybe other people can live a lie, but I couldn't. I know the crap you believe, because I heard it all my life. I don't care. What your Bible, your minister, your friends, or your parents say. It would have been great to have a family who could acknowledge it, let alone accept or embrace it, but it didn't work out that way for me. I can't say I don't care about that, because deep inside, I do. I always will, but that's just something I have to live with. I can't change you; you can't change me."

Beverly stood up and walked to the kitchen sink, staring out the window. Shane looked at his coffee cup with a sullen expression and said, "Is that it?"

"I just want to be clear about this. There was a time, if I *had* been given a choice, that I would have chosen not to be gay. Not anymore. I'm fine with who I am. But again, I had no choice. That's it. Have a good day on the links. I'll see myself out, Beverly."

I drove to the Hampton Inn and got the key and directions to the cabin from Frank. Then I wrote a letter and slid it under Gretchen's door, knowing she would understand my need to be alone. Once I was on the highway, I allowed myself to breathe. I had no idea if what I'd done would ever be of any help to Nick, but hopefully I'd given his parents something to think about against the day he might tell them what I'd never been able to tell mine.

I stocked up on groceries before finding Frank's cabin, which I was relieved to discover wasn't the primitive place I'd expected. It was a comfortable little cottage with every amenity, including a computer with a cable modem. I should have known that a businessman like Frank would never strand himself without access to his company.

I made myself something to eat, then plugged in my laptop. First I composed an e-mail to Adam, explaining where I was and thanking him and Jeremy for letting me stay there. Then I began dealing with

Lillith Allure e-mails as I read them in order. After about forty of them, I got a surprise when I hit "Next" and found one from my nephew.

> *Uncle Blaine,*
>
> *I heard you talking to my parents this morning. Way to go!*
>
> *Love,*
> *Nick*

I rubbed my eyes, then kept my hands over my face. Had I actually thought that Nick needed me to save him? It was starting to be obvious who was rescuing whom from the lonely silence imposed by the Apple Dunhill Gang, as Jake always called us.

I sent my nephew a simple reply to thank him and tell him I loved him, then I did the most shocking thing I could think of. I powered off my laptop and returned it to its case.

Six days. Without e-mails, phone calls, or news. I didn't want to deal with anything else at the office. No one was indispensable, and I needed a vacation. Frank knew where I was. If there was really such a thing as a crisis that couldn't be managed without me, he'd know how to reach me. If Gretchen needed me, she'd know to call Frank, because I'd told her in my note that I was using his cabin.

I didn't want to read a newspaper, including Lola Listeria's damage control on why her dire predictions about Sheila's wedding had not come to pass. I didn't want to talk to my friends about everything that had happened in Eau Claire, either before or after the wedding. I was going to have six days disconnected from the world if it killed me.

Not that I wouldn't work. I thrived on work. But with silence, punctuated by hiking and swimming, I could go back to New York with the full Gods of Mythology campaign mapped out.

I called the airline and changed my point and time of departure. By flying out of Chicago on Saturday night, I'd be able to walk into a quiet apartment without fanfare, rest and catch up on e-mail on Sunday, and be ready for the corporate world on Monday. Meanwhile, I had six relaxing, Blaine-only days ahead of me.

CHAPTER 12

I had a spring in my step as I climbed the five floors to my apartment at one in the morning. Shutting out the world had been the best gift I'd ever given myself, and I couldn't wait to crawl into my own bed, wake up to Gavin's breakfast, and find out what the pesky Dexter had been up to in my absence. I managed to get into my apartment without making a sound because I didn't want to wake Gavin.

I needn't have worried. No one noticed me, and I silently shut the door and tried to figure out the meaning of the tableau spread before me. Every light in my apartment was on, the television was blaring, and Dexter was nowhere to be seen. I assumed that was because Rowdy was snoozing as if oblivious to the chaos around him.

Violet and Gavin were sitting on floor pillows at the coffee table, which was littered with Chinese takeout containers. They were deep in conversation with Frank and Lillith Allure's attorney, Ryan Sloane. Barbara, Lillith's assistant, was lightly snoring from the end of the sofa. Lillith herself was ensconced in my armchair, with one of her many advisors at her feet. He was using one corner of the table to cast what I assumed were rune stones. For all I knew, they were I Ching stones, since it was apparently Asian night at Blaine Manor.

"As long as *Secret Splendor* isn't issuing an outright denial, people are going to assume the story is true," Gavin was saying.

"Employers aren't obligated to make public statements about their employees' private lives," Ryan said.

"Including our company," Frank added. "Even if they eventually print Blaine's name, it will be up to him how he responds to it."

"Peorth," Rune Reader intoned. "Signifies something unresolved in one's life."

"But whose life?" Lillith asked. "And which lifetime are we reading? I'm so tired."

"Daniel's a celebrity. The show can't keep dodging the question. Or at least Daniel can't. It will come up in any interview he does in the future. They'll keep asking until he either confirms or denies it," Gavin said.

"That's Daniel's problem," Violet said. "I'm only worried about Blaine. *Please* give me his phone number at the cabin. He isn't answering his cell phone or returning my messages."

"None of this has anything to do with Lillith Allure," Ryan repeated. "So what if Lola names Blaine in a future column? He doesn't owe anyone an explanation."

"Backlash," Gavin said. "Gay people are consumers, too. We boycott companies that piss us off. If everyone issues denials about something that's obviously true, there could be a boycott of *Secret Splendor*'s sponsors. And Lillith Allure's products."

"Ice counsels caution. The best action is no action," Rune Reader chimed in.

"How many gay men buy Zodiac?" Ryan scoffed.

"The men's line," Lillith moaned. "What if they don't buy our new men's products? Assuming Blaine isn't too distracted to create an ad campaign for them."

"I know he'd want to hear it from me first," Violet insisted. "Instead of seeing it in the paper."

"Would anyone like to tell me what's going on here?" I asked.

Rowdy sat up with a quiet *woof;* Barbara continued to doze. Five pairs of stunned eyes turned to look at me as the television reminded us that we had only hours to take advantage of a limited offer, and Rune Reader said, "Eolh reversed. Danger with a negative outcome."

"Blaine!" Violet exclaimed. "We were just—"

"Talking about me? I heard. What's this about?"

Since they'd been talking over each other before they knew I was there, I expected them to all speak at once, but I only got stares. And another soft snore from Barbara.

"Just give him the paper," Lillith said, finally breaking the silence, and Violet, as she had so many times in the past, handed me the *Manhattan Star-Gazette,* folded open to Lola Listeria's "Lo-Down" column. I scanned the text, but I didn't see anything pertaining to Sheila or Daniel.

"The pictures," Violet said.

"Ah," I said, my eyes traveling to the row of grainy black-and-white photos to the right of the column. My first reaction was surprise that, in a picture of the bride and groom dancing, Sheila looked less than stunning. Her mouth was hanging open and her eyes were glazed. Apparently Lola had lost her infatuation with Sheila. The caption read, "Sheila Meyers an exhausted bride in her nuptial dance with groom Josh Clinton."

The second photo showed Mr. T handing over his mushroom cap to Faizah, but when I dropped my eyes to read that caption, I zeroed in on the next picture. Daniel holding me—although my back was to the camera—in our dance outside the tent. That picture, and the three that came after it—one in which the two of us were in profile, still dancing; one in which Daniel was kissing me; one in which we were pulling away, but still staring into each other's eyes—were all untitled. The final picture, which must have been taken just before we turned to walk back inside the tent, clearly showed our faces, and beneath it was printed, "Lola now understands that she was 'steered'— get it?—in the wrong direction regarding Daniel and Sheila. The portrayer of *Secret Splendor*'s Angus obviously grazes on the other side of the fence."

Rowdy let out a soft whine and lay back down on the floor with a heavy sigh, and I said, "I know how you feel, buddy." I looked up to see them all still staring at me, even Rune Reader and the newly awakened Barbara, and I felt the first stirring of my famous Dunhill temper. I looked at Gavin and asked, "Has Daniel called?" When he shook his head, I looked at Violet.

"He hasn't called the office either. Have you been checking the messages on your cell phone?"

"No," I said.

"He may have left one there. Although your voice mail is jammed with my messages."

I crossed the room to look down at Daniel's apartment. Tiny

white lights twinkled around his plants, but his apartment was dark. So he was in the city, but either out or asleep.

"Violet did beg for your number at the cabin," Frank said. "It was my decision not to bother you. I thought you deserved your vacation."

I turned around and said, "It was a working vacation. Lillith, don't worry. I have an advertising strategy for the men's line. I'll present it to you and Frank on Monday." I looked at Violet and said, "I'm sorry if I've caused you anxiety. I know you'd do anything to take care of me, but you can see that I'm fine. Just tired."

"I'd like to strangle that redheaded bitch, Lola Listeria," Violet said.

"Karma," Lillith warned her.

"Erase, erase," Rune Reader said, looking heavenward.

"We should leave and let you get some rest," Frank said as he stood up.

Gavin, Violet, and Barbara began clearing the table while Rune Reader packed his stones and Ryan helped Lillith retrieve her belongings. I continued to lean against the windowsill, and Frank crossed the room to me after turning off the television.

"I didn't loan you the cabin so you could do nothing but work," he scolded.

"Trust me, working on the men's line without distractions was exactly what I needed. I felt great at the cabin," I assured him, taking the key from my pocket and handing it to him.

"Then you came back to this," he said, glancing around.

"Has the story been picked up? With any more details?"

"A few of the entertainment shows seem interested. So far, there have just been generic 'no comment' statements from unnamed sources connected to *Secret Splendor.*"

"I wonder how Lola got the pictures? I thought Adam's security people thoroughly screened the press."

"They aren't professional shots," Frank said. "Apparently someone sneaked a camera in."

"Trust Lola Listeria to find that person. Or maybe she set it up."

"Gavin told us earlier that *listeria* is a food bacteria also found in sewage," Lillith said, joining us at the window.

"How appropriate is that?" I asked.

I was grateful when they were all gone. I left Gavin cleaning the kitchen and shut my bedroom door behind me. Dexter was asleep on my pillow, which he knew was forbidden, but I ignored him and took my cell phone from one of my bags.

There were no calls before Wednesday, but Violet was right. My voice mail was full. After hearing the third message from her asking me to call about an urgent matter, I began deleting hers, but listened to the others.

"Hi, sweetie," Gretchen said in a message from the night before. "You might want to get your hands on a copy of the *Star-Gazette* before you come back to the city. Civil Liberty and I are fine. We took a vacation, too. Call me when you get back."

"Blaine, it's Ethan. Your assistant tells me you're out of town. Give me a call when you get back."

"Hi, Uncle Blaine. Hey, was the wedding you told me about the one with that actor from here who's on a soap? I think something happened to him, but I don't know what. I'll e-mail you if I find out." So as of last night, apparently, my picture wasn't in the Midwestern papers. Or else Nick hadn't seen it.

The last few messages were from Violet and had filled my mailbox. If Daniel had tried to call, he wouldn't have been able to leave a message. I dialed into my voice mail at work, but it was empty, so I assumed Violet had handled everything there.

I sat on the edge of the bed, too tired to think but unable to stop, and the only thing on my mind was Daniel. What a miserable few days he must have had. First finding out about the baby, then this spiteful act by a scandal-hungry woman who didn't have the grace to admit she was wrong. She'd used her little bit of power to strike out at him. If he hadn't stubbornly, stupidly walked out on me, I'd be doing whatever I could to help him through it. Although I knew that was his choice, I couldn't help but feel guilty.

Even after I put Dexter out of my bedroom and went to bed, I lay awake thinking in circles. Everyone who knew Daniel would tell me that my best option was to wait for him to come to me. I fought my impulse to get dressed, go to his apartment, and force him to see me.

It was a relief to open my eyes the next morning and realize that

I'd slept. I took a shower and unpacked before I went to the kitchen, where Gavin was waiting with a cup of coffee.

"Did you sleep at all?" he asked, looking at my bloodshot eyes.

"Not much." I took the coffee and walked to the window. No sign of life at Daniel's.

After I ate breakfast, I called Gretchen, forestalling any discussion with a terse request that she let me come over. She agreed and within the hour was ushering me into her loft.

"You look like hell. You saw the paper, I assume?"

"Yes, after I got home last night." I told her about my welcoming committee, and she shook her head.

"Daniel hasn't decided what he wants to do yet," she said. I appreciated her ability to know what was uppermost on my mind. "The network wants him to do nothing. Bonnie and the Seaforth Chemical people are leaving it up to him. But everyone's giving him advice, and it's making him crazy. You know Daniel. He's reeling and needs time to process."

"At least he's talking to you," I said.

"Yes," she said and gave me a sympathetic smile. "Don't look so worried. He's okay, and I'm sure he'll get in touch with you soon. He probably thinks you're still out of town."

"He knew?"

"I told him. I'd better tell you everything from the beginning."

"Okay," I said, sitting down.

"I didn't come home from Eau Claire right away. Once I got your note, I decided I could use a few days off, too. Gwendy knew I was still there, so on Tuesday night she asked me to have dinner with Daniel and her. I don't know how she talked him into it, but I thought it was a good idea. After I explained everything to him, he was mostly concerned for my health. Things were friendly enough between us that we agreed to fly back to New York together on Thursday. Which we did, with neither of us knowing what had been printed in Wednesday's 'Lo-Down' column. One of my friends told me about it. I was finally able to talk to him Friday, and that's how I know what little I know. I'm sure he was probably ready to talk to you about the baby, but of course, all this has pushed that to the background. He's got a lot of decisions to make."

"I feel like I should be helping him."

"Let him come to you," she said.

"I knew you'd say that. Can you believe Lola Listeria, though? Okay, enough about that. How are you feeling?"

"I'm great," she said. "So is Civil Liberty. My amnio's been scheduled. I know you wanted to be at all the ultrasounds, but do you want to be there for this procedure, too?"

"Of course," I said. "You told them we don't want to know the sex, right?"

"Yes. We won't have the results for about three weeks after the procedure, but they agreed to keep that out of the report. Of course, all my friends think I'm crazy. Now that the news is out, prepare yourself. Everyone, and I mean everyone, is an expert on pregnancy, childbirth, and childcare. But amazingly, none of these experts agree. Tell me again, why did we want to tell people we're pregnant?"

"Baby gifts," I said. "For years, I've had to shell out money for wedding presents, anniversary presents, congratulations on your divorce presents, and baby presents. I'm expecting a big payoff."

"I never realized you were so greedy. Would you really use our innocent child to—"

"Where have you registered so far?" I cut her off.

"I've done it all online. Wait'll you see all the cool stuff we're asking for."

I managed not to think of Daniel more than a dozen times an hour over the next few days. Lillith and Frank reacted favorably to my Gods of Mythology men's line pitch. The entire advertising staff was inundated with samples so we could work with Lillith's metaphysical and marketing experts to match myth to product. Gavin said I came home every night smelling like a whorehouse, although I wasn't sure how he came by his knowledge of such places.

Adam called to apologize for the breach of security at the wedding. We agreed it was pointless to speculate on Lola's infiltration method. We also agreed that Sheila was going to be livid over the photo of her chosen for "The Lo-Down." Neither of us had heard from Daniel, nor had Jeremy. But Adam said so far, there'd only been one small reference in the local newspaper to Daniel, as more of a footnote to ongoing stories about Sheila's splashy wedding in the society section. He assured me that hometown coverage of Sheila would be much more to her liking. The photos were fantastic and she was regarded as Eau Claire royalty.

I had an e-mail from Nick that explained how he'd come by his information about Daniel. Although the Eau Claire paper wasn't running the story, apparently whatever chat rooms Nick visited online were full of people who'd seen the pictures or heard the story and were speculating about whether or not Daniel was gay and would come out. It was clear that my nephew hadn't heard any rumors about the man with Daniel in the pictures, and I wasn't sure if there was any reason to tell him it was me.

The night before Sheila and Josh were expected home, I met Ethan for dinner at their favorite restaurant, Julian's, to get myself into a Sheila frame of mind. Ethan greeted me with an enthusiastic hug, made small talk until our orders were taken, then sat back.

"So," he said. "I saw the pictures. You and Daniel are back together?"

"Oh, no," I said. I caught him up on everything, monopolizing the conversation while he ate in silence. I took special pleasure in skewering Martin for his bachelor party antics, since Ethan and Martin were friends. I finally finished with, "The irony of it is, Daniel was okay with the idea that I'd had sex with other guys. I didn't have sex with Gretchen, but he freaked out over our news."

"Hmmm," Ethan said. When I waited for more, he went on. "He'd probably prepared himself for other men. But the baby thing—you have to admit, that's not something a man hears about his ex-lover every day."

"No," I admitted reluctantly.

"And he didn't find out under optimal circumstances. Maybe if you and Gretchen had been able to prepare him for it—"

"Whose side are you on?"

"Besides, if Gretchen's right, he was already starting to deal with it. Until Lola's bomb exploded. I noticed in subsequent columns, no mention has been made of Daniel or Sheila."

"My assistant told me that, too. I've been avoiding any kind of entertainment news, but according to Violet, in the few gossip columns or shows that have mentioned it, the word from Daniel and company is still 'no comment.' I wish I knew what he planned to do. I keep thinking my name's going to pop up any minute."

"How do you feel about that?" Ethan asked.

"I honestly don't know. Other than the feeling that it's something I can't control, so the best course of action is no action." I frowned, wondering why that sounded familiar, then remembered Lillith's rune stone reader. I expressed surprise that Ethan actually laughed after I told him that story.

"Lillith is quite the character. I know her through Bonnie Seaforth-Wilkes."

"That's right! I'd forgotten that Bonnie's a friend of yours. Have you talked to her about any of this Daniel stuff?"

He shook his head and said, "No. That was one reason I called you. To find out how you and Daniel wanted it handled. I have a certain amount of influence with Bonnie, and if I can be of any help, I will be."

"You could always ask Martin for Daniel's thoughts on the matter, if you don't want to talk to Daniel yourself. As for me, I'm clueless."

"Martin," Ethan said, shaking his head with another smile. "Speaking of characters. Martin always has good intentions. You're too hard on him."

"He's a pain in the ass," I disagreed.

When we stepped outside the restaurant to be assaulted by the sultry July night, Ethan said, "I always swear I won't be in Manhattan at the end of summer. But somehow I never plan things right."

"I'm glad you're here," I said, realizing how much more relaxed I felt after talking things over with him.

We stood on the sidewalk, and I wondered if he, like me, was trying to decide if this was the end of our evening. Then I felt like someone was staring at me, and I spotted a couple of men intently looking our way. I was trying to figure out if I knew them from the gym or something, when one of them softly spoke to the other, and realization dawned on their faces.

"It *is* him," I heard one of them say, and they headed in our direction.

"One of my summer indulgences is that I never take the subway," Ethan said, stepping smoothly between me and the approaching men to open the back door of a cab. I slid in, saying nothing when he gave the driver his address. "You can keep the cab after he drops me off," Ethan told me. "Since the windows were down, I didn't want to risk those guys hearing your address."

"Maybe they were heading for you," I said. "You're the famous author."

"Except for a handful, most writers are faceless," Ethan said.

"Lucky for you," I said, "or Lola's next column might say, *'Brave Indian—get it?—takes back the range, claims Angus's mystery man as spoils of war.'*"

"You're a little too good at that," Ethan said, and we spent our ride coming up with increasingly worse photo captions. He paid the fare when the driver stopped at his building, then said, "You're welcome to come up, of course."

I wasn't ready to go home and brood about Daniel, so I followed him from the cab. I liked his apartment immediately, in spite of its nod to his metaphysical interests. It was sparsely but comfortably furnished with mission pine furniture set off by beautiful Missoni rugs with geometric patterns. The bookcases were full of books, and I scanned the titles while he got us something to drink, wondering how a man with Ethan's spiritual interests could be friends with Martin.

When he returned and noticed that I was staring at a drum hanging on his wall, he said, "All of these drums were given to me by various Native American craftsmen. They're used in Shamanic ceremonies." He lit candles on a little altar between two windows, and I watched the light flicker over various animals carved from stone. "Don't worry. I won't force you to participate in any bizarre rituals."

"I don't remember complaining about any of your bizarre rituals at Happy Hollow," I said and tried to smile at him.

He gave me a measuring look, then said, "Tell me what you're feeling right now."

"I feel like a star," I said. His look of distaste made me shake my head and explain, "I don't mean a celebrity. I mean it literally. A star."

"In what way?"

"Like I'm a hundred light-years away, so everyone can still see me. But I burned out. There's just dark space where I used to be."

"Blaine, that's so sad," he said, the compassion in his eyes making me look away. He took my glass and set it next to his on the table, then put his arms around me. "The Menomini say a falling star leaves a fiery trail, but it doesn't die. Its shadow goes back to the sky and shines again."

"You're making that up to comfort me," I mumbled against his shoulder.

"I am not making it up. But I would like to comfort you." I nodded my assent, and he led me to his bedroom.

We took our time with each other. I appreciated his familiar scent, skin, and hair, but especially the energy that was his alone. It was a mystery that he could both stimulate and calm me, but I savored every minute of it. Later we lay on our sides, facing each other, while I played with a strand of his hair.

"Remember the fox?" he asked.

"At Happy Hollow? Of course," I said.

"I always associate a fox with you now," he said.

I frowned and asked, "Sly? Cunning?"

"No," he answered with a laugh. "Foxes are always sniffing. They have a keen sense of smell and use it to hunt and survive. When you make love, I feel like you're inhaling me. It's not surprising that you ended up using your advertising expertise in fragrances and cosmetics." I blushed, thinking of how I always sniffed Daniel, and felt a pang of remorse that I'd so easily ended up in another man's bed. Ethan smiled and said, "Relax. You're not doing anything wrong. I'm your friend. He's your lover."

"He *was* my lover," I corrected.

"Love is a state of being, not a matter of action," Ethan said.

"I have no idea what that means," I said.

"Neither do I," Ethan admitted. "But for a second, it sounded profound." We laughed, and he left me alone, returning with a towel and our wine.

We talked for hours, especially about our families, as I knew from the things Ethan had told Gretchen and me at Happy Hollow that his estrangement from his family was similar to mine. He was touched to hear more about how Jeremy had been helping my nephew navigate his way through the realization that he was gay.

"Jeremy's a good man," Ethan said.

"It's funny; I always think of him as a boy," I said. "But he's older than I am. Now, Adam, he's a man. And a sensational kisser. You should have found that out when you had the chance."

"How do you know I didn't?" Ethan asked, then laughed at my expression. "I didn't. From the time I met him, Adam's heart was set on Jeremy."

"That hasn't changed," I said. "You're right. Jeremy's a good man. Although I'm not sure how much Nick actually needs him. My nephew has a better perspective than I did when I was his age. In fact, every time I get an e-mail from him, I feel like he's got more of a handle on things than I do."

"Of course," Ethan said. "That's why teenagers are so tricky. They're great at saying the right things. In other words, telling us what we want to hear or what they think they should be saying. But that doesn't mean they don't often feel like their lives are spinning out of control. They've got all the emotions of adults, and they're having adult experiences, but they don't have the larger perspective offered by time. Everything is life and death to them because they can't see beyond it."

I nodded thoughtfully and said, "It's the difference between being smart and being wise."

"Exactly. Think of yourself at that age. What would your parents, friends' parents, and teachers have said about you?"

"That I was no trouble," I said. "Good grades, good athlete, responsible."

"Were you happy? Did you feel like the perfect kid?"

"Hell no. I was terrified somebody would find out I wanted to suck cock. I wouldn't even let *myself* think about that, and everything I did was to cover it up."

"Then don't be so sure Nick has it all together," Ethan said. He shuddered as he added, "I wouldn't be a teenager again for anything."

"Me, either," I agreed.

As shafts of sunlight touched the bed, we made love again, then I fell asleep, comfortable within his strong, solid grasp.

I realized how hard I'd slept when Ethan had to nudge me awake to offer me a cup of hot tea. I missed Gavin's coffee, but sipped the tea appreciatively after my trip to the bathroom, where I grimaced over my morning hair. I was staring at a table on Ethan's side of the bed when he came back and perched next to me with his own cup of tea.

"How'd you sleep?" Ethan asked.

"So hard," I said. "Did I snore?"

"If you did, I didn't hear you. I guess that means the Daniel 'over voice' was silent?"

I laughed and said, "Voice-over. You make him sound like something out of Middle Earth. *The Over Voice.*" I could tell by the way he tried to suppress his smile that he'd done it on purpose. I pointed to the array of wooden and metal boxes of various sizes on the table and asked, "What's all that stuff?"

I became engrossed as he took each box and opened it to reveal its treasures, including stones and pebbles, dried leaves and flowers, and tiny bits of memorabilia collected from his travels. His stories about places and people revealed a deeply sentimental streak that I hadn't expected. I grinned when one of his boxes held an acorn and a leaf from our sojourn in Happy Hollow.

"That's a little history of Ethan Whitecrow," he finally said, returning the last box to the table. "I hope it wasn't boring."

"It wasn't boring at all. You're a man of substance. Really good looking. And great in bed. It doesn't make sense that you're single."

"You're right," Ethan said. "Will you marry me?"

I laughed and pulled him to me. We fooled around awhile, but I finally got up and started dressing. Ethan rested against his pillows and watched me with an affectionate expression. When I was dressed, I sat down again.

"Among your other mystical traits, do you also predict the future?" I asked.

"Never. But I don't have to be a fortune-teller to know that you're not going to marry me," he said, and put his hand over his heart in mock despair.

"I'd like to think we'll always be friends," I said, and although I kept my tone light, he could tell I was serious.

He reached for my hand and pressed his palm to mine, saying, "It's not safe to be blood brothers anymore. But I vow my loyalty and friendship."

"Me, too," I said, and kissed him. "Don't get up. I can let myself out. I want to take the vision of you in bed when I go."

"And the scent," he said, laughing as my face reddened at the realization that I'd been sniffing him again.

Although I knew that Sheila and Josh were due back sometime during the day, I didn't expect to hear from them. I hoped they'd prolong their honeymoon for as long as they could, shutting out the world. Especially the world of Lola Listeria. Saturday was always Gavin's day away, so I wasn't surprised to find an empty apartment. I ate, fed Dexter, then grabbed my gym bag and went to bodyWorks, taking a long, hot shower after my workout. I felt better than I had in days. It was obvious that I'd become a man who slept best when he was in another man's arms.

After working awhile at home, I changed channels on the TV until I found a golf tournament, one of my favorite things to sleep to. Dexter curled up on my chest and we napped together. When I woke up, the apartment was dark, and I was starving. As was Dexter, who communicated that information to me with urgent kneading of my bare chest.

"Stop that, you freak," I said, pushing him to the floor. After I filled his bowl, I stared without interest at the contents of my refrigerator. It was too hot to cook or even be interested in cooking. So I washed my face, dressed, and headed for the Renaissance Diner. Since this had always been a meeting place for Daniel, Sheila, and me, I was indulging a secret hope that I might run into him.

I was greeted warmly and led to our usual table, but I was quite alone. Fortunately, I'd brought a book with me, a new novel called *My Best Man.* It seemed like an appropriate title considering recent events in my life. I found it so engaging that I barely noticed when my food arrived, eating absently and muttering my thanks whenever my water glass was refilled. But at last I became aware that my waiter wasn't leaving my table, and I tore my eyes from the book to look up.

Her hair was pulled back and covered by a Yankees cap. She wasn't wearing makeup and was dressed as low-key as possible. But even without her golden tan and brilliant blue eyes, Sheila would have drawn the stares of my fellow diners because of the expression of controlled fury on her face.

"She is an evil bitch." She enunciated each word from between her teeth, then dropped a copy of Lola's column on top of my novel.

"I've seen it," I said, regretting my words when Sheila narrowed her eyes at me.

"Don't banter with me, Blaine. I've been wandering from restaurant to restaurant in search of either of you, like some kind of stalker."

"I'm so glad you found me first," I said, jumping up so I could pull out a chair for her. It was obvious that she would require some handling.

"How dare she print those pictures of the two of you—"

"At least we look handsome," I said cheerily. Another mistake.

"Oh, right, I look like Mr. Rochester's deranged first wife in Jane Eyre's wedding dress," she spat. "Even Mr. T looks more beautiful than I do. Where's Daniel?"

"I don't know," I said. "I haven't seen him since the wedding." When she gaped at me, speechless, I went on. "I have some things I need to tell you. But maybe not in a public—"

"Start talking," she said.

"No scenes," I ordered, looking around nervously. I half expected Lola and a photographer to be sitting three tables over, waiting for Sheila to do something outrageous.

"I never make scenes," Sheila said in an injured tone.

After the waiter set down her water and decaf, I began my narrative with Gretchen's proposition of four months before and finished with my return home after the wedding, including my feeling that I was living in limbo until I heard from Daniel. I'd never known Sheila to be quiet for so long, except when she was sleeping. She didn't even visibly react to the news about the baby.

"Say something," I begged.

"I feel awful," she said.

"Why?"

"You and Gretchen had this huge news, and you wouldn't tell anyone because of my wedding. And I spent my honeymoon thinking that you and Daniel were as happy as Josh and me, but all this was happening, and I didn't even know! You must be crushed."

"I'm worried about Daniel. I'm disappointed that things didn't work out for us. But I have so many other things to focus on that—"

She kicked me under the table and said, "How could you not tell

me that you're going to be a father? I *hate* it that you can keep secrets. Is Gretchen okay? Is she having natural childbirth? Is she going
to have a midwife? Has she considered one of those underwater
birthing things? What kind of workout is she doing? I've heard yoga is
great. How much weight has she gained?"

I held up my hands to stop her, remembering Gretchen's warning
about the "experts," and threw the mother of my child to the wolves
by saying, "You really need to ask her. I'm sure it's been hard on her
not to talk about all this woman stuff with you."

"That's going to change immediately," Sheila promised. "From
now on, I'll be there for her every single minute." When I smiled, she
frowned. "I'm not done with you, Blaine. To my way of thinking, it's
like you and Daniel have broken up a second time. Only this time,
I'm not going to cower around, afraid to give you my opinion. The
two of you need to get your shit together. I intend to tell Daniel the
same thing."

"Good luck with that," I said. "Where's your husband?"

"Oh, my god," she said and whipped out her cell phone. "Hi,
honey. I found one of them at the Renaissance Diner . . . No, just
meet me at home. I've got a lot to tell you . . . I love you, too." After
she snapped her phone shut, she said, "We divided restaurants. I
think he succumbed to hunger at Vinyl Diner."

"Poor Josh. Eating all alone on his first night home."

"Believe me, after I saw Lola's column, 'poor Josh' was happy to
get rid of me," Sheila said. "There has to be a way to get back at that
evil woman."

"Adam and I can't figure out how she pulled it off," I said. "Unless
she's gotten better at disguises since the Lillith Allure gala—"

"Lola was not at my wedding reception," Sheila assured me. "As
soon as I saw that picture of me, I recognized whose handiwork it
was. It was my freshman yearbook all over again."

"What are you talking about?" I asked. "You think Patti or one of
your friends—"

"It was a shot of me coming down the stairs after second period,"
Sheila said dreamily. "I had on the greatest outfit, and it was a good
hair day. But I was talking to a friend, and I didn't know my picture
was being taken. My mouth was hanging open. I looked like I had
two chins. And my eyes had a vacant look, just like in this one." She

tapped Lola's article and glared at me. "You don't remember that picture of me? It was in your senior yearbook."

"No," I said.

"Sydney was on the yearbook staff," Sheila hissed. "I told you months ago that she'd find a way to mess up my wedding and make your life miserable. And she did."

I started laughing and said, "Sheila, you're being paranoid. Don't you think somebody would have noticed Sydney if she'd been there? Like me, for example?"

"Not if she was careful. Most people who know her would have assumed she was invited. I did invite her parents; they sent their regrets. She could have used their invitation to get past security. When you and Daniel were dancing, did you see anyone taking pictures?"

"No," I admitted.

"It was that hag, Sydney," Sheila said. "I know it was. What are you going to do about it?"

"What do you mean? You want me to ask Sydney—"

"I already *know* it was Sydney," Sheila said impatiently. "What are you going to tell your family?"

"Nothing," I said. "I'm done with them. Besides, Lola didn't print my name. I doubt anyone in Eau Claire has seen the picture. According to Adam, the local paper's focus has been on you, with one little mention of Daniel. The fact that they're not making a bigger deal of his being at your wedding makes me think they don't intend to do anything with this story. You know how Midwesterners value people's privacy."

"Daniel hasn't made any statements?"

"Not that I'm aware of."

"If Daniel's not mad at Gretchen, why is he giving you the silent treatment?" Sheila asked.

"You'd have to ask him."

"Trust me, I intend to." She grabbed her purse and said, "I have to go. Will you promise me something?"

"What?"

"No more secrets."

"I promise to try to keep you at least one step ahead of Lola Listeria," I said.

She gave me a look then hurried from the restaurant. I exhaled. I had the idea that the baby news hadn't been a complete surprise to her. Although Josh hadn't known Gretchen was pregnant, at some point he must have prepared Sheila for that eventuality. That didn't bother me any more than when Adam had told Jeremy. It was a couple thing to share information. Too bad Daniel and I had never learned how to do it.

Monday morning, I was eating breakfast, reading the paper, and listening to CNN, which was on in the living room, when the phone rang.

"I hate to bother you," Gavin said, covering the telephone receiver with his hand, "but—"

"Take a message," I said, still chewing a bit of ham and eggs. I swallowed, then added, "Please."

"Normally, I would," Gavin assured me, "but it's Daniel." He held the phone toward me, and after I wiped my mouth with a napkin, I took it. Gavin scooped up Dexter from the floor on the way to his room, saying, "C'mon. Let's give Blaine some privacy."

I counted to five in my head, then said, "Hi."

"I think your manservant hates me," Daniel said.

"That's an opening."

"Original?" he asked.

"Not really," I said, smiling, even though he couldn't see me. "Third time today. You can't be serious, though."

"It's not what he said," Daniel explained. "It's the way he said it."

"What did he say?"

"He said, 'Good morning, Dunhill residence.' "

"That beast!"

Daniel continued, still pretending to be angry, "When I introduced myself and asked to speak with you, he said, 'One moment. I'll get him.' "

"I'll fire him, posthaste," I said. I pushed my breakfast around my plate with my fork. "Although he's an excellent cook. Couldn't I wait until after dinner tonight? Besides, he's one of your biggest fans."

"Oh. In that case," Daniel said, suddenly chipper, "keep him. At this point, I need all the gay fans I can get."

"Which, I assume, brings us to the dreaded photos?"

Daniel sighed and said, "Yeah. I figured you should know what's been going on."

"I've been wondering how you are," I confessed. "I hope your career isn't taking a hit because of what happened."

There was a long pause, then he asked, "Could I come over? I know you must have to go to work soon, but I think we should talk."

I was torn between longing and exasperation. I wanted to see him because I hoped we could start working things out. But since he knew it was a workday for me, it was obvious that he didn't want a long visit, so I wasn't sure what the point was.

"I guess I can be late for work," I said. "I have a production meeting this afternoon, so I only have a couple of hours. You'd need to get here soon."

"I'll be over as soon as I can figure out how to get past the reporters outside my building."

Before I could question him, he hung up. Though he lived on the next street up from me, I hadn't walked by his building in quite some time. I went to the window in the living room and looked down at his garden, but of course couldn't see the street in front of his building. Remembering the phalanx of reporters in Eau Claire during Sheila's wedding, I shuddered. At least then there was a driveway for distance and a security team keeping them at bay. I couldn't imagine what it would be like to have them camped on my doorstep, and wondered how Daniel could leave without leading them to my door, like some pied piper of paparazzi.

"Blaine, I'm leaving," Gavin said as he came into the room and interrupted my thoughts. "I'm dropping off your suits at the cleaners, then I have a massage client in an hour. I'll be out of your hair while Daniel is here. Leave your dishes in the sink, and I'll wash them later. This time, rinse them off, okay? You don't know how annoying it is to scrape—stop glaring at me like that. I was kidding."

"Not that. Daniel. How much did you hear?"

Gavin shrugged, then said, "Everything. This is a nice place and all, but it's too small for privacy."

"Why haven't I moved yet?" I asked Dexter, who'd leaped onto the table and was eyeballing my breakfast. I picked him up and waved goodbye with his paw at Gavin, who resembled a pack mule as he left with his massage table and my dry cleaning.

The phone was still in my hand, so I speed-dialed Violet.

"Oh, good," she said in lieu of a greeting. "I just got the mock-ups from the art department for the men's line packaging. Are you on your way in?"

"Violet, do you sleep in the office?" I asked. "Don't you have a home?"

"Are you on your way in?" she repeated, ignoring me.

"No. That's why I called. I'm going to be a few hours late."

I held the phone away from my ear when she yelped, "A few hours! What do you mean? The production meeting has been pushed up and is now at noon. You need to look at these mock-ups and choose a direction for the packaging before the meeting. Plus you need to go over the numbers the financial department just faxed me. Not to mention the—"

"Violet," I interrupted, "you work for *me,* right?"

"All the other department heads are going into this meeting today with the assumption that you're prepared. Rumor has it that Lillith will be there, too. I'd hate for them to be disappointed."

"Daniel's coming by," I said casually. "I think we're going to talk about the photos."

"Oh," Violet said. There was a long pause, until she said, "Fine. But get rid of him before eleven-thirty, because that's when I'll be knocking on your door to drag you into the office. I'll have the packaging samples and reports with me so we can go over everything quickly in the cab. Okay?"

"As if I have a choice," I muttered.

"And, Blaine? Yes, I work for you," she said before she hung up.

I managed to finish my breakfast, wash the dishes, shower, and put on a light gray Armani suit before the doorbell sounded. I buzzed Daniel into the building, and as I tied my tie, my eyes darted around my apartment, looking for things that were out of place. I needn't have worried, because Gavin kept the apartment neat as a pin.

A light knock let me know that Daniel had reached my floor. I opened my apartment door and slammed it shut again when I saw a woman with a blond bob. She wore sunglasses, a charcoal gray suit, and a white silk blouse, and she had a purse dangling from a strap over her shoulder and was holding a briefcase.

When she knocked again, I pressed my back to the door and hollered, "If you're from the *Manhattan Star-Gazette*, I have nothing to say to you!"

"Blaine, it's me," I heard Daniel say. "Open the fucking door."

Startled, I cautiously opened the door and peered at the woman in the hallway.

"Are you going to let me in?" she asked, and it finally dawned on me that I was looking at Daniel in drag. "I promise that everything we say will be completely off the record."

I let him in, still saying nothing, and watched as he set down his briefcase by the door, stuck his sunglasses in a pocket, then sat down on my leather sofa. Keeping his knees together, he reached down and pulled off his black high heels, saying, "These things are killing me. They're like torture chambers."

"What the hell are you doing?" I asked.

"I'm massaging my feet," Daniel said. "They must have grown since I bought those shoes. Of course, your feet do swell during the summer. You know, when it's hot outsi—"

"I meant," I cut him off, "why are you wearing a dress?"

"It's not a dress. It's a skirt," he said, smoothing his skirt over his knees. "Technically, it's a suit. Anne Klein. Do you like it? I got it half off a long time ago, and it still fits me, thank you very much. If you keep making that face, it's going to stick that way, Blaine. This was the only way I could get past the reporters outside my building. I couldn't exactly throw on a trench coat and fedora and expect to go unnoticed. Besides, there's not a cloud in the sky. I figured they'd be on the lookout for me, not a businesswoman on the go. I was right, because I walked right by them, and they didn't give me a second glance."

If Daniel had been dressed as he usually was, in jeans and a T-shirt, or anything else from his wardrobe of casual designer clothing, I would have been happy to have a rational discussion with him. Or I would have been tongue-tied with lust for him. But I wasn't prepared to watch him while he sat on my sofa with a face full of makeup, adjusting the seams of his stockings.

He brushed the hair from the wig out of his eyes and said, "You look just like you did three years ago when you drunkenly confessed that you'd watched my act at Club Chaos. I see you're still afraid of drag. Ignorance is so unattractive, Blaine."

"I'm not ignorant," I said. "I just prefer my men to look like men."

Daniel opened his purse and fished out a tube of lipstick. He pulled off the top, ran the lipstick over his lips, rubbed them together, then blotted them on a tissue. He then said, "It's a good thing I'm not *your* man, isn't it?" I glared at him, and my suspicion that he was deliberately trying to provoke me was confirmed by his next words. "Speaking of drag, you should apologize to Martin. You were horrible to him at Josh's bachelor party. You bruised his arm. Not to mention his fragile ego. He was only trying to liven things up and give Josh a laugh. There was no need for you to act like a big ape."

As he returned the tube of lipstick to his purse and stuffed the tissue inside, it occurred to me that Daniel in drag reminded me of his Aunt Jen. The thought made me almost laugh out loud, but I covered my mouth with my hand and stifled it. After I composed myself, I said, "Okay."

Daniel raised his head, looked at me quizzically, and asked, "What was that?"

"I said okay. You're right," I agreed. "My behavior was churlish and unacceptable." Daniel, still looking puzzled, turned his head, and I asked, "Why are you staring at the window?"

"I was waiting for the swarm of locusts," he said. "Enough of all that. Sheila called me. What a way to cap off a honeymoon. We agreed that at least now all those silly rumors about her and me being a couple will be put to rest."

"Rumors that you and she started, remember?" I reminded him. "Even though that is a fortunate outcome, don't try to tell me that you engineered this whole thing to stop what the two of you started."

"You got me, Blaine. I actually own the *Manhattan Star-Gazette*," he said, rolling his eyes. "Give me a break. I'm only trying to look at the bright side. Unfortunately, that's all I've been able to come up with."

"What's been happening at work?" I asked.

"The show's executives don't care if I'm gay, straight, or a eunuch. As long as I know my lines and pass the drug tests the insurance company makes us take, they're happy."

"That's good," I said. "So you wait until this blows over, which it will, and everyone's fine."

"Not really. The network brass doesn't want anyone to comment. They're afraid of Seaforth's reaction if there's negative viewer response."

"Isn't Bonnie an executive producer? Have you seen her or asked her what the Seaforth board is saying?"

"She's been supportive of me personally," Daniel said, "but she seems to be in the 'no comment' camp. I don't think Seaforth will get involved unless there's more publicity."

"I have a feeling that you're not going to keep quiet," I said.

"It would be like lying. Or a lie of omission. I couldn't live with myself if I walked past people who ask if I'm gay and pretended that they weren't there. I'd feel like a hypocrite after all those years performing as Princess 2Di4, encouraging gay people to be proud of themselves. And trying to hide the life I've lived would be ridiculous. It would only take a quick search on the Internet for anyone to find out about Princess 2Di4. There were articles about me in *Interview Magazine, HX,* and the *New York Blade.* Actually, I'm surprised it took this long before someone put two and two together."

"It just proves that you're a good actor," I said.

"Thanks. I think," he said, smiling. "Regardless, I'm going to make a statement to the press and say, 'Yes, I'm gay,' and get it over with."

"I think it's the right thing to do," I said. "I admire your honesty and the risk you're taking."

"If they write me off the show, they'll have to buy out my contract. If there is a negative reaction and I don't work for a while, I've got a nest egg from the town house sale, so I won't hurt for money. Don't start frowning again. I'm not going to name names. I know how you are about your family."

"My family knows," I said. "Well, I told my brothers. I'm sure it's just a matter of time before they tell my parents. But I don't care if they do."

Daniel looked momentarily nonplused before he smiled again

and said, "That's good. I'm proud of you, Blaine. That must have been difficult."

"It was surprisingly easy," I admitted. We were silent while I thought things over. Although I didn't care what my family might find out, I had no desire to endure the public scrutiny Daniel was probably in for. There were still some things I wanted to keep private, namely Gretchen and our baby. I finally said, "If you could leave me out of your press conference, I'd appreciate it."

"Not a problem. I'm going to tell the truth, remember? I'll just say the man in the photographs with me *was* my boyfriend, but we broke up and now I'm happily single. I held off making a statement because I wanted to talk to Sheila and you first. I figured you'd both be affected by the outcome, and we should all be on the same page. I see that as far as you're concerned, I needn't have bothered."

"That answers that question," I said. Daniel looked confused, so I explained, "I wondered if you only came over here to talk about the photos, or if you wanted to talk about our relationship, too."

"One crisis at a time, please," Daniel said.

"What makes you think I want to sit around waiting for you?" I asked, suddenly angry. "I'm tired of you putting me off and walking away from me all the time."

"Trust me. You don't want me to say everything that's in my head right now," Daniel warned.

We both looked at the door when we heard someone knock. I glanced at my watch and said, "It's Violet. I have to go to work." Daniel said nothing as he put on his shoes and picked up his purse. I opened the door for Violet and said, "Hi. Give me a couple of minutes."

"It's okay," she said. "I've got everything with me for the meeting."

Violet walked into my living room, but stopped in her tracks when Daniel stood up from the sofa. He gave her an appraising look and said, "And *I* make you uncomfortable? That's rich, Blaine."

I assumed he was talking about her resemblance to Jennifer Lopez, although I could have told him that wasn't deliberate.

"I'm sorry," Violet said. "I didn't mean to interrupt."

"Daniel was just leaving." I picked up his briefcase and held it out. He strode past Violet, and as he took the briefcase, I said, "If you're talking to the press today, I hope you're not wearing that outfit."

"Maybe I will," Daniel said. "What of it?"

I knew he wouldn't go to the press in drag, but I said, "Nothing. That skirt makes your butt look fat. That's all."

Violet and Daniel gasped audibly at the same time, and Violet said, "He's angry. He didn't mean it."

"Thank you," Daniel said to her. "You look fabulous, by the way. Is that Calvin Klein?"

Violet put her hand over her jacket and said, "Yes."

Daniel glanced at me and said, "Uh-oh. He's frowning again. It was nice to meet you." He swept through the open door, and I listened to his heels tapping on the stairs.

Violet eyed me cautiously, obviously testing the waters, before she said, "I take it things didn't go well?"

"If your idea of things going well includes snide remarks and being taunted by your boyfriend—excuse me, ex-boyfriend—showing up in drag, then yes, things went well," I said. I found my briefcase and added, "Let's go. Suddenly I can't wait to be in a boring business meeting."

CHAPTER 13

Gretchen's doctor was paged to do an emergency C-section before he could examine her, so the staff at Preston Women's Healthcare Center put us in a patient room and even ordered a fruit plate for me while we waited. I glanced up from my laptop to watch Gretchen as she aimlessly flipped channels, her feet propped on a pillow. She looked so comfortable on the hospital bed, with its crisp white sheets, that I wanted to trade places with her. The center was famous for considering the comfort of its patients, but the visitors' chairs left something to be desired.

She'd been complaining about being huge. Other than the fact that her waistline was finally expanding, I thought she looked great. Her face was a little puffy, but even though I knew it was a cliché, she really did glow. She'd stopped getting her hair colored while she was pregnant and claimed to be too busy to get it cut, so she'd started French braiding it close to her head, minimizing the contrast between its chestnut roots and blond streaks. I thought the style softened her and made her look more feminine, but I didn't dare tell her so.

"Sheila's on *Zandra's Chick Chat*," I said, looking at my watch.

"I hate that show," Gretchen said. "It's like what would happen if Barbies could talk."

"I think Faizah is on, too," I said, smiling when Gretchen changed the channel just as Zandra and her guests gathered around the set's kitchen counter.

"—so I make casseroles, but I wouldn't dare eat them myself," Sheila was saying. "Well, maybe a nibble or two, with salad. No dressing."

"If she delivers one more casserole to me, she's going to be wearing it," Gretchen muttered.

"That's how Sheila nurtures," I said.

"I had a casserole dish once," Faizah said. "It made a great water bowl for my dog, because it was heavy. Faizah orders in."

"Sorry, Blaine, I can't handle this," Gretchen said, and hit the channel button just in time for us to see Cressida Porterhouse cowering at the rim of a volcano and bursting into tears on *Secret Splendor.* "Sorry, Blaine, *you* can't handle *this,*" she said, then turned it to CNN.

"These aren't new, but I know you two must be bored," a nurse said, coming into the room with a stack of magazines. "We just got word that Dr. Griffith is finishing up in surgery. As soon as he gets here, we'll move you to the examining room."

"Thanks," Gretchen said.

I took the magazines, then rolled my eyes when I saw Daniel's two-week-old *Us* magazine cover. It seemed he was everywhere I turned. I handed Gretchen *Architecture Magazine,* hiding the *Us* behind a *Town & Country* so she wouldn't know that I was reading Daniel's article again.

Were you surprised when you were "outed" with pictures in Lola Listeria's column, the "Lo-Down," in the Manhattan Star-Gazette?

I was surprised to see unauthorized photographs of me at a private function, a friend's wedding, sharing a private moment. But I take issue with the idea that I was "outed." At no time in my career as a performer have I ever pretended to be straight. I don't discuss my private life, because it has nothing to do with my work. I've never denied being gay.

What about the rumors that you were involved in a romantic relationship with supermodel Sheila Meyers?

I suppose you'd have to look at the source of those rumors. I don't think you'll find any kind of statement from either Sheila or me that we had that kind of relationship. She and I have been friends for several years. Sheila's relationship with her boyfriend—now her husband—Josh, has been public knowledge for as long as they've been dating. They attend functions together, they've done interviews together, their apartment was even featured in an issue of *Ultimate Magazine*. If a few reporters chose to present the story from a different perspective, they were misleading their readers and viewers.

Still, your show, Secret Splendor, *and the network, while not issuing any kind of denial, have refused to answer questions about your sexual orientation.*

I think they're showing me the same courtesy they show any actor on one of their shows. The degree to which we make our private lives available to the public is up to us. There are actors who don't want pictures of their families printed. Who don't want their families to be the focus of articles. The network, and my show, are going to respect that.

For your bosses, then, this is a nonissue.

You'd have to ask them, of course, but it seems to be. There's been no pressure on me to deny the story, or any sense that if viewers know I'm gay, my job is in jeopardy.

Some sources say there are plans to diminish your role as Angus Remington on the show.

Really? We finished shooting a major storyline around Angus in early July. I took several weeks off after that, so in the coming weeks, there'll be less Angus, because I wasn't taping. My absence was written into the storyline. But now I'm back at work, and the diabolical Angus is wreaking as much havoc as ever. Those episodes will start airing in about three weeks, I think. And I still have a little over two years on my contract.

Is the man in those pictures someone special in your life?

I haven't changed my policy. I still don't discuss my private life. I'll talk about my role as Angus, my public appearances, or anything about my career. I appreciate my fans, and I hope they appreciate my work. But my private life is just that.

Wouldn't a bit of candor help generate more positive attitudes about gay people?

I would hope so, if you mean being candid about my orientation. Like I said, I've never denied it. I have no trouble saying that I'm gay. If I were straight, I'd still be a private person when it comes to my personal life.

What other roles did you have before you became Angus?

(Laughs) That's a short list. I had small parts on *NYPD Blue, ER,* and *Chicago Hope.* My characters usually died really early. I've done a few commercials. No theater. A lot of extra work here and there. But Angus was my big break, and I love the show and the character. We've got a great cast and crew at *Secret Splendor.*

You began your career as a performer fairly recently then.

No. I've been performing professionally since I was eighteen. I began as a female impersonator, and after a few years, I developed a character based on the Princess of Wales called 2Di4. She was my longest run, but I stopped performing as 2Di4 when Diana was killed, as a gesture of respect. I was never as big as RuPaul. Then again, she's seven inches taller than I am, and her heels are higher.

What's the reaction of your fellow actors on the set after all this publicity?

Nothing's changed, since it was never a secret that I'm gay. Although one of the younger actors on the set did ask me if I thought I could get Elton John's autograph.

Can you?

I doubt it. If you're reading this, Elton, call me.

If it hadn't been for Sheila, I'd have had no inkling of the ordeal Daniel was going through at work. The network was unhappy with his decision to come out, and several of his fellow cast members had begun to distance themselves from him, as if they hadn't always known he was gay. For the time being, his job appeared to be safe, but the writers had been ordered to make Angus more masculine. This included sex scenes with Angus's heretofore wife-in-name-only, Cressida Porterhouse. According to Sheila, they'd reached an impasse, because Jane-Therese threw a tantrum and refused to do love scenes with Daniel. It was anybody's guess if they were going to come up with another plausible love interest for Angus or kill him off again—Angus apparently had more lives than Bonnie and Lillith combined—and buy out Daniel's contract.

"Gay or straight, that is one sexy man." The nurse voiced my thoughts as she looked over my shoulder at Daniel's picture. "Dr. Griffith can see you now."

Gretchen smirked when she saw me drop the magazine like it was burning my hand, but at least she didn't say anything when we followed the nurse to the examining room. I waited outside until I was told I could go in. Gretchen had changed into a gown and the ultrasound tech was getting the machine ready.

"Good morning," Dr. Griffith said as he joined us. He shifted Gretchen's file so he could shake my hand, then he rested his hand on her shoulder. As usual, I appreciated his calm, friendly manner. Even though it had surprised me when Gretchen chose a male OB/GYN, her instincts had been good. I always felt reassured and comfortable after our appointments. "I think I explained last time, this is just a routine ultrasound. Did you have any cramping after the amnio?"

"Not at all," Gretchen said.

"Good. The results are in. Absolutely normal." He opened the file and rattled off some tests and figures that made little sense to me, but it didn't matter. All I needed to hear was that things were okay. "You two still don't want to know your baby's gender?"

"No," Gretchen and I answered in unison.

"Let's take a look, then."

The tech squirted gel on Gretchen's belly. This was our third ultrasound, and Gretchen had told me the gel was warm and, except for having to endure a full bladder, she found the entire procedure calming. I, on the other hand, always felt charged up when I saw Civil Liberty on the monitor, and watched with fascination as Dr. Griffith pointed out things I'd never have been able to see on my own. The baby was just a mysterious gray blob to me.

Later, while we listened to the heartbeat, I felt anxious when I saw Dr. Griffith frown as he skimmed through the file. But he'd already told us everything was normal. He scribbled some notes on Gretchen's chart and said, "I'm seeing a trend with your blood pressure, Gretchen. It's getting a little higher each visit. Nothing to be alarmed about, but just to be on the safe side, I want to put you on a low-sodium diet. We've got some material to help you with that."

"Can't high blood pressure be caused by stress?" I asked.

"Sure. But stress is a fact of life. It's easier to control our diets than the world around us."

"Blaine's just looking for a reason to lecture me," Gretchen said. "I'm not the one who's stressed. He is. Put him on a low-sodium diet, too."

"I'm not stressed," I argued.

Dr. Griffith closed the file and said, "The only thing Blaine needs to do is ease up on the Gravitron machine at bodyWorks." He winked at Gretchen and left the room.

"How did he know—"

"You can be so dense sometimes," Gretchen said. "You never realized he was family?"

"Why am I always the last to know these things?"

"Total lack of gaydar, as usual," Gretchen said. "Go away. I want to get dressed and get out of here."

Once we were standing on the sidewalk, I asked Gretchen if she wanted to share a cab. I was going back to the office and figured we could split the cost. She hemmed and hawed and finally said, "That's okay. I'm going downtown."

"To your office?" I asked. A look of annoyance washed over her and her eyes darted skyward. "Didn't you hear what the doctor said, Gretchen? No stress. You should go home and start thinking about a leave of absence."

"I'm fine," she said firmly. "The doctor said to watch my sodium intake. He said nothing about taking off work."

"Don't get upset," I cautioned.

"I'm not upset!" she yelled. Several pedestrians jumped away from her or eyed her cautiously as they walked by.

"Okay. I'm sorry," I said. My cell phone rang, and Gretchen started frantically looking around for a cab. I looked at the Caller ID. "Lillith?"

"We need you back at the office immediately. When you get here, meet me in Conference Room A," Lillith said. She sounded like a secret agent setting up a rendezvous. I almost expected her to demand that I wear a white carnation in my lapel and bring a billion dollars in small denominations along with the stolen microfiche. "The short notice can't be helped, Blaine. This is very important."

"It's okay," I said as I watched Gretchen step into a cab, wave at me, then speed off downtown. "I was on my way there anyway."

When I got to Lillith Allure's headquarters, I found Violet, but she had no information about Lillith's urgent meeting.

"Sorry, Blaine," she said with a shrug. "I got the same summons as you. I did my best to find out what's going on, but nobody seems to have any answers. We'd better get moving."

Since Violet was rarely out of the loop, I felt nervous. Was Lillith purposely keeping us in the dark? What was I about to walk into? I composed myself while we walked down the hallway to the conference room. Although I knew I looked calm and collected on the outside, inside I felt like the pain and discomfort sufferer in a Tums commercial.

We found Lillith seated at the table next to our attorney, Ryan. Standing behind her was a woman dressed all in white, who was waving her hands through the air above Lillith's head. A second woman sat on the other side of Lillith and was looking through a long computer printout, while occasionally entering information into a laptop. Adam Wilson sat across the table from them, his mouth slightly open while he stared at the woman stirring the air above Lillith's head.

"Oh, good," Lillith said when she noticed our entrance. "Please, sit down. The others will arrive shortly. That'll do, Hibiscus. My aura feels much clearer now, thank you."

Hibiscus stopped waving her hands around and left the room. Violet and I sat next to Adam, who leaned over to me and whispered, "Just when I think it can't get any nuttier here, it does."

"What? Oh, Hibiscus," I said. "I guess I'm getting used to it. How scary is that? What are you doing here?"

Before he could answer, the phone rang, and Lillith answered it. "Thank you. Yes. Send them in," she said, and replaced the receiver. "The rest of the attendees are finally here."

The door opened, and Bonnie Seaforth-Wilkes, Daniel, Ethan—who I assumed was with them as Bonnie's spiritual advisor—and three stony-faced men in suits filed into the room. When Daniel met my eyes, his gaze seemed to convey that he was as mystified by this meeting as I was. I relaxed, grateful that he didn't look angry, upset, or like a woman.

"First of all," Lillith said, "I'd like to apologize for the air of mystery surrounding today's meeting. Noreen, my astrologer"—she gestured to the woman with the laptop and computer printout, who looked up briefly and gave a small wave—"assured me that surprise is the best plan of attack in business proceedings today."

"Enough with the drama, Lillith," Bonnie commanded. "Would you get on with it? Why am I here? Have you finally come to your senses and realized that amulet is mine? Did you want witnesses around us this time, in case things get ugly?"

"This has nothing to do with the amulet," Lillith said. "Besides, you know perfectly well I don't have it. *You* probably have it and are saying these things to drive me mad again. I'm sure that's why you were born thirty years before me—"

"*Thirty?*" Bonnie gasped.

"—to get your hands on it before I could," Lillith spoke over her. "You'd like to see them put me in an asylum, like they did three life-times ago. Do you know what they did to me?"

"Hmmm, yes," Bonnie said. "Aren't they making a movie about it? Called *Quills?*"

"I was *not* the Marquis de Sade," Lillith snapped.

"Ladies, please," Ryan said, holding up a hand. "Arguing about past lives isn't going to help us."

"Actually, that's not true," Ethan said. "Oftentimes, it helps us grow when we—"

"Be that as it may, we *are* off track," Lillith interrupted. "Maybe I should turn the floor over to Adam. I invited him because he has interesting information regarding our respective Web sites."

"For those who don't know," Adam said, nodding at Ryan and the men with Bonnie, "I'm Adam Wilson. I maintain the Web sites for Lillith Allure Cosmetics and Seaforth Chemicals. Lillith asked me to monitor the e-mail from both sites and keep a tally of reactions after the photos of Daniel and Blaine ran in the *Manhattan Star-Gazette*. Of course there have been negative responses, but not in the numbers you'd think. Around eighty percent of the e-mails have been positive reactions to Daniel and Blaine."

"Why would there be any e-mails about me?" I asked. I'd been sitting quietly, wondering where the meeting was headed and trying not to squirm about being in the same room with Daniel and Ethan. Now that my name had come up, however, I found it difficult to keep my mouth shut.

Noreen typed on her laptop, hit "Enter," and said, "Friction between Taurus's heart and head are affected by Mars. Don't let your career path be affected by your personal path."

Lillith sagely nodded her head in agreement with Noreen and said, "Let Adam finish, please."

"On Bonnie's site, Blaine's name hasn't come up at all," Adam said.

"Why would it? I haven't told anyone who he is," Daniel said.

"Sixty-five percent of Seaforth's e-mails regarding the pictures completely support Daniel. Fifteen percent completely support Angus Remington. Ten percent favor Angus's new relationship with the mystery man in the photos over his marriage to Cressida Porterhouse. And ten percent of the people who e-mailed think Daniel is going to hell. However, they'd be willing to keep watching *Secret Splendor* if he'd repent."

"Not on your life," Daniel muttered.

"Virgo men reel amid chaos," Noreen said, again consulting her laptop. "Saturn will turn chaos back into order during the next crescent moon."

Bonnie looked at Noreen with annoyance. Then she turned to Adam and said, "Ten percent isn't bad."

"The same goes for Lillith Allure's e-mails," Adam said.

"Why would Lillith Allure get e-mails about Daniel?" Violet asked.

"Lots of reasons," Adam said. "Mainly because of Sheila's friendship with Daniel. If they're fans of Sheila's, they're fans of Zodiac. So they go to the Lillith Allure site and learn everything they can. Which leads us to your question, Blaine. The creative team behind Zodiac is detailed on the Lillith Allure site, where there's a whole page—with a photograph—on you."

"So it stands to reason that people are beginning to realize that it was Blaine with Daniel in the *Star-Gazette,*" Violet said, catching on. "I get it now."

"Aries will fail to maintain a charade," Noreen said to Violet, who looked momentarily stunned. Daniel snorted derisively.

"I'm a Capricorn," Violet said.

Noreen looked baffled as she consulted her laptop and said, "No, you're not. You're an Aries."

"Blaine, everyone knows you're the tour de force behind Zodiac's ads," Lillith said. "You've been on *Entertainment Tonight,* there have been magazine articles and advertising industry awards, all with your name and face attached." She pointed from Daniel to me as she said, "The press already knows. It's only a matter of time before someone prints it."

"This story was supposed to die, not get bigger," Bonnie complained with a frown.

"You said there'd be no repercussions if I came out," Daniel said.

"Disharmony is at its peak when—"

"Noreen, please," Lillith spoke sternly.

"Well, no," Bonnie said awkwardly to Daniel. She glanced at two of the men she'd brought with her, introducing them as a network representative and a lawyer. They took their cue and began a tag-team discourse.

"*Secret Splendor*'s numbers haven't dropped. In fact, they've gone up," the network rep admitted. "That's not surprising. Our research has always indicated that the show has a large gay viewership. Seaforth Chemicals has advertised heavily to that market. But the shows that precede and follow *Secret Splendor* have different demographics, and their ratings are falling."

"Advertising costs are tied to the numbers," the attorney said. "Those shows' sponsors have the legal right to demand lower rates or pull their ads. We can't let one rotten banana spoil the bunch."

"I believe it's apple," Violet said.

"Either way, it's fruit," the attorney said. This remark was met with dead silence, as Ethan, Adam, Daniel, and I all stared at him with irritation.

"We can't afford a loss in advertising revenue. It would be cheaper for us to buy out Daniel's contract," the network rep said.

"Fine," Daniel said. "Buy me out. I'm not lying or hiding the truth about myself."

They were now speaking my language, and I suppressed a smile, remembering Gavin's prediction about backlash. I leaned forward and said, "It would be cheaper in the short run. You'd get rid of your immediate problem. Your other shows would be safe. It would probably be the end of *Secret Splendor,* though."

"One character doesn't carry the show," the network rep disagreed.

"No, your 'large gay viewership' carries the show. You'll see the effect first among the Manhattan viewers, since Daniel is a highly regarded performer here. Then it'll spread outward, possibly becoming a national boycott. You're familiar with that word, right? Florida orange juice? Coors beer?" I turned to Bonnie. "Your sales will be the next to suffer if you continue to sponsor the show after they dump Daniel."

Bonnie blanched, and Lillith emitted a peal of laughter, then said, "The solution is obvious, Bonnie. Keep Daniel. Seaforth Chemicals should buy the commercial time any other companies drop."

"Our advertising budget is determined months in advance," Bonnie said. "You have far more autonomy with your little company. Why don't *you* buy the commercial time?"

"Why would I advertise on shows with falling ratings?" Lillith asked.

"Scorpio is wise to practice thrift in business matters," Noreen said, and Lillith looked smug.

Before Bonnie and Lillith could continue sparring, Adam said, "Blaine's right, but I can take his thinking a step further. If the responses I'm seeing on the Seaforth and Lillith Allure Web sites are accurate, the network must be getting similar reactions. Rather than worry about alienating that small segment of negative viewers, why not try to pick up *Secret Splendor*'s gay and gay-friendly viewers for your other shows?"

"How do you propose that we do that?" the network rep asked in a condescending tone.

"Use the gay media," Ethan said. "It's good for the gay community to have an out, gay actor who's on everyone's television set. Now that Daniel's come out, the gay media will want statements and interviews with him, the show, and the network that carries it. The entertainment media will pick up the story; you'll get plenty of publicity."

"Negative publicity. Backlash works both ways," the attorney said. "When the general public feels someone's advancing a gay agenda, they retaliate. You're familiar with that word, right? Ellen Degeneres?"

"Maybe we should drop *Secret Splendor* altogether. Soap ratings are falling on all the networks," the network rep said. "It's a dying form of entertainment."

"Oh, God," Bonnie said, pinching the bridge of her nose with her fingers. The rest of us sat in silence. Even Noreen, who could obviously find no cosmic platitudes on her laptop to offer as an answer.

I could feel Daniel watching me, and I stared back at him, trying to figure out what he wanted. I was willing to fight on his behalf. I saw determination in his eyes, and I knew he wasn't going to back down. He had no intention of scuttling back into the closet, whatever the cost. I was filled with respect for him. When I smiled, he returned the smile. It felt like we were the only two people in the room.

Both of us jumped and broke eye contact when Adam suddenly said, "You're a couple!"

"A couple?" Lillith asked, bewildered.

"Adam's a Gemini," Noreen said. "Twins hinder business deals with frivolity today. Pay him no mind."

"No!" Ethan exclaimed, nodding at Adam. Noreen frowned and checked her laptop again. Ethan went on, "Adam's right. Blaine and Daniel are a couple."

"We broke up," Daniel said.

"The press doesn't know that," Ethan said. "If the two of you do interviews together—"

"I don't get it," Bonnie said. "Will someone please tell me what's going on?"

"If Daniel and Blaine present themselves as a stable couple, it might be more palatable for mainstream America," Ethan explained.

"They wouldn't be so threatening," Violet agreed. "There's nothing more boring than a couple."

"I still foresee losses in revenue from initial bad press," the network rep said stubbornly.

"How do you know there'll be bad press?" Violet asked. "Lots of prime-time shows have gay characters now. *Friends* has lesbian co-parents, and they never went off the air. What about *Will and Grace*? It's gotten high ratings. I'll bet their network is raking in the dough."

"Scorpio is wise to reconsider investment decisions," Noreen said. "Virgo needs your assistance."

Lillith looked down her nose at her, but before she could speak, Ethan said, "I think Lillith is right, Bonnie."

"Excuse me?" Bonnie asked, giving him an ominous look.

"For the greater good, Seaforth Chemicals should help allay any advertising losses on the other shows. You'll be repaid many times over. You'll be known as the company that stood up for fairness when other companies faltered. Consumers will respect you, and sales will soar. Just as importantly, your own spirit will grow in strength, and the universe will reward you, not only in this life, but in ones to come. Your karmic path may even lead you to—"

"The amulet," Bonnie whispered.

"Noreen is right," Lillith said quickly. "Daniel, the universe is directing me to help you."

"As well you should," Bonnie said, "since it was your executive who was in the pictures that got us into this mess."

"Your actor would barely be a blip on the celebrity radar screen if you hadn't tried to turn him into Susan Lucci," Lillith snapped. "You grabbed any chance at publicity you could, including connecting him to my company's spokesmodel." The two women glowered at each other, until Lillith turned to Daniel again and said, "Lillith Allure is introducing a men's line of toiletries called Deity. Rather than going with models, I want to feature daytime television actors in the ads. We'd like to offer you the opportunity to be the face of Narcissus."

My mouth fell open. Violet's sudden death grip on my arm stopped me from cursing out loud. Obviously she was just as shocked as I was. It was supposed to be my job to choose the male models for the ads. The same ads I had yet to worry about, since we'd only just agreed on a packaging concept. I wanted to leap over the table and strangle Noreen when she said, "The best action for Taurus is a path of silence."

"Narcissus?" Daniel barked. "Very funny, Blaine."

"I didn't—"

"We can start the Deity ads now, to pique the public's curiosity," Lillith spoke over me. Though I wanted to disagree, I heeded Noreen's advice and kept quiet. Lillith continued, "In addition, they'll send the message that Lillith Allure is behind you and *Secret Splendor*. In fact, we'll help offset Seaforth Chemicals' costs and buy advertising time on the network. The Deity commercials will be raw. Masculine. They'll give the press something other than your acting career and your relationship with Blaine to focus on."

"I don't want to lie," Daniel said. "We're not a couple, boring or otherwise, and we're not going to pretend to be. Right, Blaine?"

"I don't have to be part of a couple to be boring," I said. "I'm just a businessman. No one cares about me. Even if they did, there's nothing to write about."

Bonnie turned to the third man who had accompanied her and gave him a nod. He whipped a tiny spiral notebook out of his pocket, opened it, and recited, "Blaine Michael Dunhill. Lives with a massage therapist named Gavin Lewis. Frequent meetings at home with his assistant, Violet Medina. Visited by a blond female corporate type who travels between his apartment and Daniel Stephenson's. Dinner meeting at Renaissance Diner with Sheila Meyers dressed incognito. Dinner with Ethan Whitecrow at Julian's Restaurant; left Whitecrow's apartment the next morning. Last week, had a mixed fruit smoothie at his gym, bodyWorks, with an unidentified male companion. Later visited companion's apartment for an hour and a half. This morning, was at a women's hospital with a pregnant lady."

"A pregnant lady?" Violet repeated blankly.

"You tricked with someone from our gym?" Adam asked in a surprised voice.

"I'm being followed?" I exploded.

"See how easy it is to gather information about a supposedly boring person and put a salacious spin on it?" Bonnie commented with a shrug.

"Bonnie, this is completely unacceptable," Ethan said, shooting me an apologetic glance.

"Unbelievable," Daniel said, looking from Ethan to me. "I'm out of here."

"Daniel, wait," I began, but as was his habit, he walked out without looking back.

"You've really gone too far this time," Lillith said to Bonnie.

"Compared to Blaine's, Daniel's report is the boring one," Bonnie answered.

"This is a complete invasion of Blaine's privacy," Ryan said. "We ought to sue you."

"That would certainly help matters," Bonnie said in a tone rife with sarcasm.

"Who's pregnant?" Violet asked.

I turned to look at Adam when he said, "I didn't know about this part of the meeting, Blaine. I swear. I didn't even realize that you and Ethan were friends."

"Friends," I mused. "Considering today's input from you two, I'm starting to rethink that whole concept." I turned to Violet. "Gretchen is pregnant, but it's not relevant to this discussion. Lillith, I'd like to meet with you another time to talk about the Deity line. Right now, I have other things to take care of."

"Of course," Lillith said with a nod. As I left the conference room, I heard her say, "I wonder how much bad karma you've racked up over this, Bonnie?"

By the time I got to the elevator, Ethan, Adam, and Violet were on my heels. I turned around and held up one hand, saying, "No more wisdom, advice, or questions out of any of you. I'm going home, getting out of this suit, and—never mind. Too many people know too much as it is."

"I was trying to be supportive of Daniel's career," Adam said. "And also give the two of you a reason to spend time together so you could work things out."

"Remember what I told you once?" Ethan asked. "That avoiding people is never a good way to solve problems?"

"It's not their fault Daniel walked out," Violet added. "Bonnie's the one who had you followed."

"You know whose fault it is?" I asked. "Once again, I've made it possible for someone I love to be publicly hurt and humiliated."

The elevator doors closed between us. I was producing enough adrenaline to run home, but I walked the thirty-plus blocks, hoping the August heat would melt my anger. I wasn't happy that Daniel had walked out, but I didn't blame him. He'd been subjected to a net-work weasel, Bonnie and Lillith's bickering, a homophobic attorney, and surprising revelations about his ex-boyfriend, all while a job he loved was being threatened.

I knew how he felt. I was furious at Lillith for springing her idea to use him in our Deity ads. I was even angrier that Bonnie's people had been spying on me. But most of all, I was mad at myself for being part of something that had hurt Daniel.

When I got to my building, Gavin was just coming out the door with a duffel bag that I assumed held my laundry. He smiled at me when I approached, but the smile quickly disappeared after his eyes focused on my expression.

"I'm on my way to drop off your laundry. Your shirt is soaked. If you want to go up and change, I'll wait here, then I can take that one, too."

"No. It can wait," I answered curtly, not wanting to unleash the rage that had only intensified on the long walk home.

"Bad day?" he asked, dropping the bag on the sidewalk.

"I don't want to talk about it."

"Sometimes talking helps reduce tension," he said, putting his hand on my shoulder. "Damn, you are tense."

I heard a clicking sound coming from somewhere behind me. I turned around, suspicious after what had happened at the meeting. For all I knew, Bonnie's gumshoe was following me again.

Nothing looked out of the ordinary. Pedestrians crossed the street, cabs tore up the avenue, and cars were parked bumper to bumper along the curb. An old lady stopped to clean up after her dog. Her cane tapped against the side of a small metal fence around the base of a tree, and I decided that must have been the clicking sound I'd heard.

"Gavin, have you noticed anyone following me?"

His forehead scrunched up as he thought. He was probably trying to visualize every moment we'd been in public together. "No, I haven't. Why? Is this about the photos from the wedding?"

"I just found out how un-boring I can seem to be."

"I don't follow," he said.

"Some of the people that Daniel works for had me followed, noting all my comings and goings. I'm furious. I don't want my private life invaded."

"Look," Gavin said, turning me around to quickly work my shoulders, "this thing will blow over soon, then you can go back to living the normal life you lead."

Gavin's magic hands began to smooth out the taut muscles in my shoulders. Unfortunately that didn't alleviate the boiling in my veins. I decided a long, hard workout at the gym was called for. I winced with pain and pleasure as Gavin hit a particularly tight spot on my back.

"I'm going to the gym. If anyone calls, tell them I went to Bermuda. Alone."

When I went to the office the next day, there was a buzz and crackle in the air. I wondered if the meeting with Lillith and Bonnie had generated more gossip. If so, no one was saying anything to my face.

I hastily skimmed new mock-ups from the art department and asked Violet to schedule a meeting with Lillith to resolve our ideas about the Deity line. Though I realized that Lillith and Frank had final say over how their products were presented, I still felt as if my concept had been pirated.

As I approached the office door, Barbara looked up at me and smiled. "Lillith will be ready for you in a minute."

A few seconds later, the red light on Barbara's phone began blinking, and she ushered me into Lillith's office. The familiar dragon-headed chairs were situated in front of her ornately carved desk. Antique bookcases and shelves were littered with the same small figures of gargoyles, mystical icons, and stones. Unlike her former rooms in Baltimore, however, her new office was flooded with sunlight, causing the royal blue walls to glow. Plants were situated on stands near the windows, bringing life to the room. The new office felt more alive and inviting, leading me to believe that Lillith was happier since she'd moved to New York.

"Lillith?"

She looked up and calmly set down her pen, then motioned for me to sit across from her. She then turned to her companion, who fanned out some cards he held.

Lillith waved her hand over the cards, drew two, and put them faceup in front of me. On one card was a picture of a tall stone tower being struck by lightning, captioned *The Tower.* The other card depicted a bearded man wearing a tall hat and pointing one hand upward. It was titled *The Heirophant.* Lillith seemed pleased by whatever mystical message these cards supposedly divulged.

"What do these cards mean to you, Blaine?" she asked.

Although I was impatient to talk about the Deity line, I decided to humor her. "I wish I could tell you," I said, thinking, *But then I'd have to kill you,* and added aloud, "but I don't read tarot cards."

She gave me a piercing look that made me wonder if she could read my mind. "But you have a mind for analyzing visual representations. That *is* what advertising is all about. Give it a try; you'll be surprised how simple it is."

I took in the details of the finely rendered cards. "This one," I said, pointing at *The Tower,* "would seem to represent some kind of trouble, as the man who's falling has lost his crown. Furthermore, it looks like this trouble was caused from an outside, uncontrollable source, as represented by lightning striking the top of the building."

I looked up at Lillith. She widened her eyes as if to say, *Go on.*

"This card"—I pointed to *The Heirophant*—"reminds me of Renaissance-era paintings of popes. The vertical design exudes power. The pope, historically, is a figure of wisdom."

"Now," Lillith interrupted, "what do you suppose this means in relation to our situation?"

I laughed and sat back in my chair, realizing that I'd played right into her hands. I felt myself calming down as I thought about it. "To put it bluntly, a wise figure has emerged during a time of crisis."

She didn't elaborate or embellish my final reading and waved her card reader out of the office. "Now, let's talk about the Deity line."

I opened my portfolio to the first three sketches that I'd received from the art department. My brief glance at them prior to the meeting hadn't prepared me for how similar the artist's rendering of Narcissus was to Daniel. In the ad, a blond man was looking into a pool of water shaped like a bottle of cologne. His feet seemed to be growing out of the ground, and his face had a dreamy, faraway look. It reminded me of Daniel when he would get lost in thought while sitting in his garden.

As I flipped through the sketches, Lillith's face brightened. "Let's continue on this course. Daniel is perfect for the Narcissus ad. I want to see more ideas."

"I'll have them for you within the week," I said.

Later, after fleshing out more concepts for the Deity line, I left the office and headed for the gym. One good thing about being stressed was that it fueled my workouts and forced me to push myself.

When I'd finished an extended routine of cardio and weight training, I felt like my limbs were made of spaghetti. I was also starving. As I pulled my phone from the pocket in my gym bag to let Gavin know I was on my way home, I glanced at two men who were standing at the juice bar. They were whispering to each other and making it perfectly obvious they were talking about me. I overheard the skinny one say, "It is him. It's Blaine Dunhill."

I pretended to look at my cell phone, but watched the two men from the corner of my eye. The taller man, who looked like he ate steroids for breakfast, pulled a newspaper from the counter of the juice bar and looked from the page to me then back again. I heard him say, "You're right. It's him." When he dropped the newspaper, I could see the banner.

I bolted from the gym without calling Gavin, running to a newsstand to shuffle through papers until I found a copy of the *Manhattan Star-Gazette.* I flipped through the pages until I found what I was looking for. The newest "Lo-Down" featured the headline REAL LIFE GAY SOAP OPERA: IS ANGUS'S BEAU A CHEAT? Below it were photos of me with Gavin. The first one was a close-up shot of me with my mouth open and eyes closed in what could be perceived as ecstasy. The angle distorted the distance between Gavin and me. It looked like he was holding me close to his body, with his hands on my shoulders. In the second photo, I was looking behind me at Gavin and smiling. Again, the angle distorted the truth. It looked as if we were about to kiss.

I crumpled the paper in my hand when I saw my name mentioned in the first sentence. All the tension I'd worked out was back in my muscles, tightening my body from head to toe.

"You gonna pay for that, buddy?" the cashier asked.

I dug into my pockets, pulled out two quarters, and slammed them down on the counter. I then stormed away from the newsstand. As I was crossing the street, my cell phone piped up, and I checked Caller I.D.

"Gavin?"

"Blaine, have you seen—"

"That bitch," I said, cutting him off. "As if I didn't have enough going wrong."

"So you have seen it."

"Has anyone called?"

"No, not here," he said.

"I'm on my way home," I said and disconnected the call. I held the phone away from my ear and noticed the envelope symbol on the face of my phone, signaling that I had voice mail.

"Hi, Blaine, it's Ethan. I saw the 'Lo-Down.' I know you're probably still mad, but if you want to talk about it, give me a call."

I knew what he wanted to say to me, and I didn't want to hear it. Now that the press had announced that Daniel and I were in a relationship and possibly in trouble, it would be best to represent ourselves as a happy couple being unfairly treated by a vindictive gossip columnist. But as far as I was concerned, Daniel had made the decision for us. I was not going to oppose him.

Over the following days, Violet and Gavin ran interference for me, fielding calls from gay reporters across the country who wanted some kind of statement. But neither of my assistants could protect me from my friends or what they were going through.

I hadn't heard from Sheila since she'd told me what was happening to Daniel at *Secret Splendor*. She'd left a message on my voice mail at work, but it had nothing to do with Daniel. All she'd said was, "I hate you, Blaine. You know I can't stand snakes!"

After her honeymoon, she'd gone back to work posing for Zodiac. The Libra ads were photographed on the terrace of Lincoln Center with Sheila, a male model, and forty extras all dressed in formal wear, as if at a party. All eyes were on Sheila and her paramour while they danced, charming the guests at the party, until they ended up playfully splashing in Lincoln Center's fountain. Reflecting the characteristics of people born under the sign of Libra, the ads were luxurious and grand, yet playful and gregarious.

The Scorpio ads were a different story. Sheila and her paramour from the Libra ads posed in the Lobby Lounge at Manhattan's Four Seasons Hotel. When her partner's head was turned by a beautiful woman, Sheila's Scorpio rage was manifested by snakes curling around her arms, waist, neck, and shoulders. The snake handlers had assured me that there would be no poisonous snakes used in the photos. However, I erred on the side of caution and had a representative from Poison Control on hand, just in case. I couldn't imagine what all the fuss was about, and never bothered to return Sheila's call.

After Gavin and I appeared in Lola's column, I felt nervous about going out the following weekend. I stayed home to catch up on paperwork in front of the television. Dexter "helped" by napping on folders, papers, and spreadsheets that were scattered around me on the living room floor. Shooing him away for the tenth time and flipping through channels with the remote, I paused on a program that was showing an overview of entertainment news from the past week. What caught my eye was Sheila and Josh being stopped on their way to the premiere of a movie in Los Angeles.

"Hi! This is Claire Jennings at the *Bring It On* premiere. In addition to the stars of the movie, lots of celebrity guests are showing up on the red car—Oh, look! It's Lillith Allure's Zodiac model, Sheila Meyers. Can you talk with us for a minute, Sheila?" the overenthusiastic correspondent asked.

"Hi," Sheila said agreeably. She looked none the worse for wear after the Scorpio photo shoot. She and Josh were dressed similarly in jeans, T-shirts, and leather jackets. I wondered why they were in L.A., and briefly allowed myself to buy into Lola's speculation about Sheila being the next Bond girl. But I quickly dismissed the idea, deciding their jaunt to California was more likely due to an assignment Josh was doing for *Ultimate Magazine*.

"Are you excited about the movie?"

"Sure! I hear it's very funny," Sheila said.

"Were you a cheerleader in high school?"

"Yes. For two years. If this is where you bring out my old yearbooks, I'll be forced to hurt you," Sheila warned. I laughed as Josh looked at his watch and began to playfully pull on Sheila's arm. "I'm sorry. We really should be going in."

"Before you go," Claire Jennings hastily said, "just one question.

Care to comment on your friend Daniel Stephenson's recent coming-out interview in—"

"No. Not really," Sheila interrupted.

"The man photographed with Daniel Stephenson in the *Manhattan Star-Gazette* was identified as Blaine Dunhill. He's the man who creates your Zodiac ads, right?" Claire Jennings persisted, her plastic smile never faltering.

"Yes," Sheila answered.

"Oh, shit," I moaned.

"The two of you went to high school together, and Mr. Dunhill was on the football team. Was there a cheerleader-football player romance going on? Oh! I guess not if he's gay, right?" Sheila and Josh, like me while I watched, looked at Claire Jennings as if they were waiting for her to bring out a white sheet and a burning cross. "Rumor had it that you and Daniel Stephenson were dating," Claire Jennings babbled on. "And now you and Josh Clinton are married."

Sheila finally regained the use of her tongue and said, "Are you suggesting that I'm turning men gay?"

"Look! It's Anthony Edwards," Josh said, pointing off camera. "He's cute!"

Sheila and Josh laughed together, then Sheila said, "Oh my gosh, you may be right! It's happening to me, too!"

She leaned over to the unwary Claire and kissed her. Claire struggled and pulled back, Sheila's Capricorn Crimson lipstick smearing her lips.

"Tasty!" Sheila said as a laughing Josh dragged her away.

Claire, apparently thinking they'd stopped taping, sputtered, "Did you see what that dumb dyke did? I've interviewed dozens of closet cases, and none of them ever tried anything with me."

While I considered asking Lillith if I could borrow her attorney, the entertainment program's anchor appeared on my screen. "In a related story," he said, "Claire Jennings was given a leave of absence after pressure from the ACLU and gay-related media watchdog organizations. Questions surrounding Daniel Stephenson and Blaine Dunhill remain unanswered from *Secret Splendor,* as well as the show's sponsor, Seaforth Chemicals. Stephenson's publicist has also declined to comment about the actor's personal life."

I tried to get in touch with Josh and Sheila, but couldn't be sure if they were still in L.A. or back in New York. Their cell phones were off and Call Notes picked up when I tried them at home. I wanted to call Gretchen, but decided not to. Unloading my stress on her wouldn't help either of us. I finally ordered in, and three bacon cheeseburgers later, talked myself into believing that nothing further would happen now that Claire Jennings had been removed from the entertainment news scene. That lasted until the next day, when Jake Meyers called me at my office.

"Blaine, this is getting weird," Jake said. "Some reporter called me from a gay paper in Minneapolis and wanted to interview me about Daniel. I said that I barely know him. Then he asked about you."

"What did you tell him?"

"That I didn't want to be interviewed and he should call you. I figured that was the end of it. But then someone called from *The Advocate*. *The Advocate*, Blaine. That's national. When he realized that I was familiar with the magazine, he asked if I was gay." Jake laughed when I groaned. "It doesn't bother me, but what do you want me to do? They seem to know I'm your best friend. I don't want them to think my silence means I have a problem with you being gay."

"You don't have to say anything. They'll eventually leave you alone."

"They're obviously doing their homework if they're calling me. What happens when they find someone who might be willing to talk? Like Sydney, for example."

"According to my nephew, Sydney's in Europe," I said. "By the time she gets back, this will be old news."

"Your nephew? You've spoken to your family?"

"No. Nick and I have been e-mailing for a while. He says my parents are oblivious to it all. Or at least they're pretending to be."

"Big shock. Where did Sydney get the money to ship her paintings? Please tell me you didn't give it to her."

"No. Sheila thinks she got it from Lola Listeria and the *Star-Gazette*."

"It wouldn't surprise me," Jake said.

A few nights later, Jeremy showed up at my door. He accepted the beer I gave him, listened as I caught him up, then said, "This is not what you signed on for, is it? People in the business crave attention.

We start reciting Oscar acceptance speeches to the mirror when we're barely out of kindergarten. I'm sure it's not easy being the private half of that equation."

I frowned at him and said, "I'm not half of anything, remember? I wish Adam and Ethan had never put that idea into Lillith's and Bonnie's addled brains. Don't you start, too."

Jeremy crossed the room, making no secret of the fact that he wanted a look at Daniel's apartment, and said, "What about him? How's he handling it?"

"How would I know? It's not like we call each other to compare notes. I'm surprised he's not telling you, both of you being 'in the business' and all. Why are you in town?" I asked to change the subject.

"Adam is still here on business, and I flew in for my parents' wedding anniversary. We're staying with them in Brooklyn." He turned back to me. "I'm worried about him."

"Adam?"

Jeremy rolled his eyes and said, "Daniel. I hate it when he shuts down like this."

"Give me a break," I said. "There's nothing wrong with Daniel's coping skills. You should have seen him the day he showed up here in disguise. He enjoyed shoving his drag persona in my face."

Jeremy frowned and said, "You never even tried to understand that side of Daniel. Drag wasn't just a way for him to perform."

"I know," I said. "He raised tons of money and helped the community."

"That's not what I'm talking about. For Daniel, being in drag offered the kind of safety the closet gives some people. It made him feel secure when he was scared or nervous. Like wearing a mask, so no one could see and possibly reject the real him." He paused to let that sink in, then said, "I wish he'd return my calls. He knows I'm in town."

"Maybe he's just dodging unsolicited advice," I suggested.

"Like you, huh?" When I emphatically nodded my agreement, he said, "I gave you advice once before, about talking to Daniel before you and Gretchen made a decision. Was I wrong?"

"Probably not," I admitted.

"I also told you to follow him after the wedding reception so you and he could have it out. You let him leave. How'd that turn out for you?"

"I get your point," I said. "Say what you have to say."

"Stop walking on eggshells around him. Stop listening to other people. They don't know him the way you do. Neither do I, but I've come close. Take my word for it, giving Daniel too much time and space, or letting him magnify your relationship with Ethan out of all proportion, is a bad idea. Not to mention your gym tricks and the rumors about your live-in help."

"Adam is a font of information, isn't he?"

"Believe it or not, Adam, not Daniel, is the reason I'm here. He feels like hell because of the meeting with Lillith and Bonnie."

"That wasn't Adam's fault," I said. "I'll call him and tell him so."

"Thank you."

We both turned when the lock clicked and Gavin came into the apartment. I introduced them, surprised by how reserved Gavin was. Months before, when he'd first found out that I knew Jeremy, his star-struck gene kicked in the way it had on the day we saw Daniel in Whole Foods. But after a polite exchange with Jeremy, Gavin went into the kitchen to noisily put away groceries.

Jeremy regarded me a few seconds then said, "Do you love Daniel?"

"Of course I do."

"Do you want the two of you to work this out?" When I just stared at him as if he had to be kidding, he smiled. "Then find a way to make him face you. You're creative. I'm sure you'll think of something."

After Jeremy left, Gavin came back to the living room, saying, "Is there anything I can get you?"

"No, thanks. You were a little distant to Jeremy. What was that about?"

"I never liked his sitcom. Too much sit and not enough com. Besides, I don't know who's an enemy anymore."

I gave a startled laugh and said, "Is that what it's like around here? A war zone?"

"It's tense," Gavin admitted. "Maybe you could use a massage."

"No," I said. "Not right now." I started to take Jeremy's half-drunk beer from the windowsill and paused, staring down at Daniel's patio.

He'd turned on the lights and was kneeling, doing something to the plants next to his fountain. "Could you hand me the phone, please?" I exchanged the beer bottle for the phone and dialed Daniel's number, watching as he walked to the door to screen the call. "Hi, it's me. Please pick up."

He walked inside and a few seconds later said, "Hi, Blaine."

"Are there still reporters in front of your building?"

"I don't know. Probably. Why?"

"I want to come over. We need to talk."

"I can't guarantee that you won't see your picture somewhere tomorrow."

"I'll be there in a few minutes."

Just in case there were reporters, I combed my hair and changed shirts while I thought things over. Jeremy was right. There was a way to make Daniel spend time with me and maybe work through some of our differences, and it could also spare our friends public scrutiny.

When I rounded the corner, I saw three people relaxing on the stoop of Daniel's building. It was obvious they didn't really expect anything to happen but intended to stick it out, just in case. I took a deep breath and walked purposefully toward them. Tonight they were going to get lucky.

I was on the third step before one of the photographers recognized me. He jumped to his feet, which alerted the others. Daniel had anticipated them, and by the time I was at the door, he opened it, jerked me inside, then quickly pushed it shut.

"Thanks," I said.

"I didn't want you to be stuck ringing the buzzer with those jackals nipping at your heels," he said. I followed him to his apartment, then froze when it occurred to me that I hadn't been inside since the fight that broke us up. Daniel saw the look on my face and said, "We should have met somewhere so you wouldn't have to put up with that crap."

"It's not that," I said. "Anyway, where would we meet, Daniel? I feel like I'm always looking over my shoulder. Gavin and Violet have to screen my calls. I've been accosted going into my office building several times. Usually after somebody's done a story on you. I can't go near Sheila and Josh's place. People stare at me at the gym—"

"They always did," Daniel said with a slight smile.

"—and Gretchen and I have to act like CIA operatives to see each other. This is ridiculous. Elections, mad cow disease, global warming, people fighting over Cuban children—wait, hold the presses, because America must know: *Are Daniel Stephenson and Blaine Dunhill a gay couple?* How fucked up is this? I want to go to work, come home, go to the gym, have an occasional dinner out, walk through Central Park without someone saying, 'Hey, are you that guy?' I never minded being recognized for my accomplishments. Attention is okay if it's something I worked for. But this is so . . . so . . . ."

"Artificial?"

"Or superficial. I want my life back."

"I'm sorry," he said quietly. "My family is going through the same thing you are. I never meant for anyone else to get sucked into my little nightmare."

I nodded and said, "In spite of all the bitching I just did, I don't really give a shit what they're doing to me. It's everybody else. Sheila. Jake. Our friends. What if they start bothering Gretchen? She doesn't need the stress. She's already having blood pressure problems. What if some unscrupulous reporter like Lola Listeria finds out Gretchen's pregnant with my baby?"

Daniel opened his mouth as if to make a quick retort, then stopped himself, finally saying, "If they're willing to print lies to sell tabloids, how do you keep them from printing the truth? There are some things you can't control, Blaine."

"What if we do what everyone else suggested?" I asked. "Pose as a gay supercouple until everyone gets tired of us. Anne and Ellen just broke up. We'll carry the torch now. If we're willing to give interviews, maybe reporters will stop hounding the people who know us."

"You want us to lie," Daniel said.

"I want us to take the heat so no one else has to," I said. "We do a few interviews, smile, and profess our love for each other. The story dies, and we all go on with our lives. Privately." When he stared at me, saying nothing, I realized that I'd wanted him to tell me that we did love each other, so it wouldn't be a lie. That obviously wasn't going to happen. "Never mind. Lying would probably only make things worse. Forget I asked."

He didn't stop me from leaving. There were now eight people on his stoop, all of whom I ignored as I walked through them. I was a few steps down the sidewalk when I heard Daniel call my name. I stopped, turned around, and waited for him to walk to me, keeping my face empty while the cameras flashed.

"You forgot this," Daniel said, wrapping his arms around me and giving me a long kiss.

The kiss was wonderful, even though I knew it was only for show. I pulled away, forced a smile, and said, "You could have answered me inside."

"Be careful what you ask for," Daniel said, smiling as insincerely back at me. "See you in the papers."

CHAPTER 14

Violet arrived for breakfast with a wary look on her face. I saw Gavin give her a reassuring glance, then they both sat down at the table with me. Violet filled her plate, lifted her fork, then set it back down.

"I can't eat," she said. "Blaine, if you're about to fire me, just do it."

"Fire you?" I asked. "Are you nuts?"

"Why am I here? Something isn't right."

"You're here because I need you. Both of you." They listened silently while I described the effect the unwanted media attention was having on my friends and Daniel's friends and family. I finished by telling them the decision we'd made. "A few days ago, we agreed to go public with our relationship. Or rather, with the pretense that we have a relationship. Last night we taped an interview that will air on Daniel's network tonight. We're hoping if we're more accessible, everyone else will be left alone."

"How can we help?" Gavin asked.

"Violet, all you'll have to do is coordinate my schedule with Gavin. Gavin, if you're willing, you'll work with Daniel's publicist, Ronald, to manage whatever interviews or engagements the two of us need to do. We'd like to keep that to a minimum. I think you have some idea what we may be in for if you've followed the stories of other gay celebrities and politicians who've come out. I understand it can get a little crazy."

"I can handle it," Gavin assured me.

"I'm not a public figure and never intended to be. But Daniel is.

He's also very honest, so this isn't an easy game for him to play. But he accepts it as the fastest way to put an end to something neither of us ever wanted. We feel like we've been backed into a corner, so we'll play the game for a few months, then we can both move on with our lives."

Violet nodded, took a bite of food, then dropped her fork again. *"Months?* There's more, isn't there?"

"Yes," I said. "I need to apologize to you both. I gave you a hard time about the apartments we looked at because I couldn't be honest with you." I told them about Gretchen's insemination and our December due date. "When we first started looking at apartments, we didn't know if Gretchen was pregnant. Then I got too busy to worry about moving. But when I do, I need a place big enough so that my child can occasionally spend nights with me."

"Congratulations," Gavin said, grinning at me. "It's great that you're going to be a father."

"I already suspected as much," Violet said, also smiling, "after hearing that Gretchen was pregnant. I'm happy for you both."

"Don't worry; you won't end up being nannies," I promised. "Gretchen is already interviewing people for that position. Her health is my main concern. Her doctor wants her to avoid stress as much as she can, so she doesn't need to be subjected to what my other friends are going through. Plus, this is the one thing I want kept private, no matter what. Gretchen and I are not exactly *Rolling Stone* cover material like Melissa Etheridge and David Crosby, but as far as I'm concerned, any press is bad press when it involves my child. If Daniel and I appear to be a happy couple, no one will try to dig up dirt about us. And on the bright side, at least we're being honest that we're gay. You never know. That could help someone."

"It will," Gavin said. "Including you and Daniel. You shouldn't worry about pretending that you're a couple. I think the well-being of an expectant mother is a pretty compelling reason to do what you're doing." He looked at Violet and added, "I admire honesty, but I've never been a fan of outing. People should be allowed to share things about themselves on their own terms."

"Yeah, it's too bad Lola Listeria took that choice away from Daniel and me," I said. "So you two are okay with this?"

"Yes," Violet said.

"Totally," Gavin agreed.

"Good. Can we eat now? Violet's getting a Dexterish look of hunger in her eyes," I said.

That night I went to Gretchen's to watch the interview. The network had chosen the most dignified, understated of their entertainment reporters to question us. It was hard watching myself on television, but fortunately Daniel was the main focus, and I admired his poise and his ability to keep things light. His publicist had prepped us, but Daniel's innate acting ability helped him carry it off.

Although I'd been with him and already knew what he was going to say, I found myself affected by his description of how it felt to have our privacy invaded and our lives turned upside down. Even when I spoke, the camera couldn't stay away from Daniel, whose face conveyed affection for and approval of me. I was sure that if we hadn't been honest with our small group of friends, they would never have guessed that we'd arrived separately, spoken very little to each other, and parted quickly after the interview was over.

Gretchen turned off the television, looked at me, and burst into tears.

"What's wrong?" I asked. "Is this another hormonal moment?"

"No," she said, taking the Kleenex I held out. "I'm sad because it's not true. You're doing this to protect me and the baby, but I want it to be real. I feel like it's my fault that it's not."

"Daniel and I broke up months before you and I made our decision."

"I know, but you almost got back together at the wedding. Why can't this be real? Why can't the two of you stop fighting and work this out?"

"Please don't get upset. That's exactly what we're trying to avoid."

"I'll be fine," she said. "But what about you and Daniel?"

"Did we look like we were suffering?"

"Not on camera."

"We're tired of being at the mercy of people like Lola Listeria. You have no idea what a relief it is to finally feel in control of this situation. If anyone's going to tell lies about me, dammit, it's going to be me."

Gretchen managed a weak smile and said, "You're awfully good at it."

"He's an actor. I'm in advertising. Would you expect less?"

"Hand me the phone and go home," she ordered. "It's time for your friends to do a postmortem."

"I wanna hear," I whined.

"No. Trust me, the phone lines will be busy, and you're better off not knowing."

"Why? Did I look fat on television?"

"Are you still here?" she asked.

I laughed, gave her a hug, and left as she was dialing the phone. My cell phone rang before I was a block from her building, and I looked at the display with a smile.

"You'd better be calling to tell me how good I looked," I said.

"You both looked great," Ethan said. "You came across as intelligent and funny. I'm afraid it's going to be a while before you bore them into leaving you alone."

Over the next couple of weeks, thanks to anonymous calls from Gavin and Violet tipping off the press, Daniel and I were "caught" going to the movies, having dinner together, and attending a performance at Lincoln Center. On each occasion, we'd be as affectionate as possible and offer a quick sound bite professing our love for each other. Other than a photo in the *New York Times* "Styles" section capturing Daniel and me shopping on Madison Avenue, captioned, "Can dashing Daniel liven up bland Blaine's fall wardrobe?," reactions to our stepping out as a couple were favorable.

Gavin was able to confirm what Daniel's publicist, Ronald, had told us might happen. Requests and calls from the mainstream media dropped off when the story began to be perceived as less of a scandal than as "another gay couple trying to promote their agenda," as one of my least favorite talk show hosts put it. With occasional guidance from Violet and painstaking coordination with Ronald, Gavin began providing us with lists of interviews and public appearances to choose from.

Daniel's friend, Andy Vanedesen, owner of Club Chaos in Greenwich Village, hosted a benefit at his club for God's Love We Deliver, which we attended. Andy talked Daniel into singing one song, and Daniel dragged me on stage with him. Holding hands, smiling, and ending with a kiss, we sang "Together, Wherever We Go," much to the delight of the audience. It was actually a nice evening for us, and I started feeling hopeful that our ruse might have a positive outcome. Pictures of us embracing with microphones in our hands ran in *HX* and *NEXT* magazines the following week.

Our social calendar began to fill with a cavalcade of confusing acronyms. I'd dash home from work to change and discover which group would be garnering an appearance from Daniel and Blaine, Gay Supercouple.

"I know I just came from the office, Gavin," I said one night, "but could you call Violet and ask her to memo the Deity shooting schedule to the other departments? What am I dressing for? Where are Daniel and I going tonight?"

Gavin consulted his PalmPilot and said, "Tonight is ELBOW."

"Who's elbow?" I asked.

"Empire Lesbian Bowlers of Woodside," he said.

"You've got to be kidding. We don't bowl. We're not lesbians. What could they possibly want with us? Is it too late to back out?"

"Tonight is their Bowling for Breast Cancer benefit," Gavin explained. "You and Daniel will show up, tell a few jokes, introduce the league president, bowl a little, and have your picture taken. Oh, yeah, and have fun."

"Why was I thinking tonight we were supposed to be dancing somewhere? I would've remembered ELBOW. I thought you said something about dancing. Or a bake sale. Not bowling."

Gavin shook his head and said, "No. You're thinking of BACON. Bears and Cubs of Newark. You and Daniel are judging their dance marathon this weekend. The bake sale for SIQC is tomorrow."

"Sick? Is that a health group?"

"Staten Island Queer Coalition," Gavin clarified.

At every event where Daniel and I cut ribbons, spoke, or put in an appearance, we were photographed hand in hand, smiling at each other. If the press asked about our relationship, our only comment was that we were simply a couple in love offering support to our gay brothers and sisters.

Unfortunately, the social whirl began taking its toll. What we didn't let anyone see were the arguments that began to precede and follow every appearance. The problems that caused our breakup remained unresolved and added to the tension. Sometimes, smiling for the camera, we'd whisper terse comments through clenched jaws, squeezing each other's hands a little harder than necessary. I endured it, hoping that sooner or later these meaningless fights would force our more serious issues to surface.

The most significant, immediate payoff of our farce was that the more approachable we became, the less our friends were bothered. There was only one reaction I'd been anxious about, and it came in an e-mail.

Hi Uncle Blaine,

Boy, once you decide to do something, you do it in a big way. I thought it was a big deal when you came out to my mom and dad, but now you're doing TV interviews and all kinds of stuff. It's kinda cool, kinda like having someone famous in the family. Not that anyone in the family talks about it. It's like it's happening to everybody but us.

Remember the time you saw me at that PFLAG meeting? I know I probably didn't seem glad to see you, but I didn't know what to think about you being there. I was afraid you'd say something to my mom or dad or someone. I didn't think about how you'd have to explain what you were doing there, too, until later. But I've thought about things a lot since then. You asked me then if I was gay, and I said I was confused. That's what I tell people when I'm not sure how they'll react. But I wasn't really confused, and if I was even a little, I'm not now. It's just not easy to be gay, in Eau Claire, and a Dunhill all at the same time. I guess you know that. I wish sometimes I could be anywhere but here.

I told my family that I'm gay. I figured if you could do it, so could I. Mom cried, and Dad walked out of the room. We don't talk about it, and that sucks. But I'm not going to be someone I'm not just so everyone else can be comfortable. I don't think Chuck and Tony were surprised.

I decided to come out to a few of my friends. No big deal. Everyone basically said, "Yeah, I already knew," or "I

*thought so," or "Really? Cool." One of the other kids at
PFLAG warned me that I should watch out for bashers.
But I've always done that. I'm careful what classes and
teachers I take. You learn pretty quick who you can
count on, and to find a way out of PE or stuff like that.*

*If there's one thing I'd like to know, it's when you knew
about yourself. I've always known I wasn't like everyone
else. I just didn't know what it was about me and couldn't
figure out how come I didn't fit in. Was it like that for
you, too?*

*Gotta go.
Nick*

Remembering Ethan's warning that teenagers tell us what they think we want to hear, I put everything else on hold and wrote a long response, describing the adolescent fear and denial that had led to my dating Sheila and marrying Sydney. I told him how much I admired his courage and honesty, reminding him that if things got difficult, he could talk to his PFLAG contacts, especially Jeremy. Finally, choosing my words with care, I assured him that he could always tell me anything, especially about problems he experienced with our family.

It chilled me to think of how much like my father Shane was. When I thought of my baby, I felt a mixture of joy, fear, hope, and humility. Had my father ever felt that? Had Shane felt that way when Beverly was pregnant? If so, what happened after a child was born that closed a parent's heart?

Maybe it wasn't a lack of love, but a need to control. You couldn't control the world, or the things your child would have to endure, so you tried to control your child. To make him into someone the world wouldn't hurt or reject. Daniel had often chided me about my need to control people. My scheme to use our fifteen minutes of fame to force him to spend time with me seemed to confirm his accusations. I hoped that didn't mean I was doomed to repeat my family's mistakes with my child.

Then again, Daniel wasn't a child, nor was he the most pliable of accomplices. Our public appearances were proof that he was only too eager to challenge my opinions and goad me into arguments.

"Is that what you're wearing?" Daniel asked one night when we were off to another benefit.

"No. It's an illusion done with smoke and mirrors. I'm really wearing a sequined ball gown," I growled.

Since the press no longer found it necessary to camp on our doorsteps, Daniel and I felt free to try to get the bitterness out of our systems. He glared at me as we stalked angrily to Ninth Avenue to hail a cab.

"All I meant was," he said, "if we're going to make people think we're a couple, you should start dressing a little more—"

"Like you?"

"Yes," he insisted. "Remember that photo in the 'Styles' section? I don't mean to sound conceited, but I'm known for being a stylish dresser."

"I know you don't mean to sound conceited," I said. "It just comes naturally to you."

Daniel scowled at me but let the insult slide, saying, "If you want people to believe we're dating, you should refresh your wardrobe so it looks like I'm influencing you."

We slid into the backseat of a cab, and I recited an address that Gavin had hastily scribbled for me to the driver. "We want people to think we're a couple. I'm not in this alone, you know," I said to Daniel, resuming the discussion. "And you're being ridiculous. I never altered my style when we actually were dating. Why should I do it now?"

"I'm just saying it's an idea. Lots of couples take on each other's characteristics when they're in love. Style is sometimes one of them."

"If that was true, David Arquette wouldn't be on *People*'s 'Worst Dressed List' all the time. And why would I have to be the one to change? Why couldn't you start wearing suits? Or be the responsible one for a change?"

Daniel took a deep breath and opened his mouth as if to start yelling, then looked at our driver and stopped himself.

"What?" I asked.

"I'm afraid we're going to end up on *Taxi Cab Confessions* or something," he whispered.

"That's insane. Those people have to sign releases before they 'confess.' It's a skewed version of reality," I said.

"Just like us," Daniel said. He fell silent until he asked, "Where are we going?"

"BATS is throwing a fund-raising benefit party at some club down-town. I have an early morning meeting, so I don't want to stay too late. Violet tried to talk me out of going. She's worried I'll oversleep and miss my meeting."

"What the hell is BATS?" Daniel asked.

"Brooklyn Area Transgender Support," I said.

"No wonder she didn't want you to go," Daniel said, hiding a grin behind his hand and looking away from me.

"Why?"

"Blaine, you really are clueless sometimes. Violet used to be a man."

"No, she didn't," I said, looking at him like he was crazy.

"Okay, you could be right. I don't know what stage of the process she's in. But she's definitely transgendered. You do know what that is, don't you?"

"Of course," I said, holding up a hand so he wouldn't go into graphic detail.

"Until now, I thought you knew about her," Daniel said. "I finally understand why she always avoided meeting me. Considering my past as Princess 2Di4, she probably figured I'd spot it immediately and tell you."

"But that would mean she was keeping it a secret from me," I said, dazed by his revelation. "If that's the case, it worked. I thought she was a woman."

"She *is* a woman," Daniel said. "She used to be a man."

"Right. But why would she want to keep that a secret from me?"

"Blaine, I'm not trying to start another fight," Daniel said, "but sometimes you can be very intolerant."

I met Daniel's honesty and his sympathetic stare with silence. Rather than fly off the handle like I normally would, I carefully weighed his words. I thought about Jeremy's criticism of the way I usually reacted to Daniel's past profession as a female impersonator and, most recently, when he'd shown up at my apartment in drag to elude the press. I was sometimes hostile, but usually changed the subject. I'd embed it in the past, as if drag were a bout of chicken pox that Daniel had caught but would never experience again. Which was how Daniel treated the subject of my ex-wife, Sydney. The difference was, I shared Daniel's feelings about Sydney. Daniel, on the other hand, regarded his years of performing as 2Di4 with fondness, as if she were a real person he loved and respected, who had moved to another country and was sorely missed.

"I'm sorry," I said.

"For not knowing Violet was once a man?" Daniel asked, looking perplexed. "That's nothing to be sorry for. She's beautiful. It took a few hard glances for me to be sure."

"No. Not that," I said, pausing to get the words right. "I'm sorry that I always reacted so badly whenever the subject of 2Di4 came up. Not only because of how that must have made you feel, but because I missed sharing a part of your past that made you who you are today."

Daniel stared at me, his mouth slightly open, until the cab swerved to avoid colliding with a bus and he grabbed my arm to keep from being flung across the backseat. He finally said, "Okay," very quietly. When he realized that he was still holding my arm, we both watched as he slowly let go and retreated into silence.

"Do you know anyone else who's transgendered?" I asked.

"Uh-huh. Bernice at Club Chaos," he answered.

"Bernice?" I asked, shocked.

"Yeah. You know her. She runs the sound system there."

"I know who she is," I said, remembering the time Daniel and I had borrowed Bernice's truck to pick up my leather sofa from a showroom in SoHo. "I didn't know she was a man."

"Is a woman," Daniel said, correcting me. "Really, Blaine. If we're going to be hobnobbing with transgendered people tonight, you should watch what you say."

We were almost banished to the long line of people waiting to get into the club because the doorman didn't have our names on his list.

"I don't mean to be an asshole," Daniel began.

"But he does it so well," I said.

The doorman laughed, but fell silent when Daniel got in touch with his inner diva and said, "I was performing in this club when you

;uring out how to masturbate. Now get your head out of
l let us in."

ho'd come from inside the club asked, "Is there a prob-

he doorman said, gesturing to Daniel and me. "These
should—"

"Holy shit! It's Angus! I mean, Daniel Stephenson," the other man said. He pulled aside the velvet rope and led us into the club, babbling the whole way. "I'm so glad you two made it. Daniel, I'm sure you know Taylor? The club's owner? He's doing an interview with the director of BATS right now. I know they'd love to get a picture with both of you. Come on."

We posed for a few pictures, and Daniel, speaking for both of us to the reporter, said, "It's high time that legislation to extend civil liberties to transgendered people was introduced to City Council. There were nineteen transgendered people murdered this year. Blaine and I feel that transgendered people have a right to feel as safe and protected in this city as anyone else."

When we joined the party and hit the dance floor, Daniel wrapped his arms around me and started moving slowly to the music, although a fast dance mix was pulsing through the club's sound system. It felt good to have him close to me, and it was easy to forget all of our arguments, but I reminded myself that there were photographers around and he was only portraying his role as the doting boyfriend.

"I didn't know I felt so strongly about transgender equality," I said in Daniel's ear.

He pulled back from me and said, "I'm sorry I spoke for both of us."

"No. It's fine. I'm all for it. Now that I know someone who's . . ." I trailed off, unsure of what I was trying to say.

"What?" Daniel yelled.

"Never mind," I shouted. Daniel shrugged and kept dancing, although he no longer felt compelled to hold me. I spied a familiar face across the room and said, "I'll be back in a minute."

When I reached the bar, Violet handed me a martini. "It's dirty," she said. "You showed up."

"Yes. Despite your protests," I said, sipping the drink so it wouldn't spill. "Hey, speaking of dirty little secrets—"

"Found me out, huh?" Violet asked.

"Daniel told me," I said.

"Speaking of dirty little secrets," Violet mimicked me. She glanced at the people around us and motioned for me to follow her to a corner of the room where nobody would overhear our conversation. "How's it going?"

"Dammit, Violet," I said. "I find out I know less about you than I thought I did, and you want to talk about me and Daniel?"

"Could you know less? When's my birthday? Where do I live?" she asked. I cringed when I realized I had no answers. "Here's a hint. You're at a benefit for an organization with Brooklyn in its title."

"I'm sorry. I suck," I said. I was relieved when she laughed.

"No, you don't," she protested. "You're a busy man, and I'm your assistant."

"But I think of you as my friend, Violet, above all else. You're like my spine. I'd be a mass of quivering Jell-O if it wasn't for you." She looked embarrassed, albeit in a pleased way. I remembered our meeting with Lillith and said, "You're a Capricorn. I know that much."

Violet exclaimed, "Ha! Technically, Noreen was right. I am an Aries. Four years ago, I had my final operation on January twentieth, so I consider that my birthday now."

"No wonder poor Noreen was so confused."

"Yes. Especially since all my legal documentation lists April twelfth as my birthday. I'm sure that's on her company astrology charts."

"How come you never told me?" I asked.

"I don't like a fuss on my birthday."

"Not that," I said.

"I was afraid," Violet said. She stared into her martini as she continued, "I applied at Breslin Evans because I heard they were extending benefits to partners of their gay and lesbian employees. When I found out that was your idea, I asked to work for you."

"I didn't have *that* much to—"

"Blaine, please," Violet interrupted. "This is my story."

"Sorry," I said, failing to suppress a laugh.

"However liberal Breslin Evans tried to be, there was nothing in their antidiscrimination policies that said they couldn't fire me because of my being transgendered. So I didn't tell anyone. Why should I? I'm a woman."

"Despite my being here, I know little to nothing about transgendered people," I admitted.

"No offense, Blaine, but that's not a huge revelation," Violet said, winking before she sipped her martini to let me know she was teasing me.

"But didn't you have to show HR a driver's license or something?" I asked.

Violet replied in a patient tone of voice, like a teacher talking to an eight-year-old, "I don't drive, but the name on my license is Violet Medina. Female. Same name on my social security card. It's all legal. I wasn't trying to pull the wool over your eyes."

"If you were, it would be a fashionable wool hat, I'm sure," I joked. "But I hear you. It's like when Gavin said that people should be allowed to reveal their secrets on their own terms. I completely agree with that. Although recently, I've been told I can be intolerant to what I don't understand."

Violet craned her neck to look at the dance floor, then turned back to me and said, "Daniel looks okay. I guess you didn't rip his face off for saying that. You're making progress."

"I'm not that bad, am I?" I asked.

"I wouldn't have worked for you all this time if you were," Violet assured me. "Nor would I go through all this trouble helping you deceive the gay media. How's it going?"

"It's tough. The deception is bad enough, but what's really difficult to deal with is Daniel. If it were anyone else, it would be a whole lot easier."

"If it were anyone else, you probably wouldn't be going through all of this," Violet pointed out. "Is it worth it?"

Before I could answer, Daniel walked up and said, "Hi. Hope I'm not interrupting anything serious."

He was wiping sweat off his brow, as he'd been dancing nonstop since I left him to speak with Violet. His face was flushed and he smiled bashfully, obviously thinking he looked a mess. He looked fantastic, and I was painfully aware that I was staring at him, so I polished off the rest of my martini and said, "Violet was discussing the Deity line with me, letting me know that Josh is available to shoot ads this month as long as they're in New York."

"Do you two ever stop working?" Daniel asked.

Violet and I looked at each other and said simultaneously, "No."

Daniel shook his head, and Violet said, "I need to go home if I'm going to get to the office in the morning. And you should, too," she said, poking my shoulder. "Daniel, it was nice to see you again."

"You, too, Violet," he said.

As she walked away, she hesitated, then walked back to Daniel and said, "Before I go, I've wanted to tell you something. A long time ago, after the Pride Parade, I was at the pier dance and you—well, Princess 2Di4—gave this wonderful speech about what pride meant to you and how important our families are to us."

"Violet, please don't say it was 'a long time ago,' pumpkin," Daniel said. Running his fingers over his face, he turned to me and asked, "Are my wrinkles showing?"

"Yes," I insisted.

"What I mean to say," Violet went on, "is that I loved Princess 2Di4, and she gave me a lot of courage to become the person I am today." Violet leaned forward and kissed Daniel on the cheek. "I just wanted to say thank you."

"You're welcome," he said, before she smiled at him, waved at me, and left us standing there. Daniel bit his bottom lip as he watched her leave. I could tell he was trying not to cry.

"She's amazing," he said.

"You're amazing," I said.

Daniel composed himself, took my hand and said, "Yeah, well, smile for the cameras, darling. We're leaving."

Since the night hadn't gone too badly, I was tempted to prolong it. Once we were in our cab, however, Daniel practically hugged the door opposite me, and I bit off whatever suggestion I'd been about to make. By the time I reached my apartment, I could tell it would be a Sominex night. Not that I ever took anything like that. I preferred to stare miserably at the clock while it ticked away the possibility of sleep.

"Welcome home," Gavin said, after I shut the door behind me.

"How did you know?" I asked, looking around. Gavin's massage table was set up, the top sheet pulled back invitingly. The air smelled of rosemary, chamomile, and lavender. Ambient music played softly in the background, and the only light came from dozens of votive candles flickering throughout the room.

"Violet called. She thought this might be a good idea."

"She was right. I'll be ready in a minute." I went to my room and undressed, wrapping a towel around my waist. When I came back, Gavin was washing his hands in the kitchen, so I removed the towel, lay facedown on the massage table, and started doing the deep breathing he'd taught me.

Once Gavin started the massage, I shut out Daniel by thinking about Violet. Although she hadn't been reproachful, it bothered me how little I knew about her life. Or Gavin's, for that matter. I turned my head and asked, "What do you do in your spare time? Do you date? Do I give you enough time off to have a life?"

"Facedown," Gavin commanded. "I can't get into those muscles when you're all twisted around." I did as I was told, and he went on. "I'm not dating anyone right now. By choice. I go out for dinner and drinks, or to see shows and movies, with old friends. I have no complaints."

I was quiet until he had me turn over, then I said, "Since you and Violet have been acquaintances for a long time, I guess you knew her secret. Was she afraid of telling me because I'm an intolerant pig?"

"No! The day we looked at apartments, you left us to meet someone, and Violet and I had dinner to talk things over. How we both fit into your life. How we could work together. She told me that she loved working for you because you're not a 'supposed to' person."

"What does that mean?"

"Some people do things because they know they're supposed to. Flowers on Secretary's Day. Lunch or dinner on a birthday. Violet told me that you don't operate on that level. You act from impulses of gratitude or generosity."

"Sometimes I act that way as a means of persuasion," I said.

"So what? At least you're honest about what you're doing. Anyway, Violet said she didn't tell you up front because she didn't know you, and she'd been burned by a few people when she was honest. By the time she understood you better, she knew it wouldn't matter. If you found out, you'd be okay with it. Not because you're *supposed to,* but because it was irrelevant. She was right, wasn't she? It is irrelevant."

"She's always right," I said, and closed my eyes. After a couple of minutes, I opened them, looked at him, and said, "What about you?

Are you going to spring any secrets on me? Manservant by day, suave cat burglar by night?"

"My life is an open book," Gavin said. "Stop talking and practice your breathing."

Whatever détente Daniel and I had reached at the BATS party had apparently dissolved by our next outing together. The following Wednesday we were slated to appear at a gala hosted by *Ultimate Magazine.* Wearing a new Armani tuxedo and trying to remain optimistic, I greeted Daniel on his stoop with the brightest smile I could muster. My smile quickly faded when he said, "Hi. I thought you'd be wearing your beaded ball gown tonight."

"I don't get it," I said.

Daniel handed me a newspaper clipping as his front door shut behind him. My eyes were drawn immediately to a photo to the left of Lola Listeria's column. It was a picture of a blond girl holding a guitar.

"Isn't that the girl from *Family Ties*?" I asked. "What was her name?"

"Tina Yothers. Look a little closer," Daniel urged.

"Christ on a cracker. It's you," I said.

"I don't know where Lola got that," Daniel said. "Or how. 'The Tina Yothers Comeback Special' only ran at Club Chaos a few times. And it was never publicized."

"The Tina Yothers what? Never mind. I just hope it wasn't Andy who sold the picture to Lola," I said, thinking about Daniel's love-hate relationship with his former employer.

"No," Daniel protested. "Andy may be a lot of things, but he'd never do that. Besides, I called him and did a lot of yelling just to be sure, and he swore he didn't. I believe him. He reminded me that 'The Tina Yothers Comeback Special' happened before I officially worked for Club Chaos. Andy hardly liked me enough then to want to hang on to any keepsakes of the moment. Some queen must've cleaned out his closet, found the picture, and figured he could make a few bucks from it."

"Martin," I said vehemently.

"Jesus Christ, Blaine! Martin is my friend. Why would he sell that picture to Lola? I didn't even know him at that time. Besides, what would he have to gain from this? Nothing!" Daniel yelled.

"That's true," I said. "I mean, if it would hurt me in some way, he might. But this is about you."

"Well . . ." Daniel said, trailing off and looking nervous.

"Oh, fuck," I said and scanned the article. There was only one section about us, which was adjacent to the photo of Daniel impersonating Tina Yothers. I read it aloud. " 'Oh, that Daniel Stephenson! What a ham! Lola dragged—get it?—this alluring photo of our favorite daytime devil from the archives. That's right, readers. Our soap stud wore drag duds in a show called 'The Tina Yothers Comeback Special.' Lola wonders why that's not on the *Secret Splendor* star's résumé? Sha la la laaaa! Lola also wonders if Daniel Stephenson's boyfriend, Lillith Allure's Creative Director, Blaine Dunhill, knows about this? Does Blaine dress up like Justine Bateman or Meredith Baxter? Our boys have been appearing at every event in the city, proclaiming that they're just a normal couple like everyone else. If dressing up like Tina Yothers is normal, Lola's catching the next bus back home to Boise . . . Speaking of freaky, guess what Lola heard about a certain not so innocent . . .' " I stopped reading and gritted my teeth to keep from screaming.

"Go on. I didn't read that part. What does she say about Britney?" Daniel asked. I grimaced at him and he said, "Never mind. Look, it's not that bad."

"Not that bad?" I bellowed. "Now people are going to think we sit around in petticoats drinking tea."

"That's ridiculous," Daniel said. "Nobody wears petticoats anymore. Maybe a nice Chanel suit."

"Sure, Daniel. Make jokes," I said.

"What else can I do?" Daniel said, his voice growing louder. "Nothing! It's a gossip column. Nobody takes Lola seriously. A few months ago, she thought I was trying to break up Sheila and Josh. Was that true? No. Everyone knows they're married and very together. Maybe people will think this is more of her moronic ramblings."

"Illustrated with a picture," I reminded him.

"You can't handle another reminder that I used to perform in drag," Daniel huffed.

"No. You're wrong," I protested. "What pisses me off is that she's setting us back to square one. We've spent weeks doing all this work to make people think we're a normal gay couple, and now it's all for naught."

"Normal," Daniel scoffed. "I guess you blame me, as usual. Once again, I can't live up to your idea of respectability. Anyway, her column is old news. I was truthful about my past as a female impersonator in *Us*. Nobody cares."

"Oh, forget it. Let's just go to this stupid function and pretend like we never saw this." Trying to lighten the mood, I looked at Daniel's tux, obviously new and created by some designer I'd never heard of, and said, "Is that what you're wearing?"

Daniel looked horrified for a moment, then rolled his eyes and followed me to the car that was waiting by the curb.

Ultimate Magazine was celebrating five years in the publishing business by throwing a gala dinner at the Waldorf-Astoria Hotel. Not only was the magazine celebrating its success, but tickets to the party were sold to benefit People for the Ethical Treatment of Animals. When we arrived, the hotel's opulent ballroom was crowded with formally attired magazine staff, society's elite, celebrities, and their pets.

"This is like *Lifestyles of the Rich and Famous* meets Noah's ark," Daniel said.

"I should've brought Dexter."

"He's better off at home," Daniel said. "The society pets would all laugh at the state of his fur coat."

"Don't say 'fur coat' so loud," I joked. "Chrissie Hynde might kick our ass."

"I love Chrissie Hynde. I used to impers—she can kick my ass anytime she wants to," Daniel said.

Josh and Sheila spotted us from across the room and rushed over to greet us. "You look so familiar," Sheila said, pretending to study my face. "I know we've met."

"Very funny," I said. "I know I've been busy lately. But I'm not the one jetting back and forth across the country."

"I take it you saw our red carpet encounter in L.A.," Josh said.

"You mean the one where Sheila, who never makes a scene—"

"The upside is that the media's avoided me ever since," Sheila said, cutting me off. "A little embarrassment works wonders. You two should try it next time you're in a pinch."

"We're trying to create a positive image," I reminded her. "What were you doing in L.A.?"

"Sheila was invited to that movie premiere. I was on assignment. Our next issue is entirely devoted to PETA. I was taking pictures of celebrities and their pets," Josh explained. "I spent an entire afternoon at Pamela Anderson's house. She's practically running her own zoo."

"I thought you might be there auditioning for a movie," Daniel said to Sheila.

Sheila replied, "Nope. I was just along for the ride. The dutiful wife follows her man. One big happy family. Hey. Speaking of families, how's Gretchen doing?"

Josh placed a cautionary hand on her shoulder, but it was too late. Sheila's gaffe had done its damage, which was evident when I winced and Daniel turned scarlet.

"Oh, shit," Sheila said helplessly. "I'm sorry. I thought maybe you two had—"

"Worked that out? No. Not so much," Daniel said, interrupting her.

"That would be forbidden topic number—what are we up to now? Twenty? I can't keep track," I said, glaring at Daniel.

"Guys, bring it down," Josh said, keeping his voice low. "I don't think this is the time or place to—"

"Be honest for once?" Daniel said. "Is that what you want, Blaine?"

"Josh is right, Daniel. Let's save this for later and put our party faces back on," I said, smiling to emphasize my point.

"Oh, look. It's Tina Yothers. I can tell her I just made a movie with her mother," Daniel said and walked away.

"I'm gonna go . . ." Sheila said, her voice trailing off as she followed Daniel.

"What the hell just happened?" Josh asked.

"It's like this every time we get together," I said. "We fight, the insults start flying, and we're horrible to each other."

"Defense mechanism," Josh said and patted my shoulder. "Hang in there. You guys are doing fine."

"I hope Sheila can calm him down," I said. "I can't believe she mentioned Gretchen in front of him."

"They'll make up. They always do," Josh said. "I hate to leave you, Blaine, but I have to find my editors and schmooze. Are you going to be okay?"

"Yeah, sure," I said. "At least Daniel and I are no longer avoiding the fights we should have had months ago. It's just not doing much for his mood."

"When I shoot the Narcissus pictures for Deity, I'll see what I can do to lift his spirits," Josh offered.

"Good luck. I know he's not too thrilled about posing for Lillith Allure. I think the best way to lift his spirits about any of this is for me to steer clear of that particular session," I said. Josh looked like he was about to protest, so I shooed him off, saying, "Go. Mingle with the people. Talk to the animals."

I walked aimlessly through the ballroom, pausing only to politely say hello to people and pet their dogs, cats, or lemur. As I did, I scanned faces for Daniel or Sheila, but couldn't find either of them. Instead, in a grand hall off the ballroom, I found a group of people lined up to pamper their pets with massages offered by a local holistic animal center. Among the men and women soothing the savage beasts, I was surprised to see Ethan resting his hands on the back of a Doberman pinscher, his eyes shut in deep concentration. When he finally opened his eyes and handed the dog back to its owner, he saw me and broke away from the other therapists.

He gave me a sociable hug and said, "What a pleasant surprise. Did you bring your cat? I'd be happy to do some energy work on him."

"Dexter's at home washing his hair," I said. "I didn't know your work extended to animals."

"Animals not only guide our spirits, but they give so much to our energy," Ethan said. "It's important to give back energy and heal them whenever possible. A wise man once said, *True love needs no company, it can cure the soul, it can make you whole, if dogs run free.*"

"What?"

"Bob Dylan. Are you okay, Blaine?"

Before I could answer, Daniel appeared, looking less than pleased to see Ethan. Though they greeted each other and attempted to make small talk, it was obvious Daniel was just going through the motions. Ethan excused himself by saying he had to get back to his energy work.

"Why were you so rude to him?" I whispered to Daniel after Ethan left.

"Don't start with me," Daniel warned.

"It's time for dinner," I said, noticing that people were starting to take their places at the tables in the ballroom. "Let's just eat, make a few more rounds, then we can leave."

"In separate cars, I hope," Daniel said, taking off for the ballroom.

I followed him to our table, where we were served several delicious courses of vegetarian fare. I immediately thought of Gretchen, but wisely kept that to myself. I needn't have bothered being discreet. We were seated with a few people from the publishing industry, who only talked to each other. Daniel wouldn't talk to me at all, as he was seated next to Tina Yothers, who he conversed with nonstop from the moment we sat down.

After dinner, the guests were treated to a performance by The B-52's. When they started playing, I decided to use the noise to my advantage and squirreled Daniel away to a corner of the ballroom to have it out with him.

"What's wrong with you?" I asked. "The plan was that we go to these events as a couple. People are more likely to believe you're dating Tina Yothers, since you haven't said one word to me all night."

"Just as they're more likely to believe you're dating Ethan Whitecrow," Daniel said. "Did you know he would be here? Is that why it was so important we come here tonight? So you could be with your fuck buddy?"

"No," I said quickly. "Your publicist and Gavin arrange our appearances. Other than shelling out money for the tickets, I had nothing to do with this. I had no idea Ethan would be here."

"Yeah, right," Daniel scoffed.

"Sure, Daniel. You got me. Ethan's whole spiritual thing is a complete ruse. It's all an act just so he could see me tonight," I said sarcastically. "In fact, those two books he wrote? I wrote them. Yeah, that's right. I wrote them to add credibility to this whole plot. I guess the jig is up. Maybe I should find Ethan and let him know."

I turned to walk away, then spied a camera crew from *Entertainment Tonight* headed toward us. Looking over my shoulder, I saw Daniel scowling at me, obviously getting ready to rival The B-52's in terms of volume. I panicked and grabbed him, quickly pulling him to me and kissing him. Daniel struggled in my grip for a moment, but soon gave in to the kiss and even opened his mouth to touch my teeth with his tongue. I felt warm lights from the television crew turn on us, and someone said, "Having fun, guys?"

I broke our kiss, spun Daniel around, and dipped him, as if we were Fred and Ginger. We both grinned maniacally, and I said, "This is our song."

The *ET* correspondent laughed and said, "'Rock Lobster' is your song? That's great. Thanks, you two."

When they left, Daniel punched my arm and said, "Let me up." I did, and he continued, "We came, we ate, we fought, and we got on TV. I'm leaving. Feel free to walk out with me if you want. First, I'm going to say goodbye to Tina."

I watched him storm off and thought briefly about finding Ethan. I decided that would do more harm than good, so I stood locked in indecision about my next move. I felt a hand on my shoulder and turned.

"You look like you just lost your best friend," Frank said.

"I see yours is with you," I answered, bending to rub Rowdy's ears. "Is he enjoying the evening?"

"I just discovered he doesn't like ferrets, but other than that, we're both having a good time. What about you?"

"I like ferrets okay." Frank gave me his fatherly look, and I confessed, "I feel like I'm trying to sell a product that should be recalled. Like Firestone tires." When Frank stayed silent, I said, "If you were gay, that would have been your cue to make jokes using the words 'blow' or 'rubber.' What I mean is that Daniel and I have these moments when we connect, like in the old days, then it always goes to hell. Two steps forward and three steps back."

Frank gave me an understanding nod and said, "It seems to me that the two of you have done enough. Why don't you tell Gavin to curtail your joint appearances?"

"Because . . ."

When I showed no indication that I intended to finish my sentence, Frank said, "Because at least this way you get to see Daniel. Beneath your public ruse is genuine feeling."

"Thank you for recognizing that. Daniel sure doesn't."

"Do you acknowledge that it's the same for him?"

"I don't think it is," I said.

"It's been three months since the wedding," Frank said. When my face clearly showed I didn't understand his point, he went on. "You and Daniel almost reconciled then. I assume he made it clear that he loved you and wanted to work things out. As little as I know him, I do know you. I don't think it's possible for him to stop loving you in three months."

"You're right," I said after thinking it over. "But love needs to be nourished. We're giving it junk food."

"That's why I suggested it may be time to step away from the table," Frank said. "Until you're both hungry again."

Daniel and I were quiet as we rode home later. I didn't know what he was thinking about, and I decided I might as well follow Frank's advice.

"I think we should cut back on some of this stuff," I said.

Daniel stared out the window and said, "Suits me. You tell Gavin. I'll tell Ronald."

His indifference made me reluctant to explain my motives. Apparently Frank was wrong. Daniel would rather not see me at all than take the crumbs these public appearances offered us.

CHAPTER 15

The next few days were peaceful, as I declined all invitations to public functions or private evenings with my friends. I'd decided my next move would be to meet with Daniel alone, hopefully to settle some of the unresolved issues between us. So I was annoyed to find out that we were committed to tape an interview for some gay Canadian cable show that I'd never heard of. At least they were doing it in Daniel's apartment, so I didn't have to go far. Afterward, I was supposed to meet Gretchen at the healthcare center for a doctor's appointment, which hopefully precluded another fight with Daniel following the interview.

By the time I got to his place, everything was already set up in the patio garden. After a quick session with their makeup person, they seated me next to Daniel on a bench, and the interview began. Different interviewer; same drill. I could do it in my sleep now.

Until we were thrown a curve when the interviewer, Geoffrey, said, "This is where it all began. Daniel worked in his garden, and you watched him from your window in the building behind us, Blaine. It's a romantic beginning, like something out of Shakespeare. When was that?"

"Three years ago," Daniel said automatically.

"An eternity in gay years," Geoffrey said, smiling as if he found himself wonderfully clever. "It must be one of the longest courtships on record."

"Courtships?" Daniel asked.

"Seems like yesterday," I offered, unsure why Daniel was frowning.

"It very well could have been," Geoffrey said, "since nothing's changed. You two still live apart. Isn't that a little unusual for two crazy kids in love?" We sat in stone silence until Geoffrey said, "Take your time. We'll edit out the dead space later."

"We've both shopped for a bigger place," I finally said. At least that was the truth.

"But Blaine has his mind set on a town house, and I want something a little different," Daniel said.

Apparently it was going to be war between us today. I kept my face pleasant and said, "The real estate situation in Manhattan is fierce. Just when you think you've found the perfect place, someone snaps it out from under you."

"Yes, you can't really take the time to consider whether it's the right place with everyone demanding a fast answer," Daniel said.

"Or if you walk out before a deal can be finalized," I said. "It's daunting for Daniel to uproot himself. Or rather, uproot this garden. He's always growing new things I don't know about. In fact, you could call this Daniel's secret garden."

"It's quite lovely," Geoffrey said.

"Not to mention how busy Blaine is," Daniel said. "Between work and indulging his various physical interests."

"Oh, honey, you know you're as busy as I am. All the drama of *Secret Splendor* and your friends. Daniel takes into account where his friends live when he ponders moving."

"Plus Blaine's need for space gets bigger all the time. There's the child to consider."

"Child?" Geoffrey asked, perking up, while my face got hot and all capacity for speech left me.

"Dexter," Daniel said sweetly. "Our cat. Cats get very attached to the places they live, you know."

"Don't we all," Geoffrey said. "When you two finally find the right place, we'd love to cover your housewarming party."

"When we move in together, you'll be at the top of our list," Daniel vowed. "Geoffrey, I'm afraid Blaine's run out of time."

I managed a cordial exit and went to Daniel's bathroom to wash my face. I could hear the sounds of the crew packing up when Daniel slipped in behind me and closed the door.

"I'm already late leaving to meet Gretchen," I warned. "I don't have time to get into anything with you."

"You were right. No more interviews. I'm done with this bullshit," Daniel said.

"You managed to dish out enough to fertilize your entire garden," I said.

"You held your own," he said.

"You started it with your dig about the town house. Don't tell me you weren't trying to antagonize me. And that crack about 'the child'? Totally uncalled for."

"I just wanted to remind you that I'm not the only one who keeps secrets."

"Anything I kept secret from you happened after we broke up. You can't say the same, can you, considering your town house sale to Martin?"

"I didn't sell Martin the town house," Daniel said.

"That's what you told me on Sheila's wedding day," I said. "Changing your story again?"

"No, actually, *you* said it on Sheila's wedding day. All I said was that I sold the town house. You assumed it was to Martin. Where the hell would Martin come up with that kind of money?"

"Excuse my ignorance, but we never finished that conversation because you walked out. As usual." I dried my face. When I moved the towel away, Daniel was sitting on the edge of the tub, staring at the floor. He looked tired and drained, and all the fight left me. I continued in a more civil tone, "Who did you sell it to?"

"Blythe's father," Daniel said. "Even at less than market value, he was the only person I knew who had that kind of money and would let Martin and Blythe stay. It was *Ken's* town house, Blaine. I was trying to find a way to keep it in the family."

"Then I guess you found a solution," I said. "I wish you hadn't waited nearly a year to tell me."

"You can never let it go, can you? You always have to win." He stood up. "You're late for your appointment."

I wanted to scream when he walked out. I took out my phone and called Gretchen's cell. I was sure she'd understand if I missed the appointment to finish this fight with Daniel once and for all. She didn't answer, so I left a message. When I went back to the living room, Daniel was on the patio with Geoffrey. They were taping him as he talked about the volunteer work he did with Parks and Recreation. Apparently, I'd have to catch up with him later.

It took forever to get a cab, and traffic was heavy. By the time we got to Chelsea, I couldn't wait to get out of the cab, and I was ready to throw money at the driver and run. Fortunately, when I opened the door, I looked toward the building.

Gretchen stood on the steps in the artificial light of a film crew, speaking into the microphone a reporter held. While my driver impatiently repeated how much I owed him, she pointed toward a building down the street. As the reporter looked in that direction, she met my eyes with a tiny shake of her head. I slammed the door and said, "Take me to that diner down the block. Don't worry about the meter." I handed him a twenty and he happily drove me another half block, where I got out and slipped into the diner. I didn't have to wait long before Gretchen came in.

"That was close," she said.

"I'm sorry I was late. What the hell happened? Who was that? What was he asking you?"

"Geez, one question at a time. Buy me a bottle of Poland Spring water. My mouth is dry." When I came back with the water, she said, "Don't worry about being late. For once, Dr. Griffith was running ahead of schedule. The exam was fine. Civil Liberty is doing exactly what she should be."

"Your blood pressure?"

"Still high. Anyway, that reporter is a journalist I know. A really nice guy. Hillary had just made a campaign stop there, and his crew was packing up to leave when I walked out. We started chatting, and I saw it as an opportunity to talk about the center's baby-holding program. Don't worry. He wasn't asking about Daniel or you. But Blaine, if he puts me on TV, how fat will I look? I hate thinking of all my ex-girlfriends chortling over that."

"You don't look fat," I promised. "Your coat covers your stomach."

"Oh, so usually, I do look fat," she said. Before I could redeem myself, she asked, "How was your interview?"

"Horrible. We're not doing any more of them. The veneer is cracking, and it's not pretty."

"I don't mean to cut you off, but I have a meeting," she said. "Are you free tonight?"

"Yes."

"Why don't you come for dinner, and we can talk about all of this?"

"I could bring takeout—"

"No, I'm in the mood to cook. Amazingly, my kitchen is now nearly as well stocked as the one at Happy Hollow. Being pregnant has changed my brain chemistry, I think. I'm getting all domestic. Just get to my place around seven."

I worked late, but skipped going to the gym, so I got to Gretchen's a little early and found the elevator in use. Since the doorman knew me, he allowed me to take the stairs and said he'd call to let her know I was on my way up. I was looking forward to having dinner with her. I'd been spending so many nights in places I didn't want to go, being someone I didn't want to be, that I welcomed a relaxing evening with just the two of us, without flashbulbs or microphones.

She was holding the service door open when I got to her floor, and hurried me past the kitchen to the living room, sparing me the necessity of finding something tactful to say about how she looked. I'd been right that morning to assure her that her coat concealed her pregnancy. What I couldn't figure out was when she'd gotten so huge.

I stopped short when we walked into the living room and Daniel turned from the stereo. The record he held fell to the floor and shattered into several pieces.

"What's he doing here?" Daniel asked.

"What record was that?" Gretchen asked anxiously.

"Probably some singer named Joan. Aren't they all?" Daniel asked.

"What's *he* doing here?" I echoed Daniel.

"I've had that album since I was fourteen," Gretchen said, then it dawned on her that we were glowering at each other. "Dinner. You're both here for a friendly dinner. You remember those, don't you? We've had them before."

"Memory fails," Daniel said.

"It's the second thing to go," I retorted.

"Knock this shit off," Gretchen said. "You know I always have a reason for the things I do. If you want an explanation, sit down and pretend to be civilized human beings."

"We're good at pretending," I mumbled.

"Some of us better than others," Daniel said under his breath.

"Who wants what to drink?" Gretchen asked.

"I'll have a Manhattan," I said.

"I'll have gin with a hint of tonic, please," Daniel said and sat on the sofa.

I watched as Gretchen poured a splash of sweet vermouth into the shaker at the bar and plopped a cherry into my glass with the smoothness of a professional bartender. When she started making Daniel's drink, I glanced at the floor and said, "Are the broom and dust pan in the kitchen? I'll clean up Daniel's mess."

"No!" Gretchen said, freezing.

"I said just a hint," Daniel calmly reminded her, as the tonic she was pouring flowed over the rim of the glass. "Blaine, you want to clean up Gretchen's mess, too?"

From the kitchen, I heard a noise that sounded like a lid being replaced on a pan. "Is somebody else here?" I asked.

"I can't do this," Gretchen moaned, setting down the tonic and turning to face us.

"It's just a gin and tonic," Daniel said. "Gin. Tonic. You pour them in a glass. If you can make a Manhattan, you can make a gin and tonic."

The kitchen door swung open, and Gwendy came out carrying a tray of hors d'oeuvres. Daniel's mouth dropped open, and I squinted at her as if she were a mirage.

"What's she doing here?" Daniel and I asked in unison.

Gwendy set the tray on the coffee table and bent next to me to pick up the broken record. "Joan Baez," she said. "I always thought of her as Bob Dylan in drag."

"You're gonna need this," Gretchen said, handing Daniel my Manhattan.

Gwendy gently propelled me toward the sofa, and I sat next to Daniel. He and Gwendy had always had a contentious relationship. I felt sorry for him. After all he'd been through over the past few months, a surprise visit from Gwendy could only add to his agitation.

I decided it would be best if I was supportive of him. If the two of them started another of their arguments, it would add to Gretchen's stress. In fact, it was possible that Gretchen had invited me so I could buffer her.

Gretchen handed me Daniel's gin and tonic before she sat in a chair across from us. It wasn't like her to be so absentminded, but pregnancy had changed her. I switched drinks with Daniel without commenting.

"Will someone please say something?" Daniel asked.

"Have an hors d'oeuvre," Gwendy said. "I'm a lesbian."

As Daniel choked on his drink, something clicked into place for me. Gwendy had always reminded me of someone. I finally realized it was Gretchen.

"Is that a joke?" Daniel asked. He took my Manhattan from my hand and gulped half of it down. "You're not a lesbian. If you think you are, it's just a phase."

"Who are you, Jerry Falwell?" Gwendy asked. "Trust me, I'm a lesbian."

"When did you figure this out?" I asked in a friendly tone, trying to give Daniel a chance to process the news.

"In college—"

"Everyone's a lesbian in college," Daniel interjected.

"—when I started sleeping with the Law Review president," Gwendy finished.

"So you're a slut. You're not a lesbian," Daniel said.

"Fine, I'm a lesbian slut," Gwendy said. "You really should try one of these crab puffs."

"I don't want fish," Daniel said.

Gwendy and Gretchen looked at each other and laughed, but wisely didn't make a joke out of that.

"It's great, isn't it," I said, "to get that secret out in the open? I remember how I felt—"

"Wonderful," Daniel interrupted. "When you tell our parents—"

"They've known for months," Gwendy said. "Why do you think they joined PFLAG?"

That left him momentarily speechless. I understood. It had taken Daniel and his parents years to come to an understanding about his sexuality and be comfortable enough to talk about it to one another.

"Fabulous," he said. "They barely spoke to me for a decade, but for you, they're marching in parades."

"No, Daniel," Gwendy said impatiently. "They joined PFLAG because they needed support. Finding out they had two gay children left them wondering if they'd done something wrong. Why can't you ever see anything from their point of view?"

"You owe Daniel a lot," I defended him. "He paved the way for their acceptance of you."

"I agree," Gretchen said. "We owe something to you, too, Blaine. The Stephensons respected your relationship with Daniel because they love you. That made things easier for Gwendy and me."

"Gwendy and you?" I asked, disconcerted. As I stared at them, realization dawned. "You mean you two are . . . you're . . . together? How long has this been going on?"

"It all goes back to the wedding, doesn't it?" Daniel demanded. "You've been skulking around ever since Josh and Sheila got married."

"Actually," Gretchen said, "it all goes back to lunch at Le Madri. Remember? The day Aunt Jen met Frank?"

"I remember the lunch," I said. "But you two barely spoke to each other."

"We made a date right under your nose," Gwendy said, rolling her eyes.

"Yeah, how could you miss that?" Daniel asked. I looked at him, then realized that his sarcasm was directed at his sister and not me.

"I tried to talk to you about it later," Gretchen said to me. "But you kept turning the conversation back to your relationship with Daniel." She looked at Gwendy. "Is something burning?"

"Oh!" Gwendy said, jumping to her feet and heading toward the kitchen.

"I'll help her," Gretchen said, following.

I took a deep breath and said, "Well," as I exhaled.

"How could you not know this?" Daniel asked. "How many times a week do you see Gretchen? You go to doctor's appointments with her. You're having a baby together, for God's sake. You never noticed anything?"

"Don't blame me for this," I said. I couldn't believe he was turning on me after I'd tried to be supportive of him.

"I've had enough of these sneak attacks," he said.

"I didn't know anything about it. I was surprised to see you here tonight. I thought I was coming for a relaxing dinner with Gretchen. I definitely didn't know Gwendy was here."

"I find that hard to believe. But I guess you have your hand in so many pies these days, you'd put Mrs. Smith to shame."

"Look, this is a shock to me, too," I insisted.

"I'm sorry; am I being unsympathetic? I just found out, under the pretense of having a long overdue dinner with one of my best friends, who is pregnant with my ex-lover's child, that she's sleeping with my sister, who's gone years without telling me she's a lesbian. And my ex-lover, who I seem to be saddled with on an almost nightly basis while we play America's favorite gay couple, and who I've seen enough of for one week, wants to sit here and share coming-out stories, until he finds out *he's* affected, too."

"Would you lower your voice, please? Do I have to remind you that one reason I'm doing what I am is to protect Gretchen's health?"

He gave me a look that could freeze lava and stood up just as Gretchen came out of the kitchen.

"Dinner's almost ready," she said, looking from me to him. When she saw his face, her pleasant expression was replaced by a look of concern. "Daniel? Are you all right?"

Daniel gave her a contemplative look and said, "Yes. It's been a long day, and I shouldn't have had two drinks on an empty stomach. Is there anything I can do to hurry dinner along?"

I had to admire his acting ability, because Gretchen stopped frowning and said, "Everything's under control. I'm sorry. I know this was a lot to throw at you. I hope after you have time to think it over, you'll be happy for me. You've always said that I need to find someone responsible, who's able to take care of me in a way that I don't take care of myself. Someone who takes her professional life as seriously as I do, but is able to relax and have fun when the day is over, so I can learn to unwind. You're the one who's—"

"The brother of your new girlfriend," Daniel finished. "We've been friends so many years, Gretchen. You know I want you to be happy. But you have to give me some time to take all this in."

I sat in silence, once again understanding Daniel's need to process things. I needed to process this one a little bit myself, especially as I watched the ease with which Gretchen and Gwendy finished getting our meal ready. They were obviously comfortable with each other, and I couldn't understand how Gretchen had been living what amounted to another life without my having some clue about it. Then again, after Daniel and I had begun our charade, my time with Gretchen had tapered off. We talked on the phone every day, but now that I thought about it, she'd mostly listened while I complained.

Our conversation after we sat at the table made us sound like four food critics analyzing each dish at a new restaurant. I'd almost convinced myself we were going to pull it off when Daniel suddenly spoke. "I can't believe you're a lesbian. How many years did you give me shit about being gay?"

"I did not," Gwendy said. "I gave you shit because you're my brother."

"You can't be gay," he said. "This is so weird."

"You're sounding awfully intolerant," I said, using one of his favorite adjectives for me.

"Don't start with me." Daniel waved his fork in the air.

"I could hardly be Gretchen's girlfriend if I wasn't a lesbian," Gwendy said with a snort.

"I'm not finding the humor in this," Daniel said.

"Maybe you should be?" Gwendy suggested.

"What's that supposed to mean?" Daniel asked.

"Here we are, brother and sister, gay and lesbian, sitting at a table with your ex and my current. Isn't there some humor in that?"

"I'm sure when I get home, I'll double up with laughter," Daniel said.

"As long as you're getting used to the idea," Gretchen said slowly, "you should also know that Gwendy's moving in."

"What?" I was shocked.

"Blaine, you had to know that I might not stay single forever. I got lucky. I found a great woman who loves me and wants to be a part of my whole life."

"What about the baby?" I asked.

"The baby is part of my life," she pointed out. She looked at Gwendy and said, "We may as well put it all out on the table, along with the food no one's really eating. I know I'm not the only reason the two of you are playing the game you are. But I do appreciate the way my privacy has been ensured because of it. Blaine, you wanted me to take a leave of absence for my health. Gwendy has made me realize it's a good idea. She and I are going to distance ourselves further from the drama by going to Happy Hollow for a while. I can't turn on the TV or go to the supermarket without seeing you on some talk show or tabloid. It would be like going to a convention of gay coffee table book retailers and not seeing John and Ron on display."

"Bob and Rod," Daniel corrected.

"Whoever," Gretchen said.

"Why does no one remember that they broke up years ago?" I asked. "What does your doctor say? Don't you have more frequent appointments during the next few weeks?"

"He referred me to a doctor who's less than ten miles from the resort," Gretchen said. "I'll continue to be monitored. I'll definitely be back before the baby's born. You'll be with me during labor and delivery. I promise."

"I have to go," Daniel said, pushing himself away from the table.

I didn't say anything while Gwendy got Daniel's coat and Gretchen walked him to the door. All I could think of was that once again, he was walking out on me. Now that we'd agreed to no more appearances together, he'd be able to stay away from me indefinitely.

After he was gone, they returned to the table and sat down.

"Blaine, I've always liked you," Gwendy said. "You know that. Maybe things are going to be different from what you imagined now that I'm in the picture, but try not to see that as a bad thing. I know you want to be a full-time father, and I'm not going to try to replace you in her life. She'll have more than two parents. It happens all the time."

"You know the sex of the baby?" I asked, starting to get angry.

"No," Gretchen assured me. She sighed. "This wasn't supposed to be a bad evening. Gwendy and I have found something special in each other, and we wanted to share it with the two of you. It was supposed to be more of a celebration."

"I guess with all the parties Daniel and I have been to over the past few weeks, we're celebrated out," I said. "Gretchen, could we talk? Alone?"

Before she could answer, Gwendy picked up our plates and said, "I'll be in the kitchen."

When she was gone, I turned back to Gretchen, saying, "Look, I know I haven't been around much lately. I'm sorry if you felt neglected."

Gretchen let out a short laugh and said, "I'm not your wife, Blaine. I didn't turn to Gwendy because you weren't around. Falling in love with her took me by surprise, but I'm happy. Just be happy for me."

"I am happy for you. Both of you. I understand how Daniel feels, though. I need time for this to sink in. Will you keep me apprised of your plans? About going to Happy Hollow?"

"Of course," she said.

The chilly autumn air hit me when I stepped out of her building. I watched as a couple walked quickly down the opposite side of the street. They looked like they were physically attached to one another rather than just holding each other tightly. I wondered for a minute how new their relationship was. Did they have problems?

What if Gwendy and Gretchen had problems? Would that affect the future of my child? I wanted to talk to somebody. No, not somebody. I wanted to talk to Daniel, to work our way through this news together. But of course, he'd made that impossible.

I pulled on my gloves and walked down the steps. As I turned toward home, I saw him leaning against the building, his breath making clouds in the air.

"You should have waited inside," I said. "What if I'd been a long time?"

"I'm here," he said impatiently. "Let's finish what we started this morning. Nothing left unsaid about our friends, the baby, the town house. No more of your secrets to catch me off guard."

"I don't have secrets," I said.

"The hell you don't."

"You know about the baby. I wish you'd found out in a different way, but you of all people should understand why I wanted to wait for the right moment to share the news. God, it took you nearly a year to tell me the details about the fucking town house."

"Blaine," he said sharply, "I've told you everything about the town house. Maybe I should have told you sooner, but I didn't. I feel like you want me to change the past."

"You can't. We can't. The town house is irrelevant compared to the bomb they just dropped on us. Your sister is going to be involved in raising my child. How do you think that makes me feel?"

"How do you think it makes *me* feel?"

"How does it affect you? It's not your child."

He stared at me for a moment. The look on his face made it seem like he was lining up all his mental soldiers for one last battle. "How could you not have told me you were going to have a baby with my friend?"

"Gretchen is my friend, too. You and I were broken up. It seemed to me that we were through and I was left to make decisions for myself again."

"You always make decisions for yourself and help yourself to whatever is available."

"What do you mean by that?" I asked.

"It was supposed to be you and me," Daniel said. "A baby was supposed to be what we did together." I didn't know what to say. The look in Daniel's eyes was hard to read, and his words left me disarmed. He made a disgusted sound. "Just as I thought, no good response."

When he walked away, my heart sank. I didn't know how he could leave now that we were finally approaching the issue that had been looming between us like the Rock of Gibraltar. I wanted to say something, anything, to get him to come back, but the words caught in my throat.

Daniel stopped four doors down from where I stood. He crossed his arms over his chest and looked up at the sky, as if searching the few dim stars for some kind of answer. He slowly turned around. His face reflected a renewed strength. I couldn't help but feel a glimmer of hope that he would stick this out instead of running to the safety of his garden or friends.

He stopped in front of me. He looked serious, his arms still defensively folded across his chest. His voice was soft when he spoke. "Blaine, do you remember when Martin and I were fighting and couldn't stand each other after Ken died?"

"Of course," I said.

"Martin kept Ken's ashes until we were able to dispose of them in a way Ken would have wanted."

"What does this have to do with—"

"Do you want to find out, or should we just part now and vow never to speak again?"

"Please stay," I said.

"Martin and I always knew we'd fulfill Ken's final wishes together, but we couldn't do it until we were all right with each other. If Martin had taken the ashes by himself, without telling me, and spread them in Greenwich Village, how do you think that would have made me feel?"

"Betrayed," I said. "Left out."

"Right. And like he gave up. Like all the planning we'd done, the importance of doing it together, meant nothing to him."

"Daniel, when we split up, you made it pretty clear we weren't going to get back together."

Daniel's bottom lip quivered, but his eyes showed no sign of weakness. I, on the other hand, felt like my feet were sinking into the concrete, and if I didn't move soon, I would become part of the sidewalk.

"You still don't get it," he said. "Think about how Gretchen and Gwendy just made you feel. Does that give you any insight into how I've been feeling?"

"Yes," I said quietly.

"It's a good thing we don't have any more interviews," he said. "I can't fake it anymore. I think it's best if we finish our business with Lillith Allure, but after that, I don't know."

I felt defeated, but not hopeless. Daniel shot a halfhearted smile at me before he turned to leave again. He shoved his hands in his pockets as he turned the corner to go back uptown.

The entire day had left me reeling. Rather than follow him and head toward home, I walked east, finally ducking into a diner that was only half full of people, most of whom were reading in solitude at their tables. I slid into a corner booth and ordered coffee from a waitress who thankfully didn't seem inclined to make small talk.

I tried to sort through my feelings about Gretchen and Gwendy. If I took the baby out of the equation, I knew that I'd be happy for them. I liked and admired both women. It was apparent that Gretchen had finally conquered her tendency to get involved with the worst possible girlfriend. The happiness she'd worn like a partic-

318 Timothy James Beck

ularly flattering outfit over the past few months hadn't been only because of her pregnancy. She was in love with someone who knew how to treat her. Especially how to take care of her, since Gwendy had been able to accomplish the impossible—persuading Gretchen to take a leave of absence from work.

I also agreed that their decision to go to Happy Hollow until just before the baby was born was sensible. Gretchen needed to get away from the public farce that Daniel and I had been living, not just to avoid the possible leak of our secret, but for her own peace of mind. The past couple of months had been stressful for all of us.

What bothered me was the strange sense of disconnection I had. I remembered Adam's cautionary words when I'd told him what Gretchen and I were considering: *What about when she gets involved with someone? That's one more person involved in how your child is raised.*

It was an issue that I'd had no reason to think about, but now I couldn't dodge it. For the rest of Gretchen's pregnancy, during her delivery, and every day afterward, Gwendy would have an intimacy and access that excluded me. I'd gotten used to being the person Gretchen relied on. I'd felt like we were partners. And even though we wouldn't be living together, I'd anticipated being a solid half of the parent dynamic.

Gwendy would be living with my child. Gwendy would gradually know more than I would about how to take care of him and meet his needs. It would be Gwendy who changed his diapers, comforted him after a bad dream, and celebrated all his firsts with Gretchen. When he started crawling, walking, and talking. When he got his first tooth.

But he was *my* child. All these things were supposed to be what *I* did. No matter what happiness I took from the news that two people I loved had found something beautiful and affirming to celebrate together, I couldn't deny that it left me feeling jealous, shut out, and—

"Oh, fuck," I said out loud, tilting my head back to stare at the ceiling. "Daniel."

I should have told Daniel what I was thinking of doing before I gave Gretchen an answer. I should have made him part of the baby decision from the very beginning. Not just as Gretchen's friend and my ex-lover, but because I finally understood what he'd been trying to tell me.

I'd not only excluded him, I'd taken one of our dreams and given it to someone else. The baby wasn't conceived the day Gretchen was inseminated. It was conceived as an idea, a possibility, and a promise in Daniel's bed.

We were always safe; but in spite of our vow of fidelity and our consistently negative test results, and even though we didn't really believe we had reason to worry, whenever we got tested we experienced a giddy euphoria after hearing that everything was okay. The last time we'd been tested, we'd gone to Daniel's doctor instead of the usual anonymous clinic, and Dr. Canady, who was gay, had asked to speak to us together before we left. After commending us for staying safe and healthy, he'd suggested we both continue to get regular checkups. Some of his patients had testicular and prostate cancer, and he brought up the idea of sperm banking.

"Is there an ATM machine for that?" Daniel had quipped.

Dr. Canady laughed and said, "Seriously, it's protection. A lot of my patients are straight, so they preserve semen samples as insurance against something going wrong and preventing them from having children. But more of my gay patients, too, want children these days. Should either of you ever decide to go that route, you can store clean samples without worrying about HIV or other complications, like cancer, impotence, or some physical disability. Things happen. It's better to be prepared."

We'd taken the information for a lab he recommended and gone on our way. That night, in bed, Daniel had run a finger over my stomach and said, "Here they are. All our unborn babies mingling together."

"Maybe we should do it," I'd said.

"Where were you the last hour or so?"

"Not that." I laughed. "Bank our sperm."

"You've always been the fiscally responsible one," Daniel teased.

"Both of us," I insisted.

We stayed in bed for hours, talking about the future, the possibility of having a child, and how it would change our lives. It wasn't the first time we'd talked about it, but it seemed more real that night as we discussed adoption, insemination, surrogate mothers, and women we might be able to coparent with. Gretchen's name had come up, because Daniel knew she wanted a child. Just before we fell asleep, we'd come to the conclusion that of all our options, the one that seemed the least complicated was a surrogate. Some kind stranger who would carry our baby for us, then hand it over and vanish from our lives.

We contacted the lab recommended by Dr. Canady and found out things were more complicated than we'd expected. We couldn't just play around at home and proudly deliver our plastic chalices to the lab. Instead, we had to abstain from any sexual activity for three days, go to the lab, provide our samples, wait ten days, do it again, then repeat the process a third and final time. Which essentially made it a month-long commitment, with at least nine days of abstinence.

"I've found, pledged eternal love, and broken up with boyfriends in less time," Daniel complained.

"I'm sure the idea of not having sex with me is agonizing," I said. "But you'll survive."

The first time, we went to the clinic together. We'd hated our solitary little rooms, but both of us were horny and managed to provide our samples without much trouble. The second time, I'd been out of town, which helped with the abstinence, but I felt sad about the fact that we'd gone separately to make our deposits. The third time, I was just over it. The room looked drearier than ever, and I couldn't get hard. I zipped up and sat on the uncomfortable plastic chair, kicking at a loose piece of tile. I was even more disgruntled when I heard Daniel outside his door talking to the nurse. Apparently *he* wasn't having any problem.

I opened my door and glared at the two of them, saying, "It's hard—"

"It's supposed to be," the nurse joked.

"—to concentrate with you two out here whispering."

The nurse looked from Daniel to me and said, "When we bring you back here, we leave you alone. Do not contaminate the sample with saliva or anything else." Then he shoved Daniel into my room and shut the door.

"You can't do it either?" I asked.

"I can now," Daniel said, grabbing me.

It was hot and exciting and sneaky, even with the ridiculous plastic cups labeled with our names. After it was over, while I leaned against the wall gasping, Daniel got an evil gleam in his eye.

"You know, I could mix these up, give them half and half, and we'd never know—"

"Don't you dare," I said. "If they figure it out when they test it, they might make us come back. I'm done with this place."

"Oh, all right," Daniel said. He hit the call button and the nurse returned, grinning like an idiot when he took the samples from Daniel. I wondered if they had hidden cameras. If so, we'd provided a hell of a porn scenario.

I had no idea which of my samples had been sent by my lab to Gretchen's clinic, but it didn't matter. Daniel was justified in feeling that I'd taken his baby, *our* baby, and given it away. I hadn't discussed it with him. I'd kept it a secret for months. He'd found out in a way that was unsettling and humiliating, because it had been clear that not only Gretchen and I, but Adam and Jeremy, had known something he hadn't. As if all that wasn't enough for him to deal with, it was obvious from what he'd said earlier, *You always make decisions for yourself and help yourself to whatever is available,* that Gretchen had told him we'd used my banked sperm. She'd had no idea what effect that might have on him.

The anxiety and sense of exclusion I had felt after hearing about the town house, and especially after being told Gretchen and Gwendy's news, was exactly the kind of thing that had tormented Daniel for months. And the charade for the press I'd asked him to go along with was a mockery of everything we'd shared and lost. I'd never felt so dishonest, not even with Sydney.

I paid for my coffee and walked home, climbing the five flights to my apartment like my legs were made of lead. When I put my key in the lock, Gavin opened the door to greet me with a wary look on his face.

"Brace yourself," he said.

"No. I don't want to." I started to walk into the apartment and was appalled when Gavin blocked the doorway.

"You have visitors."

I pushed past him to my living room, and my sister-in-law Beverly stood to greet me. Standing at the window with his back to me, Nick was enveloped by a floor-length black trench coat. From behind, he looked like a goth gunslinger.

"Blaine, we need to talk."

"Hello to you, too, Beverly. Welcome to my home."

Beverly took a shallow breath and let it out audibly. She smoothed a loose strand of hair into place and said, "I'm sorry. It's been a long day—week—month—months. I need your help. *We* need your help."

"What's wrong?" I asked.

During our exchange, Nick remained standing with his back to me. I thought it odd, since Nick and I had established a bond, that he wouldn't acknowledge that I was in the same room.

"We need your help with him." She gestured over her shoulder toward her son. "He's out of control, and I don't know where else to turn."

"I'm not sure I follow you. Out of control how?"

"Show him, Nicky," Beverly said to her son's back.

"No," came the reply.

"Show him," his mother asserted more forcefully.

"*No,*" he answered with equal passion.

"Okay," I interjected, "let me explain something. I've had a long day—week—month—months, too. All I want is to go to bed and slip into a coma. Let's cut to the chase. What happened, and why are you here?"

Beverly continued to stare at Nick's back. No one spoke as my disgruntled mood permeated the room. Nick slowly turned to face us, exposing a black eye.

"Oh, geez," I said. "What's that?"

"It's a black eye," Beverly said.

"Yes, Bev, thanks. I can see it's a black eye. Who gave you that? What happened?"

"You should see the other guy," Nick said with a half smile.

"His brother gave him that," Beverly answered. "And you *should* see 'the other guy.' Nicky attacked him."

"Nick, what happened?" I asked. I couldn't believe someone as thin and wiry as Nick would go after one of his athletic brothers.

"Chuck called me that name one too many times. I guess I snapped."

I didn't have to ask what the name was.

"You know," Beverly began, "I'm not sure what you hoped to accomplish by telling Shane and me what you did when you were home—"

"*This* is my home," I said.

"—but you made an awful mess that I've spent months trying to clean up. He's been sullen and out of touch ever since he overheard that conversation." She misinterpreted my quick glance at Nick and went on. "Yes, that's right, he heard it when you talked with your brother and me in the kitchen. I can't even list for you all the things he's done since then. Do you know what he did? He came out"—she used her fingers to make quotation marks—"at school! Tony's away at college, but do you know what that's done to Chuck? All the other boys in the locker room have been badgering him ever since. Somehow, things got back to one of his friends' parents, and now they're saying things to Shane at work. At work! Can you imagine? We don't live in New York City or San Francisco. We live in Eau Claire! People aren't anonymous there like they are here.

"So his brother called him a fag after having been taunted all day, and Nicky hit him. Chuck hit him back, and the next thing I knew, the two of them were rolling all over the floor, knocking things over, trying to kill each other. They even broke some of my Lladro statues!"

I suppressed my urge to pull out my checkbook, knowing it was the kind of thing my father or Shane would have done.

"Oh! And tell your uncle what you did in your social studies class," Beverly said. Nick looked at the floor and mumbled something, so Beverly asked him to repeat himself.

Sounding defeated, yet more audible, Nick said, "I had to do a report on England's main export."

Beverly set up the scene by saying, "So he stood up in front of his class and said—go on. Tell him."

Again, Nick mumbled at the floor.

"What?" I asked.

"George Michael's ass," Nick repeated with more clarity to the floor. "I said that Britain's main export was George Michael's ass."

The sound of a dish breaking in the kitchen caused Beverly to turn her head. When she did, I regained my composure and held back my laughter by biting my finger.

Gavin stepped into the room and said, "Sorry about that. We're down to service for five now."

Beverly looked mildly annoyed by his interruption and said, "I'm at the end of my rope, Blaine. Talk to him. Something. Excuse me. I need to freshen up."

I directed her to the bathroom. When she left, Gavin whispered, "George Michael's ass. That's brilliant, Nick. Keep him, Blaine. Pay the lady. Whatever you have to do. This kid belongs here. Not in Wisconsin."

"Gavin, he's my nephew, not a puppy. This isn't one of those 'Gee, Mom, can we keep him?' things. Where would we put him? Nobody said anything about me raising a teenager." It occurred to me that we were having this discussion about Nick as if he weren't in the room. I looked at him, and he continued to look at the floor. "Considering everything, I can't believe they want me anywhere near you. Whose idea was it for you to come here?"

"Mine," he said.

"Did you just need to get away from the pressure? Do you need to talk to me privately? Should I ask your mother to give us some time alone?"

"I'm not running away from Eau Claire," Nick said quietly. "I had a plan."

"Go on."

"I got accepted to Broadway High School for the Arts. Mom and Dad didn't know I'd applied, but they said they'd pay what my scholarship doesn't cover."

"Scholarship? What did you get a scholarship for?" I couldn't help feeling proud.

"Visual arts. I paint." He briefly looked up. "They offered me a partial scholarship, but the term doesn't start until January."

"Is it a boarding school? A day school?"

"Day school," he said, dropping his eyes again.

I began to understand and said, "You need a place to live."

He looked up again, and his expression held an admission and a plea. "I don't want to go back to Eau Claire." I couldn't argue with that. I didn't either. "I'll sleep on the floor. I'll clean the apartment if you want."

"Careful, kiddo," Gavin warned with a smile. "You're stepping on toes."

I drew a deep breath and let it out, hoping Gavin noticed that I was practicing my breathing. I thought about the possible ramifications of Nick's request. I didn't want to involve him in the mess with Daniel. It would be too much for someone his age to handle. But

Daniel and I had decided there wouldn't be any more interviews, and the invitations to do public appearances had been waning. I couldn't stand the thought of sending my nephew back to face more conflict.

Beverly returned, having applied a fresh coat of makeup. She looked softer and somewhat calmer. "Blaine, I'm sorry if I came off a little strong, but we really are at our wits' end. We've never dealt with anything like this before."

"Nick just told me about his scholarship. Is this what you and Shane want? For him to stay here with me?"

"Nicky's father and I don't know how to handle this. Maybe no parent does. But the conflict is affecting all three of my sons. Maybe a separation will give all of us time to learn how to deal with it and each other."

"But if school doesn't start until January—"

"I could finish this semester at a public school," Nick interjected.

"Blaine, this doesn't mean I don't love Nicky. I worry about him every time he walks out the door. I worry about how the kids at school will treat him."

"Kids are the same everywhere," I said. "What makes you think it will be different here?"

"The difference is that he won't have to put up with the same thing at home. I'd worry less about Nicky being in Manhattan with you, even without me watching over him, than I would if he were at home."

I knew what she wasn't saying. She couldn't count on my brother to help her protect their son from his own family. I even respected her for not disparaging his father in front of Nick.

I regarded him carefully and finally said, "I want you both to understand that I wouldn't see Nick as an imposition. I'm touched that you trust me to provide the acceptance and care I wish I'd had at his age."

"I do trust you," Beverly said.

"My house. My rules. You do your part, and you can stay. Okay?"

"Okay," Nick said quietly, but his face lit the room with a smile. "Can I stay here tonight?"

Beverly gave me a helpless look and said, "I'm staying at the Park Savoy. His luggage is there."

"I can go with you and pick it up," Gavin offered.

"Okay," Beverly said with a combination of resignation and relief. "Will you be able to help me find the right public school to enroll him in?"

I stifled my immediate impulse to call Violet and said, "Of course."

Beverly walked to Nick and touched his face. Their eyes met for a moment, and she put her arms around him, then finally let go and turned to face me. "Thank you, Blaine."

"Don't thank me yet. You may get him back."

One side of Nick's mouth turned up, and I smiled at him. We both knew I wouldn't be sending him back to Eau Claire.

CHAPTER 16

It wasn't as hard as I'd feared to adjust to Nick's move to Manhattan. Beverly and I were able to enroll him in school, and I began to feel a grudging respect for her when I realized that she hadn't lied. She wasn't dumping Nick. She was trying to find the best way to take pressure off her entire family. Since Shane wasn't much help, I saw the two of us as allies on Nick's behalf.

Once Beverly flew back to Eau Claire, we settled into a routine. Although he slept on the sofa, I told Nick to feel free to use the computer, television, and stereo in my bedroom during the afternoons and early evenings after school. I remembered how much I'd liked privacy when I was a teenager. As small as my apartment was, Nick and Gavin needed the ability to close doors between them. I wasn't sure if they did, since whenever I came home, they were usually in the kitchen talking and laughing while Nick helped Gavin get dinner ready.

I found myself looking forward to getting home every night. The two of them had hit it off, and Gavin was more relaxed with Nick around. In looking after my nephew, he and I became more like partners than employer-employee. I figured Nick liked interacting with a gay man who wasn't related to him and didn't know he'd always been regarded as the problem child. He didn't even mind the way Gavin teased him about his mode of dress, calling him "Gloom-cookie" and "Gothboy."

Jeremy called with a suggestion that turned out to be helpful. Since Nick was interested in art, and Blythe was an artist, he told me to hook the two of them up. She'd been the person who helped

Adam navigate Manhattan when he'd first visited the city, and because she and Nick were closer in age, as well as sharing similar interests, she was a good guide for him.

It was also great having Nick to focus on after Gretchen and Gwendy left for Happy Hollow. They stayed in town only long enough to vote, and considering the fiasco the election turned into, I had to admit that it had been a good idea for Gretchen to get out of the city. She took her politics personally. Even though she'd had a feeling Gore wasn't a shoo-in, as evidenced by her nervousness over the stock market and our financial portfolios, she was nonetheless appalled at the strange chain of events set in motion by the hotly contested presidential race. At least she had the comfort of knowing that Hillary was our new senator.

My secret feeling about the election was relief. Hanging chads and confusing ballots were the news of the day, even in the gay media, and the Daniel/Blaine story faded into well-deserved obscurity. After a few days' respite from our drama, I called Daniel, who sounded a little leery when he heard my voice.

"I've been doing a lot of thinking," I said. "I owe you an apology. Regardless of how things stood between us, I should have told you about the baby before I made my decision."

After I relayed some of the thoughts I'd had following our last fight, Daniel said, "Thank you for calling and telling me that. How did things ever get so out of hand?"

"When we were together, or are you talking about the past few months?"

"All of it, I guess. I'm so glad we stopped doing the publicity stuff."

"So am I. Too much stress."

"For you and me both," he said. "Let's give each other some breathing room, okay? Before we ruin any chance we have of being friends again."

"Sure," I said, knowing he was probably right but still feeling disappointed. Friends. I supposed that was better than nothing.

By the time Thanksgiving came and we hadn't talked for a couple of weeks, I wasn't so sure. Thanksgiving was when we'd always officially celebrated our beginning as a couple, and I didn't even know where he was. I tried to call him, but when I got the machine, I hung up without leaving a message.

I'd offered Gavin time off to go to Baltimore, but he insisted that Nick needed to have a festive Thanksgiving, including turkey and all the trimmings. I gave in, not wanting my nephew to be affected by my melancholy. I'd noticed Nick's tendency to watch me too closely now that he had all the facts about my breakup and farce with Daniel, as well as the news about the impending birth of my child. I didn't want him to feel like he'd traded one dysfunctional family for another.

That night, Nick was napping, stuffed from dinner, and Gavin had gone out to meet friends. After I hung up from a call to Gretchen, I had no idea what to do with myself. Dexter jumped on the windowsill, and I walked over to pet him, looking down at Daniel's dark patio. I felt restless, but I wasn't in the mood to go out. I had no interest in finding some other lonely soul who was spending the holiday feeling nostalgic for better days. Not to mention I hadn't tricked since the day Bonnie's detective, or whatever the hell he was, had announced that I'd gone home with someone from bodyWorks.

Besides, I wasn't really in the mood for sex. I was in the mood for a friend. I picked up the phone to call Ethan, wondering how he'd spent his Thanksgiving.

"Quietly," Ethan said after I asked. "How was Nick? Any sign that he's homesick?"

"Not unless he's eating to cover it up," I said.

Ethan laughed and said, "I remember that age. I ate everything in sight."

"I still do," I admitted. "I'm sure it'll catch up with me one day. I'll end up sloppy and alone."

"Oh, you're in one of those kinds of moods," Ethan said. "I hate those."

"Are you ever in a bad mood?" I asked. "Don't you just light a candle to the Buddha or something?"

"It's better to light a candle than—"

"Sit in the dark and sulk," I finished. "Why don't you bring your candle over here?"

"Sure," Ethan said. "I'll bring maize and tobacco, too. It'll be just like the first Thanksgiving."

"Good. I've got blankets and smallpox."

"I can hardly wait," Ethan said.

I straightened up the apartment as best I could and uncorked a bottle of wine. Just to be on the safe side, I heated water and pulled out some of Gavin's herbal tea. Then I checked on Nick, who was still sprawled across my bed, sound asleep. I took out a blanket and put it over him, smiling at how young and fragile he looked, in spite of the earrings and black bracelets. It was probably only a matter of time until he asked for a tattoo. At least I hoped he would ask first.

Dexter had followed me into the bedroom and was busy pretending he had no interest in jumping on the bed. "Good idea," I whispered. "You can stay in here. Charming as you are, I don't need a chaperone."

I softly shut the bedroom door, went to the bathroom to make sure I didn't look as scruffy as Dexter, and within minutes I was letting Ethan in. He smelled of cold air when he embraced me, and I wouldn't let go. It felt so good to have a man's arms around me. When I finally pulled away, he reached into his jeans pocket and brought out a birthday candle, saying, "Would you light my candle?"

"I loved *Rent*," I said.

"Me, too."

"I was wondering if that was a candle in your pocket or you were just happy—"

"Don't you dare," Ethan said, looking at the tiny candle. Then he glanced around and said, "Nice place."

"Don't be rude. It used to seem roomy. It was definitely less cluttered. I've got to get a bigger apartment."

Ethan took a step toward the window and asked, "Is that the one that overlooks the famous garden?"

"It's dark right now," I said. "You can't see anything."

"Already checked it out, huh?"

"Tea or wine?" I asked, ignoring his question.

"Wine," Ethan said. "Maybe some tea later." When I came back from the kitchen, he said, "Where's what's-his-name?"

"I don't know. Probably in Eau Claire." Ethan started laughing and I said, "What?"

"I meant your assistant."

"Oh. Gavin," I said, blushing. "He went out with some friends tonight. Am I as pathetic as I sound?"

"It's just that mood," Ethan said. "Why have all your friends let you spend a holiday alone?"

"We usually go to Happy Hollow for Thanksgiving, but that would be a bit much for Gretchen this year. She and Gwendy are there. Sheila and Josh are in Wisconsin. Everyone's probably at Adam and Jeremy's. But it's okay. I had a good day with Nick and Gavin."

We sat on the sofa, and he nudged at my leg until I gave him my feet to rub. We were quiet awhile, until he said, "I saw *Rent* with Martin."

"That name," I groaned.

"He's the best person to see shows with."

"I'm sure he's full of all kinds of catty stories and sordid backstage gossip."

"A little," Ethan admitted, "but really, he's as enthralled as a kid seeing it all for the first time. What gay man doesn't love a show? Even you loved *Rent;* don't act immune."

After a pause I asked, "So what kind of sordid backstage gossip did he tell you?"

Ethan burst out laughing, and neither of us heard Gavin come in until he was standing in front of us.

"Hi," he said, giving Ethan a somewhat dazed look. "You're Ethan Whitecrow."

"I am," Ethan confessed, his eyes still dancing.

"Ethan, this is the man who keeps me sane, Gavin Lewis."

"It's so great to meet you," Gavin said. "I've read your books. I practice your seven steps to Shamanic insight. It's really made a difference to my massage practice." He looked at our glasses and said, "Let me get you some more wine."

When he walked into the kitchen, Ethan looked at me and whispered, "He's so cute!"

Before I could answer, Gavin was back with the wine. He sat down and began asking Ethan excited questions about Shamanism. It was obvious he had no intention of disappearing to his room, and it began to dawn on me that I was the one who needed to disappear. I brooded over that a minute, then looked up as Nick came in, yawning and holding Dexter close to his chest.

"Dexter's hungry," he said after politely acknowledging his introduction to Ethan.

"Maybe you could give him some turkey when you make yourself a sandwich," I said wryly.

"Okay," Nick said, trying to sound as if starvation hadn't been his reason for joining us. "Does anyone else want anything?"

"Was it free-range turkey?" Ethan asked.

"I think it lived with a sweet old lady in Scarsdale until it died of a happy old age," I assured him.

"I'll make us a tray," Gavin said, following Nick into the kitchen.

"I can't believe I invited you over here to get me out of a pissy mood, and you're about to elope with my manservant," I groused.

"I promise to be a great manservant-in-law," Ethan said. "He is totally hot."

"Aren't you supposed to be telling me what a beautiful soul he has?"

"I was too busy looking at his hands. I'll bet he gives a great . . . massage."

Over the next couple of hours, I actually enjoyed watching the two of them flirt under the guise of discussing their work. Nick was obviously enthralled by the energy flowing between them. But when I stifled a yawn, Ethan looked remorseful.

"I'm sorry. I lost track of time."

Gavin, like a gracious host, protested, "No, this has been great. I could talk for hours about this stuff."

"It's not that late," I said. "Just because I'm a slug doesn't mean everyone else has to be. Of course, we are sitting on Nick's bed. You two should go out and talk over a drink or something."

"Oh, no, I need to clean up," Gavin said.

"I'll do that," Nick volunteered. "I have to pull my weight around here." He began gathering up dishes and went into the kitchen.

Gavin looked at Ethan, who said, "I'm not tired. Is there somewhere in the neighborhood—"

"A million of them," I said, getting to my feet. "Anyway, Gavin, this was supposed to be your night off."

"Let me get a heavier coat," Gavin said and went to his room.

When I helped Ethan into his coat, he said, "You don't have to be so eager to get rid of me."

"I'm bowing to the inevitable," I said. He turned around and hugged me, and my hands caught for a second in his beautiful long hair. "Okay, I'll admit it. I'm a little envious. I know what he has to look forward to. But I'd be disappointed if the two of you didn't see where this leads."

"Did you ever have a moment where you look at someone and you feel this little *yes!* inside?"

"No!" I said. "I'm kidding. It's destiny, and I don't even believe in that crap." Ethan laughed and pulled away when Gavin came back. Gavin's look held a question, as if he was seeking permission, so I smiled and said, "If it's a late night, don't even think about getting up early. I'm sleeping in, and Nick knows his way around the kitchen."

"Thanks," Gavin said.

Then they were gone. I stood there a minute, bemused, and looked at Nick when he came from the kitchen.

"Did he just—are you and Ethan—"

"Friends," I said. "I think he and Gavin would make a good couple, don't you?"

"I love New York," Nick said. "This is exactly the way I thought it would be."

"Me, too," I said, remembering how scared and hopeful I'd been, and how Daniel had been the answer to all the questions I'd been afraid to ask. "And then I found out real life . . ."

"Yeah?" Nick prodded when I trailed off.

"I found out real life is better than anything I'd imagined."

Lillith took advantage of the holiday shopping season by flooding the market with the Narcissus ads. She even threw a party at the Four Seasons, inviting a number of the soap actors who would be featured in upcoming Deity ads. Normally, I'd have been front and center, both as Lillith Allure's Creative Director and as Daniel's escort, since he was the star of the night. Frank had managed to thwart Lillith on my behalf, however, sending me with Sheila to Los Angeles to launch Zodiac's Capricorn campaign. I was sure Daniel was relieved, and Sheila and I enjoyed a few drama-free days. When we weren't touting our products, we went on a shopping frenzy, checking names off our Christmas lists like Santa on crack.

The next week, I holed myself up in the art department going over various sketches for the Deity line. The artist I normally worked with was on vacation, and I was ready to wring the neck of his assistant, Randy, who seemed to have difficulty thinking outside his art school box. He'd drawn Thor as a burly man who was pounding down on a lightning bolt with a large, carnival-type sledgehammer. It was drastically different from what I'd envisioned.

Randy groaned when I gave him a list of corrections longer than his arm. He brightened when the phone rang, offering him sudden salvation from my annoyance. He answered it, then passed it to me, saying, "It's Violet."

"There you are. I've been calling all over, trying to find you," Violet said.

"I told you I'd be here. In the art department," I said.

It occurred to me that I'd left my office while Violet was at lunch and that I hadn't left her a note. The same thought must've crossed her mind, since there was a short lull, which I assumed meant she was quickly weighing the pros and cons of correcting me. Finally she said, "At any rate, Bonnie Seaforth-Wilkes and Lillith would like to meet with you."

"Do you know why?" I asked.

"No. They didn't elaborate. They just said they need to talk to you."

"I'm busy shaping young Randy's vision of our Thor campaign," I said. "I'll be able to meet in a couple hours, or maybe tomorrow." Violet's words finally permeated my brain. "Wait, they *said?* I assume they didn't conference call you."

"No. They're waiting in your office. Together. You might want to get up here."

"Okay." I sighed. Randy looked relieved when I turned to go. As I walked away, I said, "Before I leave for the day, I'll be back to see those revised drawings." I went to my office, pausing at Violet's desk before going in to ask, "They're really both in there? Just the two of them?"

"I should warn you, before you go in," Violet cautioned ominously, "it's a real battle zone in there."

"Oh, great," I groaned and opened my office door.

Lillith and Bonnie were both seated behind my desk, staring with rapt fascination at my computer monitor as they pounded on the keyboard and shrieked at each other.

"That's their leader!" Bonnie yelped. "Take him out! I'll hold off the platoon."

"I'm trying!" Lillith roared. "Use your flame-thrower, you imbecile. Don't waste ammunition!"

"I'm not the one who ran over a land mine with our tank," Bonnie snarled.

"Oh, what I wouldn't give to have that tank right now," Lillith mused.

"Watch out! He's got a grenade!" Bonnie screamed. A loud explosion emanated from the computer and both women sank back in their chairs, looking forlorn.

"Don't take it too hard, Bonnie. Try as I might, those boys in the shipping department always win," Lillith assured her. Instead of laughing, I pretended like I'd just walked in and cleared my throat. Lillith jumped up and said, "There you are, Blaine. Good of you to drop whatever it was you were working on. We need a word. Rather, Bonnie does."

I walked toward the sitting area, and they moved to join me, taking opposite ends of the sofa. They left a demilitarized zone between them, which somehow comforted me after witnessing their camaraderie against the shipping department on the company's computer system. I'd had no idea that this was one of the customs Violet brought with us from our days at Breslin Evans, but if Lillith didn't mind, it had nothing to do with me. I took a chair opposite the two women and asked what was going on.

"Have you heard of *The Robby and Rhonda Show*?" Bonnie asked.

"No," I answered. "I don't have much time to watch television."

"I suppose not," Bonnie said. "It's new. It's barely made a dent in the daytime ratings, even though I've poured money into it. That's why I'd like for you and Daniel to be guests—"

"I'm sorry to interrupt, Bonnie, but no," I declined.

"Blaine, don't be impertinent," Lillith sternly said. "Bonnie's come all this way to make her request. The least you could do is hear her out."

"There's really not a lot to say. I was only thinking of our boys, and how *The Robby and Rhonda Show* would be a good opportunity for Blaine and Daniel to cement their public image in a positive manner.

The hosts of the show are gay, so it would be a comfortable environment."

"Frankly, Bonnie, I've told everyone involved that I'm done with interviews and appearances."

"Is this show on before *Secret Splendor*?" Lillith asked Bonnie, ignoring my comment.

"Yes, it is," Bonnie said, brightening. "After that horrible meeting we all had, I pitched an idea for a gay talk show to the network. They jumped right on it, knowing we could hook *Secret Splendor*'s gay viewers. We're still testing it, though, so it's only local right now. But I know it will take off."

"I'm sure you're right," Lillith said, peering intently at Bonnie. "I can tell by your aura."

Bonnie looked pleased. She turned back to me and asked, "Are you sure you won't reconsider, Blaine? Even if Daniel is willing to do it?"

Daniel had been so relieved when we agreed to end our public appearances together that I felt confident enough to say, "Sure. If you can get Daniel to do it, then I'm in."

Bonnie clapped her hands twice and said, "Perfect! I'll fax Violet with the details."

"What?" I asked, confused.

"That's very good of you, Blaine," Lillith said, rising from the sofa. "This will do wonders for your karma. You'll see. I'll walk you out, Bonnie."

Before they left, I collected my wits and said, "One condition. This has to be it. I'm a busy man, and I've done more than my share for *Secret Splendor*'s image. Let alone another one of your shows."

"Agreed," Bonnie said. "I'll get back to you later today."

An hour before I left for home, I returned to the art department, ready to be presented with another mutation of my vision. I was pleasantly surprised. Randy had done away with his original version. This time, Thor emerged from the thick haze of a cloud, his left hand holding an anvil-shaped bottle of cologne with a lightning bolt etched into the glass. Thor's other hand had lightning shooting from his fingers. It wasn't exactly what I'd described, but it was much closer to what I wanted.

"Thank you. This is a lot better, Randy," I praised. He smiled bashfully, and as I watched him begin work on another revision, his phone rang.

"Art department," I said, grabbing the phone so Randy wouldn't be distracted.

"Don't tell me Lillith demoted you," Violet teased.

"Don't forget we're nearing Christmas bonus season," I said. "What's up?"

"I got a fax from Bonnie. Are you going to be on something called *The Robby and Rhonda Show*?"

"Yes. When is the taping?" I asked.

"Wait, I just saw this. There's a condition," she said. "Daniel has agreed, but only if you two can publicly break up."

I was startled by the news and got a sinking feeling in my stomach. I shouldn't have been surprised that Daniel was looking for a way to put a permanent end to our farce. But the small flicker of hope that I'd had for us slowly faded.

Violet continued before I could reply, "I don't get it, Blaine. I thought the two of you were done making appearances together."

"Bonnie and Lillith managed to railroad me into doing it."

"It sounds like this will free you from doing any more," Violet said. "I'll send the details to Gavin after I add them to your calendar."

I took off work the following Friday and encountered Violet on my doorstep when I left to go to the studio where *The Robby and Rhonda Show* taped.

"What are you doing here?" I asked.

"I know these appearances with Daniel can be strained," Violet said. "I figured you could use a friend."

I stared at her while she readjusted her scarf and tucked its ends into her black leather coat. She looked at me expectantly, perhaps waiting for me to protest and send her to the office. Instead, I put my arm around her shoulder, steered her up the block, and said, "I can't think of anyone else I'd rather have in my corner. The studio's only eight blocks away. We're walking."

At the studio, we were ushered to the green room by a phalanx of handlers, interns, and producers. I was surprised to see Lillith standing at the end of a hallway with Bonnie, but since they seemed preoccupied, I didn't try to get their attention. When I was asked if I wanted to reserve seats in the audience for friends, I scoffed and said, "No offense, but I haven't told my friends I'm doing this show. I don't want any of them rehashing it over and over. I just want to tape this thing, then forget it ever happened. Is Daniel here yet?"

"Mr. Stephenson is around here somewhere," a woman in horn-rimmed glasses said. "Let me see if I can find him."

After she left, I was taken to a makeup room. When I returned to the green room, all the others were gone except for Violet, who was sitting on a leopard print sofa next to Daniel. He looked annoyed.

"I can't believe you agreed to do this," Daniel said. "I've been up since four this morning. I had to rush my scenes early so I could come to this stupid show."

"Hold on to that bitterness. It'll come in handy for our fake breakup scene," I said casually. "Don't blame me. The only reason I said I'd do this was because Bonnie told me you were okay with it."

Daniel shook his head and said, "If you're going to be a father, you need to wise up. Bonnie and Lillith played you like a ten-year-old trying to get a later bedtime. I didn't agree to anything. Bonnie let you believe I did."

I cringed, ashamed that I'd fallen for Bonnie's ploy, until Violet said to Daniel, "For that to work, both parents have to fall for it. You're here. She played the same trick on you, huh?"

Caught, Daniel bit his lip, then said, "What could I do? Not only does Seaforth Chemicals underwrite *Secret Splendor,* but Bonnie's also one of our producers."

Before Violet and I could discuss the merits of his contract and the benefits of his membership with AFTRA, the segment producer came in to prep us for the show. He told us to expect the same line of questioning we'd probably had from other interviews, and urged us to relax and have fun. He seemed content with our blasé agreement and left us, saying he'd return in ten minutes to escort us to the stage.

"This is stupid," I said. "I wonder if it's too late to back out?"

"Yes, I'd say it is," Daniel said curtly. "Besides, we agreed to put an end to this together."

"I don't remember signing anything," I said, turning away from him.

"Would you two stop?" Violet said. "I'm sure the only reason you're sniping at each other is because you're nervous. You've both done interviews together. This will be a piece of cake."

"I guess so," Daniel said quietly.

"Whatever," I mumbled.

"Besides, this is just a local talk show," Violet continued. "I did a little research on the Internet the other day. It's only been on the air about a month, but if the ratings don't pick up, it will probably be canceled by January. And the hosts are complete nobodies." Violet took out her PalmPilot and read, "Rhonda Goldfarb is a psychologist and used to have an A.M. radio show on the West Coast. The other host—"

"We're ready, guys," the producer said, bursting into the green room.

"The other host is a failed stage actor," Violet hastily said. The producer frowned at her, but continued to rush us out of the green room. He directed Violet to the backstage area where Bonnie and Lillith would stand. Before he could take us onstage, someone from the crew stopped him to ask a question.

While he was distracted, I turned to Daniel and said, "Don't do it. Please."

"Don't do what?"

"Don't fake our breakup in front of all these people." When he stared at me, puzzled, I added, "Maybe you've forgotten that it was this time last year when we broke up. But it's been on my mind a lot, and it still hurts. I don't want to relive it in public."

"I haven't forgotten," Daniel said.

Before he could say anything else, the producer turned back to us, and I could hear the announcer boom, "It's *The Robby and Rhonda Show*!" There was sufficient pause for applause, then, "With Robby!" More applause. "And Rhonda!" Still more enthusiastic applause.

The producer said, "After a few minutes of patter between the hosts—"

Daniel cut him off and said, "Okay, Blaine. I won't do it."

"On today's show, Rhonda chats with a bipolar lesbian nun! It's a story you won't believe. Then Robby learns how to bake cookies from Mrs. Fields herself!"

"You won't do the show?" the producer asked in a panicked tone.

"But first, Robby and Rhonda get to chat with a real-life gay super-couple! From *Secret Splendor,* Daniel Stephenson! And his significant other, the creative genius behind the blockbuster ad campaigns for Lillith Allure Cosmetics, Blaine Dunhill!"

"No, we're doing the show," Daniel assured the producer. He looked at me and said, "We'll do the happy couple thing one last time."

"And now, here they are, Robby and Rhonda!" The announcer dragged out the last syllable of Rhonda's name as if he was waiting for his doctor to examine his tonsils. I saw Robby and Rhonda bound onto the stage, and the crowd bestowed their approval by cheering wildly.

"Welcome, everyone, welcome!" Robby gushed.

"Thank you so much! You're so sweet!" Rhonda chimed in.

"Oh, my fucking god!" Daniel blurted out after a moment. Although I agreed that the two hosts' opening remarks were excruciatingly saccharine, I didn't understand Daniel's reaction. Daniel glanced at the producer and said, "Robby is Robert *Orso?*"

"It ain't Robert Kennedy," the producer answered.

"Who's Robert Orso?" I asked.

"The slut who broke up Jeremy and me," Daniel said.

I took a closer look at Robby. He was reasonably cute, but certainly not in the same league as Daniel or Adam, which made me question Jeremy's judgment.

"I'm confused," I said. "Do you want me to hit him? Or thank him?"

"Get the nun," Daniel said to the producer. "I'm not doing an interview with Robert Orso."

"We have such a great show for you today," Robby was saying. "Don't we, Rhonda?"

"Bonnie assured me this would be painless," I said to Daniel.

"We sure do!" Rhonda gushed. "You get to work with the kitchen queen herself, baking those scrumptious cookies! I can't wait to get my hands on them!" The audience applauded madly, as if they, too, were going to get cookies when all was said and done.

Bonnie, alerted by the wild gesturing of the producer, hurried to us, asking, "Is there a problem?"

"Daniel says he's not doing it," the producer hissed.

"And you," Robby was prattling to Rhonda, "get to help Sister Mary Michael share her ups and downs with us. Just wait until you hear what she has to say!"

"Not doing what?" Bonnie asked.

"This show," Daniel said emphatically.

"But first," Rhonda and Robby both faced the camera, "we have a special treat for you. We're going to spend some time with a couple who's been in and out of the limelight over the past several months. You might know half of this supercouple as Angus Remington, from our network's hit daytime drama, *Secret Splendor*."

"That's right, Rhonda. Ladies and gentlemen, my good friend, Daniel Stephenson!"

Daniel opened his mouth as if to protest, but Bonnie gave him a shove that propelled him onto the stage. He had no choice but to smile at the applauding audience, and I had no choice but to follow him.

"His partner," Rhonda continued, "is less recognizable to most of us, although with a face like his, I'm not sure why we haven't seen him somewhere before! The man who stains the lips of lesbians everywhere, Blaine Dunhill, the creative genius behind Zodiac cosmetics!"

I grinned stupidly when the audience greeted me. Robby and Rhonda led us to armchairs that sat perpendicular to theirs.

As the applause dwindled, Robby reached over and put a hand on Daniel's knee, playfully shaking his leg back and forth and saying, "So how are you? It's been so long!"

"Great, thanks," I heard Daniel say in a faraway voice.

"Hi, Blaine," Rhonda said. "How did you two meet anyway?"

"He saw me in the window, and he just had to have me," I said. The audience laughed and clapped, and our hosts joined them. "Seriously," I continued, since I could see that Daniel was still rattled by seeing Robby, "we met as neighbors and slowly got to know each other over time. It's been great seeing Daniel go from performing on small stages to becoming a successful actor on daytime television with an audience of millions. I'm so proud of him."

As the audience applauded, I leaned over, kissed Daniel on the cheek, and whispered, "Score one for the home team."

I could tell Robby had understood my dig about his less successful acting career by the way he briefly narrowed his eyes at me, but his voice kept its forced cheerfulness as he said, "You two have really taken the show on the road, huh?"

"We tried to keep the show off the road, but I guess you could say we got forced into the fast lane," I said, continuing to field the questions.

"We tried to keep our private lives quiet," Daniel explained, having pulled himself together. "This is Blaine's first foray into public life, so it's been an adjustment. We really are just a couple of ordinary guys who live an ordinary life. Part of our intention in going public with our relationship was to show just that."

"Ordinary? I'd say after the research we've done for this show, there isn't anyone who'd call your lives ordinary!" Rhonda said. Robby looked at her, flashing a smile that would make the queen from *Snow White* jealous. Daniel and I exchanged a nervous look through ever-smiling faces.

"What Rhonda means to say is that we have a little surprise for you. A couple of surprises, really. We know you've been interviewed, taped, questioned, and quoted into a stupor, so we wanted to do something a little different today. You know how it's been, and we've seen the interviews. Fresh young reporters asking hard-hitting questions, trying to pin you down and make you crack so you'll spill the beans—"

"Mixed metaphor, anyone?" Daniel asked. The audience laughed.

Robby continued, "We wanted to do something different. We didn't want to ask hard-hitting questions."

"Good." I breathed a little easier.

"Yes. We saw this as an opportunity to do some good," Robby said.

"That's been our goal all along, too," Daniel said.

"So many interviews have focused on the two of you that we thought we'd shed some light on the other people in your life. Certainly the support of those around you has helped you to be as safe and secure as you are today, right?" Rhonda asked.

Suddenly I felt as "safe and secure" as a tightrope walker. I was distracted for a moment, thinking of Zodiac's future Aries ad. Sheila . . . on a tightrope . . .

"We thought we might share the stage with some of your closest friends," Robby interrupted my thoughts. "Let's bring out the first of our guests, Martin Blount!"

I nearly had a stroke and looked at Daniel, who shrugged help-lessly. Martin ran from the backstage area with the enthusiasm of the Kool-Aid Man after being named an honorary citizen of Nebraska. He waved to the applauding audience with a maniacal grin on his face. He bent to hug Daniel, but merely smiled at me from a safe distance.

"Martin, welcome! It's no secret to a lot of our viewers that before Daniel assumed the role of Angus Remington, the two of you shared a spotlight. Tell us a little about what that was like," Robby baited him.

"Whatever he says, it isn't true," Daniel said with a smile. I knew that he was trying to signal Martin that this should be a nice inter-view, not a bitchy one, but I didn't have much faith in Daniel's ability to tone him down.

"Oh, you," Martin said. "We did share a stage, but rarely a spot-light. Daniel was the star. When he performed as Princess 2Di4, and I performed a myriad of characters at Club Chaos, there was no one who could hold a candle to him." I glanced at Daniel, who gave me a *See?* look, as if to remind me that Martin wasn't always an evil bitch. Then Martin added, "He was practically shellacked in hairspray, Robert! The fire hazard was far too great!"

I smiled sweetly at Daniel, who pretended not to see me when he said, "Martin is too modest. It was a pleasure to work with him, and I always look back fondly on that time in my life. Martin and I have had our ups and downs—"

"Like the bipolar lesbian nun!" Martin said.

"—but we remain close to this day," Daniel finished.

The four of them continued to exchange quips. I was grateful that I didn't have to say much of anything, and I started to relax again, until Rhonda said, "We don't want you two to feel like you're on an episode of *This Is Your Life,* but we do have another surprise for you. Ladies and gentlemen, an argument for the gay gene theory, Daniel's sister, Gwendy Stephenson!"

"And her girlfriend, Gretchen Schmidt," Robby added.

Daniel and I both went slack-jawed as the curtains on the side of the set parted briefly and Gwendy and Gretchen came out. After ex-changing a bewildered look, we plastered smiles on our faces and stood as they approached, clapping like trained seals. Gretchen hugged me, and Gwendy hugged Daniel. We both asked, at the same time, through locked jaws, "What are you doing here?"

Gretchen patted me on the back and whispered, "Don't worry; we've got it under control."

"We'll be back after this message from Deity's Narcissus, the new fragrance by Lillith Allure!" Robby exclaimed.

Someone shouted, "We're off!" Robby and Rhonda left us without a word and retreated behind the curtains. I turned around, looking in every direction for Lillith, but Violet was standing alone. When she saw my frantic expression, she grabbed a pitcher of water and hurried to join us.

"You're all wearing microphones," Violet spoke quietly. "Somebody drink water, so I don't look like an idiot." Daniel and I both gulped down a glass, while Gretchen and Gwendy watched with amused expressions. "Never send a man to do a woman's job. For the rest of the show, the two of you need to—"

"Fasten your seat belts," Gretchen finished with a Bette Davis impression so bad that Martin and Daniel flinched.

"What the hell is going on here?" I whispered.

Gretchen smiled, gazing out at the spectators, and said, "This is only live for the studio audience. Trust me, when we're finished, this tape won't be shown in Manhattan or anywhere else."

Gwendy pretended to accidentally disconnect her tiny microphone. As it fell to the floor and a couple of techs headed our way, she quickly said, "While the two of you can do nothing but piss and moan, thanks to being alerted by Violet, the rest of us have been doing research and gathering reinforcements. It's time to kick some butt."

"The rest of you?" Daniel voiced my thought.

Gretchen looked adoringly at me and said, "Laugh like I said something funny so nobody catches on."

We all threw back our heads and roared with laughter. Robby and Rhonda came back and sat down, and Violet retreated to the wings.

"Isn't this fun?" Rhonda squealed.

"I can't remember having a better time," I answered.

"Well, there was that time—" Martin started, but stopped when I locked gazes with him.

"All right, folks," the producer said, "we're back on in three," then used his fingers to show *two, one,* then pointed to Robby and Rhonda.

After a brief reintroduction by Robby, our hosts asked Daniel and Gwendy questions about growing up in Wisconsin, a conversation that thankfully excluded me. I certainly didn't want to talk about my family, especially after all the plugs Gwendy was making for PFLAG.

I began to feel calm again, only half listening while Gwendy talked, then I glanced at Daniel when he shifted in his chair. He was looking at me, so I stared back, wondering if he was trying to send some silent communication my way. After a few seconds, I realized I was feeling it again—that giddy sense of euphoria that watching him sometimes gave me. The corners of my mouth turned up slightly. His expression became softer, even happy, and the only thing I could think about was how much I loved him, even after our tumultuous year apart.

I wanted to give in to my impulse to reach for him. No one but our friends would be surprised. Everyone else already thought we were a couple. But my attention was diverted when I heard Robby say, "Gretchen, you look like you've had an exciting year! When are you due?"

I swallowed hard and felt my protective instincts well up inside me in spite of the fact that Gretchen seemed to have the situation under control. She radiated serenity as she answered, "Next week."

"We hear so much about couples in your situation choosing to have children. I think it's just wonderful," Rhonda said. "Did you use artificial insemination?"

Daniel had already stopped looking at me, and at that question, his face went blank.

"I sure did. I've been very fortunate through this whole process. I have friends who support me, and Gwendy to help indulge my late-night cravings."

"Er, cravings?" Robby asked, looking a little nonplused by Gretchen's suggestive expression.

"Yes. I have a voracious appetite for—"

"Cookies warm from the oven," Gwendy said. "When do we get to meet Mrs. Fields?"

"We're having so much fun, I'm not sure we'll have time for our other guests," Rhonda said.

Martin looked crestfallen and asked, "Not even the bipolar lesbian nun? I used to perform as Sister Mary Amanda Prophet, and I'd hoped—"

"We do have another surprise for you," Robby smoothly interrupted. "We'll be bringing her out after this message from ToothTape, the revolutionary new denture adhesive from Seaforth!"

"We're off," the producer said.

Robby and Rhonda sprinted to the side of the stage to confer with their producer, and I felt my stomach tie into a knot. I wondered what else could possibly be in store for us.

"Why don't they let Robby bake his cookies, already?" Daniel asked impatiently.

"Where are Lillith and Bonnie?" I asked. "They got us into this. They need to—"

"The fun's just beginning," Gretchen insisted, her eyes glittering in a way that made me even more nervous.

Robby and Rhonda joined us again. "Ready to wrap this up?" Robby asked me.

"You can't imagine," I said.

"We hope you've had fun," Rhonda said. "We sure have enjoyed having you all on the show!"

"Thank you," Daniel said, exchanging a look with Robby.

When taping resumed, Robby addressed the camera. "There's been a lot of publicity about this young dynamic couple. Some of it has been true, some of it has maybe been stretched a bit. Haven't they been good sports to answer our questions today?" The audience applauded on cue. "But we'd hardly have a show if it wasn't for the tenacity of one reporter who introduced us to this amazing story in the first place. *Manhattan Star-Gazette* columnist Lola Listeria!"

As Daniel went pale, I felt my own face flush. Lola came onstage in a yellow suit, her flaming red hair spilling out from under a huge, yellow-feathered hat, making her look like a cross between Bette Midler and Big Bird. The chairs on the set had been arranged so that Lola sat on the other side of Robby and Rhonda, apart from the rest of us. Wise choice.

"Hello, Lola!" our hosts chorused.

"Hello, darlings! Lola is so happy to be here! You know, since I broke this story, poor Lola's phone hasn't stopped ringing!"

"Neither have my ears," Daniel muttered.

"Why does she talk about herself in third person?" I heard Martin whisper. "Who does she think she is? Bob Dole?"

"Our little lovebirds thought they could hide in their nest, but Lola knows what the people want to hear, and Lola knows how to deliver!"

"Like Domino's," Martin added a little louder. Lola shot a scathing look his way.

"How do you get these stories, Lola?" Robby asked.

"Darlings, all I had to do was look into Daniel's résumé. It didn't take long before I could see all the good he'd done for his community. I felt that shining some light on his perfect relationship would be an example for all to aspire to. I just needed to give him a little push."

"I'd like to give you a little push. Right off the Brooklyn Bridge," Martin muttered.

"But you know, darlings, Lola's eyes and ears can't be everywhere—"

"—like her hat," I said.

"—like her nose," Gwendy added.

"—like her ass," Martin said at the same time. The three of us exchanged admiring glances, and Daniel laughed.

"I've noticed you rely on a lot of anonymous sources for your stories," Gretchen spoke over us. "It must be difficult to balance the public's right to know with an individual's desire for privacy. I was speaking to my dear friend Jane Gorman, the Hollywood producer. Maybe you've heard of her?" When Lola gave her a vacant look, Gretchen continued. "Jane's an out lesbian, but she talked about what a tough time all women have in the entertainment industry, which is why so many Hollywood lesbians prefer to keep their sexual orientation private."

I wondered if Gretchen's plan involved boring the audience to death with some political rant, but my eyes were drawn to Rhonda, who'd scooted to the edge of her chair. Her eyes were wide, and her complexion had suddenly become blotched with red spots.

"I think Lola wants to introduce us to one of her sources," Rhonda quickly followed up Gretchen's remark.

"I wonder which Hollywood lesbian Rhonda slept with?" Daniel said in an undertone.

"Yes!" Lola gushed. "I want to give credit where it's due, so I'd like to take this opportunity to welcome and thank a new friend who worked tirelessly with me on this story, the renowned artist, Sydney Kepler-Dunhill!"

I literally saw red, since Sydney strolled onstage from the opposite side of the set wearing a bright red dress. My pulse doubled when I looked at her, and I felt my heartbeat pounding out a rapid rhythm in the veins in my neck.

"Redheads should never wear scarlet," Martin said disapprovingly, applause making his comment inaudible except to our group.

"Especially not in front of an angry Taurus," Daniel said.

I tore my gaze from my ex-wife to look at him. I was in no mood for astrological jokes, but once I saw his amused expression, I couldn't help but return his smile, because it was genuine. He'd obviously decided to stop letting any of this get to him. I wasn't sure I'd ever loved him more than I did at that moment, because his smile was all it took to make my anger evaporate.

"Hi, Sydney," Robby greeted her after she settled next to Lola. "Is it just a coincidence that you share a name with one of our other guests?"

"It's not a coincidence," Sydney said. "It was more like a mistake. Wouldn't you say, Blaine?"

"One of my biggest," I answered dryly.

"Sydney helped so much on the legwork of this story," said Lola. "She's quite a resourceful gal, and very handy with a camera."

"Speaking of cameras," Gwendy said, facing the camera and emulating Robby and Rhonda's cheesy banter, "here's a woman who's no stranger to cameras! Her husband is a major fashion photographer, and she's the daredevil spokesmodel for Zodiac Cosmetics. Let's welcome Sheila Meyers and her friend, Faizah!"

The audience, though perhaps confused about who was hosting the show, reacted accordingly and applauded when Sheila and Faizah strode onto the stage. They bypassed Robby and Rhonda, who were gaping at them, and sat down in the chairs that Martin and Gwendy vacated.

"Hi, Robert," Sheila said, reaching over to pat his arm. "I think it's so fantastic that you landed this hosting job. I mean, a person can only do so many performances of *Anything Goes,* right? Oh, wait. Did that close?"

"Child," Faizah drawled, "Faizah saw Robby in that show. What a bomb! And I don't mean that in the street slang kind of way. It stunk up the theater like burnt cookies! And Faizah should know what—"

"Cookies!" Rhonda trilled. "Isn't it time to bring out Mrs. Fields?"

"Why?" Martin asked as he situated himself into a kneeling position at Gretchen's feet. "Is she the famous lesbian you're sleeping with?"

"Mrs. Fields is a housewife!" Robby gasped.

Faizah shook her head in disbelief and said, "Don't you know better than to call an entrepreneur a housewife? If my mama heard you, she'd snatch you baldheaded." Faizah turned to Gretchen and said, "Mama sold Avon back home in Maine. Only thing on earth that kept those mosquitoes away."

"Faizah! You can't talk about Avon when this show is sponsored by Lillith Allure. Or while I'm on it," Sheila reprimanded.

"Why not?" Faizah asked. She pointed to Lola and Sydney and said, "They look like an Avon representative's wet dream. Look at those clogged pores. Faizah feels like she just performed a lunar landing."

Sydney's upper lip curled as if she was channeling Billy Idol. Lola looked miffed. Though I imagined she was more upset by Faizah's commanding use of the third person, rather than the slight to the condition of her skin.

"Sydney and I have been exchanging makeup tips since we were girls together in Eau Claire, Wisconsin," Sheila said. "I remember how pretty she was the day she married Blaine. I was *invited* to their wedding."

"Robby. Rhonda," Faizah said, leaning forward in an inviting manner, "what you may have missed in Sheila's polite statement is the underlying tone of anger and betrayal she feels because Sydney not only crashed her wedding, but took pictures with a camera. Obviously not a good camera. If she had used a good camera, it would be one thing. No. She used one of those cheap cameras. Disposable. Just like her integrity."

"Sheila is appalled," Sheila chimed in. Faizah nodded and high-fived her friend.

"Well," Rhonda said, trailing off and looking to Robby for help.

"*Anything Goes* did *not* bomb," Robby said. "The revival I was in had one of the most successful runs in Broadway history."

"Faizah stands corrected," Faizah said. "I meant you, specifically. If you plan on singing during this little gabfest, Faizah's out of here."

"Who invited you?" Sydney asked.

"You're one to talk!" Sheila exclaimed. "You crashed my wedding. I crashed your show."

"It's our show," Rhonda said, gesturing to herself and Robby. "Just in case anyone was wondering. Let's get back on track."

"Yes. Let's!" Gwendy said. "I want to hear about Sydney's illustrious art career."

"Thank you for asking," Sydney said. "I just had my first successful—"

"—face-lift," Martin interrupted.

"—independent thought," Gwendy interjected.

"—orgasm," I said at the same time.

"—show in London," Sydney continued, glaring at us. "It received rave reviews."

Sheila extracted some folded pages from her jacket pocket and said, "I took the liberty of downloading a few of those reviews. Would anyone like to hear the highlights?"

The audience applauded while Sydney blanched. Rhonda looked offstage to her producers for guidance. Robby slumped back in his chair, apparently having given up trying to maintain control of his unruly guests.

"The *Guardian Unlimited* called Sydney's work 'trash that never should've left the sidewalk,'" Sheila read.

"Ouch," Daniel said.

"They didn't understand what they were seeing," Sydney protested.

"Neither did you when you put on that dress and looked in the mirror," Martin said.

"The *Telegraph* says, 'If great art is like giving birth, this is afterbirth.'"

"Speaking of birth," Sydney said, her voice rising above the laughter of the audience, "shouldn't one of you be enough of a gentleman to proudly claim paternity of Gretchen's baby?"

There was a brief pause, until Daniel and I chorused, "I am."

"They're lying," Martin said. "It's me."

"You're all wrong. Faizah's Gretchen's baby-daddy," Faizah said.

"Back off, Amazon queen," Gwendy said.

"Really. I'm the father," I said, laughing because it was true, but nobody would believe it now.

When Gretchen held up her hand, we all held our collective breath and waited to hear her answer. She inhaled deeply and said, "I think my water just broke."

"Oh, my god," Martin said. "What a cliché."

CHAPTER 17

She was one month old, and as I rested on the bed next to her, I realized that the past four weeks were a blur. I tried to make linear sense of it, but all I got were images. I could barely remember *The Robby and Rhonda Show,* but I never was into drama, and that day was over the top—both the show and Gretchen's sensational exit from it.

My most vivid memory of the day my baby was born was how amazing Gwendy had been. Calm, funny, and strong. Both of us stayed with Gretchen during labor, and any resentment or anxiety I'd felt about Gwendy disintegrated when I saw how tactfully she managed to support Gretchen without making me feel extraneous. Both of them laughed at me after the baby finally made her entrance into the world and I stood there speechless at the realization that my son was a daughter.

Looking at her now, it was hard to remember that I'd spent nine months certain she was a boy. She was exactly who she should be; I wouldn't change a thing. The day after she was born, with Gwendy and me flanking the bed, Gretchen looked up from nursing her and said, "As lovely as the name is, I'm afraid I can't inflict her with Civil Liberty. Any thoughts, Blaine?"

"I only had a boy's name picked out," I admitted.

"Some boys' names work for girls," Gwendy said. "What was it?"

"Rex Stetson," I said. Gwendy looked confused, and after Gretchen recovered from her laughing fit, I said more seriously, "Kenneth."

"For Ken," Gretchen said, looking down at our daughter. "That would have been sweet, Blaine. But I'm not naming our daughter

Kenneth. Ken's been on my mind a lot, though. He and I used to talk about names, back when we thought we'd be doing this together."

"Did you ever agree on a girl's name?" I asked.

Gretchen nodded and said, "Emily. He said it was feminine and traditional and might protect her from some of the craziness of life with me as her mother. I'm sure he could never have imagined how unconventional her conception, birth, and family were going to be. Lucky child."

The three of us looked at the baby, then Gwendy and I met each other's eyes. It was clear she was biting her tongue, and I grinned at her.

"I like the name 'Emily,' " I said.

"Emily Dunhill Schmidt," Gwendy suggested.

Gretchen looked at the two of us and said, "We're all in agreement?" When we nodded, she smiled. "I hope that's a sign of things to come. Maybe not such a lucky baby. It won't be easy growing up with three strong-willed, stubborn parents."

"I'm sure she'll be the alpha infant in no time," Gwendy said.

It is true that there is something tyrannical about babies. They determine the schedule, mood, and activities of a household. I knew it was tougher on Gretchen and Gwendy, who were with her all the time. Although I saw Emily every day, I didn't live with her. I could go home and sleep through the night. I could go about my daily schedule, losing myself in work or the gym or the other activities of my normal, adult world.

The biggest change in my life was that Emily's existence buffered me. I had no idea if anyone was still talking about Daniel and Blaine, Supercouple, or if there had been any fallout from *The Robby and Rhonda Show*. I didn't know what movies were being rushed to the screen in time to be Oscar contenders. For the first time in my professional memory, I had no idea how much Super Bowl commercials were going to cost. The final outcome of the presidential election barely registered with me, although I was sure my friends were in shock.

It was actually my friends who helped keep me out of touch. Along with Gavin, Violet, Lillith, and Frank, they were letting me take a vacation from the world on Emily's behalf. I could focus on my work while I was in the office, then I either went to Gretchen's or to the gym and then Gretchen's. Gwendy and I pampered "our two girls," as she called them, cooking, taking care of household duties, or making sure visitors didn't wear them out.

There were a lot of visitors. Gretchen's father came from Pennsylvania to meet his only grandchild. I liked him; it was easy to see that he was the reason for Gretchen's down-to-earth, sensible attitude. Years before, she'd been at odds with her family, but began visiting them after her mother became ill. By the time her mother died, they'd made peace. Mr. Schmidt didn't ask many questions about Gwendy and me. He seemed satisfied with the knowledge that his grandbaby was going to be well loved.

If my family knew about the baby, I had no indication of it. That was fine with me. Emily would have her Cousin Nick to represent the best of the Dunhills. He loved his new school and was coming into his own in New York. He sometimes joined me at the Tribeca loft, doing his homework while the rest of us treated Emily like she was better than *Must See TV*. Even though he affected teenage indifference, I often caught him watching me when I held Emily and talked to her. On those nights, I'd insist that we walk home instead of taking a cab, eager to give him my undivided attention while he talked about whatever came into his head.

One night after Gretchen teased me about Emily's gender, Nick was quiet on our walk. We were waiting for a light to change when he finally said, "Does it bother you that you had a girl? Did you think it was a boy because that's what you wanted?"

I redid his scarf to provide better protection against the winter chill and said, "It doesn't bother me. After all, I got my son, too, didn't I?"

He rolled his eyes, but when he turned his head to step forward as the light changed, I saw his pleased smile. I, myself, was grinning like an idiot. The next day, he and Gavin helped me put a baby bed together, although Gretchen wouldn't allow Gwendy or me more than a five-minute walk with Emily, and then only if the sun was shining. I had no idea when my daughter would be allowed to come to my apartment, which was supplied with everything she could possibly need. The baby bed sat in my room as a reminder that I needed more space. I'd promised Violet and Gavin that we could resume the apartment search after the new year.

Sheila adored Emily and visited her often, bringing Josh and his camera so that every nuance of my daughter's waking and sleeping moments could be captured for posterity. Adam and Jeremy also visited when they were in town for the holidays. I knew that Martin came, too, but only during the day, when he was sure that I'd be at work. I did run into Blythe one night, smiling when she explained that the pastel pink streak among her magenta strands of hair was in honor of Emily's birth.

Frank liked to drop by a couple of evenings a week, bringing Rowdy, who would lie at the feet of whoever happened to be holding Emily. On a night that one of Frank's visits coincided with Sheila's and Josh's, Josh snapped a picture of Frank and Emily that I loved. She was holding tightly to one of his fingers, staring up at him as if spellbound. I had that one matted and framed, keeping it on my desk at work. Every time I looked at it, I was reminded of how I'd realized at Sheila's wedding that families were often what we created from the best parts of our lives.

Lillith, of course, had her own retinue of people who needed to be involved. Fortunately, Emily's mothers found humor in the smudging, aura fluffing, charting, and blessings that Lillith deemed necessary. The most profound of these events occurred when my daughter was two weeks old. I'd just finished filling the dishwasher when Gwendy took a call and handed me the phone.

"I'm sorry for doing this to you," Ethan said, "but would it be okay if I stopped by with a couple of friends? It's a necessary step to restore harmony to the universe."

I was intrigued by the amusement in his voice, and after clearing it with Gretchen and Gwendy, I gave him the go-ahead. A half hour later, he entered Gretchen's loft with Bonnie and Lillith, looking altogether too satisfied with himself.

"Where is that precious angel?" Lillith asked, and she and Bonnie practically ran over each other in their attempt to be the first to reach the sofa, where Emily was sleeping on Gretchen's lap.

"Beast," I said to Ethan.

"I apologized in advance," he reminded me.

Bonnie managed to claim the space next to Gretchen on the sofa, so Lillith sat on the coffee table, saying, "Bonnie and I have a gift for your daughter. Ethan?"

He shrugged off his coat, pulled a black velvet pouch from his pocket, and walked across the room to them. Both women reached for the pouch, but he held it away from them with a stern look and handed it to Gretchen. Gwendy and I walked behind the sofa to watch as Gretchen untied the silk cords and pulled out a pendant hanging from a thick copper chain.

"The amulet," Bonnie breathed, her eyes glittering.

"The stone is lapis," Lillith said. "It traveled between our families from prehistoric times, providing protection, before it ended up in Egypt, where it was set in faience, which is a ceramic. The sheen comes from a copper glaze. It's thousands of years old, Gretchen."

"I can't possibly—"

"We know it's not the kind of thing you want lying around the house," Bonnie said, cutting Gretchen off. "It's priceless. It's also caused quite a bit of controversy over the centuries. With your permission, Gretchen—"

"And Blaine," Lillith said.

"And Blaine," Bonnie concurred, "we want to donate it to the Metropolitan Museum's Egyptian Art collection. The placard will state that it's the gift of Emily Dunhill Schmidt, daughter of Gretchen Schmidt and Blaine Dunhill."

"But we've also commissioned a replica, which Emily can keep for her own protection, and pass down to her descendants," Lillith said.

"Thank you; Emily and I accept," Gretchen said.

"I'm honored," I said. I didn't believe in their past-life nonsense for a minute. I suspected they'd seen the piece—and each other— for the first time at some gem show and tried to outbid each other for it. After the fact, one of them had no doubt invented an ancient feud to justify her greed, and the other had followed her lead. I met Ethan's laughing eyes and asked, "What I really want to know is, where did it turn up? Who had it?"

"That," said Ethan, "is a story I will carry to my grave." The grateful looks Lillith and Bonnie cast his way made me certain that his position as their spiritual sovereign was guaranteed for life. At least this lifetime.

Louis and Joyce Stephenson flew in from Wisconsin for a few days before Christmas. It was obvious that they regarded Emily as their grandchild, which gave me a pang. She could have been theirs through Daniel and me. Instead, she was theirs through Gwendy and Gretchen. They'd taken Nick with them when they returned to Wisconsin, but he flew back to New York immediately after Christmas, seeming none the worse for having spent time with his family.

As for Daniel, I knew he hadn't seen Emily because Gretchen would have told me. Nobody talked about him when I was around. I didn't know if they were uncomfortable or didn't want me to be uncomfortable. I let it slide, appreciating the break from a year's worth of roller coaster experiences and emotions where he was concerned.

"You'll love Daniel," I whispered to Emily as she lay sleeping. "He's Gwendy's big brother, so I guess he's your uncle. But he's your father, too. He was with me the day you were started."

I wondered if Emily would ever know or understand the way she came to be. Maybe by the time she was old enough to hear it, no one would be having babies the old-fashioned way. It was overwhelming to think about the world my child had inherited and how it might change in her lifetime.

I looked up as Gwendy came into the room to check on us. "You're not asleep either?" she asked. "Gretchen tried to doze, but I think she has cabin fever."

"I do not," Gretchen said, walking in to sit on the bed next to us.

I sat up to give her more room and said, "You both look exhausted. You're supposed to catch up on your sleep when she naps."

"I can't believe it's snowing again," Gretchen said. "Ten inches brought in the new year—"

"Not in front of the baby!" I gasped.

"Hush. We don't have ten inches of anything around here but snow," Gwendy said.

"You don't know what you're missing," I said.

"I know you're shy of ten by several inches," Gwendy said.

"If you're going to disparage my manhood—"

"Oh, what's it like to be outside in the snow?" Gretchen moaned. "Any other time, I'd be out walking in it, getting into a snowball fight, enjoying it before it turns to slush."

"Then do it," I said. "Here you are, with the woman you love. The city's blanketed in white. The two of you should go out and play.

Stop somewhere for hot chocolate. Talk about legal briefs and quarterly taxes, or whatever it is you talk about when Emily isn't dominating you. Take a break. I'm here."

"I wouldn't get ten feet from the door before I'd be overcome by separation anxiety," Gretchen said.

"It's true," Gwendy said. "I've tried to send her out for walks, Blaine. She won't go."

"Sounds like it's time for me to put my paternal foot down. In fact, I'll make it harder for you to run back. Let me take Emily to my place for a couple of hours."

Gretchen put her hands around her throat as if she were strangling and said, "Stop. I can't."

"You stocked my place with everything I'd need," I said. "I'll take bottles of your expressed milk. Emily can travel in the sling, under my coat, dressed in warm clothes. Traffic is light. Cabs have been ordered by the city to drive slowly. We'll be buckled up and safe. You can take your cell phone and call if you panic. And I can call you if I need anything."

Gretchen's eyes filled with tears, and she said, "You think I'm neurotic, don't you?"

"I think you've got baby blues," I said. "Come on. How many Manhattan babies have two residences? It's time Emily found out about the dynasty she was born into."

"You call that dump you live in—"

"If I remember correctly, you once told me it was a great apartment. So it's a little crowded right now. She won't mind. She already knows Nick and Gavin. It's time she met Dexter."

"That ought to make her eager to come back home," Gwendy said. "He's the ugliest cat I've ever seen."

"He has character," I argued.

"And really bad breath," Gretchen said.

"And bad hair," Gwendy added. "Sounds like my senior prom date."

"You went to the prom with a guy?" Gretchen asked. "I actually went with a girl."

"See all the things you don't know about each other? You need quality time alone. Emily and I are going to Blaine Manor."

Gretchen took a deep breath and said, "Okay. I'll do it. But only two hours. Promise me. And you'll call if—"

"I promise."

It was an hour before they finally put us into a cab, satisfied that I had every possible thing I could need for the drive home. I glanced back to see Gretchen standing forlornly on the curb, staring after us as we drove away. Then Gwendy put an arm around her, and the two of them turned to trudge down the sidewalk. Gretchen's arm slid around Gwendy's waist as they walked, and I smiled. They looked sweet together.

I felt like an idiot carrying the diaper bag when I stepped into the deli after the cab dropped me off. Since no one could see that there was a baby under my coat, it looked like I was carrying a hideously unstylish, oversized pastel purse. I really had to find Gretchen something more chic before she started venturing out with Emily. This one had been a gift from somebody.

"Mr. Blaine," Amir called from behind the counter. "How are you today?"

"I'm great," I said. I unbuttoned my coat and said, "Come meet my daughter, Emily."

I was gratified by the way everything ground to a halt as Amir and assorted relatives examined Emily and congratulated me.

"You shouldn't have her out in this weather," Amir scolded.

"I'm going home," I promised. "I thought I should take a treat for Dexter to fend off sibling rivalry."

"I'll wrap some tuna for you," Amir said, hurrying behind the counter.

"Blaine."

I turned, startled, to face Daniel. His eyes were riveted to Emily, who continued to sleep against my chest. His preoccupation gave me a chance to study him. In spite of the color the cold air had given his cheeks, he looked tired. It made my heart hurt.

"Would you like to hold her?" I finally asked.

He met my eyes and said, "I can't. The show's taping scenes in the park today, and I need to get back."

"That explains the red snow gear," I said.

He smiled faintly and said, "Cressida is going to be missing after an avalanche. Of course, everyone will suspect that Angus caused it."

"It'll be the first time the snow up Jane-Therese's nose didn't come from South America," I said.

He gave a surprised laugh and said, "You're right. Funny, Blaine."

"I have my moments. Emily, wake up and watch Uncle Daniel trying to hide those cigarettes so I won't know he's smoking again."

"Just now and then," Daniel said. "She looks so tiny against your chest."

"She'd look even smaller if Gretchen and Gwendy hadn't layered her in so many clothes."

"I keep meaning to . . . but I wasn't sure . . ."

"They'd love to see you," I said, adding tactfully, "Christmas sort of slipped by all of us, but things have settled down now."

He nodded and said, "I have to get back. I'll call—"

"See ya," I interrupted with our old litany.

"Yeah. See ya."

I watched him stop outside the door to light his cigarette, then he was gone. By the time I walked home and climbed the five stories to my apartment, I was struggling not to cry. Gavin took the diaper bag and the tuna while I busied myself with Emily until I could regain my composure.

"Where's Nick?" I finally asked.

"Out shopping for CDs."

"Great. We'll be living in hip hop hell."

"It is great," Gavin said. "He's with a friend."

Something about the way he said it made me repeat, "A friend?"

"A boy," Gavin said. "His name is Pete, and he's totally adorable."

"No," I moaned, looking at Emily. "It's supposed to be years before I have to start worrying about boys."

"You get to practice with Nick," Gavin said. Dexter strolled in, took a look at Emily, and made a quick dash for the kitchen. "Hmm. Maybe I should give him the tuna."

I slouched on the sofa, pulling my legs up so I could prop Emily against them while I told her what a fine cat Dexter was. I looked up to see Gavin staring at us with an odd expression.

"What?"

"I don't know. That's kind of—there's something sexy about a muscular man holding a baby. A weird contrast of strength and gentleness."

Too bad Daniel hadn't thought so. I pushed that thought out of my head and dedicated myself to my daughter's visit. She only cried once, and the bottle I heated stopped that. A couple of diaper changes, two tentative examinations by Dexter, and three phone calls from Gretchen later, I bundled her up again and took her home. I had to give a full account of everything we'd done while Gretchen checked her for damage. I left out the part about seeing Daniel. I didn't feel like being interrogated, especially by Gwendy, whose legal training made her formidable.

Instead of going back to my apartment, I took a cab to Central Park, wondering if I could find the *Secret Splendor* shoot. Without thinking, I fell into the walking routine Daniel and I had developed long ago, ending at Bethesda Fountain, which looked beautiful but so cold against the snowy landscape. I stared at the angel and said, "Come on, give me a miracle. How many times did we sit here admiring you, sharing ourselves with each other and you? I know he's in this park somewhere. Make him remember. Make him miss me as much as I miss him."

People came and went, rushing to get out of the cold. Daniel wasn't among them. Once the light began to fade, I knew my opportunity had passed. The crew had undoubtedly stopped shooting, and the actors would have hurried away to get warm.

If it hadn't been for the red parka, he would never have caught my eye when I turned to walk home. He was on the bridge, his chin propped on his hands, watching me. I stopped and stared up at him for a minute, then we both started walking until we met on the road.

"I'm so cold," he said, his teeth chattering.

I wrapped my arms around him, frustrated by his bulky clothing, and said, "How long have you been waiting?"

"Forever. Don't make me talk. Just hold me."

"If I talk while I'm holding you, will you listen?" I felt him nod. "I'm sorry. For all the things I said that hurt you, and for all the things I didn't say, too. For not telling you about the baby. For the ways you found out about that and about Ethan. For forcing you to pose as my boyfriend and letting you think it was only for Gretchen and our other friends. I wanted to make you spend time with me. I thought it would help us work out some of our problems. Instead, it gave us new problems, made you tired and miserable, and pushed us farther apart. I proved you were right when you called me controlling and stubborn."

"You always think," he began haltingly, "that because I'm older, or because I've been around more, that I'm the strong one. I can't always be the strong one, Blaine."

"I know. You don't have to be," I said. "Your whole body is shaking. Let's get you home."

"I can't," he said. "I have to meet Kyle."

"Oh," I said, wondering who Kyle was. I felt hurt and stupid that I'd apparently misread what was happening between us. "Could we get together later? To talk?"

"You could go with me."

"Go with you?" I repeated.

"Kyle is my realtor. I'm meeting him to look at an apartment."

"Oh," I said again, my elation that he wasn't meeting a date diminished by the news that he was moving. Moving on. Without me.

"You've been looking for a place, too, right?" he asked. "Maybe if this one isn't right for me, it'll be right for you."

"Where is it?"

"Fifty-seventh." His voice sounded flat when he added, "You're probably looking for a more fashionable address."

"You make more money than I do now," I pointed out.

"I don't want to leave the neighborhood," he said. "I'm sentimental that way."

I could have reminded him that I'd lived in Hell's Kitchen longer than he had, since I'd moved from Wisconsin a few months before he'd left the Chelsea apartment he once shared with Jeremy. But I knew he wasn't criticizing me. He didn't have the energy.

"Sure, I'll go with you," I said.

We didn't talk as we walked toward Columbus Circle. I wasn't sure when he started crying, but he let me guide him out of the park and down the nearly deserted avenue to Fifty-seventh, where he seemed to get control of himself. He led me to an eight-story building before he stopped, looking a little lost.

"You're still shivering," I said. "Do we have to wait out here?"

He shook his head and said, "I've got the key."

I was glad that no one was at the concierge desk to make Daniel feel embarrassed about his tear-stained cheeks. We took the elevator to the seventh floor, then I followed him, taking the key from his fumbling hands to unlock the door. When we were finally inside the empty apartment, he seemed unable to go any farther. He sank down next to the door and drew his legs up, hugging them and resting his head against the wall while he cried.

I knew how much he hated breaking down in front of me, so I busied myself for a few minutes, testing switches until I found one that turned on frosted wall sconces, bathing the room in soft light. I looked around for a radiator or some kind of heater. The fireplace held what I assumed were gas logs, but I finally spotted a thermostat in the hall, turned it on, and felt a rush of warm air. I found the bathroom and took the roll of toilet paper from the holder, then went back to Daniel. He slid off his gloves and took some to wipe his face.

I pulled him to his feet and said, "Geez, your fingers are like ice." He let me help him out of his coat, then I took mine off and pulled him to me. "Keep your hands against my chest so they'll get warm."

I continued to hold him close while he rested his head against my shoulder, his sobs finally subsiding to an occasional shudder that tore at my heart.

"I'm sorry," he said.

"Shhh. Breathe." I wasn't sure what else it was safe to say. I turned my face so that my lips were against his hair, inhaling the scent of smoke and snow and the aroma I loved most in the world—Daniel.

"I'm okay," he finally said, but he didn't pull away.

"Is this guy gonna show up? You need to get out of these wet clothes."

"I'm almost warm," he said. "He left a message saying he'd be late. Good thing, huh?"

"We could tell him you get really emotional about central heat," I said gently.

He laughed a little and pulled away to look at me, saying, "I didn't mean to fall apart on you. I'm a wreck."

"No you're not." I gently dabbed his face with toilet paper. "Blow." He laughed again and blew his nose. "You want to check out this place before your realtor gets here?"

He nodded, and we looked around. The walls were freshly painted in ivory, except for the dining room, which was wallpapered below the chair rail in a dark blue. The six-inch baseboards were stained the same honey tone as the hardwood floors, and there were built-in bookcases on either side of the fireplace.

Our shoes made a hollow sound on the floor when we explored the rest of the apartment. It had two bedrooms and two bathrooms which, although small, gleamed with new tile and fixtures.

"Do you think it lacks charm because everything is so new?" Daniel asked as we went to the kitchen.

"Who cares?" I said, looking at the stainless steel appliances and thinking of my fickle oven. "Gavin would fall to his knees and worship that stove."

"Maybe *you* should buy this place," Daniel said.

I couldn't read his expression, but his red-rimmed eyes looked like they could overflow again any minute, so I decided to keep my conversation matter-of-fact.

"I don't know what I'm going to do. I need at least three bedrooms, and I should have four. I don't think there's anything in Hell's Kitchen that can meet my needs. What if I have to move to Connecticut or something?"

We turned when the door opened and Kyle came in. Daniel introduced us. "He's trying to buy, too, Kyle," Daniel said. "You should give him your card, Blaine."

"Sure," I said, taking one out of my wallet and handing it to him. Violet would be shocked that I'd managed this much without her. "It seems like a nice building."

"It's still being renovated," Kyle said. "They're working their way down from the top. They just finished the fourth floor. There are several available apartments. In fact, the reason I'm late, Daniel, is because I have one to show you directly above this one. It's not on the market yet; the owner just found out his company is moving him to London. It's only one bedroom, although it has a small study that could be converted to a second bedroom. The square footage is less because it actually has a terrace. I know you wanted garden space. Do you want to look at it? I have the key."

"Yes," Daniel said, finally looking happier, and my heart sank. He couldn't possibly resist a top-floor apartment that would accommodate a garden.

While we waited for the elevator, Kyle and Daniel told me about the history of the building and its friendly co-op board. Listening to them, it dawned on me that Daniel's celebrity had been a drawback with some of the boards in other buildings. Apparently, it wasn't a problem here. Kyle dropped the names of a few other famous residents, and Daniel mentioned a Hollywood couple waiting for renovations to be completed on the third floor, where two apartments were being combined to give them the space they wanted.

"This may be a mess," Kyle warned as he put the key in the lock. "I know the owner is having stuff put in storage, and movers have been getting the rest of it ready to ship. His urgency works to the advantage of the buyer, though."

When he let us in and turned on the lights, I heard Daniel catch his breath. I looked around with understanding. Although the layout was basically the same as the other apartment, the blue walls emphasized that color in the beautiful Oriental rugs. The artwork, the books on the shelves, and the furniture showed what the other apartment could become once it was occupied.

The single bathroom and small study allowed the master bedroom to remain spacious in spite of the terrace that it accessed. I could tell by Daniel's expression that he loved everything about the apartment. While he and Kyle talked, I stepped onto the terrace, bracing myself against the freezing wind. I looked at the view, which wasn't bad, since Hell's Kitchen residents were known to voraciously fight high-rise development in the area.

When I finally went back inside, Kyle was gone. Daniel gave me a measuring look and said, "What do you think?"

"It's great," I said quietly.

"I could definitely see myself here," he said. He walked past me to step outside, so I returned to the terrace with him. "I can't believe how big this space is. I think I could even use my fountain, don't you?"

"It would probably fit over there," I said. "Your garden will be flourishing again in no time."

"I've even seen people glass in their terraces," Daniel said. "I'd have to check into the building codes—"

"I'm kind of hungry," I said sharply. "I probably should take off."

"How's Ethan?" Daniel asked.

"He's fine," I said, trying to figure out where that question came from. After a few seconds of awkward silence, the reason for Daniel's question flooded me with warmth, in spite of the freezing air. Choosing my words with care, I said, "He's like anyone who's falling in love. Absentminded. Romantic. Obsessed with sex."

"You don't have to—"

"He even sends flowers. He calls two or three times a day. He's like a teenager in love for the first time."

"How do you feel about that?" Daniel asked.

"I think it's great," I said. "You don't seem very happy about it." He pushed past me and went inside, but before he could go anywhere, I caught up with him, grabbing him and turning him around. "You're not walking out on me again, Daniel."

"I wasn't leaving. It's too cold to talk out there." After a few seconds, he added, "I just let down all my defenses with you, so I'm feeling a little fragile. I don't want to hear about how happy you are, okay?"

"Would you rather hear how unhappy I am?" I asked.

"Yes."

"I just endured the most miserable year of my life, but there were a few high points. Leaving Breslin Evans Fox and Dean to work for Frank at Lillith Allure. Sheila's wedding. My nephew coming to live with me. Gretchen's pregnancy and Emily's birth. And watching Ethan and Gavin fall in love with each other."

He thought that over, then said, "You were just tormenting me?"

"Sort of like you were tormenting me with your plans to move into a great new apartment."

He wrapped his arms so tightly around me that I couldn't move my own arms from my sides. We leaned into each other, and I inhaled deeply.

"You smell like smoke," I complained.

"Let me do this, so you can get the other one out of the way," he said, then kissed me hungrily.

When he finally broke away, I said, "And you taste like an ashtray."

"That's the one," he said and kissed me again. "I love you."

"I love you, too. Can we please go back to your place?"

"Here and now," he said. "Not later. Right now."

When he started undressing me, I felt a momentary qualm about being in some stranger's bedroom, using a bed that was stripped of sheets and pillows. Then it started seeming hot in a forbidden way. In any case, I knew better than to stop him. I understood that he wanted to take back some of the control he felt he'd lost when he allowed himself to cry in front of me. If the power games we played were unnecessary, even foolish, they were our games, and I was tired of being sidelined. He was mine. I was his. That was the way it was supposed to be, however flawed and infuriating it could get.

Making love equaled things out, and afterward we lay on the bare mattress, staring at each other and trying to breathe.

"It was the most miserable year of my life, too," Daniel finally said. "It's over."

"I hope so." Neither of us spoke for a while, until he said, "I'm sorry, too. For shutting you out and letting you feel guilty about everything. You didn't force me into the couple farce, Blaine. I thought if we spent time together, I could get you back."

"You never lost me," I said. "No matter how hard you tried."

"It's too bad neither of us had the guts to admit what we wanted, isn't it? We wasted a lot of time."

"At least we finished that fight that was started over a year ago."

"I do all the wrong things when we fight," Daniel said. "I dredge up the past. I say things I don't mean. I get defensive."

"And you walk away before the fight is finished," I reminded him.

"You can't resist pointing out my shortcomings, can you?" Daniel asked.

"No. I never learned how to fight, either."

"I know. Even when I felt sorry for myself, what made me feel worse was what I'd done to you. I couldn't forget the lonely boy you used to be. How you trusted me to love you and make a home with you. Every day I wanted to take back the angry things I said to you."

"At least you cared enough to fight. All I ever got from my family was silence."

Daniel smiled and said, "Yeah, you can't say I never yelled at you."

"Except on Sheila's wedding day."

"Are you still looking for punishment for kissing Adam? Who wouldn't, given the chance? Besides, it was such an obvious ploy to irritate me and grab the attention from Martin."

"Let's not bring him into this, please," I said. "I wasn't talking about the kiss."

"The baby?" Daniel asked. "If you couldn't tell that pissed me off, even without me sticking around to scream at you—"

"Before you found out about the baby. In our room. If you'd told me that *you'd* been seeing other guys and having sex, I'd have gone off the deep end. I'd have wrung every detail out of you, and made you tell me, one by one, all the ways they didn't measure up to me. But you said you didn't care."

"I never said I didn't care," Daniel argued. "I said I *understood*. I didn't want any details because I'm different from you. When I found out about Ethan, when I had a name and face, that's when it became torture for me."

"Torture?" I asked.

"Yes, and you've had enough fun with that for one night. Blaine, you couldn't have been unaware of my feelings. Even the night we broke up, I never said I didn't love you. Before the wedding, the few times we talked or saw each other, I was floating. But that weekend, you got surly about Martin. I got blown away by Gretchen's news. All I needed was some time until I could remember why I trusted you. Then all that other stuff got in the way."

"I know. The night we fought outside Gretchen's building, I finally tore up my mental list of grievances. When you made me see things through your eyes, I couldn't find a single reason why you should want me back. I agreed to do that stupid *Robby and Rhonda Show* because I thought it might give me one last chance to let you know how sorry I was."

"Believe it or not, I was happy that day," Daniel said. "When the women in our lives transformed themselves into our avengers, I realized none of that other stuff mattered. Sydney, Lola, the publicity. It started being funny. Especially when you turned gay."

"When I *what?*"

"You and Gwendy and Martin were like a comedy team. It made me realize how things could be if we'd both swallow our pride and stop being pissed off at each other and everybody else."

We lay quietly for a while until I said, "If you were ready, what kept you away after Emily was born?"

"Ethan," he said. "I thought—"

"Never even close," I said. "Ethan is a good friend. I hope you can deal with that."

"It's only fair. You dealt with Jeremy."

"Jeremy's all right. Martin's the problem."

"I wish you'd make peace with him. He had no idea what Robert was planning. He only agreed to be on *The Robby and Rhonda Show* because Gretchen told him to. You have the wrong idea about Martin. When Blythe's father and I started the town house negotiations, Martin was like a little kid, anticipating how happy you were going to be when we got our own place. He drove me crazy, calling me every day to ask if you knew yet. When he told you about Mrs. Lazenby and Blythe's move, he wasn't taunting you. He was trying to force me to tell you because he couldn't wait. He was mad at me after you and I broke up. He couldn't believe I let it turn out that way."

"All right," I said. "Martin is not Satan in a silk dress. I get it."

"After we broke up, you shut everybody out. They all came down on me. If I had to hear the words 'poor Blaine' one more time—"

"Are you joking? I thought everybody blamed me."

"Hell no," he said. "I thought I was going to have to befriend that coke-snorting bimbo Jane-Therese. That's how bad it got."

"Poor Daniel," I said helpfully, and he narrowed his eyes at me. "But you had Sheila."

"She was my rock. I know that caused problems between the two of you, but I honestly don't know what I'd have done without her."

"I guess that was fair, too," I said, "since I took Gretchen."

"Yeah, at least I didn't knock Sheila up."

"He can make jokes about it now!" I said, and he laughed. I pulled him to me, running my face over his shoulder until I buried it in his neck, inhaling him. Finally I surfaced to say, "I love you in ways and places that defy rational thought. All I want in return is everything."

"Funny, I happen to have everything." He looked around. "Possibly even a new apartment."

"There's not enough room here," I argued. "You're not moving anywhere without me, and I need more space. For Gavin, Nick, and a nursery."

"I'm sure as hell not living in Connecticut," Daniel said. "While you were moping on the terrace, I pitched an idea to Kyle. What if I bought both places and combined them into one, like that Hollywood couple? We could have stairs put in. Kyle said he'd present it to the co-op board. But if not here, we could do it somewhere else."

"Sounds expensive," I said.

"You have no idea how much I got when I sold the town house," Daniel said.

"Really? I always wanted a rich boyfriend."

"Me, too. You can take care of things like maintenance fees, real estate taxes—"

"Or renovation costs," I said, catching his enthusiasm. "It could work. You and me up here. The study turned into a nursery. This dining room could be office space. Gavin's and Nick's rooms would be downstairs, and we could use that kitchen and dining room for family meals. We'd all have room and privacy."

"See how smoothly things go when you let me have my way?" he asked.

I smiled and wrapped my arms around him again, regretful that we'd had only one condom between us. I dreaded the thought of going back into the cold night and wished this was already our apartment.

"Wait a minute," I said. "If you thought Ethan and I were a couple, why were you asking Kyle about combining two apartments?"

Daniel propped himself on one arm and stared into my eyes, saying, "Because I intended to fight for you. I figured once the luster wore off your new relationship, you'd realize that with Ethan, you get a man who spouts New Age garbage, kisses Bonnie's ass, and would never tolerate your temper and possessiveness. Whereas with me, you get—"

"A man with a big . . . apartment?"

"A man who never had sex with Martin Blount," he said and laughed when I grimaced.

I kissed him hard and said, *"Now* can we go to your place?"

"I'm finally warm," he protested.

"I'll get you warm again," I promised.

"I love it when you're insatiable."

We left the keys to both apartments with the concierge and picked up food on our way. While Daniel was in his kitchen getting everything ready, I called Gavin to tell him that I'd be spending the night away and to ask him to take care of a few things for me. After I talked to Nick, I called Violet at home.

"You promised these were snow days," she said. "No work."

"This is personal," I said. "I'll give you genie pay if you can achieve another miracle for me."

She listened quietly while I told her what I wanted, then stoically promised to do her best. In turn, I had to promise to answer my cell phone to help her work out any details.

The next day, *Secret Splendor* had again planned to take advantage of the snow in Central Park. We woke up before sunrise and put together a hurried breakfast. I tantalized Daniel with descriptions of Gavin's cooking. He was sure that even when we lived together, Gavin wouldn't get up at dawn to cook for him. When I set our eggs on the table, I saw the key placed next to my napkin.

"Take it back?" Daniel said, making it a question.

I nodded and said, "Until we get new ones."

We left his place together. I went home to change clothes and make a few calls. Gavin had packed a weekend suitcase for me. I dropped it at Daniel's apartment, then walked to the park to keep him company between takes. Fortunately, it wasn't a Jane-Therese day, since Cressida Porterhouse was supposedly buried in snow, so things went smoothly.

"I'm not as cold today," Daniel said at one point when I was rubbing his hands.

"Must be love," the makeup artist said, shooing me away.

"I think you two are great," an intern gushed as she handed me a cup of coffee. "You're both so honest and open about your lives—"

I didn't hear the rest of what she said because Daniel and I met each other's eyes and started laughing.

After six hours of scurrying between the overheated production trailer and the taping site, we started our weekend by walking to his apartment, picking up lunch on the way. We spent the afternoon tangled together on his bed, talking about a year's worth of emotions and experiences. When we finally subsided into silence, he caught me glancing at the clock.

"Do you see her every day after work?"

"Or after the gym," I said.

"You can go. I understand."

"Do you want to come with me?" I asked.

"Next time. You talk to them first, and let them know we're back together. Maybe then I won't feel like I'm on stage when I see her."

I felt a little uneasy about the plan I'd asked Violet to carry out, but merely said, "You do that so well."

"Hurry back," he said.

Gwendy was at the library, and Gretchen said I was just in time to help bathe Emily. I filled the baby tub with warm, soapy water, then sat on the counter and handed Gretchen things as she needed them.

"All right, it's obvious you aren't going to tell me unless I ask. Is it true? What Violet told me?" she asked.

"Daniel and I are officially the couple we professed to be," I assured her.

"Are you happy?"

"Oh, my god," I said, giving her an ecstatic look.

She crowed with laughter, then hammered me for details. I prudently left out the sexy parts, but she seemed satisfied by my account. Later, as I was leaving, I said, "Okay. I'm not coming tomorrow. I want to devote my whole day to him. We need our privacy and solitude. I'll see you Sunday night, right?"

"You don't have to feel guilty, Blaine. There'll be days you can't see Emily. I know there's a world out there. Just because I'm becoming agoraphobic—"

"Yeah, well, fixing you is my next project," I interrupted.

"Really? How do you propose to do that?"

"The usual way," I answered. "I'll tell Violet to handle it."

"It's reassuring to know that some things never change," she said.

Saturday and Sunday with Daniel were like a dream. We had food delivered and ignored the television and his phone. My cell phone never rang, which I took as a good sign.

Sunday evening we were back in bed when Daniel said, "I keep waiting for the next thing."

"The next thing?"

"For months, every peaceful moment was followed by a fight, a reporter, a news story, or a boss breathing down our necks. All this peace and quiet is making me edgy."

"Good," I said, "because I made plans for us tonight."

"To do what?"

"You'll know soon enough."

"Oh, already the secrets and battle for control start," he said.

"And the bitching," I countered.

"All right, have it your way. It's pointless to fight. You always have to be right."

"And you always turn everything into an ordeal," I said.

We got into the shower together, still grousing at each other, until he put a stop to it by grabbing me and saying, "It's so good to feel secure enough to bicker, even if we're only pretending."

"Who's pretending?" I asked, but ruined the effect by laughing.

"I love you," he said over and over, between kisses. "I'll go anywhere with you."

Later, when I gave the cab driver the address, Daniel's jaw dropped, and I reminded him, "You said anywhere."

"I don't have a problem with it," he said, sitting back and turning away so I couldn't see him smile.

Martin had on his best hostess face when he opened the door to us. "Isn't this a surprise?" he trilled.

"Please," Daniel said. "After the last few months, I know a setup when I see one."

Martin pushed us to his sofa, fluttering around and offering us drinks before he finally sat across from us, waiting expectantly.

"My cue," I said. "Martin, according to Daniel, you're like the Dr. Ruth of our relationship."

"Zat is correct," he said, channeling the diminutive German therapist. "Most problems can be traced back to sex. In fact, perhaps if you show me your penis—"

"I want to apologize for the anger I directed at you about the town house," I said, refusing to laugh at him. "And for shutting you in the closet at the bachelor party."

"Again, perhaps if you vere to vip out your penis, all vud be forgiven."

I doggedly went on, "You didn't deserve to be treated that way, and I'm sorry."

"Is that it?" Martin asked.

"You wouldn't say that if you saw my penis," I said. "Did I do something else to you?"

"You had your way with one of my former suitors, then hooked him up with your houseboy. It's really cut down my social life."

"Martin," Daniel warned.

"Oh, all right," he said. "I accept your apology."

"I think you can do better than that," Daniel said.

"I'm sorry for contributing to the *Robby and Rhonda* ordeal. I had no idea Robert was that diabolical. He used to be so nice before Daniel and Jeremy—"

It was my turn to say, "Martin."

"I guess this whole reconciliation thing isn't going to be any fun for me," he huffed. After a sigh, he added brightly, "Gretchen and Gwendy are upstairs at Blythe's. Should I call them?"

"I knew it was a setup," Daniel said. He met my eyes and said, "Yes. It's okay."

When they joined us, Gwendy was holding Emily, which gave Gretchen the chance to hug Daniel. I couldn't hear what she said to him, but when he let her go, he looked at his sister and used his Angus Remington voice to say, "Bring me the child."

It broke the tension, and we all watched when Daniel sat down with Emily and checked her out.

"I think she has Blaine's coloring," he said.

"Um, I think she's soiling her diaper," Gretchen said. "Her face is red because she's—"

"I think we get the picture," Martin said.

I grabbed a diaper and baby wipes from the hideous pastel bag and said, "You want to help me change her?"

When Daniel glanced up and saw all four of us waiting for his response, he said, "I'm afraid not to. Is this a test?"

"Come on," I said, and he followed me into Martin's bedroom, watching as I efficiently handled the diaper change.

"You're so sure of yourself," he said. "I'm scared of her."

"Get over it," I said, thrusting Emily at him so I could dispose of the diaper and clean my hands. "I love leaving this in Martin's wastebasket. I hope it takes him a while to figure out what the smell is."

I joined him when he sat down on the bed with her. "I'm going to let myself believe she started with our third sperm donation," he said. "If you know otherwise, don't tell me."

"Actually, that's what I believe, too," I said. "That was hot."

"Plus it allows me to say that my sister is the mother of my baby."

"Is that what you really think?"

"That my sister is the—"

"That she's your baby," I interrupted.

"Of course she is. She was ours before she was Gretchen's. Or Gretchen and Gwendy's. Don't worry, Emily," he said. "Your life won't be all flannel and Jeeps. With me, you get fashion advice and limos."

"Oh, boy," I said with dread. We sat shoulder to shoulder, staring down at our daughter, until I said, "I have a confession to make."

"Oh, boy," Daniel mimicked me.

"It really bothered me when you told me how everybody blamed you for our breakup. I wanted to make things right with our family. Violet helped me put together a little surprise party. Upstairs at Blythe's. I doubt Gretchen and Gwendy will stay long, because of Emily, but it should be quite a gathering."

"Sheila and Josh?"

"Yes, and Jake flew in with Adam and Jeremy. I also asked Gavin and Ethan to bring Nick. Frank is with Aunt Jen and Rowdy. Not necessarily in that order. Violet's there, and Martin helped her include some of your old friends from Club Chaos. Oh, and Faizah. It wouldn't be a party without Faizah."

"What about Mr. T?" Daniel asked.

"You never know," I said. "Everyone loves a party."

"That's a drag queen. Everyone loves a drag queen."

"You're right," I said, leaning over to kiss him.

ABOUT THE AUTHOR

TIMOTHY JAMES BECK is the author of *It Had to Be You* and *He's The One*. He divides his time between California, Texas, and New York, where he's hard at work on his next novel. Visit his Web site at www.timothyjamesbeck.com.